# Listen to the River

*Drifters,*
*Book Fifteen*

## SUSAN RODGERS

Edited by Colleen McKie of Savvy Fox Author Services
Cover design by Alanna Munro. All rights reserved.
Book design and formatting by Valerie Bellamy, Dog-ear Book Design.

ISBN: 978-1-987966-19-0

'Close your eyes and listen to the river.
Open your heart and let the water flow.'
—Lukas Bloom (adapted)


'Rivers know this: there is no hurry.
We shall get there someday.'
—A.A. Milne

Contents

*I*nitially it wasn't a creak on the narrow wooden risers that alerted Alice Sutherland to her husband's inability to sleep; instead it was the empty space in their bed, still warm from the heat of his body, which she discovered when she laid a hand across where she expected him to be.

Rolling over onto her back, Alice cocked an ear and listened for him. There it was, sign number two—a telltale creak on the stairs, followed by another and then another, the first audible signs that William was up and moving into his day.

Alice clasped her hands in prayer. Repetitive whispered appeals to the angels she believed guided her through her days calmed her worried heart. The continuous hopeful dawns of daily sunrises, followed hours later by the sinking of solitary suns, made it that much harder to judge whether William was really okay or whether he was just going through the motions. Days and nights were passing by at the same rate as always, yet they were like waves, rolling into each other in nightmare crashes of salt and spray, dispersing into liquescent valleys so benign and quiet they almost went unnoticed. Every day—every wave—sank the valley of William's soul just a little lower.

At seventy-one, his quiet nature had intensified. He had always been a man of routine, a hard worker who appreciated a certain distinct structure to his days. In these last few difficult years, however, he was slowing down and changing some things up. This was cause for concern to Alice. To her, the man she married fifty years ago was now a barely ticking clock with a low battery.

Downstairs, a metal measuring cup clinked against the side of a small pot. William was dumping in a daily ration of steel cut oats so his breakfast would be ready when he got back from his walk. Alice heard this sound every morning, yet for some reason it always tugged at her heartstrings. She pictured her husband's hands, always strong, steady, until a few short years ago. Lined with the grace of an honest man's work in the outdoors, they shook these days with a barely-there tremor only Alice noticed. The clink on the pot was her reminder. There would be a few scattered oats on the stovetop, left to burn into oblivion while the rest bubbled in homey unconcern.

For the thousandth time, Alice wondered how she could help her husband.

Easing up onto her side, she squinted at the digital clock radio by her bedside. Red numbers came into focus, their hazy truth more easily decipherable when she leaned closer to her nightstand.

*4:21.*

Exasperated, Alice fell back onto her pillow and stared at the ceiling. "Too early for me," she grumbled, throwing her floral duvet off anyway so she could pad down the hall for a pee. The fresh morning hour was also too early for her husband, but Alice was well aware that voicing her opinion to her introspective, quiet man would only serve to push him away. He was hard enough to talk to before the accident. Now William was just plain impossible to reach. He went about his days with a solemn dignity and curved, heavy shoulders, trudging through the toils of grocery shopping, church and meals with barely a look in her direction.

"Fifty years of marriage," Alice sighed as she did her business, "and this is what it comes down to. Silence."

She flipped on a tap. Without bothering to wait for the water to heat up she ran her hands under the faucet, one at a time. Catching sight of herself in the framed oval mirror above the sink, Alice paused, a hand towel hanging from her cold fingers. Absently, she touched her silver curls.

Medium-length, cut just below her chin, her layered hair was natural, untouched by even a hint of color over a lifetime of work as a cashier at the Food Mart in the nearby town of Kensington, Prince Edward Island, twenty minutes away. She didn't see the point in masquerading as someone she really wasn't. Alice was all about staying true to herself; she'd lived her whole life that way. Sometimes that meant wearing an outrageous hat she crocheted herself. Sometimes it meant giving her customers' children stickers when they passed through her checkout. And sometimes it meant saying exactly what she felt, when she felt the time was right to say it.

Except where William was concerned.

The man Alice knew the best was the only person she feared upsetting.

She tiptoed back to their shared bedroom.

A betraying creak filtered up the stairs. The antique plum velour chair by the front door of their small one-and-a-half story home was talking to Alice, communicating her husband's path on this cool morning. He was lowering his tired body into it. The chair was old when they got it, a cast off that William, in better days—when their only son was maybe fourteen or so— had plucked out of someone's side-of-the-road junk pile. Curbside, the ragged chair had surely been waiting for the waste truck to come by, to carry it away and end its suffering; to fulfill its destiny after a life well lived. Jeffery, Alice and William's son, had noticed it first. He'd asked his father to pull over.

Proud as peacocks, William and Jeffery had brought the rustic, damaged chair into the family's small home and set it—on the three legs it had left— in front of Alice. Remembering the day clearly, Alice's eyes brimmed with tears at the way she had berated her boys, at how she had sniped at them for bringing junk home from the side of the road.

*How nice it would be to have new things*, she'd often thought in those days. New things mattered, then. Unmarked, unscratched things, furniture that didn't reek of a family's business; furniture that wasn't missing parts and stained by spilled food, and sometimes even marked by rusted, stinky cat piss sprays.

The chair was removed, the hurt in Jeffery's eyes replaced with a burning resentment toward his mother for not seeing the value—the good bones— in the carved walnut arms, in the magnificent legacy of old world craftsmanship, of a lengthy unknown provenance worthy of one's daydreams and imaginings.

A week later the chair was back in the house, its horsehair cushion repaired. Brand new upholstery was snugly fitted over it with small tacks, and a fresh cotton muslin dust cover protected its belly underneath. The chair's arms, legs and Victorian scrollwork at the top back were polished— not entirely unscathed, because some scratches, some history, remained. Yet its walnut frame was shining with the joy wrought by the chair's rebirth. It was proud, that chair. And elegant and quite comfortable, Alice mused at the time, once she got used to the odd lumps of the horsehair innards. The side-of-the-road find became a showpiece in their home and a reminder to Alice to look beneath the surface of things, and of people.

For William, it jumpstarted a comfortable business.

Not that he was active in the business now. Restoring antique chairs was something William used to do with Jeffery, in the old days. It was their thing, their father-and-son thing. Each day William would patter away at one piece of furniture or another in contented quiet solitude until Jeffery, fresh off a yellow school bus if it was a school day, would run up the long lane that led to their house from the quiet Sutherland Road, and dump his knapsack on a chair by the door of his father's dusty workshop.

In those days, Jeffery was so anxious to get to work that he didn't even bother ducking into the house for a snack. Like his father, he was most at peace sliding his fingers over the aged patina of antique walnut and rosewood, urging new life from furniture pieces most people would easily consider garbage. If Alice were home she'd drop into the weathered red barn where the guys were working. Suspended in her capable hands would be fresh-baked blueberry scones, or cinnamon rolls, laid out on a tray alongside tea for William and chocolate milk or orange juice for Jeffery. Before she stepped out of the dimly lit barn Alice always took the time to stay with her boys and watch them work. Eventually William and Jeffery built new furniture too, based on age-old designs. Their work was detailed, skilled and in demand.

The family had two horses back then, a palomino and a chestnut, Gilligan and Ginger. Jeffery, who got a kick out of classic TV and liked to watch *Gilligan's Island*, named them. While father and son worked side by side, the horses snuffed and snorted and pawed their approval in stalls just down from them. Some days the work was done early. After a late dinner, William and Jeffery liked nothing better than to saddle up and go for a moonlight ride on the beach behind the house, or through the fields, depending on the season and on the weather. If there was homework, it got tossed aside and was hastily completed just before bedtime.

The beach was icy now, not a safe place to walk a horse, but there were no longer horses to ride up and down alongside the bay anyway. It was early May, springtime, but in Prince Edward Island spring was occasionally laden with late season ice storms.

A creak downstairs refocused Alice on the present. William was getting up from the plum chair now. A slow tap tap tapping marked his weary footsteps to the front door. Ragging at him about putting Ice Traks on in the house did no good. He found it easier to slip the ice grips over his boots when he was sitting in the low plum chair.

"And besides," William once said in rebuttal to Alice's scolding, "I just walk on the mat anyway." The mat was a ten dollar jobbie from Kent Building Supplies in Kensington, so in his humble opinion it was no biggie if it got the occasional hole ripped in it. Alice was not in agreement. His unconcern for the way things looked drove her around the bend, even after fifty years of marriage.

The door opened and closed, jarring the house just slightly, even though William was always careful to make his morning routine as soundless as possible so as not to disturb his supposedly sleeping wife. Alice heard him march down the outside steps, and soon the low crunching of his boots and the Ice Traks with their spiked prongs faded off into the distance.

In a rectangular pattern, he'd go up through one field, into a small clump of trees, then trek down the other side of the field until he reached the beach. Along the beach he would tread carefully, Alice hoped, knowing she would not relax until his familiar footsteps started back up the outdoor steps. It was still icy out there and William was a stubborn man who had no interest in owning a cell phone.

The hardest part of the journey, of William's daily morning walks, was always when he strode up off the beach at the dead end part of Sutherland Road. There the road emptied onto the beach; a wide path connected the two. Walking up off the beach meant meandering up by a one-hundred-and-fifty-year-old mid-Victorian home built by William's great-great-grandfather in 1865. Seeing the grand two-story white house today, with vehicles parked outside, would be tough on William. For a long time the home was vacant, a 'for sale' sign hanging from a post out front, squeaking in the blustery breeze of the Prince Edward Island winter.

Today, Alice knew, her husband would come home with no reserves of strength left. Tired, bone-weary, he would work at piddly little projects all day until fatigue got the better of him and he gave in to a nap. Some random technical manual would do a nose-drop on his face when William dozed off, which would be around four o'clock. He would get up for dinner when Alice called him. Together they would sit at the small square table by the front window in their 'open-concept' home that, if you wanted to call a spade a spade, was really just a modified, insulated one-and-a-half-story cottage. No words would pass between them; no exchange of information would take place. That was the legacy Jeffery left them.

Closing her eyes, Alice moved her lips in silent prayer. When Jeffery crossed her mind, she always said the *Hail Mary* three times. Mary got Alice through the loss of her son and then through the subsequent move of Jeffery's wife, Heather, and the only two grandchildren William and Alice would ever know, back to Ontario.

When she finished praying, Alice tilted her silvery curls and listened for wind. There was none. "Good," she whispered to her snowy pillow, rolling over onto her side and hugging its downy softness close. "William won't be cold, at least." Their little corner of Prince Edward Island—on the north shore in rural Hamilton, near the seaside summer resort area of Darnley— was often windy, and thus often chillier than the more enclosed, populated areas of the island. They lived on the shore of Malpeque Bay, world famous for its oysters and once a bustling shipbuilding hub back in the days when wooden ships rigged with canvas sails dotted the waters off P.E.I.

Sleep was weighing on Alice's eyelids. Determined to wait for her husband's safe return from his icy pre-dawn walk, she fought the sandman with another round of *Hail Marys* but her good intentions fell flat. Alice was snoring before she got to say pray for us sinners, now and at the hour of our death.

Downstairs on the couple's old white stove the oatmeal was bubbling away in its cozy way, ready to offer William comfort and warmth upon his return. Only a mere few feet away, the restored antique plum chair sat in stoic silence.

Down the narrow lane from the Sutherlands, in the large house built by William's ancestor and most recently owned by William and Alice's son

Jeffery, Josh and Jessie Sawyer and their four children nestled under warm duvets and dreamt restlessly of strange, new lives. Outside, the frosty bay bordering their home whispered a frigid, yet hopeful, welcome.

# Chapter One

Emily-Grace was supervising Dylan and David when she saw a beige Toyota Corolla sedan pull up to the P.E.I. house. It drove slowly, cautiously, as if the driver wasn't sure exactly where to stop. In the end it ground to a halt just beyond the Sawyer family driveway, a short, paved lane that led off Sutherland Road to the right and widened into barely enough parking area for one vehicle, much less the three already situated at the house.

The kids were running around outside on this, their first full day in their new east coast Canadian home. There were interesting things to explore, like tracks in the little bit of snow that had fallen from the gray sky overnight. *Are those bunny tracks?* Emily-Grace wondered. Behind the rambling house were small, matching outbuildings the kids' dad told them not to go into until he had a chance to be sure they were safe. One had a large happy face painted on its wide door. Someone had decorated another with a bright spring-like hand-painted spray of yellow and red flowers. Emily-Grace thought both paintings were likely a child's work, but whose?

Not too far away a pebble-dotted sandy beach lined a bowl-shaped expanse of cold looking dark blue water that wasn't at all inviting, unlike the warm aqua green ocean the family left behind in the Caribbean. This body of water was still partly ice covered, even though it was now May. Even Momma and Daddy seemed shocked at that when they pulled up to the house yesterday. The whole family was tanned from their days in the sunny Caribbean. Didn't seem like those tans would stick around for long in this freezing province. Worse, Emily-Grace had overheard talk of all of them having to keep their distance from people in the near future since no way would the tanned look jibe with their new home.

A silvery-curled woman got out of the passenger side of the beige Corolla. She was carrying something—*a pie*, Emily-Grace thought, since it was some kind of round pastry and was held high in two hands in front of the woman's chest. A man followed from the driver's side, but he seemed hesitant. Judging by the couple's gray hair, Emily-Grace figured them for an older couple but they weren't anyone she knew, and she was fairly certain her parents weren't expecting anyone. Reaching behind her, she grabbed Dylan's hand and called out to David at the same time.

"In the house," she ordered with as much big sister authority as she could muster. "You know what Momma and Daddy said."

Dylan tried to wrench his arm out of his sister's grasp. "They said we could play outside," he whined, "while they carry in the groceries that Arnie got. They said!"

"We're not supposed to see people." Adamant, Emily-Grace yanked on Dylan's arm until he had no choice but to follow grudgingly along behind. After they walked a few feet, she halted in her tracks. Behind her and Dylan, David wasn't moving. He was staring at the couple, the corners of his mouth turned down in an uneasy frown.

The woman seemed friendly enough. She called out to them. "Hello, kids. Is your mother or father home?" She was getting closer.

Emily-Grace panicked. "David!" she hissed. "Come on! Now!"

All three kids jogged up a set of wooden stairs and disappeared inside the house without a word to their company, which left their visitors momentarily stunned.

Inside, as he manipulated his boots off one at a time, Dylan's complaining was more vociferous in the presence of his parents. "I want to play outside! There's animal tracks, Daddy!"

Josh was handing Jessie a container of plain Greek yogurt for her to slide into the open refrigerator. He caught the look of fear crisscrossing his daughter's face, but spoke to Dylan first. "Could be a fox, Dylan. Or maybe a bunny. I'll come outside with you later and we can investigate, okay buddy?"

"Soon, okay, Daddy?" Dylan tossed off the new winter coat and snow pants the family'd found waiting at the house when they arrived. Emily-Grace picked them up off the floor and hung them, together, on a hook. David was already out of his winter things, and was hanging them up alongside Dylan's in the small side porch mudroom.

"You got it," Josh said, ruffling his son's messy hair as Dylan sank into a chair at the round kitchen table. "Real soon." He turned his attention to his daughter. "Is there a reason you came inside, Emily-Grace?"

Jessie cut in. "Besides the fact that it's bloody freezing, you mean?" she griped, setting the yogurt in the stainless steel fridge and frowning at Arnie's bleak attempt at covering up a small half smile. Her frown flipped over and she grinned at him.

Josh chewed on a lip and studied her with a pensive silence.

Looking over at him, Jessie shrugged. "Well, it is. You want me to lie?"

"There are people outside," Emily-Grace piped up, shrugging off her coat, which drew Josh's attention back to her real quick.

"Here?" Josh asked, rather stupidly he chided himself afterwards. They were living at the end of a barely inhabited country road with almost zero traffic on it. There was only one house anywhere nearby— a small dwelling well across the road from them, built way back into the field, accessed by a long, narrow dirt lane. Far enough away to give all of them—including their neighbors—some much coveted privacy.

"The lady has a pie in her hands." This was from David, who was already licking his lips. He was remembering a grandmother and a live-in housekeeper he desperately missed. They used to bake together a lot in Vancouver. Plus when they hugged him cozy, loving flowery smells always radiated off of their bodies.

As one, the adults' eyes all darted to the west side of the house, to the large high window facing the road. The visitors, who were standing outside looking confused, seemed to be engaged in a discussion about what to do since they were each shooting guarded looks toward the house. The woman started walking up to the steps.

"It's just neighbors," Jessie muttered to no one in particular, eyes downcast. Her unspoken words haunted them anyway. Josh touched her hand in a shared knowing before he turned from her and moved over to the door.

Arnie's voice stopped him. "Stay inside," he demanded.

"It's my house, Arnie," Josh snapped, leaving no room for discussion. "They're local people, not the," he glanced surreptitiously toward his kids, "Alberta mafia. They won't know me, anyway." Lifting a hand, he touched his new beard, which was quite intentionally a little on the scraggly side.

"What's the Alberta mafia, Daddy?" David had a feeling that whatever it was, it wasn't good.

Emily-Grace confirmed his suspicion with a glare and a, "Sshh." In her mind, most things to do with Alberta were painful. Any mention of the province where Daddy used to work on *Sacred Peace* made her heart race and sweat break out on her forehead.

"Never you mind, David. Daddy was just making a joke." Leaping after Josh, Jessie grabbed a baseball cap from a hook near the side door. "Here," she said proudly. "Now you'll fit in. They'll think you're native to the land of red mud, potatoes and freezing cold spring weather. The truck outside's a dead giveaway too." Caps like this one—dark blue, emblazoned with the logo of the local junior hockey team, the Summerside Capitals—were staples in Jessie's life. When she and Josh were in P.E.I. for part of the summer years ago, they both had ball caps just like it stashed in their vehicle at all times. They came in handy for trips to the Frosty Treat for cookie dough flurries and milkshakes. Matt and Charles had stocked some in the Sutherland Road house when they flew to Prince Edward Island to make sure all was well for the move.

Crossing her arms, Jessie rocked back on a heel and cocked her head at her husband. "Sexy." She winked. "And the beard adds just the right amount of," she raised her fingers in quotes, "rural vibe."

"Thought we agreed beards were trendy," Josh growled, heading for the door with Arnie right behind him.

"More redneck than trendy," Jessie teased with a twinkle in her eye as Josh and Arnie left the kitchen through the mudroom. "But then again," she smiled at her observant children, "Daddy's really a hardcore redneck anyway, isn't he, kids?"

David put a finger to his lips in his usual inquisitive way. "What's a redneck, Momma?"

"Ask Daddy, Mr. Curious." Jessie giggled. "He'll tell you."

Emily-Grace dropped into a vacant chair on the opposite side of the kitchen table. "Are we always gonna have to hide from people, Momma?" she asked.

Jessie's smile did an about face, and turned upside down. She blinked three times in rapid succession before looking away from her daughter toward the big window. She and Josh had agreed before making this move that they would not blatantly tell the children they were 'hiding.' For their own sakes too, Josh and Jessie did not want to approach their new lives with the fear engendered by 'hiding' hanging over their heads as if it were always going to be a standard part of life. Instead, they'd had a frank talk with their older children about being cautious around people.

"We need some privacy," they had said. "You know how people are always following us and taking our pictures? We don't want that anymore." The explanation made it easier to convince the children to take on new names. "Just for when we're out in public," Josh and Jessie told them.

Everyone had new haircuts. David's—short, and adorably spiked—was driving him nuts since he still inadvertently kept trying to brush a longer strand behind his ear. Emily-Grace's was a shiny, aristocratic, below-the-chin bob that she liked because it reminded her of her grandmother. Dylan's was a mussy mess of short curls instead of his usual wild gypsy shoulder-length cut. Carlotta's sister had flown in to the Caribbean to do the cuts. When she finished trimming the children's hair, she colored Jessie's a dreary mousey brown, ordered her to straighten her big curls on the days she planned to venture into town, and to always wear ponytails or hats. Josh was easier. She trimmed the split ends from his long hair, highlighted it blond, and suggested he let it continue to grow.

As a result Josh was wearing his hair longer than ever, which sometimes necessitated pulling it back into a long ponytail at the nape of his neck or twisting it into a man bun so it didn't drive him crazy. The Harley was locked up in Vancouver, but just for fun Jessie had badgered Josh about it anyway, telling him that with his scraggly hair and beard all he needed was gang colors to fit the stereotypical Harley mold. Josh's changed appearance undoubtedly gave him a 'rough around the edges' vibe.

That particular good-natured teasing only lasted a half day. It drew to a quick close at a gas station yesterday after Jessie took the time to have a closer look at her husband. His much-loved eyes were buried beneath a knit toque Josh put on just before he slipped out from behind the wheel of his truck to pump gas. Jessie was sorry to see that. Josh's expressive bottomless, sad, liquid chocolate eyes—the windows to his soul, the reflections of his joys, the keys to his hurts—were practically submerged.

The Sawyers and Arnie had only been on the island a day, having landed in nearby Halifax, Nova Scotia and driven over to P.E.I. the day before. Already Josh was averting people's gazes by staring at his feet or at the floor in front of him. Yesterday after crossing the Northumberland Strait via the thirteen-kilometer long Confederation Bridge, he was clearly in hiding mode when they stopped at the gas station on the south side of Prince Edward Island. He practically shrank into an old leather jacket, a mid-thigh length dusky brown one, when he inserted a shiny new bank card embossed with the name Joe McIver into the gas tank's payment slot. Covertly watching him, Jessie didn't think Josh was feeling scared exactly, but a waterfall of hair cascaded over both cheeks beneath the toque when he looked down to nervously toe the asphalt while pumping the gas, and he didn't bother to tuck it behind his ear. The knit toque was tugged so low over his brow that Jessie wondered how he could see at all.

At the time, Josh collected his receipt and stopped by Jessie's window to see how she, Emily-Grace and Micah were handling the drive from Nova Scotia. Arnie was at the wheel of the vehicle they were riding in, a four-year-old cranberry 'mommy van' Matt and Charles had insisted Jessie drive in order to better fit in to the general population. Josh was parked in front of the van. He was driving a truck, albeit not his usual luxurious King Ranch. His ride was a blue Ford F-150, also more than a few years old. Matt and Charles had picked up a used Jeep for Arnie and parked it at the Sutherland House for him.

At her open window, Jessie had reached up and taken Josh's hand when he leaned both forearms on the door. Lifting the much-loved fingers to her lips for a kiss, Jessie closed her eyes, sighed, moved his hand against her cheek and held it there for a few extended seconds before she let him go. These days, with a change this big, there didn't seem to be a lot to say. Actions spoke for them most days, and were doing a damn good job as substitutes for words. Going through the motions was the order of the day over this last while.

In the kitchen, bringing her focus back to the present, Jessie absently tossed a box of pasta back and forth between her hands before deciding she ought to answer her daughter's question. Rounding the end of the counter, which wasn't a kitchen island but which jutted out from the main cabinet where the sink was, creating an L-shape, Jessie dropped the pasta on the table and slid into a chair next to Emily-Grace. David had gone over to the window to take a closer look at their visitors, and slumped into a wooden rocking chair near the door when he decided the couple outside were just ordinary folks. Dylan was bending down in front of Micah who was gleefully kicking his arms and legs in a baby seat Jessie had set inside a travel playpen to keep him safely out of the busy family's way while they unpacked groceries. Making weird faces and waving a fabric rattle in front of him, Dylan was contentedly coercing giggles from the good-natured baby.

"Emily-Grace," Jessie said, taking in the pleasing sight of her two youngest boys before looking away from them and grasping her daughter's hand in hers, "we just need to get a feel for this place, for how things are going to be here. It's important that we keep our distance from other people for at least a little while, to start." She snuck a glance she hoped was covert out of the window, where she saw that Arnie and Josh were just approaching their visitors.

"I want to go home." Big tears welled up in Emily-Grace's pale eyes. "I miss Grammie and Grampie."

"We all do, sweetheart. But they'll be around lots. You'll see." *I miss someone too. And he won't be around. Ever.* It only took a second for Jessie's eyes to fill too. Rallying, she heaved up her shoulders and said, "How about we get these groceries put away so we can make room to bake cookies?" This new reality would be a lot easier to bear, Jessie figured, if she injected some normalcy into it.

That brightened the two older children up. Cookies were an instant mood lifter since wonderful memories were associated with baking.

Dylan was harder to please. He stopped waving the rattle in front of

Micah. "I wanna know about the tracks outside." An outdoor boy like his daddy, he added, "I need to know about those tracks. Cookies can wait."

"You and your stupid tracks." David shrank lower into the rocking chair and gave it a glum half-hearted push.

Dropping the rattle in Micah's lap, Dylan crossed the floor in a second flat. Launching his wiry body at his brother, he hit David three times before his mother could jump up and come to the rescue.

It took Jessie a minute to get a grip on him. "What's this about, Dylan?" she asked, hanging on tightly while he flailed in her arms. "Ouch! Jesus, stop kicking!"

"I'm so tired of David always picking on me!" Going limp in his mother's arms, Dylan started to sob.

In the rocking chair, David drew his knees up to his chest and shoved his face into a makeshift cave.

Scanning her kids closely, Jessie turned Dylan around so he could wrap his arms around her and lay his head on her shoulder. "Okay," she said, aware that Emily-Grace was nearing breakdown mode too, "I know we've got a lot of adjusting to do. Whining about who and what we've left behind, and picking on each other, is not gonna do any of us any good. We've got to make the best of things, kids. Dylan, hitting your brother is not allowed, and David, you're older, don't pick on Dylan."

Nobody answered.

"Look," Jessie tried, rubbing Dylan's back as his sobs quieted, "let's just treat this as a little holiday. When Grammie and Grampie come to visit they'll be wishing they lived here too. You know I lived here when I was a kid, right? P.E.I is where I was born."

That piqued some interest.

"Can we go see where you used to live?" Emily-Grace was the most curious.

Jessie's heart hitched. *Bedeque. Her dad. Memories. Crosswinds. George.* "Yes, one of these days we'll take a drive to Bedeque. We'll get puppy paws ice cream at the village store." Emily and George were still on the island, in their Clinton nursing home. But that would be a visit Jessie would be making alone—in disguise just for safety's sake.

She set Dylan down. "In the meantime, we've got cookies to bake. Let's get these groceries put away. Hand me the bananas, Emily-Grace," she ordered. "Dylan, put the carrots in the crisper in the fridge. And you boys apologize to each other or you'll both be taking a time out. Let's git 'er done so we can move on to something more fun."

*Move on.* Considering the next few hours, and only the next few hours, was manageable. Moving on was relative. Jessie didn't have a clue exactly what it would mean in the long term, and dwelling on the next day and the next—unknown quantities, at this point in time—would only lead to a crippling, choking rise of anxiety.

With a sigh she plucked the pasta box off the table where she'd set it earlier, shoved it in a cupboard, and slammed the door closed with a loud, frustrated, harrumph.

*Chapter Two*

$\mathcal{O}$utside, Josh couldn't help but shuffle his feet and stare at the ground when he and Arnie approached the older couple in their dooryard. Arnie was a good judge of character. Thrusting out a hand to offer the man a handshake in greeting, he fixed a careful, cautious gaze on him, and then on the woman, in turn.

The woman spoke first. "We're Alice and William Sutherland. We live down that lane, a stone's throw from the beach." She gestured to the small house a ways behind her before looking back and meeting Arnie's eyes a second time. "That's our place. We just wanted to say hello. To let you know that if you need anything, anything at all, don't be shy. Just come knocking."

"Barney's my name," Arnie said, not unkindly. "I'm this guy's buddy. This is his place; I live in Charlottetown."

Two pairs of older eyes landed on Josh. "Uh, Jo…uh, Joe," he said, almost slipping and saying Josh. Next to him, Arnie licked a lip and stayed as cool as a cucumber. "My wife and I, uh, Jasmyn," Josh heaved in a breath, "Jasmyn, that's my wife's name, uh, we just moved in."

"Yes, we've been quite eagerly awaiting our new neighbors," Alice said as Arnie studied the quiet man at her side—the man who was standing a bit behind her, almost.

*He's the shy type,* Arnie figured. *The kind of man who likely prefers a zero conflict environment and so lets his wife wear the pants.*

"We saw that you have children," Alice was saying. "Three?"

"Uh, four," Josh managed, hooking his thumbs over his jeans pockets. Arnie still had a coat on, from his earlier trip to the grocery store. Josh hadn't bothered grabbing one. He shivered. After the Caribbean—heck, even after Vancouver—this was an unpleasant, damp kind of cold. It went right to his bones and stayed there, chilling him to the core. "We have a baby too," he said to Alice from under the ball cap's brim. "Five months. He'll be six months old the end of May."

"Just the one girl?" Alice was determined to find out what she could. Still standing there with the pie suspended in her arms, she teetered a little on her feet, back and forth, her husband frowning as he watched. "Three boys?" *Three boys. We only had one, me and William. And we lost him. Some people are so lucky. Or blessed, maybe,* she forced herself to think more charitably.

"Just the one girl, yep." Josh shuffled his feet and half smiled at the already melting spring snow. He toed it with a boot. "For now."

With a half-assed grin, Arnie looked over at him. Such hope in those two simple words—*for now*. He relaxed.

"I'd love to meet your wife," Alice said. "Jas…" She hesitated.

"Uh, Jasmyn," Josh repeated, glancing up just for a second. "As in J – A – S – M – Y – N."

"What a pretty name."

"She's just about to feed the baby," Josh lied. "Would another time be okay?"

The quiet man at Alice's side spoke up. Almost surprised to hear him speak, both Arnie and Josh looked quickly over at him. "You move here from Vancouver?" he asked.

"Uh…" Josh wasn't sure what to say. Scripted lines were one thing. This awkward conversation was an altogether different animal.

Arnie saved him. "Yes," he responded openly. They'd decided not to confuse things too much. Vancouver would be easy for the kids to talk about—for their parents too, for that matter. As long as their overall identities were protected, they should be okay. "Vancouver."

"You said you're friends?" This also came from the man. William, his name was, the guys remembered.

Josh chewed on a lip and stared at his boot.

"Yeah," Arnie stated a little defensively. "Friends."

"Family," Josh interjected, and shrugged, glancing up to meet William's eyes for a brief second before looking down again. "Barney and me," he almost laughed at how bizarre that sounded, "we, uh, we go way back."

"I'm just divorcing," Arnie explained, hoping he could put an end to the questions by giving the couple something, even a lie, to mull over. "When I found out these guys were moving it seemed like a good time to make a new start. All those kids…" He let the thought drift away.

"What do you work at?" The question was propelled toward Josh. It was followed up with an almost rude, "You got a job to go to?"

"What do I…? Uh, I dunno yet. I guess I'll be lookin' for something," Josh stammered.

"What'd you do on the west coast?"

*Jesus, lay off, man,* Josh fumed, feeling his blood pressure spike. He realized he was now staring at the man. Something about the fellow's eyes disconcerted him. Expecting at first that he would see anger or hostility to go with the interrogation, Josh was quick to realize that what he was actually privy to in the man's hazel eyes was a deep layer of sadness. He swallowed. These days, sadness was always easy to recognize in the spirit of another human being. Letting his shoulders down, easing off the tension he felt hijacking his body, Josh was surprised to intuitively feel he could trust the guy. He wasn't entirely sure about bossy-pants Alice, even though she was staying quiet while her husband probed for answers.

"I did a lot of things," Josh answered, in a sort of half truth.

Unable to keep himself from grinning as he listened, Arnie tilted a head toward Josh and averted his eyes from the Sawyer family neighbors.

"I was in law enforcement for a while." *Two seasons,* Josh chuckled wryly, inwardly, recoiling against the gut-clench that wrung out his intestines like a wet dishcloth at the thought of his much-loved gig on *Sacred Peace. Plus I had a few law enforcement roles in films back in the day,* he wisecracked to himself. *CIA, regular police force, you name it.*

"You don't strike me as the type."

"The beard?" Josh raised a hand to his beard and fingered it. "I left the force." He dropped his hand. "I'm celebrating my freedom."

Arnie raised his eyebrows. Josh actually seemed to be having fun with this.

William just nodded.

Alice cut back into the conversation. "I gather the children will be going to school in Kensington. The bus comes by at ten-to-eight. It drops them off at four-ten."

"The kids will be homeschooled." This dose of reality was from Arnie. "For now."

"I gather the other people who lived in this house had kids," Josh said, trying to turn a corner. "The paintings on the outbuilding doors…"

There it was, the reason for the sadness in the man's eyes. It flashed across his face like a shooting star—instant, dazzling in its intensity and quick to sizzle out. After it passed, his eyes settled back into their stoic, blank hazel.

Alice mustered up a breath. "Our grandchildren," she explained. "They moved to Ontario quite some time ago now. Almost two years. They're eight and ten now. Bobby and Lizzie." The hands holding the pie suddenly moved, thrusting the offering toward Josh, who took it with a grateful hesitancy. "Apple," Alice said. "A welcome gift."

"It must be hard to not have your grandchildren around anymore," Josh mumbled, unsure. He was looking at Alice, but out of the corner of his eye he saw William fidget uncomfortably.

"Well," Alice elaborated, softening noticeably, her gaze capturing Josh with a new, gentle, grandmotherly kindness, "our daughter-in-law needed her own parents nearby. Our son," she reached deep to say the words as William turned away, "died. It was an accident. She had no choice, really, in the end. This can be a lonely place for a young mother from away with no husband to help her out."

Both Arnie and Josh were moved to silence. It wasn't just the admission that these two seemingly caring (albeit curious) people had suffered—were still suffering, apparently—or that the house the Sawyers were now living in had suffered a tragedy. The house was old. It had strong character and an earned authenticity that was most certainly treasured and cherished by heritage aficionados, and equally appreciated by those who didn't care about history but who recognized at the very least that it was well built and well loved. A lovely, soft patina was worn into the newel post at the bottom of the stairs; patterned wooden marquetry gracefully bordered many of the floors.

Families over many years had inhabited the ancient walls. There was no way a house this old was immune to tragedy.

No, what sliced Josh and Arnie in two at the admission was the newness of the tragedy. The somewhat recent loss of a son—a husband and father, at that—hit a little too close to home.

*Could have been me,* Josh thought, taken aback. *Could have been Jessie raising kids alone. Could have been our kids without a father. Almost was.*

It was William's turn to see a shadow of sorrow pass across his neighbor's eyes. Hauling up the faux fur collar of a thick gray winter jacket he'd dug out the other day, one he thought he'd already put away for the season, he wondered what had transpired in this man's life for him to pull up roots and haul his wife and four children across the country to start anew in a tiny pissant province in a rural, remote locale.

He and Josh shared a moment, a united glimpse into each other's souls. It got heavy, that moment. It got weighted and thick. Like waterfalls, hard memories came rushing back, seizing both men's hearts with unwanted grit.

William handled the overarching grief by nodding a gruff, "So long," and heading for his car.

Josh thrust a chin toward the pie and muttered a hasty, "Thank you for this. It's very thoughtful of you. My boys will love it." He took a few steps backward, wheeled around and stumbled toward the house.

Arnie was left to face Alice alone. "I'm sorry to hear about your loss," he said, unable to keep sadness from creeping into his usually street-tough countenance. "You should know that these guys, the McIvers, have weathered some rough times too."

Alice pulled up her robust and resilient side. Proudly hunkering up her shoulders, she said, "We'll watch out for them. You make sure they know to come to us if they need anything."

"I think they would say the same thing." Arnie smiled.

"Well, that would be nice," Alice replied with just a hint of relief. "William, my husband, he really misses our son and the kids. They used to do a lot of things together."

"Sure. I'll tell them. It was nice to meet you, Mrs. Sutherland."

"Alice." Gladness added a teensy bounce to Alice's steps when she swung around and started for the car. Just as she reached for the door handle she called back to Arnie, "Do you and your ex-wife have children, Barney?"

The name 'Barney' took Arnie by surprise. He wasn't as accustomed as Josh and Jessie were to 'playing' someone else. Flushing, embarrassed, he stuttered back, "N-no, we don't. No kids." He angled a shoulder toward the house. "These kids are like my own. They're enough of a handful."

"I look forward to meeting them." Alice hesitated before she opened the Toyota's front passenger door. "McIver. That's a Kinkora name, isn't it?"

"Kinkora?"

"It's a community about ten minutes off the Confederation Bridge, toward the center of the island. I thought maybe your friend had a Kinkora connection. My apologies." By way of explanation she waved an arm matter-of-factly. "It's an island thing. We're always trying to see who belongs to who."

"I understand. But no," Arnie ascertained, starting to back up. "These guys aren't connected to any island McIvers. They don't have any family connections here." He could swear his nose started to feel tickly at the lie. Like Pinocchio, he half expected it to start growing. Emily, Jessie's mother, was still here, at least in body. Who knew where her mind spent its restless days?

"Good enough." Still, Alice couldn't let it rest. "Why here, then? As opposed to anywhere else?"

Arnie shrugged. *Nosy much?* "They need peace and quiet. Seemed as good a place as any to hang their hats."

"This is about as quiet as it gets." Alice gestured to the dead end of the Sutherland Road, which tapered down an easy, brief slope to the beach. "Unless you count the wind and waves on a stormy day." At that, she finally opened the door and slipped into the car. William already had it running.

Back in the house, Arnie and Josh stood at ease in the mudroom, ushered off their boots and considered what they now knew about the neighbors. Watching, Jessie dropped a hand to her hip and leaned the other on the kitchen counter. With the exception of Micah, the kids had been shooed to a first floor room now designated as a playroom. Digging through boxes, they were searching for coveted toys while waiting for their mother to finish with the groceries so they could get started on the cookies.

"So?" Jessie asked her two solemn men. "Details?"

"Over there." Josh gestured to the small house across from them, the distant one set back from the road. He swallowed. "This was their son's house." Not one single part of him wanted to tell Jessie that the son had died. He did not want any inkling of tragedy or sorrow to permeate these walls, or to insert any kind of wretched cracks into what he felt was a good start at healing after all that he, Jessie and the kids had been through over the last many years.

Jessie gulped. When she spoke, her voice was low. "I can read you, you big baby," she reprimanded, almost forgetting that Arnie was in the room. "What is it? What don't you want to tell me?"

It was Arnie who said it. He avoided looking over at Josh. "He died."

Jessie blinked at him. "How." It wasn't a question. It was a demand.

"They didn't say." Arnie, like Josh, waited to see what would come next.

Adjusting her stance, Jessie forced her eyes back over to Josh. "Well," she breathed. "That's too damn bad. That sucks."

Always, Josh's recent unilateral choice would stalk them, every bit as McCall did years ago. It was already clinging to Josh and Jessie, nasty and vicious in its unspeakable, almost incomprehensible way, and it would never let go, no matter how many cleansing waters or healing rituals or tender, sweet lovemaking sessions passed between them.

Something that poisonous? That deadly? A grisly choice like the one that almost killed Josh on *Sacred Peace's* exterior set could never be erased. Not ever. And sometimes it reappeared by rearing its ugly head via toxic, spiteful comments that Jessie thought she'd buried but that showed up in times of duress. Aiming frosty eyes at Josh, she said casually as if her even tone could negate the vicious barb, "I suppose he had no choice."

That was it, but it was enough. Electricity zipped between Josh and Jessie, but it wasn't the good kind. It was the supercharged blistering hot kind, the kind that burned.

Bitter, wondering how far into the future he would have to endure these kinds of nasty sarcastic digs, Josh swallowed past the hurt and strode past Jessie. He could hear the kids arguing in the next room. Deciding to mediate their fight instead of sinking into one of his own, he gratefully took the opportunity to make his escape.

Exasperated, Jessie ran a hand through her new mousey brown hair.

"What the hell did I just say to that man? Jesus. Thank God you decided to move here too, Arnie." She groaned. "We may occasionally need a neutral voice. Although lately it's really only me that seems to be doing the fighting. I don't know why I turn into such a bitch sometimes."

"That wasn't a fight," Arnie said in the most soothing, understanding tone he could manage. "That was hurt talking. Josh knows that."

"Still…no excuse, Arnie. I need to try harder. Airing my hurts to intentionally hurt him just ends up wounding us both even more." Sinking lower onto the counter, Jessie rested her chin in both hands and stared through the window at the little white house far back down the lane across from them. There were barns outside that house, and a fence. A corral. *Hmmm,* she wondered idly, thinking of a way she could maybe make her husband happy, and wondering just how amenable the new neighbors might be.

She took a new tack. Turning back to Arnie, Jessie probed for details about the older couple, about what they seemed to be like. At one point, she wrinkled her nose and asked, "They knew we moved here from Vancouver?"

"The realtor likely filled them in," Arnie explained. "In small communities like this, people go digging. They find out things."

"Whose name is on the deed, Arnie?" Jessie's eyes narrowed. "Matt bought this house." A sudden gulp telegraphed how that made Jessie feel. "He bought it for us. For me and him and the kids. He ever tell you that?"

Arnie wandered over to the fridge and opened the door. He trolled for a container of orange juice and poured himself a glass before returning the carton to the fridge and leaning back against the door. "I knew. Charles told me," he said eventually. "Matt was smart enough when he purchased the house to put it through a business name. He used one of Michael and Kelly's businesses—they've got a lot going on with real estate. He was still thinking about…" Stopping, he tilted his glass back and took a drink.

Jessie paled. She finished his sentence. "About Morgan," she determined. "Matt was still thinking I should hide from Morgan. Even though he hoped me and the kids were off Morgan's radar once and for all."

"That's right. But I guess he felt comfortable divulging the Vancouver connection, seeing as it was rather anonymous. Michael signed the deed.

From the perspective of local realtors, Michael Kelly is a generic enough
name, especially attached to an American company."

"If people around here talk, then wouldn't there be some question as to
why a Joe McIver's living here instead of a Michael Kelly?"

"Michael signed on behalf of a business. Businesses buy property all the
time, and move their people around."

"Okay. Well, that's good, I guess. Curious locals should be all right with
that, don't you think?" Jessie let her shoulders droop. She wiped her lip.
A bead of sweat had broken out across the top of it at the hard memory of
living a life that no longer included Matt. *Slays me,* Jessie sighed to herself.
*Just guts me not to have him near.*

She cheered up when, from the other room, Josh's jubilant laughter rang
out in the midst of the kids' giggles and roars. Micah was in a shining mood
too, and stretched his arms out to the closest adult, which happened to be
big tough Arnie. Happy as a clam, Arnie set his glass on the counter before
bending over and scooping the baby up in his arms.

Jessie's eyes brightened. "We oughtta get those cookies going," she said.
"I promised my incorrigibles that we'd do some baking. And Dylan wants
to explore the outdoors some more." Cornering right, she dug around a half
unpacked box for baking things Deirdre had assured her would be waiting at the house. She smiled widely at Arnie. "That baby looks some good
on you. Maybe you'll meet yourself a new woman down here on the east
coast, Arnie."

"I'm too old to have kids of my own," Arnie huffed, adjusting Micah to
cradle him upright against his shoulder. "Those days are long past."

"I wonder if Matt knows what he's getting into," Jessie thought aloud in
an abstract kind of way. "I seem to recall Shanda saying she wants kids. I feel
like she said something about adopting, at one point."

Arnie did a little back and forth sidestep to rock Micah in his arms, and
darted a peek toward the sound of Josh's voice. "You miss him," he said
plainly, deciding Jessie was craving news, any news, about her old friend.
This was not likely a discussion she would have with Josh. Josh's tolerance
toward Matt was fair and open, but had its limits.

"'Course I do." There were a few more groceries to put away. Setting a mixing bowl sourced from the baking box down on the counter, Jessie picked up a can of chick peas and stared at it, but didn't really see it. Dancing across her mind was Matt, clear as day. She ached to have him in her kitchen rocking the bobbing Micah in his arms. Not as a lover, but just as the old friend she knew and loved. "I'll always miss him." She looked up at Arnie. "This is all gonna take some serious getting used to, Arnie," she confessed. "All of it." Her voice was thick again. Jessie was on a roller coaster these days, slowly going up, up, up, and then cresting summits and flying back down at wild rates that instantly plummeted her spirits.

"I know." Always the understanding guy Jessie relied on, Arnie didn't disappoint. Moving in her direction, he rested Micah in one strong arm and took the chick peas from Jessie's hand. He placed them in a cupboard. "One breath at a time, Jessie. The days will get easier."

Turning so her back was to Arnie, Jessie sighed heavily. "You sure about that?"

"Yeah," he said, with a confidence Jessie wondered if he really felt. "You either sink or you swim. You know this, girl." Arnie gripped her shoulder and rotated her back around to face him. "It's your choice."

"Ah. A choice. Don't talk to me about choices." Biting her lip, Jessie watched her buddy for a moment; watched hard facts flit across his usually calm demeanor.

Arnie handed Micah to her. He reached past Jessie for a can of kidney beans and set them in the cupboard next to the chick peas, not so much to be helpful, but more so he wouldn't have to look into Jessie's scared, sad, lonely eyes for one more second. He worked in silence, which only served to sink Jessie's spirits further.

When Josh came back into the kitchen ten minutes later with Dylan happily suspended fireman-carry style, belly down, over a shoulder, Jessie gathered her wits enough to press her lips to his before she started out of the room. "Can you take the kids back outside so Dylan can have a closer look at those tracks?" she asked. "I need to feed Micah. I don't know if we're gonna get the cookies baked today. At the rate we're going, and all the unpacking I need to do, it might be easier to just run back into town and buy some."

"Animal tracks, is it?" Josh was whistling happily. He marched over to the mudroom and set Dylan down on a wooden bench, stopping long enough to say, "Call the other two heathens, would you, Jess?" Rummaging for outdoor clothes, he tossed a coat and pants on his son's lap. "Here, Dylan. Snow pants again, buddy."

Stealing away, Jessie passed Josh's request along to Emily-Grace and David before trudging upstairs and sinking into a rocking chair in Micah's half set up room. She trained a gloomy eye out at the partially iced over bay. "How are you doing, Matt?" she brooded aloud, cuddling Micah to her. She couldn't help but wonder whether her old friend was missing her too, even just a little bit.

Placing a kiss on Micah's soft hair, Jessie started to softly sing. Music was the universal healer. Music softened the noisy mess in her belly and lessened the ache in her heart. Outside, Josh eventually appeared and bent over some of the snowy footprints. Soon three small heads were bent over them too.

Jessie stopped singing. She could hear Arnie fishing through boxes downstairs, unpacking what he could, she supposed. A content Micah was making the sweetest soft sucking sounds at her breast. The house was cold and creaky; the late season snow was frustrating and this new life was already isolating. Yet there was hope amidst the unique sorrow.

She watched her children bounce along next to the animal tracks. Emily-Grace dropped to her knees in the snow and soon was flat on her back making an angel by repeatedly fanning out her arms and legs. David followed. Josh started a snowball fight with Dylan, who screeched and hid behind the smaller of the two outbuildings. Soon there were snowballs flying everywhere.

"Ohhh," Jessie breathed when Josh looked up at her in the window, his face rosy-cheeked from the cool outdoors. He was radiant in the pure peace of this laid-back Prince Edward Island day. "I don't suppose it can get any better than this, Micah," she whispered to her baby. "Truly."

Josh raised a hand in greeting, but it was a brief hello. He got tackled by both of his older sons at once. Picking David up, he swung him gleefully over a shoulder.

Closing her eyes, Jessie sighed into the rocking chair and held her baby close. Half-heartedly, she growled at Josh for the sore shoulder she would have to ice for him later.

"Thank you, God," she murmured sleepily. "Thank you for lighting the way."

Chapter Three

Jacob reached into a small fridge in his Austin, Texas dressing room and pulled out a large bottle of beer. He held it up to Matt and made a dramatic point of turning the bottle around so the front label was facing his friend. Peering out from underneath a wide-brimmed cherry red cowboy hat on the colorful label was a starry-eyed rodeo clown.

"Whiskey Barrel Rodeo," Jacob explained, extending the dark bottle out toward Matt, who took it with apprehensive scrutiny and raised eyebrows. "Brewed right here in the Lone Star state. Made with chipotle peppers and smoked malt. An aged stout with a healthy dose of whiskey, properly nuanced with the world's most expensive coffee. That coffee provided to you, might I add, by the internal workings and subsequent ass end of some waif-like cat creature in Peru or China or somewhere."

"Quite the combination." With a dry twist of his lips, Matt gave the cap a turn to loosen and remove it, and sniffed the beverage before taking a drink. "Vietnam," he stated aptly after swallowing the robust beer and nodding his approval. "Not Peru. Not China. Not a cat. A civet."

"What the hell's a civet?"

"Ask Josh's brother, Zach," Matt said knowingly, dropping down onto an overstuffed, comfortable yellow leather couch. "He's the coffee hound."

"So you've heard of it. I ain't lyin.' The most expensive coffee in the world is made from critter shit. Who the hell knew?" Nudging his butt up onto the make-up counter that ran one length of the dressing room, Jacob twisted off the cap on his beer and took a long pull on the heady, crisp brew. Satisfied with his first taste, he licked his lips. "Now that's a beer. Good for when you can't decide what ya want, whiskey, coffee or beer. Although in my case it'll always be beer."

Matt took a good long look at the clown on the label. "Kind of ruins the taste of a good whiskey, in my opinion. Not to mention a good stout."

A spark of joy appeared in Jacob's eyes. He enjoyed trying to get a rise out of Matt, who was his opposite in terms of being schooled in class and luxury, and definitely his reverse when it came to the finer things in life—things that required refined taste, like exquisite food and tailored clothes. "What about the coffee?" he teased.

"I don't care about the coffee."

"Jessie would. She'd rag at you for that snide remark, Matt."

"I can just imagine what Jessie would have to say about this beer." The sarcastic comment was a foil. Matt would give anything to have Jessie at his side tossing in her two cents on this crazy Texan beer.

Jacob was about to take another drink. He hesitated, his arm floating in the air for a second before he followed through and tipped his bottle back. Matt did seem a little blue at sound check and then before the show tonight—his comment about Jessie confirmed it. Jacob was no stranger to interpreting Matt's feelings when it came to anything Jessie related. His voice was a little lower when he spoke again. "I think she's tried that coffee," he said helpfully. "Seems to me we've talked about cat shit coffee before."

"Civet coffee," Matt corrected idly. "Not really a cat, Jacob. Not really the same thing at all."

"Whatever." Inching his body back so he could relax more fully on the counter, his back against the mirror—mirrors always seemed to line the fancier dressing rooms at his shows—Jacob studied Matt. His friend and security for tonight's multi-cast show was lost in a fog of remembrance it seemed, judging by Matt's long face and unfocused eyes.

Catching Jacob's eyes on him, Matt lifted his feet onto a coffee table and crossed his ankles. He started picking at the top right corner of his beer label.

"It's always weird doing these kinds of shows without her, isn't it, buddy?" Jacob sank into a slump. "The stage feels so damn empty."

Matt didn't say anything in response. He just did that blank stare thing he seemed to do so much these days, his lips curled downward as he peeled away at the metallic label on the bottle.

Jacob tried to fill the awkward pause with something he figured Matt would have no choice but to respond to. "You talk to her much, Matt? Is she liking P.E.I. okay?"

"Ask Kayla." It was practically a grumble.

"Yeah, about that. I heard you got a phone to Kayla earlier in the week. Thanks. She needed to hear her big bro's voice."

Glancing at the doorway, Matt followed up a quick panicked look with a scathing reprimand fired in Jacob's direction. "Careful, Jacob," he warned.

Jacob threw up his arms so fast he almost spilled his beer. "Easy. Jesus. You need to get back to Shanda in Calgary. Methinks my man Matt needs a good lay. Or three."

A low rumble was all Jacob got from Matt. It landed somewhere between a sorrowful whine and a defensive counter attack.

Annoyed at his glum traveling partner, Jacob glanced away from Matt. Some of the other cast who were finished their sets and who were waiting to be called back to the stage for the final number were hanging around in the hallway, laughing and swigging back their choice beverages, their boots and shoes muffled thuds as they moved about on the venue's historic back-stage hardwood floor.

Following Jacob's curious eyes, Matt took a second look out of the open doorway. One of the artists on the bill tonight was Dallas White, a well-loved forty-something long-haired country singer who, both Jacob and Matt were aware, had a fairly new girlfriend. What was really interesting about Dallas, though, was that he'd met his lady in Prince Edward Island, at a campground not far from where Jessie was living now.

Matt perked up.

In his peripheral vision, Jacob watched his friend straighten noticeably and latch his eyes onto Dallas.

Dallas was a good guy. Over the years Jacob had gotten to know him at various mutual concerts and awards shows, like the one they were doing now for environmental awareness. In the celebrity world of entertainment and gossip, it was no secret that Dallas had endured his own struggles over the past few years—serious heartache, in fact, when he split from his song-writing partner who was also his partner in love, Deborah Lacey, and high-tailed it to Prince Edward Island for some healing time.

Matt saw himself in the man's eyes. Dallas, seeming to get some kind of vibe that he was being watched, wandered to the open doorway of Jacob's dressing room. He, too, was sucking back one of Texas' finest handcrafted beers, a gift from the brewing company sponsor, stocked in each artist's dressing room.

Dallas took up a half reclining position against the door frame and raised the bottle in a jubilant, wide *hello*. Fit and trim, his gray T-shirt excited the females in the audience tonight, no doubt about that; rippled muscles were clearly visible underneath the tee's comfy cotton blend. A round tattoo armband encircled one perfect bicep; it moved slightly every time Dallas raised and lowered his bottle. Even Matt, a man more at ease with morning runs and daily workouts than Jacob, who did okay when it came to staying toned at least, noticed how good the guy looked. Dallas, with his long hair and contented smile, wasn't a pretentious kind of guy, though. He didn't flaunt his looks or seek attention. He was just a good sort of person who was known around the music block as a nice guy, and then there was that P.E.I. connection…

Jacob raised a bottle. "Haven't seen you in a while, Dal. I hear congratulations are in order. You're dating an east coast girl. Well played."

"Thanks, Jacob." Dallas was alight, all right. With a casual nonchalance, he glanced over at Matt and spoke directly to him. "Seen you around, usually in Jessie Wheeler's company. Dallas White." Shoving out a hand, he sauntered the few steps over to Matt, who half rose and shook firmly.

"Matt Kelly," Matt replied, easing back down. "Security. Jessie's taking a break."

"I heard. I'm sorry about her troubles."

Uncomfortable, Matt looked away and met Jacob's eyes across the room. The shared knowing between the men was merely a glimpse, but Dallas caught it. Wisely, he chose not to say anything, although there was a palpable sadness in the room—more, he noted, coming from Matt than from Jacob.

With the beer suspended in one hand, he recrossed the small space between himself and Matt, pivoted around to face the guys, leaned back against the door frame, and shoved his free hand in the right front pocket of his jeans. "How's Jessie doing?" he queried.

Matt tensed. Noticing, Jacob got Dallas' attention. "She's holding her own. She'll be back on stage with us in no time."

"She's a tough one." Dallas raised his bottle. "To Jessie," he said. Jacob followed suit.

Ignoring them, Matt took a drink without toasting. "You and I both spent some time in the land of the bright red mud," he said, curious. "In Darnley, right?"

"That was you? Yeah, I knew one of Jessie's guys hung out there. Good place to hide." Dallas took a chance. "Relationship funk?" he asked. "Or general all around life funk, like me?"

"Kind of both."

"I hope you got them sorted." Dallas was genuine in his concern. The dark days that landed him in Prince Edward Island were unpleasant enough to warrant serious attention. Thing was, though, Dallas was thinking this guy of Jessie's didn't look any better than Dallas himself felt the day he first steered his old pickup truck across the Confederation Bridge.

Jacob butted in. "Matt here's newly married. To a drop dead gorgeous actress, in fact. Shanda Ellis? She's in *Sacred Peace*?"

"Yeah, I watch the show. It's terrific. Gonna be different without Josh Sawyer in it, especially after what…" Dallas hesitated. Matt seemed pretty down and out. And wasn't there something about he and Jessie hooking up? There was that viral tweet from Stockholm, and some harmless gossip around the music circles Dallas was privy to. He narrowed his eyebrows and fixed his stare on Matt. "In my experience, it doesn't do to beat around the bush," he said. He pointed his bottle at his chest. "I just latched onto a new woman, and I'm over the moon." Bringing the bottle out from his body, he tipped it nose first toward Jacob's security pal. "I'd think the man who just snagged Shanda Ellis oughtta be equally starry-eyed."

Suddenly alert, Matt sat back and picked at the beer label. Studying the much-loved country artist at Jacob's doorway, he shrugged. "Jessie and I were a team for a long time," he professed. "The stage just looked empty out there tonight. That's all."

Smart enough to note the way Matt's eyes moistened when he referenced how empty the stage seemed, Dallas wondered what was being omitted from the conversation. His earlier instincts were right when Matt added, "Jessie means a lot to me. Truth be told, she was my reason for going to P.E.I."

"She's from there."

"Yeah."

"Well, it's a pretty special place, her island." Dallas was finding that there was something immediately agreeable about Matt, even though the guy was down and out at the moment. Likely it was the stage, as he'd said—the whole not seeing Jessie there thing. The first few times Dallas played with Deborah at his side after he caught her cheating on him with his best friend had been torture. He grinned. "I had the opposite problem. I wanted my ex off the stage. Girl refused to go away, at first. Drove me nuts."

"Deborah?" Grabbing the back of a high chair, Jacob hauled it closer so he could put his feet up on the seat. It screeked loudly across the floor. "She's a handful. Geez, Matt, you think Jessie goes rogue—"

"Deborah's hot-headed, I'll give her that," Dallas jumped in, "but her going rogue is mostly restricted to the bedroom." He followed it up with a convivial, "And by that I mean not always mine. Hence our breakup. We've made our peace, finally. We're both with other people now. We're good. Time's a good healer."

"You just switch that light off, Dallas?" The quiet query came from Matt's corner of the room. "Is it that easy?" Tipping back his beer, he waited for the country singer to respond.

"What light, the…oh, I get it. The one where I'm playing shows and my gal, Cassie, is home in Halifax working, and red-hot Deborah runs her erotic come hither fingers down my chest. The thing is, lots of guys would jump right back in there, if that's the light you're referencing, Matt. But there's this thing about the music world that I've learned over years of sharing beds with women I'm not in love with. You two listening?"

Jacob was watching Matt, but thinking about Kayla and their new baby. Not once had he cheated on her since they recommitted to each other on the B Boyz tour—in Prince Edward Island, no less. The few hot nights he'd shared with other women since—Jessie included, which was more of a healing kinda night—Kayla had been part of the fun. He had no desire to step out on her. Ever. He wondered if Matt felt the same about Shanda now that the two were married.

Aiming his words at Dallas, Matt spoke to both guys. "Save your breath. It's not the women you're no longer in love with that are the problem. It's the ones you still love. That's the light I was thinking about."

Jacob set his now empty bottle down on the counter. Even though he did it quietly it jarred all three of them, because the room had suddenly seemed to fill with dead, musty air. He wriggled uncomfortably on the counter. "It gets easier, Matt," he tried. "Give it time."

Dallas looked from one guy to the other and back again. His eyes eventually landed on Matt. They were a little sad. "Your island girl still has your heart. Maybe it was just too soon for the two of you. After losing her husband, I mean."

At first, Jacob and Matt stayed silent. After a bit Matt said, while picking away at his beer bottle label, "That one tweet from Stockholm musta been from a damn Ostrich or something."

"Sorry, man. It doesn't seem to be a secret. People know about you and Jessie the same way they know everything that goes on in celebrity lives. Look, maybe you ought to bring your new wife to P.E.I. for a few weeks this summer. Get some more of that famous laid back R & R."

Jacob stilled, while Matt chuckled into his beer. "That'd solve everything." He pictured dropping in unannounced on Jessie and Josh. "Can't, anyway. Shanda's tied to *Sacred Peace* until the end of September."

"Sounds like you need a break, though," Dallas said helpfully. "Some time to think things through?"

"There's nothing to think through. Look, I've made a bad impression." Setting his bottle down on the coffee table, Matt brought his feet back down to the floor one at a time and sat more upright on the soft leather couch. Leaning forward slightly, he rested his forearms on his thighs. "My wife is amazing. I chose her. I'm committed to her. But losing Jessie…well, I had to let her go. But it was like losing my shadow. Regardless, she's still everywhere.

Her ghost, I mean. On every stage this guy plays, and in Calgary on the *Sacred Peace* set where Shanda is and where I should be a lot more often."

A tentative voice from across the room called Dallas and Matt out of their study of each other. "Cutting Jessie loose is like cutting off your balls," Jacob announced. "One look into those anguished eyes and you're instantly gone again. All that strength and willpower you think you have just disappears." Hopping off the counter, he swung open the fridge door. "We need to talk about something else." It took him a minute to reach in for more beer; with his back to the guys he had to work to get his emotions under control, although for him these days the hurt was more about that empty space on the stage than it was about missing a woman he loved.

Dallas mused over what to say next. In the end he got Matt's attention with a simple sentence. "Wanna tour with me for a bit?"

Jacob was fishing for beer. At Dallas' question he stood upright and looked over at Matt, feigning surprise, forgetting that the fridge door was open. He tried not to laugh. "Can't see my boy here doing country music."

Jacob scowled at Matt's response, which was a single word. "When?"

"Not for a bit," Dallas replied easily. "Not finalized yet. Lookin' at late summer or fall."

Matt hesitated. "Prince Edward Island's North Shore Music Festival a part of that tour? Or is that too soon?"

Jacob slammed the fridge door shut.

Matt didn't budge. He was suddenly picturing a certain wild gal against the backdrop of a glorious summer island sunset. *Even just one hug…*

Dallas took in Jacob and shrugged. "From what I hear, Charles Keating currently has the most stable, loyal security team on the planet. I could use a guy like Matt here. You can let this guy go for a bit, can't you, Jacob? He needs a break from the heartache."

The whole idea rankled Jacob's nerves. "He has a stunning wife. I wouldn't exactly call her heartache."

"When Shanda's done shooting *Sacred Peace*, if our tour has started by then she can join us," Dallas said agreeably. "We have an open door policy when it comes to family. Just might be the break you need to get used to the loss of that shadow, Matt. And yes I'm doing the big outdoor P.E.I. show this summer, before the official tour starts up, actually. If you're up for it we can make that gig a test run."

With effort, Matt blew out a little *pffft* and leaned on his arms to boost himself upright. Facing Dallas, he said, "I'll never get used to the loss of that shadow. You know how it is with shadows. They're a part of us." He started toward Dallas, to go out into the hallway so he could escape Jacob's lingering, downcast, accusing eyes. Clapping a hand on Dallas' shoulder, stopping by his side for a second, he said, "Send me the details." Rooting around for his wallet, Matt used two fingers to nudge a business card out of a leather pocket inside it. Handing it to Dallas, he added, "I was around Josh Sawyer a lot in the old days. Josh is, uh, was," he blinked down at the floor and quickly back up again, "a big country fan. I can sing every one of your tunes. Word for word. Which is more than I can say about Jacob's hopeless, saccharine lyrics."

Wandering out into the hallway, Matt took up a position against the wall, crooking a knee up and watching the excited, adrenaline-fueled singers and musicians in the hallway happily carry on with each other. Some obviously hadn't seen each other in a while. There were reunions happening here—people slapping each other on the back, hugging…there were even a few tears.

*Shit, that was close,* he reprimanded himself for his slip of the tongue. He slumped unobtrusively against the wall. *Damn it, Jessie. I do okay until I get to shows like these. And looking into Jacob's sad eyes as he moves along without you only makes the hole you left behind that much deeper.*

He had a few chosen thoughts for Jacob. *You can try to fool the others all you want, Ryan. You would never have let Jessie go if you didn't have to. You've been clinging to what she left you—your musical partnership. You made your peace with that and now, with Kayla and Lily, it's easier for you to go on. But I still see the desperation in your eyes when you take the stage for sound check at a show like this, one Jessie would have done with you, and I see the same old pain there. You don't think I see it, but I do. And if you're having a hard time dealing with life without the Sawyers close by—without your son, too—then how the hell am I supposed to cope when I'm still buried in her?*

The work part was done. Matt had put almost all of his energy into the Sawyer family's move to the east coast of Canada. He, Charles and Charlie had worked closely with a trusted production designer and set dec crew to stage a plane crash in a remote area of Slesse Mountain, where Josh's medevac jet was said to have gone down. Nicely timed, Mother Nature cooperated shortly afterwards and covered the site with a few good snowfalls that added a perfect touch of realism to the area. The authorities did their thing. Supervised capably by Charles Keating's and Matt's investigative associates (paid well to manipulate evidence), they declared the crash site the proof they needed to issue a death certificate in the province of British Columbia for one Josh Sawyer.

The work, yes, was done. There was no more outrunning this drastic turnaround in all their lives, in Matt's life. The business of living had to begin anew.

Just as Matt was swallowing back a bitter longing for the wild, rebellious, troubled woman who had been at his side for so long, Jacob, inside the dressing room, was reeling. Hell, Matt almost let it slip to Dallas that Josh was still alive, that he was still on the planet. That, and all this missing Jessie bullshit, was rapidly sinking Jacob's spirits. Part of it was the notion of losing Matt, of having him potentially move on, to work with Dallas maybe, for a while. Matt was a good friend, yes—and he was also an extension of Jessie. He was a compadre in this weird new existence they—the Keating camp—were all living. Jacob didn't want to see Matt go any more than he liked Jessie and Dylan living on the east coast.

Dallas was taking a careful scrutiny of Jacob. "You mind if I ask you something?" he said.

"Shoot." Jacob twisted the top off a new beer and handed it to Dallas.

"Your friend said he was the one to let Jessie go. Why would he let her go and then instantly marry someone else? I mean, granted, it was soon after Jessie lost her husband, but you know what time is like—it flies by. Maybe he shoulda waited a little longer. Unless…"

The skin on Jacob's neck prickled. But Dallas didn't say what Jacob feared he might. Even if the slips and the references to Matt's relationship with Jessie made him suspect that something was awry, Jacob had a feeling he would keep a secret that big anyway. Dallas White was a stand-up kinda guy.

What the country singer said was, "Unless Jessie's not in love with him. She break his heart? From that tweeted photograph and just from seeing them at shows, I would have thought they'd be perfect together. They were always touching each other. Truth be told, some of the old hens around this biz figure they've been sleeping together for years."

"No." Adamant, Jacob shook his head. "Not for years. And hardly at all. Jessie cares about Matt but she has eyes for one man, and one man only. Has since the day she met him." Satisfied, Jacob leaned back against the counter and twisted the cap off another beer.

"But he's dead." The way Dallas was looking at Jacob, his head cocked to one side, his eyes curious but in an almost expressionless way, non-threatening, seemed to say that Dallas could indeed be trusted with a secret that big.

If Jacob chose to tell him.

"Not to her, he isn't," he deadpanned instead, bringing the new beer to his lips. "Not to her."

And that, no matter how you chose to interpret it, was the God's honest truth.

Jacob smacked his lips together, took a long, slow swallow, and held the bottle out to Dallas. Dallas wrinkled his eyebrows and slowly brought his bottle forward. Glass clinked when the bottles touched. "To music," Jacob said, his eyes somber but with a twinkle somewhere deep in their cobalt depths. "Its power to heal the things that hurt."

"To music," Dallas echoed, his lips curling up at the corners, accenting dimples that Jacob was well aware had the man's female fans on their knees long before he opened his mouth to sing.

In the hallway outside, Matt heard the men give their lighthearted toast to music, the wall they hid behind when things got tough. He closed his eyes. Music was not an option for him. In Matt's experience, unless he was watching Jessie play—in which case music was an extraordinary, blessed thing—music often just had the power to sink him. At least these days it did. He could barely bring himself to listen to Jessie's ballads. Even some of Matt's old standby favorites by other artists—The Stones, or some of his brother Michael's bluesy tunes—had the opposite effect of healing. With

Jessie gone from his side, with the loss of the entire Sawyer family, music just exacerbated the pain.

Music just hurt. The sad songs were sadder and the joyful ones were devoid of joy.

There was no pleasure in music for Matt anymore.

There was only a great, aching grief, and a bottomless, empty void.

*Chapter Four*

Jessie, her bum only somewhat warmed by an antique carpet runner, was sitting partway down the Sutherland House's formal central stairway, shivering in pink fleece pajama bottoms dotted with cozy white sheep, a light lace cotton tank flared overtop the pants, when Josh padded down the stairs to her sometime around three a.m. Sliding down behind her in unzipped jeans and one of his ubiquitous white T-shirts, he wrapped both arms around his wife's shoulders and hugged her arms to her chest.

"You're freezing, little one," he murmured into one ear.

Jessie tried to giggle but it came out half-assed, more like an annoyed snuffle. "Your beard," she enlightened him. "I can't get used to it. It's tickling me. Stop."

"I thought you liked being tickled," he joked with a low-toned, sexy flair. "Whaddaya say we give it a try?"

"In a few minutes."

Jessie's voice was subdued enough that Josh closed his eyes and started laying tender feathery-light kisses on one soft cheek. "What is it?" he asked, even though he kind of figured he already knew. Jessie had a burner phone dangling from one hand. Josh watched her lay it carefully on one of the many white flowers that made up the forest green carpet runner's border. "Were you talking to Dee?"

"Nope. Jacob. He was loaded."

"Nice." Raising his head, Josh started rubbing his wife's icy arms. Frowning, he stopped, grabbed the hem of his T-shirt, and pulled it up over his head.

Jessie was surprised to feel him shove the shirt, still warm from his body, over her head and down over her tank top. "Josh, no," she protested. "Babe, you need this. Your spleen, and…" She couldn't finish, and sighed in frustration instead. "You can't get sick, Josh."

"It's just a few minutes," he countered, speaking quietly so as not to wake their children or, worse, Fluffy the Maltese-Shih Tzu, who was often wired enough during the day to keep them all exhausted. The family didn't have a blanket or slipper in the house that wasn't sporting at least one hole courtesy of the dog's sharp little teeth. "So. What'd my niece's drunken father have to say?"

"Huh. That sounded freaky, considering Jacob is also Dylan's father. One of 'em," Jessie added a little too hastily. Settling into the cozy curve of her husband's chest, she curled her toes inward and snuggled up, almost into a ball. The night was freezing, acutely uncomfortable after months in the Caribbean sun. Even with the generous amounts of money the family could afford to pour into furnace oil for heat, the big heritage house was going to be hard to keep warm.

Josh laughed, a raspy, low laugh he intended as a sarcastic reference with a *father shmather* kind of vibe. "Lily's birth really confused the hell out of our kids."

"Pshaw. It's only one small blemish in the overall weird and wonderful Sawyer family history for them to sort out. At least they can never say their family is ordinary." Relishing the feel of her man's strong arms around her, Jessie kissed one muscled forearm, mouthed a silent *Thank you, God,* and dove in further. "Jacob said the show was tough tonight, without me."

"For him or for—"

"Both of them. All of them," Jessie cut in. "I don't care. I miss it, but God it's been great just being with you and the kids, Josh. It's heaven. Apart from missing everyone and apart from this new suckiness of practically living in the damn arctic, it's been surreal."

"Ahhh. Jessie Wheeler-Sawyer gets the normal life she's always wanted."

A creak in the floor below them startled Jessie. Josh was sorry to feel how quickly she stiffened in his arms. "Little one," he breathed into her neck, his eyes closed and light kisses landing in pleasurable, coveted spots again, "it's nothing. It's an old house. It's gonna creak."

"Every damn noise…" Turning her head to the side, Jessie wriggled lower and bent her nose into her husband's warm bicep. "May as well be a bomb."

"Or not. Jessie, we're safe here. Nobody knows we're here. Charles called earlier. He said the plane crash they orchestrated has everyone convinced."

"Not everyone. I was on Gabrielle's blog earlier. There are naysayers on there. Conspiracy theorists. You're up there with the mysterious Elvis now, big boy."

"Maybe you should reach out to Gabrielle again."

"I don't think I need to. She's on the 'let-Jessie-have-her-peace' side."

"Thankfully."

"Yeah."

They were quiet for a minute as they contemplated what it meant and what it would continue to mean as their lives in forced exile played out.

Josh's arms tightened around Jessie and his kisses slowed to a gradual stop. "I got to talk to Kayla, finally," he said. "Earlier today, when I went into Charlottetown. Arnie and I went for a drive along the north shore, around the Brackley Beach area. I called her from there."

"Brackley Beach…Oh, the beach past that old drive-in theater? Twenty minutes or so from Charlottetown? God, this island is all beaches. Take yer pick."

"Jessie…"

"Kayla. Oh. Good." She was rambling. "How's Lily?"

"Fine. I'd sure like to meet her before she goes off to university. Or gets married."

"I hope Jacob didn't call Kayla while he was drinking. He was on quite the bender. He was hanging out with Dallas White, the country singer who spent last summer at the campground about fifteen minutes up the shore from here."

Ignoring Jessie's anxious verbal chatter, Josh started them down a new road. "Kayla said…" He slowed, nervous about what he wanted to say because he knew it would jumpstart recent memories that would hurt. There was something to be said about starting anew, though, and a good chunk of that meant no secrets. Starting again, Josh spoke slowly, evenly, but without malice or contempt. "Kayla said you, her and Jacob had a little party of your own one night. In L.A."

Again Jessie went stiff in Josh's arms. She held her breath. "*That* night," she breathed. "Josh…" She twisted around to face him so she could place a palm on his cheek and peer into the molten chocolate eyes she loved. "It was the day I got your letter. That night. When I found out the…" She blinked unhappily up at him. "The truth."

"You had sex with Jacob. Jessie, I don't know what to make of that."

"Kayla was there, baby." Jessie's eyes were filling. "She was there, all tender and sweet, looking at me with loving eyes like yours, telling me that everything was going to be okay. It was like you were there."

"She, uh, has girl parts. She's not me. It's weird, Jessie. And Jacob…after what he did to you in Florida…I don't know how you could…"

"Come on, Josh." Abruptly, Jessie changed her tone from pleading to a more demanding one. "Jacob's actions on that one reprehensible night were the direct result of a heavy, terrible loss. Neither he nor I are looking at it any other way. We've chosen not to. I will always love him. You know that. But you should also know that nothing would have happened between him and I that night—the night I got your letter, I mean—if Kayla hadn't endorsed it."

"And been along for the ride, I gather."

"She's sweet. So sweet, your sister."

At that, Josh recoiled. "Jesus, don't tell me you're gonna fall in love with her."

Throwing her head back, Jessie laughed so loud Josh had to put his fingers over her mouth.

"Shhh," he warned. "Don't wake that damn dog."

"Or Micah." Shaking her head, Jessie curled sideways into Josh's arms. "He'll be up soon anyway. I feel like I'm living on autopilot, without help from Dee or Carlotta or even Alin and Sam. Our munchkins need a lot of attention."

"It'd be easier if we sent a few of them to school."

"Not happening. Not right away, Josh. School year's almost over, anyway."

"In September, then."

"We'll see. I don't know how Dylan would do. He doesn't like this whole pretend-you're-somebody-else game."

"Back to what we were talking about."

Jessie pshawed him. "Don't waste your breath on me having sex with Jacob. It was not about sex or lust or any of those things. I was six months pregnant and had just found out my husband didn't want to be on the planet with me or our children. I cried all day long. I needed him." Grabbing Josh's wrist, Jessie sniffled into his arm. "I needed you, Josh. But you weren't there. Jacob was, and Kayla was. Jacob and I have a history. He's my musical soul mate, someone I love dearly. Someone I had an intimate relationship with. He knew how to take my pain away. It was not about sex."

Josh considered that. "I think, little one," he said, using the endearment to cushion things, to help Jessie know he was not bringing this up in order to fight, "that what surprised me the most was that you didn't go to Matt that night. Why Jacob?"

At the mention of Matt's name, Jessie sank deeper into Josh and moaned. "Can we not talk about Matt?"

"Did you talk to him tonight?"

"No. I just talked to charming Mr. Drunk Guy."

"Were you hoping to talk to Matt?"

Jessie couldn't look at Josh. "'Course," she sniffled. "Always. I don't know where he was. And Jacob didn't say."

"I can't imagine Matt handled your passionate night with Jacob and Kayla very well."

"I wouldn't know. He and I didn't make friends again until the night Micah was born."

"Then you made, uh, good friends."

"Why are you doing this now, Josh?" It was a whisper, spoken into Josh's forearm, which Jessie was clinging to as if it were a lifeline. As if she were afraid he would take off on her again, in anger, and leave her alone with their four children and one very scrappy little dog. "You know about Matt."

"This is the thing, Jessie." Josh steeled himself for her reaction. "I don't think I knew, until Kayla told me today, how close I came to losing you this time."

Jessie held her breath. "What'd she say to you?"

"Stuff Shanda told her, mostly. That Matt shared with Shanda."

"Nice. Grrr."

"It adds up. In the Caribbean, you wanted to go back to him. You had that little meltdown the day the kids arrived. You said he told you that you could go home if things weren't working out with us. You could go home to him."

"Yes." Jessie sighed. "I would have gone too, Josh. At the time. Just so you know. But I'm glad I didn't."

Josh's next words emerged dusky and sad. He was clinging to Jessie, his arms locked around her in a tight embrace. He was strong and fit again—they had a small gym in the house, in the finished basement—but it was cold on the stairs. Bare chested and bare feet, he was starting to shiver. "I knew Matt was bringing you to me without you knowing. I just thought you weren't ready to leave Charles and Dee yet." Josh took a breath. "And because of Micah, because you needed support. I knew things had ramped up with Matt, but Jessie…Kayla said that Matt told Shanda—in the interest of full disclosure, apparently—that you and he were thinking of starting a life together. I thought it was possible but I didn't know how close you got. I'm sorry. I'm sorry because I should have paid closer attention. I should have realized before now how hard this must be for you, for him. For the two of you to have to walk away from each other again."

Jessie was shaking in Josh's arms and it wasn't because of the cold that permeated the old house like death. With her nose pressed to Josh's bicep she was sobbing in silence, her body heaving with the effort to stay quiet. Josh was weeping now too, tears like bits of ice glistening in the pale moonlight as they trailed down his cheeks. "I swear, baby girl, I often wonder why you keep coming back to me. Why you would want me." He shook his head slowly from side to side. "This time, though, it would appear you really didn't. I thought it was Dee, Jacob, Charlie, Steve, everyone else who was keeping you away. Your fear of leaving them, your fear of being with me. Your fear of leaving Matt too, yeah, I knew that would be a thing, but not," Josh swallowed, "not like the way I see it actually really is. Jesus, Jessie." Josh buried his face in her curls. "You really fucking love him."

Jessie's body was quaking in the cold and in the cruel reminder of what and who she'd had to give up. Of the hard knowing that her love for Matt almost won this round. Really, in the end, it had come down to him bringing her south. It had come down to him making an impossible choice for her.

"Truth?" Jessie said, talking in a muffled voice from inside the circle of her husband's arms. "You want the truth?"

"Does it get worse? Because if it gets worse, I don't know if I can handle it."

"What would be worse? Me going back to him?" Peeking up from behind Josh's arm, Jessie swiped a hand under her nose and hiccupped her way to a more restrained, quiet sorrow. "Because that won't happen, babe. That night in the Caribbean, we recommitted to each other. You," she punched a finger in his chest, "and me." She pointed to herself. "You promised me you would never let me down again. And so, Josh," Jessie straightened up her shoulders, "that goes both ways. I won't let you down either."

The relief in his eyes made this hard middle-of-the-night chat worthwhile for both of them. "Just tell me," Josh whispered, imploring Jessie to be honest, the type of honest that inky dark nighttime chats in creaky heritage houses called forth. "Say whatever else you need to say, little one."

"The truth, babe, is that I am really tired of loving someone I can't have. Fucking tired. That's the truth." She started to cry again, low, quiet sobs that prompted Jessie to cover her mouth with a shaking hand. "Every time I am away from you, I can't stand it. But Josh," Jessie reached deep for a big breath to help fortify her next words, "every time I am away from Matt, I can't stand it either. I'm sorry, babe. No more secrets. I miss the hell out of him."

Josh was silent, watchful, as he took that in. In the end he nodded, just once, in solemn acceptance. He cupped his wife's chin in his hands so she would have to look directly at him. The heartbreak he saw in those desperately loved sea-pearl blue eyes was almost enough to do him in entirely. "I deserve that from you," he murmured softly, with an intensity it pained Jessie to see because she knew it came from hurt. "I deserve it, because I've caused a lot of it, little one. Every time I opened a bottle or made a decision without you, Matt was always there picking up the pieces. I'd be the first to say, and you know this, Jessie, that he is one helluva man. If I have to compete with someone, I'm glad it's him. And on the other side of things, I gotta say I'm real fucking sorry for how he must be feeling right now. Because if it's anything like I feel when I'm not with you, then I know how goddamned bad it hurts."

Jessie reached out a finger and wiped some of the sadness off her man's whiskery cheek. "Thank you, Josh," she said simply. "Thank you for understanding all of this. How hard all of this has been."

"Little one...do I need to be worried?"

The dark eyes were so somber, so scared, that Jessie almost crumbled. "Nooo," she moaned, with a slow head shake to lay a foundation securely underneath the word. "No, babe. You and I have one thing Matt and I don't. And I won't say children because I swear to God there are times he has helped raise our kids every bit as much as you have. No, Josh, what you and I have that Matt and I don't is these." She raised their left hands. Their wedding rings glinted in the moonlight.

Josh's eyes widened. Scared, he stammered, "That's all?"

"It's enough," she murmured back. "It's the edge you need, Josh."

"Fuuucckkk," he said in a kind of frightened gasp.

Standing, Jessie reached for his fingers. "Come on, babe." She sighed. "We've got a little bit of footing to work with. Let's start with that tickle you promised me."

Hesitant, Josh followed her, but he felt like he was in some kind of trance now. He was not the same person Jessie married. Without a shadow of doubt, he knew that; deep in his core, he knew that. Addictions had haunted him, had fritted away a good chunk of their relationship, their marriage—never mind what caused him to go running back to the bottle in the first place. The reasons were almost irrelevant. They were almost a moot point now. He was also no longer the actor Jessie fell in love with. He was some bearded guy with no real purpose except to mind an old house, to keep older vehicles running and to entertain and feed their children (and an annoying dog). He was scarred, sore, often hurting and only above the rank of another man Jessie loved deeply by virtue of wedding vows said on a Prince Edward Island beach at a time when there was more promise in the air.

The ground had shifted; the balance had changed.

Without meaning to, Jessie drove the point further home when, at the top of the stairs, the pallid moonlight drifting in through the large window across from them highlighted the bullet scar on Josh's chest, and she reached out to touch it, to trace it. "You usually don't let me see this close-up," she said, wide-eyed, running her finger over the wrinkled, puckered skin. "Your scar, Josh. Apart from swimming, you always try to keep it hidden."

If things were lighter between them, Josh would have made a joke about keeping it covered up because it was so damn cold in the house, but there was a new icy truth in the chilled air that he had no clue how to defrost. Swallowing, he tried his best. He wrapped his big hand around Jessie's wrist and drew her fingers downward. "Matt and me," he said, drawing out the words in a husky rasp, "we both have bullet scars, Jessie. I know you look at his with honor and at mine with defeat, but one day I hope you will understand that they mean the same."

He had one more card to play. Josh led Jessie to the children's bedrooms, each in turn. Together, they pulled up blankets to tuck under chins, they lifted teddy bears off floors to snuggle under small arms and they laid sweet kisses on their babies' soft cheeks. Afterwards, Josh took Jessie to their big bed in the large master bedroom on the west side of the home. With the confidence of a man who truly loves his wife and who wants her to know it, he did what he could to try to make Jessie fully his again, but Josh knew as he pulsed inside her, and as he tented her inside his arms, that tonight there was a good chance she had another man on her mind while they made love.

In an hour, Micah disrupted their slumber with little baby-talk gurgles. Without moving or opening her eyes, Jessie stammered sleepily, "I'll get him."

Josh raised himself up on an elbow and bent over her. "I'll bring him to you so you can feed him and then you can go back to sleep," he promised. "I'll make the kids their breakfasts so you can sleep in, baby girl."

The way he said it, so sweetly, with so much fondness…

Jessie felt Josh's hand slip away from hers when he tiptoed out of the room, hauling his jeans back up over his body at the same time. She rolled half over to watch him go. The muscles on his back rippled as he moved. Would the world ever see this man's beautiful back again, on screen? Jessie doubted it. Turning away, she had to force the crippling anxiety that came with this new life back into her belly where it belonged.

Josh kept his word. After she fed Micah, Jessie slept soundly, buried under blankets and with orange foam earplugs tucked into her ears so she could filter out the happy noises of her rambunctious family as Josh fed and played with their children.

When she emerged from her cocoon a few hours later, the house was empty. Silent. The cars were in the driveway. Jessie made the correct assumption that Josh had taken the kids outside to play, or for a walk. Peering out of the side window in the kitchen, she spotted them walking away from her toward the small house across the road and down the lane. Emily-Grace was skipping, holding her father's hand; she had Fluffy's leash clutched in her other hand. Dylan and David were running, hopping and jumping. They were happy. Joyous, even. Josh had one arm wrapped around his front—he was holding Micah close in the snuggly. There was one other person walking with them—a gray-haired man.

"Mr. Sutherland?" Jessie wondered. "Hmm."

Sure enough, their older neighbor was alongside for the morning's walk. Every once in a while he bent over and the kids—and Josh—gathered around as he pointed at the ground or toward a mass of land in the bay to the north, west, or east. Jessie later found out from Josh and the kids that he was teaching them some local history about the ships that used to be built in the bay and about older generations of his family who lived in the area throughout the years.

Turning away from her family as they walked, Jessie wandered back to the stairs. She laid her hand on the round aged, worn newel post at the bottom, which brought to mind the old house across the island, to the south in Bedeque, where she spent the first twelve years of her life. It, too, had a beautiful history, and if its newel post could talk...

Well. There would be time for a drive across to Bedeque later. Maybe not today, but soon. And maybe Josh and the kids would be along. That would be interesting...a little Wheeler family history. There were things to look forward to here. Visiting her mother, and elderly George...drives across the island, detours on red dirt heritage roads...swimming at the beach when it warmed up outside...

"I'll adapt," she told herself sharply when a pang of longing, of missing everyone, accosted her so abruptly that she almost buckled over. "I have to." As far as Jessie was concerned, hers and Josh's wedding rings were enough of a reminder of what she had recommitted to, which included life here on the east coast island where she was born. They were enough of a reminder that Matt had said goodbye.

Outside, Josh ran a finger along the split rail fence on William's property. Micah was chattering adorably in the snuggly and the older three kids were running happily, playing their 'game' of new identities as they called each other by the names they would use in public—Ella, Jude and Ben. Micah was Michael.

Josh looked up at his neighbor, who seemed much more agreeable now than on the first day they met. "You ever think about having horses again?" he asked outright.

William spied a lingering sorrow in the young father's eyes. He wondered if it had to do with the wife, whom Joe said was sleeping in after being up early with the baby. William smiled. He understood about men, about having to find pursuits to combat the drudgery of everyday life. He understood about the kind of pain he saw skittering through this man's eyes.

"Horses are expensive, son," he said. "They cost a lot to feed. Plus straw for bedding's not cheap, and my stalls are old. They're in need of some repairs."

"I can fix a stall." Josh's eyes were brightening up as he spoke. "I can hammer a nail."

"I don't know what a horse costs these days, Joe. Pardon me for sticking my nose in where it don't belong, but you got old cars, a big house to heat and four kids to feed."

"And a dog!" Emily-Grace hollered as she ran by, her cheeks pink in the cool May morning. "But Fluffy's little and doesn't eat a lot!"

"We, uh, got an inheritance, William," Josh sputtered. "My wife and I."

"I see. I wondered how a man with no job could just pick up and move across the country like that."

"I can afford a horse or two."

"And a pony!" Jumping up and down, Dylan was yanking on Josh's arm. "Can we get another pony, Daddy?"

"Ouch. I dunno Dy, uh." *Jesus,* Josh cursed inwardly. "Uh, Ben." *Don't say anything, Dylan,* he begged silently. *Don't you say a damn word.* "Maybe. Or a small horse."

William puckered up his nose and frowned. "You had a pony before?"

"Yep! And horses!" Dylan yelled. "We had horses! Toby and Misty and—"

"Hey! Calm down there, kid." Josh gave Dylan a hard look that Dylan had no choice but to pay attention to. Then he turned back to his neighbor. "Mr. Sutherland, you've got stalls and fenced-in fields. All I've got is a couple of gardening sheds and a manicured lawn. I'll look after the animals."

"I'll have to ask the missus." William started walking again. "Will your wife be okay with it?"

"Yeah. She likes to ride. She's comfortable on a horse."

"The money part? Like I said, you're not exactly driving new cars."

"Uh, yeah. We're good. Really. We can rent the land from you. And the stalls. That'll maybe help you both out too."

"No need, son."

They ambled off, talking horse talk and enjoying the rowdy kids until Micah's wails signaled that Daddy time outdoors was over for the morning. At home, Josh found Jessie in the kitchen making sandwiches. Soon after, Arnie's Jeep pulled into the driveway.

A foggy distance hung between Josh and Jessie for the rest of the day. When they tucked the last child into bed that night, they went to bed themselves and reconnected through touch and love in an unspoken commitment to renewal and peace, but it was like starting over. Matt's shadow hung over them the way a fog hangs over the ocean, but instead of threatening loss, the lesson they took from him was hope—hope in themselves as a couple, which was Matt's desire when he took Jessie back to Josh in the first place.

The first days on Prince Edward Island were a baseline for greater things to come, for love to once again grow and flourish. As the island warmed, the annual lupins appeared; their dashing, aristocratic strength and beauty built into ladder-like roadside blossoms of pink and purple. The days grew longer; the fields soaked up the sun and turned a lavish green, the farmers and fishers went back to toiling on the land and water, and the pastoral island and its hardy people emerged from their frosty cocoons, encouraged by the promises wrought by each new day.

# Chapter Five

$\mathcal{E}$arly the following Saturday morning, after packing swimming bags for the older kids and a diaper bag for Micah, Jessie jogged down to the kitchen and started assembling snacks. Josh was a few minutes behind her. He showed up with shower-wet hair and a nervous frown.

"You'll wear the ball cap? And pull it down over your eyes?" he asked her as he stuck his nose into the lunch bag she was putting together, to see what she'd already plucked from their cupboards. "What do you want for drinks?"

Jessie pointed to the fridge. "There's juice in there. Fill the thermos and grab the kids' travel cups. Thanks. And yes, I'll wear the ball cap and I won't look anyone in the eye. I've got my Value Village coat that's a size too big and I'll talk to the kids again about being careful with their names and what's appropriate to share with anyone who starts asking questions." She flipped around to Josh and swept in for a hurried quick kiss. "I gotta admit, I'm really missing Sam and Alin right about now."

"Arnie's meeting you there. He can help with the boys."

"I think they've likely got a family dressing room, Josh. We're going to a decent-sized, modern complex. We'll manage. It'll be good to have Arnie along—or should I say Barney—but I don't want to be dependent on him. If we're gonna do this independent living thing, then let's go all out."

"All right. That's my girl." Relieved, Josh helped Jessie pack the rest of the bag before Dylan, their first rug rat up that morning besides Micah, sleepily padded his way down the stairs.

"I gotta go," Josh said twenty minutes later, after laying out cereal for the older three kids and refereeing a fight between David and Emily-Grace over some hand held electronic game that was quickly confiscated.

Jessie growled in frustration. Emily-Grace had run to her bedroom in a little girl funk and slammed the door. David was eyeing his mother and father from behind a big bowl of cereal, waiting to see how the fallout from the fight with his sister was going to play out. Dylan was hanging on to his father's pant leg, whining and begging to go with Josh, and Micah needed a diaper change. "Can you give me ten more minutes?" Jessie begged. "Go talk to your daughter, at least. Or change this monkey for me." Leaning forward, she dropped Micah into Josh's arms.

Josh's eyes darted to the side window. William was sauntering down the lane. "You'll have to let him in," he said. "Tell him I'm coming."

"Okay. It's all right. We don't have anything in here that he shouldn't see." Apprehensive, Jessie took a quick scan around anyway.

David piped up. "What shouldn't he see? Your Oscars?"

"Jesus, David," Jessie admonished, running anxious fingers through her hair, "for God's sake don't bring those up to anybody. Y'hear?"

"Jude, Momma," David corrected loudly so he could be heard over Dylan's wails, taking advantage of the fact that his parents seemed to have bigger things on their minds than his fight with Emily-Grace. "Not David today, right?" He was all smiles and sunshine now, spooning cereal into his mouth with so much vigor he was spilling milk. "And Grampie said you have to stop swearing."

"Grampie," Jessie muttered with a grumpy foot stomp. "Tell Grampie to come here and get all four of you ready to go out the door early on a Saturday morning. See if he doesn't start swearing himself!"

A light chuckle from Josh brought a solemn smile from Jessie. With Micah balanced in one arm, Josh tousled David's short hair and got a laugh out of Dylan by slowly walking and lifting him step by step from the room. It was easy enough to do since Dylan was sitting on Josh's foot with both arms wrapped around his leg.

Jessie tossed a few glasses in the dishwasher before regarding her oldest son from over a shoulder. "Just you and me, kid. Can you help me entertain Mr. Sutherland while I get a jump on these dishes? Then you better go get dressed, and make friends with your sister. We have to leave in half an hour." William was coming up the laneway. Jessie grabbed a baseball cap and pulled it low over her eyes just as a light knock came at the door. She moved forward to let their older neighbor in.

William had a bag of freshly baked cinnamon buns in a Tupperware container in one hand. He held them out to Jessie. "Good morning. Alice thought your kids might like these when they come out of the pool."

"Out of the pool?" Jessie met his eyes only for a second before she nervously glanced behind her at David. "Mr. Sutherland, these will be gone by the time we get to Summerside. Please thank your wife for us." She thrust out a hand but for the most part averted her eyes. "It's nice to meet you, finally."

"Good to meet you too, Jasmyn." Interested in this neighbor family, William gave the kitchen a casual once-over. "My son and I restored this old house. You're leaving it the same?"

"Oh, yes, I…we…" Taken aback, Jessie wiped a sweaty palm on the thigh of her jeans before she popped the cinnamon rolls into the big lunch bag. "We love it. You and your son did a lovely job on the house. I was wondering…since it's part of your family's history, why aren't you and your wife living in it?"

William stammered out an answer. "We've lived in the one up the lane for fifty years. This one was built by my ancestors but over the years hasn't always belonged to family. Jeffery bought it with money he made from working out west in the Alberta oil fields. When he passed his wife put it up for sale." He shook his head. "It's just not for us. Alice and I don't need this much space."

"I'm sorry if I was being intrusive, Mr. Sutherland. It's just…family's everything, right? Kinda seems to me like the house is more yours than it will ever be ours."

"It takes a family to make a house a home, Jasmyn. It'll feel like home in time."

Jessie didn't respond to that. What could she possibly say to a man she didn't know from a hole in the ground about why this big, ancient, drafty house might never feel like home?

"You should pop up to see Alice some time," William offered, still looking around. "She'd love to help you out any way she can. You've got your hands full. And call me William, by the way. No Mr. Sutherland for me."

"We call him William, Momma," David advised wisely.

"All right. William." Eyeballing her son out of the corner of one eye, Jessie gave the little fella's shoulder a gentle touch. "Jude, finish up. You need to get dressed." Grabbing Dylan's bowl from the table, Jessie was sorry to see cereal still in it. Dylan had hardly eaten a bite. She heard him laughing somewhere upstairs, which was a good sign at least. Emily-Grace's bowl was just less than half full. Jessie rocked back on a heel and ran a fretful hand through her hair again.

"Joe almost ready?" William pulled her out of her reverie, which was picturing the last few months living at La Casa before they moved to the Caribbean. Jessie was missing the cozy yellow Spanish villa and the helpful people within its hallowed walls.

"Joe? Uhh?" It took Jessie a second to come back.

David fired her an *Are you nuts* look. "Momma," he chastised, "Daddy. He's asking if Daddy's ready."

*And who are the actors in the family?* Jessie chided herself inwardly, immediately dissolving into a wide smile and planting a generous kiss on her son's unruly spiked hair. "I know, baby," she answered brightly, grabbing his bowl and rushing it off to the dishwasher. "I'm just lost in thought thinking about everything we need to bring for your first day of swimming lessons."

"Don't bother bringing Ella's swimsuit," David reminded his mother as he slipped off his wooden chair.

"Huh. Well I guess that explains her irascible mood this morning. She'll go in the water. She just needs a little help, that's all." Out from under the brim of the ball cap, Jessie stole a look at her visitor. Her voice was hushed and thick when she spoke. "Our daughter had a scare in the water. She prefers swimming with her father close by."

"Oh. I'm sorry." William's honesty was sincere. An understanding of the verity illuminating a child's fear sparked across his eyes, disarming Jessie, who was surprised to sense an instant kinship with the older man. "Look, if necessary, Joe and I can do our thing another time."

"Horse shopping?" Jessie responded after taking a moment to swallow back the dark memories of the Elbow River terror. "Nah. Ella will be okay. Barney's coming to help keep an eye on the three of them in the water." Jessie still had to reach for the new names, which irked her, but her neighbor didn't seem to notice. "My husband barely slept last night. He was vibrating, he was so excited about going to see horses with you this weekend."

The comment engendered a pink flush across the tops of William's cheeks. Muttering something incoherent that could have been interpreted as gratitude, he shuffled his feet and grabbed the top rail of David's vacated chair in order to help him stay balanced.

Jessie's smile grew wider. Clearly, this man—who had lost a grown son—was thrilled to hear that his new neighbor was excited about taking a trip with him. The men had a line on some horses for sale in Cape Breton, a small island at the northern end of the nearby province of Nova Scotia. They were so confident they would find the horses they sought that William had already sourced an older trailer to use for hauling. He and Josh had gone out last night to a farm close to Kensington and attached the trailer to Josh's pickup.

Josh's heavy footsteps sounded on the stairs. Rounding the corner to come into the kitchen, he grinned at William and handed Micah to his mother. "All set, old man?" he asked. Jessie shook her head in wonder. They were like soul mates, these two. A few years apart in age, sure, but both with the same haunted look in their eyes until they started talking horse talk.

"Let's get on with 'er," William replied, resting a hand on the door handle. "Cape Breton's a good eight hour drive. Alice will be home all day, and most of the day tomorrow except for church in the morning, in case your wife needs anything."

Reaching toward a hook by the door to grab his denim jacket, Josh turned back to Jessie.

She had to swallow past a lump in her throat. The pure joy in her husband's eyes was humbling, a rare thing these last few years.

He knew it. Sidling over to her, Josh tipped Jessie's chin up so he could better see her eyes underneath the brim of the cap. "Call me if you need anything," he demanded. They both had new smartphones, registered under their Prince Edward Island names. "I love you." A tender kiss, and he started to back away.

Jessie clung to his fingers for as long as she could. Apart from small jaunts into the Caribbean village, or out on the speedboat, or into Charlottetown or Kensington or Summerside since coming here, she and Josh had not been separated since…well, since. Certainly not overnight, as they would be tonight. A brief panic passed over her but she choked it away. "We'll be okay," she told him, so she could send him on his way without worry on his part. "Barney's close by too. We've got a fun day planned. Tonight there will be way too much popcorn and *Despicable Me*, and I have a feeling some *Kung Fu Pandas* might even make an appearance."

"My grandkids love those movies," William said, a wave of longing passing over his face.

Jessie brightened up. "Not as much as I do, I bet. Go, the two of you. Bring home some good horses. Drive safe. I love you back, Josh."

Outside, Josh had to thoughtfully rub his fingers over his lips a few times while he trudged to the truck just behind William. He was feeling guilty about sending Jessie off to the pool alone with the kids for the first time, but he fought it off. Really, what had made him decide to take this horse buying trip with his surprise new buddy was realizing how deeply Jessie's feelings for Matt ran. He needed to pull away just a little, to put some distance between them and gain a better perspective. Josh needed some space to breathe and to think. In some ways he wanted to hurt Jessie, to exhaust her by leaving her alone with their young family for a weekend, even though he knew it was a malicious thing to do.

The thing was, though, the admission about Matt—a direct result of Kayla's truthfulness on the phone—had cut Josh to the core. Horses were easy. A neighbor he planned only to get to know on a peripheral level was easy. Trying to be a man his wife would always choose first was exhausting. Trying to be a man his kids could respect was exhausting. Driving down a highway chatting with William and listening to country music, pissing at gas stations and wolfing back donuts and black coffee, was gonna be heaven.

Jessie was on the road not long after Josh. She took the opportunity of having all four kids in the van as a chance to remind them of the importance of exercising caution. "Let's practice now," she said into the rearview mirror. "Ella, let's start with you."

Emily-Grace was sitting in the back seat of the van, arms crossed and a pout the size of the Sahara Desert on her face. "I don't want to play," she mouthed off. "And I don't wanna go swimming. I wanted to stay home with Fluffy and practice my dancing."

"Fine." Steeling up her nerve, Jessie inhaled and picked Dylan out of the rearview mirror. He was whining in a pitiful kind of way, staring out of the window and missing his father. Any time the family was separated, when Josh was away from them, Dylan was usually the child who responded the most verbally with actual sadness. Emily-Grace got mad, and David usually just rolled along and brought his pain inside, although with kids there was always room for surprises. "Uh, Ben," Jessie tried, eyeing Dylan, who didn't even look up.

"Dylan!" Next to Emily-Grace in the back seat, David was behind Dylan. He poked his brother in the shoulder. Immediately, Dylan ducked his head and started to sob quietly.

"Oh, Jesus," Jessie cursed. She was already worn out and they were just turning off Sutherland Road. It would take a good half hour to drive in to the pool in Summerside.

By the time she cruised into a parking space on the west side of the low community building and thrust the van into park, the kids were all somber and quiet. The parking lot was practically full. The pool was in a large, rambling structure that housed a fitness center, three restaurants, a small casino and two rinks, the largest of which occasionally doubled as a concert venue to host world class entertainers like Elton John and Reba McEntire. Newer horse barns and a harness racing track were situated behind the building. Jessie had to park a ways back. She decided to put Micah in the stroller to more easily facilitate the diaper and lunch bags, although she gave each child his or her own swimming knapsack to carry in.

Arnie was waiting for them. He met them halfway across the parking lot.

"Aren't you a sight for sore eyes," Jessie grumped when he drew near.

Dylan was dragging his feet. In one swift movement, Arnie scooped him up and gave him a hug. "How's Ben today?" he asked. In response, Dylan kicked him and buried his face in Arnie's neck. "Ow! Geez, kid!"

"Dylan!" Jessie scolded after glancing surreptitiously around to make sure no strangers were within hearing distance. "Not acceptable. What's with all this kicking lately?" She rolled her eyes at Arnie, who raised his eyebrows at her.

"I hate that name! Don't ever call me that!" came a muffled sound from somewhere in Arnie's big, capable shoulder.

"Tell me you're coming for dinner and movies," Jessie moaned to Arnie. In a quieter voice she whispered, "How the hell'd us two lowly Downtown Eastsiders end up here, anyway?"

Arnie chuckled. "You wanted normal? This is it, your highness. This is about as normal as it gets."

Jessie harrumphed.

Inside, with Arnie's help, Jessie got the kids to their lesson groups on time and in good order, fairly certain that David and Emily-Grace would stay relatively shy and quiet, as they usually were around other kids, but she was worried about Dylan. As she and Arnie took seats in a small viewing area near the shallow end of the pool, she asked him to keep an eye specifically on her older two, while he cuddled Micah and she watched Dylan.

After about ten minutes of silence between them, Arnie interrupted Jessie's nervous observation of Dylan—who, to Jessie's surprise, seemed to be enjoying his swimming lesson—with a rather pensive remark about how Emily-Grace's lesson was going.

"I think her instructor wants to talk to you," he said.

Sure enough, when Jessie looked toward Emily-Grace's group, she spied a teen teacher on her way over. The girl had Emily-Grace by the hand. Jessie's heart dead-dropped to her toes. She yanked her ball cap down over her face. This girl would be just the right age to be a Jessie Wheeler/Jacob Ryan fan. Being known might be acceptable if Josh—as Joe—would not also sometimes be along for these weekly lessons.

"She doesn't seem to want to be here," the girl said, handing Emily-Grace over to Jessie. "Maybe she should start at a lower level?"

"That's not the problem," Jessie responded kindly. "She's a very good swimmer. I'll talk to her."

"Thanks," the instructor said. "I need to get back to my class. We can talk after, if you like."

Arnie patted Jessie's back. "I've got this," he said. "I like this family stuff. Take your daughter aside for some girl talk. Me and the boys are under control."

Jessie couldn't help but laugh, but she sobered quickly at the tears threatening to erupt onto her daughter's pretty, flushed cheeks. "Come on, sweetheart," she said softly. "Let's go find us a quiet corner."

Afraid to leave the pool area, where she could at least eyeball the rest of her children, Jessie pulled her daughter into her lap on a bench near a big tunneled water slide in the northeast corner of the pool. "That looks like fun," she said with a hint of a smile.

Emily-Grace sighed and laid her head against her mother's shoulder. "I wish Daddy was here," the little girl said wistfully.

"Hmmm. Me too. He's gonna bring us back some horses, honey. We can feed them carrot tops and apples."

"We *have* horses, Momma. Why do we need new ones?"

Hesitating, Jessie replied, "You know why, sweetheart."

"I hate this. I hate it here. I miss Stella." Emily-Grace started kicking out her leg, just enough to express her frustration but not enough to generate concern that an all-out meltdown was coming on. "I miss Precious."

"Evelyn and Gary are taking care of Precious at the ranch. Stella is coming down for a visit real soon." Jessie pressed her lips to her daughter's forehead and gave her a gentle squeeze. "We're here, sweetheart, so let's try to make the best of it."

"I don't know anyone in my swimming class. They're all looking at me funny."

"Why, sweetheart?" Jessie prodded. "Because you're feeling nervous about the water?"

"No, Momma," Emily-Grace bit off in annoyance. "Because when the teacher said Ella, I didn't answer." The tears finally spilled over. "I thought she was talking to some other kid."

"You'll get used to it. Just pretend you're acting in a movie, or on TV. This is practice."

"I'm never gonna do acting like you and Daddy. All that does is make people treat us bad."

*Yeah, like make us targets.* Jessie shivered, and tried a new tack. "How about you go in the water, Emily-Grace? Have some fun with the other kids. I bet you'll make friends super quick."

"I can't," was the subdued response. "I don't like the water when Daddy's not close by, Momma."

"Ah," Jessie stated knowingly. She hugged her daughter tight. "You're letting your fears win today, honey. What do we Sawyers always say?"

"Sawyer Strong." It was a whisper, glumly aimed at the tiles on the pool deck.

"And what do we say about fear?"

"Not to let it win." Emily-Grace sniffed and swiped a hand across her cheeks.

"The thing is," Jessie explained with a heavy sigh, "when it comes to fear, we have two choices. We can let it win, but if we do we miss out on an awful lot of good stuff; or we can take control of it. We can shove good old fear in the arse and tell it to take a hike, so it doesn't rob us of things we enjoy doing. Like swimming."

"But Momma…the deep water…I don't like swimming in water that's over my head anymore. I can't help it. I'm scared." Emily-Grace's sobs started anew.

"Oh, sweetheart." Holding her close, Jessie had to work hard to keep her own tears from pricking at her eyes. She took a look around the pool. There was David, happily paddling away with his class, apparently racing a boy he already seemed to be making friends with. Dylan was flapping his arms and splashing with his little class of six children, growing accustomed to the feel of water splashing on his face, she figured, even though he was already well used to that. On the viewing deck, Micah was a sweet bundle in Arnie's big arms; sound asleep, she hoped, judging by the way Arnie was so lovingly holding him against his body.

"This is the thing," Jessie said to her daughter as, around them, happy hollers echoed throughout the reflective, modern, glass-walled space, "you and I, we had a tough time that day, in the water." Matt jumped into her mind, on the other side of the car window, panicked, terrified. Floating there, suspended almost, desperately trying to get in, to reach the two Sawyer women he so deeply loved. Jessie hung her head and inhaled into her daughter's bobbed hair. A pungent, bedhead smell accosted her, and she forced a smile at the homey comfort.

"We did, Momma," Emily-Grace wept. Jessie knew what was coming next. "Snow. I miss Snow. Fluffy chews on everything."

"Snow would have started doing that too, honey. At least, I think so," Jessie considered. "It's something all puppies do."

"Please don't make me swim." The little girl arms went around Jessie's waist. "Not without Daddy around."

"How about this?" Jessie asked. "How about you sit on the side of the pool and just kick your feet in the water until you decide you'd like to try going in?" *You don't have to look down into it,* Jessie added to herself. *You don't have to imagine what it would look like if a car was down there, on the bottom. Our car.* "I'll talk to your teacher after. She'll understand."

The small, lithe body stiffened. "But you can't, Momma," came a thin voice from Jessie's shoulder. "You can't tell. We can't talk about it. You said! You and Daddy and Arnie and Grammie and Grampie, everyone said we can't talk about stuff like that. From the old us!"

"I will find a way to tell your teacher that it might take some time for water to become your friend again, sweetheart. She seems nice. I won't say too much. I'll just say enough. How's that?"

Slowly, the sobs quieted and the face Jessie loved appeared again. Jessie kissed away her daughter's remaining tears. "My brave, brave girl," she murmured tenderly. "I am so proud of you."

"Even if I don't swim, Momma? Ever? Even if I can't win past fear?"

"Oh, you will, honey. You will. When you're ready. Know how I know?"

"Because I'm a Sawyer," Emily-Grace said, slipping off her mother's knees and taking her hand for the walk back to her teacher. "Sawyer Strong."

"That's right. You are your Daddy's child. And he proves to us every day just how strong he is. Doesn't he, sweetheart? Look at how good your Daddy is doing these days. Us girls have to be strong right back at him. For him."

"Okay, Momma." Emily-Grace clung tighter to Jessie's hand the closer they got back to the class. Once they were there, seven little faces looked up at the little girl none of them knew from school, as Emily-Grace—aka Ella, on this day—leaned into her mother's side.

"Is it okay if for today she just sits on the side of the pool?" Jessie asked the young teacher, who nodded and said, "Sure."

"We'll talk after, okay?" Jessie asked tentatively.

"Sure. Come on, Ella." The teen reached out a hand, which Emily-Grace nervously took.

Jessie left her daughter with her class, and walked back over to Arnie just as one of her songs came over the radio speakers in the pool area. Slowing, she stared at a puddle on the pool deck and swallowed bitterly. She didn't talk to Arnie when she dropped into her seat next to him, but she was eternally grateful when he grasped her hand and exerted a little pressure.

They sat in a kind of contemplative silence, watching the children take swimming lessons on their first test day as McIver children; Jessie picturing a submerged car with a much missed man pleading from the other side of a window for her to be okay, and Arnie soaking up the family feeling of simply hanging out at the pool with a baby in his arms, glad to be part of the Sawyer fold and feeling very badly for Matt, because days like this were easy reminders of just how much the man was missing out on.

On his way to Cape Breton to go horse shopping, Josh left the radio at a low volume so he and his new friend could chat about things that didn't hurt, and rein in some joy and simply forget about life for a while. By the end of the day he was so used to being called Joe that when he called home later and Jessie called him Josh, he did a double take.

The next day, he headed home with two new horses—a frisky Palomino named Morning Star, or Star for short, and a gentle, small-framed paint that Dylan could ride, who came with the name Rusty. Saddles and gear arrived with the new mounts. Earlier in the week Josh and William had cleaned, repaired and prepared two stalls, and purchased feed and straw. When Josh piloted the trailer down to the end of Sutherland Road, his kids were out the door before Jessie had a chance to holler, "Be careful!" Jackets unzipped and small bodies running, the Sawyer children were anxious to meet their new four-legged friends.

It was a joyous homecoming. Later that night when Jessie brought her husband close for a hug and a kiss, it seemed yet another layer of the old pain had melted off his body and let him radiate a new kind of peace.

"Don't go away again," Jessie murmured into the cozy hollow between his neck and shoulder. They were standing in front of the sink just about to wash and dry the dinner dishes that were hastily tossed aside hours earlier when the men got back from their weekend trip. "I can't do this without you."

Josh was bubbling over. He chose to ignore the wistfulness in Jessie's voice. "Charlie would love that Palomino," he said, his words emerging light-hearted and happy. "He'd steal 'er and run 'er up to Calgary for *Sacred Peace* in a second flat."

Standing back, Jessie furrowed her brow. "You sound like you don't even miss it."

Josh guffawed. "What, *Sacred Peace*? 'Course I do. I just don't miss the worry that came with it. That's what I don't miss."

Grabbing the dishtowel, Jessie slapped it lightly against her thigh. She hummed in a low monotone voice and stared him down.

"What?" Josh took the towel from her and twisted it into a weapon. He chose not to use it when he recognized that her humming came with a some-what anxious, concerned frown. Her lips were pressed so tightly together they were absent of color.

Jessie wrenched the towel out of his confused hands and planted it on the counter. "You ever think you're hiding behind this place, Josh? Behind these new horses? That it's all just gonna catch up to you?"

"What's gonna catch up to me?" There was a warning in Josh's voice.

Jessie was careful before she spoke again. She tossed the mousey hair she was barely able to look at in the mirror. "What you're missing out on."

"Jessie," Josh answered, reaching for the tap and flipping on the hot water so he could start on the dishes, "I didn't think twice all weekend about work-ing. About all the shit that went down over the last few years. I think the per-son that's missing out on stuff is you." Banana-ing around her, Josh stormed over to the stove to start assembling pots to wash. "Only," he added in a gruff post script, "I don't think it's 'stuff' you're missing. I think it's a 'who.'"

"Hey, I was here with our children all weekend, Josh. Alone for the most part once Arnie headed back to Charlottetown last night. It's not exactly a stretch that I was missing people."

Josh stopped in front of her. "People?" he prodded. "Or a person." He moved back to the sink and slam dunked a pot underneath soapy bubbles. Like snow, little bits of wet white fluff spurted up and landed everywhere.

Jessie bit her lip before she answered with a single, barely vocalized word. "Person."

Slowly pivoting back around, Josh brought his wife's face into focus. "Didya wanna run?" It was a dare. "It's a Jessie Wheeler kinda thing to do. Or did you have a toke stashed somewhere that you smoked real slow to help get you through two days with your own children?"

"Really, Josh? This is what you have to give me right now? Shitty snipes about Matt and nasty crap about me being incapable of mothering my own kids without help? It's been a long fucking weekend, okay?"

Sparks flew from Josh's eyes when he fired back. "For you, I guess," he mouthed off. "For me? Not nearly long enough." Spinning back around to the sink, he angrily sponged a washcloth over the pot.

An image of Emily-Grace ripped across Jessie's mind. She was sitting alone on the side of the pool staring into its rippling, watery depths toward the bottom, barely able to summon up the courage to kick her feet, while Josh was out cruising barns in search of horses. Jessie pictured Matt again, on the other side of the Lexus' window, kicking and flailing, desperate to secure some kind of release so he could wrap his arms around his girls again. The ballad that had played over the radio at the pool started weaving through Jessie's head. The day it was recorded, with Jacob at her left as always, riffing on his guitar, seemed like so long ago now. Another dimension, almost.

"I'm going to bed." Jessie grabbed the dishtowel from the counter and draped it over the rail on the oven door. It hung there, crooked and immediately forgotten. "Leave the dishes. I'll do them in the morning."

After her stormy footsteps faded away—at the end no more than a hushed run up the carpeted stairs—Josh leaned on his arms in the hot water and closed his eyes. There were stars out tonight. It was a clear, breathless, late May night. Dylan's birthday was around the corner. That would be another tough day, because the Sawyer/McIver family would be celebrating without their usual trusted friends and family around to share in the joy for a boy going by the name of Ben who wanted nothing to do with his new existence.

"One day at a time," Josh steadied himself. "She's just tired. We're both tired." *She needs a purpose,* he considered. *Something beyond child rearing and cleaning up dishes.* He wondered whether Jessie would start to peel away from him, from them, if opportunities to play shows came up.

He didn't have to wonder for long.

Later that week, a call came in from Charles. Jacob had endured a bad fall from a bike and broken his clavicle. He had a show booked for the following Sunday night, in Boston. *Would Jessie like to take his spot?*

Josh was the one to take the call. When Charles asked, Jessie was outside wandering the property with Alice, trying to sort out the flower beds, wondering what the hell to do with them. Interestingly enough, the producer ran the question by Josh before asking him to put Jessie on the phone.

And interestingly enough, it was Josh who first said, "Yes."

Chapter Six

"I think I just said yes so I wouldn't have to see in her eyes how bad she wants this, how bad she wants to go," Josh was saying. "So I wouldn't have to bear witness to some kind of desperate, silent pleading. Instead, I'd be doing something that makes her happy. I'd see joy in those blue eyes of hers."

Outside, rippled whitecaps were lacing the bay with frenzied worry. An urgent island north wind was doing a great job of stirring things up and making the world feel fresh, but it wasn't doing a damn thing to put Josh's mind at ease. Around the house, unfamiliar clinks and clangs of yard items, like the chairs from the new patio set Josh and Jessie bought on Tuesday, were protesting the brisk breeze, undoing Josh's last nerve. He was glad for Arnie's visit. Little kids were not exactly the right sort of people to vent one's worries to.

"Jessie's not unhappy, Josh." Arnie poured a generous helping of milk into the coffee mug Josh pushed toward him on the counter by the kitchen sink. "She loves this, being here with you and the kids."

"Half of her loves this. The other half…I'm not so sure." Josh leaned back against the counter and took a careful sip of his hot French-pressed Guatemalan La Soledad.

"And you know because…"

"Because that's how I feel. And I can see it in her eyes, that same pull toward the past."

"You do a damn good job of hiding it, Josh."

"At least I've got the horses. What does Jessie have, Arnie? A longing for a life we had to flee. A longing for people she loves, for a man she agonizes over, she misses him so much." Josh angled his body sideways to face his trusted friend. His eyes were intent, imploring. "Arnie…she cries in her sleep. Since the Caribbean…since the first day she came back to me. I don't think she even knows she's doing it. It's like the old days, like when she felt she had to stay strong all day for everybody else. At night time, reality catches up to her."

A great gust of wind shook the house so hard that Josh tucked away a mental note to do a walk around later to check on the shingles. Already one of the small sheds was sporting bald spots and crying for a makeover.

Arnie cut into his thoughts. "What about the nightmares? She still have those?"

Josh deflated. "Yeah. Sometimes." If only one of those wind gusts would blow him back up, instead of draining the life out of him. Conversations like this one, that only served to bring up a troubled past, sucked. *Wish I were one of those fluffy white clouds in the sky,* he thought. *Being pushed along without having to make any effort.* "Honestly?" he said. "I don't know how she functions. Jessie's exhausted. In all seriousness, she's not in any shape to be doing a big show."

"She's on her way to Halifax, Josh. Should she be driving?"

"It's a three hour drive. She'll manage." Josh wrapped his hands around his mug and stared at his fingers. The warmth from the hot beverage was a simple, cherished comfort. "My girl loves her drives. As long as she's got music, she could drive forever."

Arnie played devil's advocate. "She's got Micah with her."

"Dan and Charles are meeting her at the airport. Once she's in their hands I'll feel better. You know Jessie, Arnie. She insisted. My wife's as stubborn as an old crow."

"Josh…since we're having an honest chat here…when's the last time Jessie and Matt saw each other?"

Josh paused and focused on a spot in the windswept bay beyond the kitchen window. There was something colorful out there riding the wind, undulating high over the waves in almost choreographed, gentle movements. A kiteboarder, harnessing nature's fury. As Josh watched, a massive yellow and green upside down u-shaped kite rose and fell like a leaf in a gale, the wet-suited body far beneath it as alert as a coiled snake. Shining with salt spray, propelled by the kite, the boarder surfed triumphantly over the waves.

For a second Josh contemplated getting a grown-up toy like that, but in his heart he had to accept that it was likely not a smart option. From the shore, kiteboarding looked easy, but riding the swells at the mercy of the waves and wind would be too jarring on his damaged body, on the steel in his leg, on the old injuries that still snuck up to haunt him on damp island days.

Refocusing, he turned back to Arnie and lifted his coffee mug to his lips. "When was the last time they saw each other?" he repeated. "When Matt dropped her off to me. February." Hesitating, Josh ducked his head. "You think he's doing any better, Arnie? Without her?"

"Sure, Josh. Yeah. Charles says he's getting by. Matt spends a lot of time on the road with Jacob, and when he's not escorting Mr. Rock Star all over the place he hangs around *Sacred Peace* with Shanda and Charlie."

*Twang.* Just like that, heartache zipped through Josh's body. He almost doubled over. "Jesus, I miss it, Arnie. I miss the whole damn circus. I wish Charlie'd get his butt down here. I need to whip his ass in a good card game, and race him down the field on horseback."

"Are Matt and Shanda coming down here with Charlie and Jane?"

Josh shrugged. "Charlie says they're talking about it. But honestly, Arnie, I don't know if it's such a good idea. The thing is…I had no idea how bad it was, between Jessie and Matt. I thought she was just clinging to him as a way of expressing her fear, I think. I didn't know her feelings ran that deep."

"Deep…?"

"Yeah. Like, it was so fucking close, man. Kayla told me, I think as some kind of warning to keep my shit together. Matt was ready to go, to run away and take her with him. And she wanted to go." He looked over at Arnie. "Did you know that?"

A tremor ran up Arnie's body. He let out a quiet breath and wondered if Josh knew the house they were standing in was originally purchased for Jessie and Matt. Deciding this wasn't the time to bring it up, he bypassed Josh's question and asked instead, "You know this, and you're cool with her going to do this show?"

Debating that, Josh hemmed and hawed before saying, "We've been doing okay, Arnie. At least, I think we have been. Apart from Jessie being bored and missing her old life, I think she and I are good. We snap at each other some, but we're under each other's feet all day. And with the kids…" He shook his head. "It's a damn handful, and that mangy little mutt of Emily-Grace's doesn't help, yipping and barking and antagonizing Jessie by pissing on the floor and chewing on stuff. But overall I think we're good."

Arnie tipped his mug toward Josh. "You better not *think* you're good, Josh. You better damn well *know* you're good."

Pondering that, Josh was quiet for a moment. After a bit he said, "Shanda gonna be there? At the show?"

Arnie harrumphed. "Hell, yeah. You think Matt would be allowed to be there if Shanda wasn't on his tail? Charlie and Jane are going down too, and Steve and Sophie. You know what it's like when Jessie plays a show."

"Yeah, all her old lovers come running." Josh let the flip comment slide out with a sarcastic grin. "Wish I could be a fly on the wall."

"You'll be picking up the pieces when she gets back, Josh. You know that, right? You ready for that?"

Josh considered that. "She'll have a three hour drive to cry in her coffee. She'll pull it together by the time she drives in. The kids will help. Jessie hates being away from them."

"I hope so."

The warmth of the coffee mug was no longer even a dull ache. It was cooling off quickly. Josh set it on the counter and gave it a shove. It skittered to a stop next to a mug Jessie had finished off and abandoned earlier. Staring at the two side-by-side mugs, Josh responded to Arnie with a wistful longing. "You know something, buddy? So do I." A last look out of the window, and he latched his eyes onto the kiteboarder. He could almost hear the shouts of joy the guy or girl was likely hollering into the wind. *Freedom,* Josh thought. *That's what it looks like.*

Beneath the rider's board, water zipped by in relentless patches swelled by nature's angst. Over the windstorm's cry, a loud *rrrippp* got Josh's attention. Another shingle went flying from the roof of the outdoor shed closest to the beach. Josh watched it spiral end-over-end toward the water.

"Arnie?" he asked idly. "Whatcha doin' tomorrow, guy?"

Jessie would be on stage in front of millions. Josh would be at home hiding behind a beard that drove him crazy, it was so damn itchy. In a pair of faded jeans and heavy work boots, he'd be minding children, and patching up holes.

## Chapter Seven

Handing Micah over to Charles, Jessie put a palm in front of her mouth to stifle a yawn. Like any proud grandfather, Charles hugged the baby tight and relished the tiny fingers that immediately wrapped around his. Dan swooped his big body into the truck—Jessie had left the van in P.E.I. for Josh and the kids—and hauled out Micah's carrier.

"So what'd that doofus do to his shoulder? He had to have surgery, you said?" Speaking to Charles, Jessie was almost grinning. Leave it to Jacob. She sobered quickly when she considered how awful he must be feeling since he was likely in pain, and missing out on a big show.

Charles elaborated on Jacob's bad luck. "He and Kayla were out for a bike ride, cruising the seawall around Stanley Park. Jacob says someone cut him off. He took a bad tumble." Unable to hide his glee, Charles was beaming. He felt bad for Jacob but for the rest of the Keating camp there was an up side to the singer's misfortune. Oh, how sweet it was to have Jessie back in his company, and six-month-old baby Micah in his arms. Deirdre would be over the moon for the next few days.

"Jesus," Jessie responded, reaching toward the floor of the back seat of the pickup to grab her guitar. "I take it he didn't have Lily in a carrier on the bike, or in one of those funky convertible strollers behind it?"

At that, Charles sobered. He eyed Jessie before he said anything. The pause was so long that Jessie, who was hauling out the guitar so she could hand it to Dan to put in their rental for the ride to the private area of the airport where the jet was waiting, spun around to look at Charles.

"Matt and Shanda were home for the weekend," he replied. "Thankfully. They were babysitting Lily."

"Oh." The hackles on Jessie's back rose in spades. Like an army of spiders, they crawled between her shoulder blades. She cringed. "Practicing for their own kids, are they?"

"You'd have to ask them that, Jessie. I don't know. I mean, can Matt actually still have kids? Didn't he get snipped once upon a time?"

"There's always adoption." Yearning careened through Jessie's heart. *It's okay, my kids are practically his kids. But gawd it would have been something to have a child with Matt.*

Immediately after thinking it, Jessie erased the longing with an imaginary swipe of her fingers across a non-existent computer touchscreen. It was easy, she just pictured Josh at home when she left that morning, scared and quiet, standing alone in their driveway in a rumpled T-shirt with both hands characteristically shoved deep in his jeans pockets. He was barefoot in the early June dew, which led to Jessie lecturing him about not getting a chill even though Josh and his absent spleen had survived something much more sinister—a bullet—not all that long ago.

He'd been standing with one ankle turned over to the outside in that Josh-like way of his, adorable enough that, as Jessie backed out, she had stomped her foot on the brake, jarring Micah, who started to cry. It was one long, last look at her husband that she craved. Her throat closed over at the same time that her heart did a little hitch-jump thing, and it was everything Jessie had in her not to leap from the truck and run back into Josh's arms. The weirdest part about it was that for some strange reason she felt like she needed to beg for his forgiveness.

*For what?* she'd wondered all the way across the width of the island to the Confederation Bridge. She kept wondering all during the creepy drive over the Northumberland Strait with its dark roiling water threatening menacingly beneath the surface of the long bridge. And all the way to Halifax after that. *What do I need forgiveness for? For running out on Josh for the weekend? Hell, he had a weekend away!*

No, the forgiveness was for wanting to see Matt so badly she almost couldn't breathe. The forgiveness Jessie desired was for nothing more than a painful, desolate longing for a life and for a man she had not been given the opportunity to say proper goodbyes to. It was for nothing more than an unspoken truth.

Jessie didn't get to see Matt until dinner, and when she did lay eyes on him he had the elegant Shanda on his arm. Shanda, his wife now who, from behind a guarded, wary mask, watched Jessie make a slow, cautious entrance into the dining room of their upscale Boston hotel.

Proud as peacocks, Deirdre and Charles were by Jessie's side. Dan was there too, standing back in his usual vigilant way mitigating issues with the keen assortment of paparazzi who were hanging around in the hotel's lobby. Jessie, a star the photographers loved and had not publicly seen since she filmed the Sakura Music interview and performance video back in early February, was the primary focus of everybody's camera lens.

There were more old friends than just Matt to say hi to. Regardless, Charlie, Steve and their gals knew their places. After hugs and ebullient *so good to see yous*—they never got to say goodbye when Jessie left Vancouver, either—Charlie discreetly took Shanda aside so Jessie could rest her eyes, for more than a lingering second, on the much-missed man who had so lovingly watched over her for so many years.

Matt offered a low-voiced observation first. Pointing at Micah gurgling and baby-talking in his grandmother Dee's arms, Matt said, "He's gotten big."

"Practically crawling," Jessie agreed in a whisper, inhaling shallowly from the top part of her chest while her heart leapt inside it. *Damn this public place,* she was thinking. There was no way everybody in the entire restaurant was not staring at her right now, or at Micah, maybe, although some of the more apt female sorts were likely eyeballing handsome Charlie. Without realizing she was doing it, Jessie wiped her palms over her thighs, once, twice, then three times. *Please please please,* she implored the universe. *Let him hug me at least. Just one hug…*

A quick intake of breath later, and she locked her eyes on the patterned rug at their feet, on the space between her and Matt. He darted his head to the side, checking out Shanda, Jessie supposed, to see if she was watching. It wasn't just the ramped-up lovemaking that was begging to be acknowledged as they stood there at an impasse. It was all those years together, of Matt bearing witness to so many changes in this grown-up version of the orphaned waif he was first charged with watching so long ago. Their history was rife with ups and downs. Like an erupting volcano their shared past was spewing over, begging for acknowledgement; in its wake was an aching need for each other that nobody but themselves—and maybe Josh and Jacob—could even begin to understand.

Jessie's eyes were floating. Forcing her gaze back up to Matt, she clenched her hands in tight little fists and made her lips move. "Please," she entreated, almost imperceptibly, tilting her head to one side so that only Matt could see the desperation in the bottomless well of her ice-blue eyes.

She was wearing a sweet little minidress that just brushed the tops of her thighs. Creamy white lace trim accented Jessie's femininity. In combination with a graceful new updo and sparkling, glittery nails, the dress gave Jessie the virginal appearance of a much younger, less damaged version of herself.

Matt was beyond enchanted. Shanda disappeared from his peripheral vision. A few short steps and he took in his arms the woman he so definitively forced himself to leave behind a few short months ago. Aware that he and Jessie were being closely scrutinized, he deftly lifted her just a bit so that he could move her sideways and turn his back to, at the very least, his wife and the other overtly curious Keating camp observers.

"Beautiful," he murmured softly, his lips pressed against one delicate ear. "You are so damn beautiful."

Almost of their own accord, Jessie's knees went weak at the intoxicating smell and feel of him. "Oh, God," was all she managed. "God, Matt." His hold on her was immense, but at this juncture it had to be brief.

Shanda, to her credit, swallowed her fear and said nothing. Elegant to a fault, she kept on smiling and nodding, trying not to look at Jessie and Matt, but failing at that as the conversation around her flowed, as wine was poured and meals were ordered. Micah was a good distraction. He entertained everyone with his amicable personality and baby-cute giggles.

Before Jessie let go of Matt, she leaned back and lifted a hand so she could run the tips of her fingers over the much-loved, much-missed cheeks.

Despondency drifted through Matt's eyes. Running across and through him, it soaked him with sheer hopelessness. The way a child's pencil runs through a maze, it led Jessie deep into the caverns of his soul.

"Baby," she whispered, her fingers stirring him, bringing him back to her through the sheer gift of touch. She was tuning into just how much her old friend was suffering simply by seeing her again, by being in her company again, yet not in the way they both once—for the briefest of time—imagined they could be. "You okay?"

"Not right now," he choked, letting his hands rest on the slender hips he once held while intimately loving—and tasting—the extraordinary woman before him. "Not so good right now." He found the wherewithal to add, "You?"

Jessie glanced over his shoulder. Shanda's eyes were piercing, and at this second they were boring holes in the quiet, emotional reunion. Swallowing, Jessie blinked rapidly at Shanda before letting her serious baby blues drift back to Matt. "We've got the wings," she murmured. "Nobody can take those away from us. You and me, Matt. The stages and the wings. They're ours."

He nodded in acquiescence, took a deep breath, and let his hands fall from the creamy lace at her hips.

Sidestepping him, Jessie sank down next to Jane on a comfortable bench seat in the exclusive restaurant. She wrapped her fingers around Jane's, sighed deeply once, and covertly watched Matt wheel slowly around, swallow twice, pick his wife out of the assembled Keating gang, and settle in where he knew he was expected to land.

～～～

The next day, Josh called his children in from the playroom just as he and Arnie were settling in to stream the concert. Halfway through the benefit, a dreamlike fairytale glamour washed over the TV stage. Wistful azure lights floated lazily back and forth—a hypnotic percussive bass thrum ignited senses and stirred watching, restless hearts. Billowy fog diluted the blue beams of light; the stage seemed to nestle into the cottony softness of a cloud. Filtering out from underneath the cave-like lights, as if blossoming into life, the first few carefully fingered piano notes of a ballad recognized as Jessie's filled the theater, undercutting the lights with a mystical, anticipatory allure.

At home in Prince Edward Island, nobody breathed.

Magic was about to happen.

A graceful, ghost-like figure waded through the mist on strappy, sky-high heels. A delicate hand lifted a silvery microphone. An enchanting, honeyed voice the world adored and missed filled the air.

"Momma's so pretty," Emily-Grace sighed, snuggling into her father's side. Her eyes were as wide as saucers. "Look at her nails, Daddy!"

Sure enough, Jessie's fingernails were glistening like sapphires in the haunting blue of the stage lights. Grasping the microphone, which at times she raised high to salute the heights of musical cadences, Jessie, too, was awed by the sophisticated sparkle of nails she'd gotten used to seeing cracked and chipped. This whole trip to Boston was a rebirth of sorts. A homecoming. In her finest adornment and glory, Jessie fell easily back into doing what she did best—entertain with music. She was in her element. Unlike her last big show, which was a stark memorial to Josh, this one was a treasured gift.

*Enough time away from the spotlight,* she decided after she brought her first song to a close with a lingering, perfectly pitched high note. *What was I thinking, with all that talk over the years about living a normal life away from the people I love? This is what I am good at. This is what I do. These people around me are family.*

Standing in the spotlight, taking her bows, Jessie never looked more glamorous or felt so perfectly fitted to her place in the world. A vision of her hair up in a messy ponytail while she bent over to wipe for the umpteenth time a child's spilled juice, or urine from a leaky dog, slid into her mind and threatened to undo her. Sneaking in alongside that vision was an image of her husband and older children watching from a drafty, unfamiliar house in Prince Edward Island.

Gathering her wits, Jessie eased her shoulders back, stood tall, and did what she always did for Josh after a show. She lifted two fingers to the corner of one eye, trailed her hand down to her heart and placed it there for a moment, and then moved it to her lips and extended it outward so it floated there, suspended, the way she felt their lives were now. Tossing her head to dispel any unwanted tears at the hard place where she felt she had been so mercilessly thrust, Jessie wondered what the media would make of the gesture, knowing, as they did, that it was meant for Josh.

*They'll just think I am mourning my ghost man,* she reasoned. *They'll just think I'm missing you.*

At home, Josh compressed his lips in a tight line and hugged his children more snugly. All three were clustered around him now, all speechless under their mother's spell, trying as always to somehow reconcile the woman who hollered at them to clean up their toys to the magical, wondrous, sophisticated creature on their television. A vision in the latest Zuhair Murad, Jessie was the picture of elegance; her eyes were shimmery diamonds, dewy, dreamy and moist, eloquently highlighted by the mystical blue stage lights.

Then, there it was—not at all a surprise, Josh thought later.

A look to stage right.

It was longer than it should have been although nobody outside of the Keating circle would clue in to the powerful longing behind it. Josh did, though; he clued in, and to his left, reclining on a big comfy chair in the old white house at the dead end of the Sutherland Road, so did Arnie.

On stage, Jessie's lips were moving. "I love you."

Stonewalled, the men in P.E.I. did not look at each other, or speak. The children were blissfully unaware. They were still in awe.

Slouching, Josh sank into the couch. A second later he slumped so far over his belly it seemed like he wanted to curl up inside himself. For one hard moment Josh wished that he did not have all of these little mini-people depending on him for comfort and support. He would have brushed Jessie's words off and said they were just a ploy to keep the hounds at bay, per se, as part of the plot to ensure the Sawyer family's safety by playing this strange game they were all so deep into now—the one that meant Josh Sawyer was dead and Joe McIver had taken his place. But he couldn't. He couldn't brush the words off. The person they were meant for was entwined in his wife's soul. Josh could no more brush them off than he could untwist the truth from his gut. The reality of what Jessie and Matt meant to each other and would always mean to each other was stuck under Josh's skin, was clawing into his organs like a tumor.

Closing his eyes, Josh counted to ten again and again until he could unclench his fists and resume some sort of regular breathing.

In Boston, in the wings, Matt's lips moved too. They whispered the same sweet sentiment back to the woman for whom the crowd, now on its feet, was raising its hands and voices in unanimous appreciation. Jessie was right. This space, the twenty feet between she and Matt, was sacred. It was theirs and theirs alone. Nobody, not even a band member, marred their eyelines.

Years of shared spaces just like this one—some smaller, some bigger—were theirs too. History was on their side. And right now, at this very moment, so was time.

Jessie made her way to Matt on the impossibly high heels Deirdre and their designer, Samantha, had picked out. There was nobody else close by to get in their way, to interrupt, to fire accusing glares at them. The camera was focused on another artist now, capturing the beginning of the pretty country ballad that followed Jessie's soulful, evocative numbers. The stage techs' eyes were elsewhere. They were busy doing their jobs.

Sighing into the welcoming safety of Matt's arms, Jessie let her eyes drift closed, and she floated away.

*Chapter Eight*

Once the concert part of the evening was over, artists, producers, managers and marketing entourages, along with special guests, gathered in the host hotel's Empress Ballroom to celebrate with a semi-formal after-party. Before Jessie joined her friends, she went back to her suite to change and to check on Micah, who she'd left safely upstairs in the care of Carlotta and under the watchful eyes of Sam and Alin. Entering the ballroom with Matt by her side, she found the Keating group gathered around a few tables in a semi-private section to the south of a large dance floor. Dropping rather inelegantly into a chair next to Charles, she avoided Shanda's eyes when Matt rounded the tables, crossed to the opposite side, and greeted his wife with a kiss.

Adrenaline from the show was still rushing through everyone's bodies, so when Steve got the bright idea to drive the recovering Jacob nuts by sending him a video of everyone having fun without him—at a show where he was supposed to perform—Jessie went right along with him.

Once Steve hit 'send,' she sat back and irreverently saluted him. "Now send one to Josh," she requested lightly.

The table fell into a shocked silence. Around them, the ballroom was vibrant and busy, arrayed colorfully with high fashion and good manners. Formally dressed concertgoers and singer-songwriters buzzed around like bees, laughing, carrying on and dancing to the angsty strains of one of Boston's best blues bands.

The full impact of what she said struck Jessie a few seconds after it hit the rest of the group. Clapping the heel of a hand to her forehead, she closed her eyes and groaned. A second later she pressed her forehead into both hands, balancing her elbows on the table. "Oh, fuck. Fuck, I hate this. This whole fucking stupid fucking game." Sending videos—or even texts, or calling— was not an option, especially at an event like this where phones might, after a few stiff drinks, get left behind in a bathroom stall or pilfered by some starstruck fan.

Steve broke the awkward silence by touching Jessie's arm. "Come on. Dance with me, little girl."

Shoving back her chair, Jessie avoided everyone's eyes but Matt's. This whole charade was his, Charlie's and Charles' attempt to save her family, with Arnie thrown somewhere in the mix too. Apart from Jessie and Josh, Matt was paying the price more than anyone. It was evident in the way he was sitting, stiff and tense, one forearm resting on the next table over, one hand curled into a fist. Across from Charles, lips markedly turned down at the corners, he was the picture of dejection.

When Jessie left the circle of friends by taking Steve's hand and rising, Charles butted into Matt's study of her. Watching Jessie navigate her way through the partiers on another pair of uncomfortable heels she was try- ing to appreciate in this fantastical old life of hers, he tossed out a question. "How do you think she's doing?"

The simply voiced query, edged with yearning and loss, threw Matt for a loop. Judging by the way Jessie had clung to him in the wings of the stage earlier, and by the way she'd touched him and murmured to him when she arrived in the city the day before, he didn't think she was doing all that well. Since the first moment Matt laid eyes on her yesterday, knowing Jessie as well as he did, something small and obtrusive had started niggling away at his stomach. It was a voice, and it was saying *maybe you didn't do the right thing by taking her choice away from her.*

Clearing his throat, with a quick look to Shanda Matt thought he should try to ease Charles' mind, especially since Deirdre, to her husband's right, was bending closer to listen. In the end he went with, "Truth? On stage tonight? She was glowing."

Shanda shifted in her seat and crossed her arms but didn't say a word. Charlie was next to her. Jane grabbed his hand as he eavesdropped.

With a second glance in his wife's direction, this one more uncertain,

Matt chose his next words carefully. "Maybe what we should be wondering is how Josh is doing. A lot of what makes Jessie okay is whether her husband is okay. Have you asked her?"

"No." Charles studied his fingers. He started drumming them against the table in an agitated, repeated thrum. Deirdre laid her long, elegant fingers over his to stop the anxious movement. He looked over at her. "We haven't really had a chance to talk to her alone. We'll get a chat in at breakfast tomorrow."

"You?" Matt's single word was aimed beyond Shanda at Charlie.

Despondent, Charlie shook his head. "No. I've talked to Josh, though. He sounds like he's hanging in there."

"Good." Charles pulled his hand out from underneath Deirdre's and started drumming his fingers against his thigh. "So he's not spending his nights and days wallowing in self-pity, drinking up a storm. Does that also mean he's communicating with his wife and kids? Bringing them up instead of dragging them down?"

"Charles," Deirdre chided. "Josh is doing great. Arnie's got a good handle on things down there."

"Addictions, Dee," Charles reminded her. "With a change this big, the truth of how permanent this new reality is will one day catch up with our boy. And when it does…"

Matt focused a good, hard stare on his boss. Charles was showing his age. Over the years Jessie had aged him prematurely. Still, every wrinkle was worth the heartache. Every tired, aged muscle was worth the pain.

She was like a magnet. Having Jessie amongst them again for these few nights, with the added bonus of her earlier absolutely enchanting performance, was a dream. Matt was sitting side-on to the dance floor. When Charles sighed and trained his eyes on Jessie, Matt followed suit. Everybody noticed, because he had to twist his head to get a clear look at her. *She's only here for a short time,* he told himself. *I need to memorize that girl before she disappears again.* Disappears…a queasy, strangled knot settled into his throat.

Charlie emitted a frustrated *mmpphh* and wrapped his fingers around Shanda's, since Jane was deep in conversation with Sophie now anyway. The song was changing. A sad, soulful saxophone was lifting its woeful missive to the luxe art deco gilt ceiling of the Empress Ballroom. "Our turn," he commanded, helped her up, and led her willingly to the dance floor. They took up positions fifteen feet away from Jessie and Steve.

Matt sat up taller, grateful to the boys for allowing him the grace and opportunity to watch Jessie largely unobserved, unless you could count the occasional distressed looks he was getting from Charles and Dee. They, too, were lost in Jessie's spell, in the way she was holding back from all of them just a little, in the way she was mostly just watching them interact with each other as if she wasn't quite ready to believe she was actually in their presence. It was as if the old homeless Jessie was reappearing, sneaking through, bringing to the forefront age-old insecurities they'd all hoped were long gone.

Together they watched as, on the dance floor, Jessie laid a toned arm casually around Steve's shoulders and tipped her head back to laugh at something he was saying. Everyone exhaled, and tried not to fixate on the woman they all missed.

About a quarter of the way through the blues piece, Matt pushed back his own chair. He did it so suddenly that everyone in the Keating vicinity was jarred into glancing over at him.

"Uh, oh," Jane said to Sophie, tapping a finger on her friend's arm. "One guess where he's going."

Always the one to try to understand the people around her, Sophie ran a hand over her long, sleek blonde ponytail twice, and raised her shoulders in a subdued *meh*. "Let them have one dance," she suggested. "One dance can't hurt."

"Tell that to Josh," Jane returned. "Remind him of the time when he showed up at that fundraiser in New York, Sophie. Not that I was there, but I got the story from Charlie afterwards. The night Jessie and Jacob got back together."

Sure enough, everyone held their breath when Matt, without even looking at Steve, laid a hand on Jessie's hip and, when she let go of her *Drifters* friend, slipped into Steve's place opposite her.

Shanda, slow dancing nearby with Charlie, narrowed her eyes over his shoulder.

"You don't have to worry," Charlie said to her at about the same second

Matt latched his intense gaze into the sea-pearl eyes he loved. "They never really got to say goodbye, you know. Not really. They just need some time to process all of this, to say a real goodbye."

"It's bizarre, Charlie." Moving effortlessly in Charlie's arms, Shanda was trying to be graceful, to 'take the high road.' He felt her body loosen up. "I know it's not the norm, with those two. I mean, everything they've been through…Their tough past, one they had little control over, joined them together in a way that is hard to explain. It's like you can't see where one ends and the other begins. That's about the deepest kind of love there is, isn't it?"

"Shanda, you'll torture yourself by thinking that way."

"Don't you get it, Charlie? I could live a whole lifetime and never get there with him."

Charlie considered that. "That's true, Shanda. You don't have the benefit of having lived out of Matt's pockets for a lot of years. And I think you can agree that the kind of fear and heartache those two have lived through is not something Jessie or Matt ever chose for themselves, or that you would ever want to go through, with him or with any man." Pondering Shanda's description of the bond that united Jessie and Matt in such a profound, infinite way, Charlie absently clicked his tongue against his teeth. "You can't focus on what Jessie and Matt have. You have to lay your own foundation with Matt and build up from there."

"Yes, but what am I supposed to do? Just step aside when she's around? Just pretend that the man I married actually knows I exist when she's in the room?" Shanda chortled nervously. "Look at him. He's so lost in her, and vice versa, that neither of them are even aware of where they are." She lowered her voice to a frantic whisper. "And what about Josh, alone in some kind of isolated  Never Neverland with their children while she's here in my man's arms?"

"Josh, above everyone, respects what Jessie and Matt have. You know why, Shanda? Because he knows where it comes from."

"I get that, Charlie, it's just that there are limits, you know? Matt almost chose her. He could have!"

"But he didn't," Charlie interjected wisely. "He took her back to her husband, tucked his tail between his legs and married the woman he's meant to spend the rest of his life with."

"Yes, his choice, Charlie. Not hers. And on that note I say that's enough stargazed love struck staring into each other's eyes for tonight." Shrugging her way out of Charlie's arms, Shanda started moving toward Matt and Jessie who were, as she said, completely buried in each other's essence.

Charlie stopped her. "No, Shanda," he directed in the gruff, business-like tone Shanda knew well from the *Sacred Peace* set, the one that refocused everyone after a debate about the accuracy of a line, or on a giddy late Friday afternoon when the weekend was close but they still had two scenes left to shoot. He had a grip on her elbow, and turned her back to face him. Following up the demand with a more gentle, "Please. Let them have this," he breathed more easily when she sighed and forced herself to give him a slight nod. She returned to him more fully, and laid her arms back around his shoulders.

Matt was dressed to the nines tonight. Always conscious of men's fashion, he was on every woman's radar in a tailored black suit and dapper gray silk tie. Jessie, too, was chic and stylish, having made the switch from her stage persona to a stunning halter-necked lace cranberry cocktail dress from a new Vancouver designer Deirdre sourced for this rare public appearance. Lost in the smoky music and in the heady company of a man she missed and craved, she gave up her attempt at self-control and let one hand rise up to Matt's face. Placing a palm against his cheek, she smiled wistfully at him. He allowed a hurting half smile back.

"So nice to see you again," Jessie murmured, curving her back enough for her to melt more deeply into him, into the encapsulating circle of safety and warmth she always found in Matt's strong arms. "So nice to touch you again. To feel your arms around me again."

Captivated by holding the actual physical presence of this beguiling woman close to him once again, Matt let his body do the talking for him. While Shanda watched, he inhaled slowly and raised his hand so he could brush a thumb tenderly, in light recurrent movements, against Jessie's cheek. The saxophone's sensuous, sultry voice wafted around them the way mist floats above a pond, its notes at once lily-soft and then, in the next lyrical phrase, fervent and dynamic, like an arched wooden bridge fortified with stones, arcing between opposite shores. The music was a Monet painting, impressionistic in its pastel tones; the melancholy couple barely swaying to it in the center of a majestic, historic ballroom were its subjects, infused by brush strokes too powerful to ignore. Bathed in the subdued evening light of a midnight waltz, Jessie and Matt were unrestrained now by such social conventions as honor in marriage. What propelled them forward was a lack of time, an unforgiving distance, a submerged car with a child's life in the balance, a troubled man who sometimes lost his hold on the earth, and a wretched, desperate need for survival. To let the worries go and simply feel safe.

A ragged *ahhhh* slipped through Jessie's open lips. Letting her eyes flutter shut, she moaned a second time as Matt, gazing up and down her body in a sort of curious wonder, let his thumb fall to an outside corner of her mouth. Without thinking, Jessie grasped his wrist and held it there, where his thumb could play with her—where it could tease her, and circle her lips, reminding both of them of their last sunrise lovemaking when he brought her fingers fully, deeply, into his mouth, and sucked hard on them before he placed them inside her panties, all the while begging her to *come.*

Desire was taking over; the memory of how good things were between them—for such a short time, not nearly long enough—was still as nascent and fresh as foggy sea smoke drifting over the new horizon of a sun kissed early morning. Almost inadvertently, Jessie gave Matt's wrist a little pressure. At the same time, she opened her mouth wider, tilted her head back, and invited him in.

The erotic sensation of her wet mouth enclosing his thumb, the memory of her tongue on his body, ripped up Matt's groin, almost crippling him with remembrance. He very nearly stumbled. His breath let go, his abs crunched tightly—instantly—and he gasped.

An awed, primal recollection swept over Jessie. Eyes closed, in a sensual retake of some good, good lovin', in smoky slow motion she moved her ex-lover's thumb in and out of her mouth, just a few times, tonguing him and sucking on him…before a hard force shoved her away, and the surreal magical reminder of what she and Matt once had, vanished.

*It was just one little taste,* Jessie told herself afterwards. *One little suck.*

*One little reminder of what I used to like to do for him. One sweet reminder of the guttural uuhhh that used to escape his mouth when I undid his belt and lowered myself to his hips for a taste.*

An older man caught her. A music producer, Jessie thought wildly as she fought for balance on the tipsy heels. Matt's hands darted out and grabbed Shanda, the violent force that sent Jessie flying. And Shanda, in his arms, was wild.

"You bitch, this man does not belong to you!" Holding up her left hand, knuckles out, Shanda fired Jessie a blatant, nasty, third finger salute. Her wedding ring caught the light, almost blinding Jessie. "He's mine. He's mine!" There were tears in Shanda's eyes. Jessie could see their wet sheen lurking underneath the surface.

But this weekend…this one dance…

"One song," she begged Shanda. "Could you not let me have just one song?"

Proudly, Shanda straightened up her shoulders. "That's the thing, Jessie. It won't just be this one song. He'll come back to me a mess of agony and heartache, and I'll be trying to put him back together for months to come." She leaned in closer, her wine-soaked breath a liquid courage she almost didn't need, she was so incensed. "You've got a man. Remember? I would have gladly taken him off your hands."

"Oh, would you have?" Jessie cried, wishing to hell Matt would let go of Shanda and come to her. Instead, Charlie was suddenly at Jessie's side, holding her steady as she catapulted angry words back to Josh's ex co-star. "The man covered in urine and vomit that you have to wash off after he goes on a bender? The one with sad little kids you have to keep quiet after those benders because he feels too damn shitty to play with them? That man? That's the one you want? Because that version of Josh comes with the sexy man whose hard body you got to run your hands all over on set, the one who fingered you and gave you an orgasm in front of the camera. It's not all roses and sunshine with him, Shanda. Not now. Especially not now."

In the close circle around them, the curious rich and famous—the entitled—grew quiet. Puzzled, they were wrinkling their eyebrows. *She's talking about her husband like he's still alive.* Most of them felt sorry for Jessie.

Obviously she was still in a state of mourning over her husband's untimely passing. Obviously she was overcome, confused.

"Jesus Christ, Jessie." Charlie was ready to lose it. "Watch what you're saying," he steamed into one angry, flushed pink ear.

Charles was storming across the dance floor toward them. This rowdy little scene was not about to get any prettier. He was there in a second. "Come with me," he huffed to Jessie, his face blooming red. "Party's over."

Jessie's eyes widened. She gasped for breath. "No!" she recoiled, trying to throw Charlie off. "In your goddamned dreams it's over!"

"Oh, fuck," Charlie mumbled, pressing the thumb and forefinger of his free hand into the outer corners of his eyes, which he squeezed tightly shut for a second. He turned to Charles. "It's one night, Charles. I'll keep an eye on our wild girl."

Charles was astute enough to get what he was saying, and the fear in Jessie's tightly clenched fists and in her scared eyes confirmed it. This glamorous night was no longer her life. Tonight was special. It was a rare, unequalled gift. He'd be an ass to take it away, to create a stomach-turning ending she'd mull over and over in the lonely days, weeks, months to come.

"It's okay. We're leaving." The trembling, hoarse voice across from Jessie was Matt's.

The terror in her eyes at those simple words shut both Charles and Charlie up real fast.

"No. Please. Don't go." Uncurling her hands, Jessie tried to unfurl her shoulders as well, to get a grip on this new turn of events, to let the people around her see that she was okay, that she could hold it all together if she tried—the lonely east coast nights, for starters, and the switching of gears to suddenly become an exhausted stay-at-home mom to four young children. The days and nights worrying about Josh, watching him meld weirdly into his new persona as if he was, and always would be, some long haired bearded stranger named Joe McIver.

Matt was still hanging on to Shanda, his hands gripping her elbows from behind. She was quiet in the presence of two of her producers, Charles and Charlie—behaving, trying to regain the equilibrium of elegance that she always presented to the world, when really all she wanted to do was spin around, clutch her man to her chest and beg him to love her *more*, for a change.

Matt spoke again, this time burying in Jessie's frightened eyes how much it hurt to say the words. "I'll see you again," he said to her in a voice that cracked and gave way under the strain of having barely seen her at all during this short reunion, and then so quickly having to let her go.

"No." Jessie could barely breathe. Slowly, she shook her head from side to side. In the end, just as Matt was forcibly turning Shanda away so they could head for the door, Jessie couldn't hold back. She appealed to the one person that had the power to give Matt back to her just so they could, at the very least, slow dance to an entire song. One song. "Shanda," she pleaded. "Please. Please, Shanda. Please."

Her producers forgotten, Shanda whipped back around. "You have a problem, Jessie, you know that? In Stockholm you knew you were losing Matt so you pulled out your biggest weapon—sex—and you fired." Raising both hands, she mimicked firing a gun at Jessie. "Kapow. Right in the kisser."

"Yeah, that's right, Shanda." At first recoiling, Jessie followed up with a threatening step toward her adversary and got right in her face. Her angry stabs at Shanda were clearly heard by everyone present, including Deirdre, who was rushing up now after missing most of the action via a trip to the ladies' room. Everyone braced themselves for what they intuitively felt was coming. And they were right. Jessie had that look on her face, the homeless mask that said *I know I'm worthless.*

With equal parts self-hate and righteous indignation, she spit out the words. "I'm that woman, the one every other woman is terrified to let anywhere near their man. You know why? Because I'm a whore through and through. I have been since the ripe old age of twelve, and I always will be. But you know something, Shanda? As the Downtown Eastside's most famous whore, I'm the kind of slut men come running to when their own women curl up in bed with a headache and say no." She pointed to herself. "This whore delivers. Ask him. Ask Matt if he liked it with me. At the same time, if you want some lessons, I'd be happy to provide."

"That's enough, Jessie." Red-faced, Charles was fuming. He snapped his fingers at Charlie. "Get her out of here."

Jessie had a little fight left in her arsenal, fired by pain and fueled by adrenaline. In one quick motion, she made a rude gesture by her crotch, thrusting her hips out to drive the point home. "If it's hand jobs you need help with, I can totally deliver. But I gotta tell you, your man, as you call him, prefers a nice little suck. Or should I say a nice loooonnnnggg suck. A long, fucking *hard* one."

"Damn it, Jessie, do you ever know when to shut up?" Charlie gave her a shove to get her moving forward. There were cell phones pointed in her direction. Normally it would be Matt who would be all over them, grabbing them from people or forcing them downward so they couldn't record. This time, as one of the subjects, he was immobile. Shanda was also rendered mute by Jessie's nasty outburst.

Charlie propelled a shaking Jessie past the couple. Matt tried not to look at her. At the last second, he sucked in a breath for courage and compelled his haunted eyes to meet the beloved ice-pearl blues one last time. In his arms, Shanda felt his legs almost give way. A pained barely-there moan met her ears.

Jessie stopped. Neither she nor Matt said a word, not a single understandable word, yet the air between them was electric with the remnants of their long, shared past—of happy jet rides, of dressing room laughter, of Jessie's years as a scared waif who, for a long time, barely spoke. The lonely years with Charlie. Happiness with Josh, a man whose deep love finally brought Jessie healing. Another man, whose music helped ease the pain.

It was all there in that one charged look.

Discouraged, Jessie shrank into herself and shook her head helplessly at Matt. Fretfully licking her lips, she swiped proudly at her eyes with a fist, and let Charlie guide her out of the ballroom.

Chapter Nine

*A*n hour later, a quiet, hesitant knock came at Charles and Dee's door. They were still up. Charles was still fuming, incensed that Jessie's brief return to the spotlight was marred with YouTube cellphone videos of her nasty rant and rude phallic gesture. Already she was trending on Twitter. The next day, radio spin jockeys would have a field day at her expense.

He opened the door to find her in demure light pink cotton pajama pants and a white lace tank top peeking out from underneath a soft pink zip-up hoodie. Bare toes jutted out from under the pajamas. Her iPhone, being used as a baby monitor in tandem with an iPad in her suite, was dangling from her right hand.

"Can I come in?" she asked.

The tear-streaked face and woe-begotten puffy eyes did the producer in. His rage subsided in an instant. Widening the door so she could slip past, at the same time he nodded his acknowledgement of Dan's presence in the hallway behind Jessie.

Jessie dropped onto the nearest couch, a beige puffy one big enough to almost swallow her up when she sank into the exact center of it and hunched over. Perched on the edge with her knees together and feet pointed in, she crossed one set of toes over the other as if she were afraid that sitting up straight or getting too casual would open her up more fully to the harsh world.

Deirdre appeared at the bedroom door, wrapping a creamy silk robe around her body and securing it with a wide sash as she moved. She didn't come any closer, at least not initially. Charles also chose to remain standing. They waited.

"I'm s-sorry," Jessie managed, forcing her gaze up from a heavy heart to scan the two of them, each in turn. "I don't know what came over me."

"Good thing you're going back into hiding," Deirdre chided. She, too, had been crying, as evidenced by the dark circles under her eyes and the pink flush across her cheeks. "The world will be hard on you for this one, Jessie. Shanda's well loved."

"It's okay." Jessie's voice was small and afraid, a complete reversal from the ballroom earlier. "I deserve it. I can take it."

"You owe Shanda an apology." With a weighty sigh, Charles eased down onto an overstuffed chair to Jessie's right. "You might want to call her before you leave tomorrow."

"I know. I will, guys, I…I will. I'll tell her I'm sorry in person, at breakfast."

Charles and Dee shared a look. "That will be tough to do," Charles said, leaning back and loosely crossing his legs. "She's no longer here."

"What?" Aghast, Jessie bit her lip.

"She left. She and Matt had words and she packed up her things."

"Oh, shit. Damn. I suck. I really suck." Edgy and nervous, Jessie set the iPhone on the cushion at her side and started to twist a ringlet in her hair. An overpowering image of Matt and his haunted gray eyes slid into her mind, momentarily blinding her. She hung her head. All of a sudden it felt too heavy to hold up.

"What was it you came here to say, honey?" Deirdre was hesitant, but at least her tone was softer.

Loosening her finger from her hair, Jessie stared downwards and studied her toes. Idly, weirdly, it occurred to her that Emily-Grace would love the new glittery polish. She made a mental note to ask Dee to get some she could take home to her daughter.

Blinking back tears when she looked back up at Deirdre, she wiped a stray strand of hair behind an ear. "It's just…I hate this. All of it." She appealed to both of her pseudo-parents. "It was one dance. That's all I wanted. One dance to give me the strength to carry me forward."

Uncrossing his legs, Charles huffed loudly and leaned on both forearms after placing them on his thighs. "None of this is ideal, Jessie. For any of us. It's hard enough trying to live our lives minus you and the kids without you hijacking the one weekend we have together by practically sexing Matt on the dance floor. At least, that's my understanding of what happened."

"Practically—what? I didn't do that. How do you sex a guy on the dance floor in not even half a song?"

"Smoky eyes. He's saying smoky eyes," Deirdre piped up, with a graceful flourish of a hand in the air. "We know what Matt means to you, honey, but you have to let him go. You have to let the past go and move on."

Jessie threw up her hands. Her voice went up an octave. "To do what? You've hired some other female singer to help Jacob with this season's *Sacred Peace* soundtrack, you never send me scripts anymore, and there's no talk of me recording a new album or going on tour. I've got news for you guys. I'm not the one who died. Josh did! Remember? Why should I be punished for what he did? Why?"

"Jessie." Charles' tone was a warning. It was late, he and Deirdre were beat, and there seemed to be no point in rehashing the old darkness.

"What?" She pounced on him, but not in a mean way, just with a quiet, exasperated frustration. "Guys, look. None of this was my choice. I needed a choice. Not about Josh and Matt—about my life. About what I am doing with it. About not having to live on the perimeter of my old life, hovering over the edge like some goddamned cliff diver about to leap."

"Jessie, language. Calm down."

"Charles, how can I calm down?" Jessie was still sitting, but a light tremor was starting in her body, nipping at her ankles and working its way upward. She wasn't yelling, but the desperate ache in her body language had transferred to her eyes. It settled there, wavering in undulating rivers with the conviction that true despair and unhappiness bring. "I feel like I'm a skeleton of myself. Tonight on stage…there was a completeness there. There was joy."

Deirdre finally sat down. She eased down next to Jessie and took her fingers in hers. "Arnie seems to think you're doing okay in Prince Edward Island, Jessie. He told us you and Josh are happy, that the kids are happy."

"Well…we are, to a point." A futile moan underlined Jessie's need to find the right words to express the impossibility of reconciling herself to her new life. "I love being with him, with the kids. I love the time we have together, the sense of freedom in letting the kids roam around the property poking sticks in holes in the ground, watching the kiteboarders in the bay, those things. I hate trying to remember everybody's new names, and I hate watching Josh have to drive a ratty old truck instead of his big King Ranch, and I hate his goddamned beard! It scratches! And it hides him from me. He's always hiding behind his long hair, peeking up at me from behind layers as if he's always scared. He looks like some kind of lonely recluse, and I wake up every day wondering if it's going to be the day he cracks, the day he realizes how permanent all of this is! And you wonder," she added tearfully, "why I just wanted one goddamned dance with Matt. One goddamned song with his arms around me, holding me up for once instead of me trying to hold myself and everybody around me up."

"Look." Charles glanced over at his wife and, at her nod, went on slowly, carefully. "Give it some more time, Jessie. There's no reason why Deirdre can't start sending you scripts. There's no reason why you can't, someday, start doing films again or recording songs."

"Someday," Jessie harrumphed. "Meaning when we're fairly certain Josh is stable? Is that the someday you're talking about, Charles? Jesus Christ. You know that day may never come. It's one day at a time with him, as I sit and wait for him to break."

"We won't leave him alone." Deirdre held Jessie's hand between her palms and rubbed it lightly, grateful for the chance to just sit with her again despite the late hour. "Sam and Alin miss the kids. Dan misses the kids. We'll send someone in to help him."

"To keep an eye on him, you mean. To babysit him. To babysit my goddamned husband."

A tiny gurgle came over the baby monitor app. Sighing, Jessie rose and reached for Dee to help her stand and to give her a warm hug. "I'm sorry," she whispered. "I'm sorry to always be the cause of stress for you guys. I love you so much. You know that, right?"

There was a day not all that long ago when Jessie would never have hugged Deirdre. She would have backed off any time her manager came near. Now, Dee soaked it up, the love and warmth and apologetic sincerity of the tragic figure in her arms who, a few short hours ago, mesmerized the world with yet another beautiful ballad.

"We'll see you in the morning," Dee said.

Charles stood and sidled over for a forgiving hug. "Stay off the Internet."

"I will. Yeesh. My stupid mouth."

In the hallway outside, Jessie waved at Dan. "I'm fine. Go to bed. I miss you, you big lug." Behind her, Charles clicked closed the door to his and Deirdre's suite.

"Miss you too, Jessie," the tall Scandinavian said, grinning at the simple joy of being in her company again. "How're my kids?"

She was just about to answer when a door down the hall shufted open. Glancing up, Jessie sidled to a stop and sucked in a breath when Matt came into view, disheveled and weary, in bare feet, his shirt tail hanging out over his expensive pants, an ice bucket hanging so low from one set of fingers that it was almost dragging on the ground. "Oh," Jessie breathed as, behind her, Dan stole quietly off in the other direction.

Matt looked up. Pausing, he shifted his weight to his right leg and helplessly regarded her.

They met at the door to Jessie's suite. A sad smile accompanied her lifting of a finger, the trailing of it down the front of his shirt. "You must hate me," she said. "Or at least be really, really mad at me."

Matt's slumped shoulders communicated his dejection. But nothing in his countenance communicated hate.

A toss of Jessie's curls preceded her upward peek from underneath damp eyelashes, from her finger on his shirt, to his eyes. The usual light gray she loved, always filled with love, or sometimes concern or sometimes reprimand or a determined serious work look, was darker than normal, all misty and floaty and filled with…longing.

Desire.

"Oh, baby," Jessie sighed. Grasping his hips, the iPhone tucked into one hand, she let her forehead fall onto Matt's shoulder. "I fucking miss you." Inhaling, she breathed in the sweaty, manly scent of him. Deciding the desperately sought-after familiar smell and feel of him was worth the risk, she tucked her nose into the hollow of his neck and secured her arms around his waist.

Matt knew Jessie well. It only took him a second to toss away any sense of honor. Reaching for the pockets of his old girl's pink hoodie, he dug for and retrieved the key card to her room. A few quick movements and he had the door open, but at the last second he hesitated.

Moving in front of him, Jessie leveraged a shoulder to keep the door from closing. She leaned her forehead against it. Almost surreptitiously, she reached behind her and searched for Matt's left arm. Grasping it at the wrist, she brought it up to her waist and slid her fingers down it to lay her palm flat over his hand.

"One night," she begged in a husky whisper. "We never had a chance to say a proper goodbye, Matt. One fucking night. Please."

He had yet to speak. Jessie caught a hint of bourbon-laced breath wafting through the air when he moved behind her, when he planted his feet in a wider stance and buried his face, eyes pressed tightly shut, in her hair. He breathed in, deeply, dropped the ice bucket, and brought his second hand up to Jessie's waist. His subdued moan when he slipped his hand underneath her hoodie and tank top so he could feel the warmth of her skin underneath his…so he could feel, under his hand, the tightness of her abs, the roundness of her breasts…set Jessie's heart on fire. Her knees were suddenly fluid. They buckled. Her breath quickened.

"Let's go inside," Matt demanded, his voice dusky, swollen with an excruciating hunger he was desperate to satisfy after bearing witness earlier to Jessie's effervescent beauty in the surreal liquidity of the blue stage lights; after holding her in his arms in the wings; after the feel of that soft, wet mouth around his thumb in the ballroom earlier. "Now."

Matt's heated, liquor-soaked breath moved to Jessie's neck; he planted kisses there, moaning again and again in guttural anticipation of having the familiar willing, lithe body clench around him, her hips arch hard into him, her body cry out in pleasure and rock from side to side while he clutched her tightly to him and set himself free.

His first hand moved upward. There in the hall, while cupping Jessie's breast, his hips starting to push rhythmically against her body, Matt clasped the zipper on her hoodie, and ever so slowly, pulled it down. At the bottom hem, when it came free, he thrust his hand down her loose pajama pants and ran his fingers back and forth over a wetness he knew, when she crumpled forward, gasped, and parted her legs, was meant for him.

"Now," he commanded again, more insistent this time. "Inside. Now."

Jessie didn't need to be asked again.

She gave the door a push, and Matt followed her into the tranquil, moon-lit darkness of her Boston suite.

On its side, the empty ice bucket lay still, forgotten, abandoned to the desires of the flesh, and to the ache of two lonely hearts.

# Chapter Ten

Shanda made a pit stop before she intended to leave the hotel. In fact, she made two—one to the public first floor ladies' room for a good cry, the second to the bar for more wine. At the bar she found Charlie and Steve soaking their sorrows in bourbon in heavy crystal glasses that were refilled twice during the short time Shanda sat with them.

The guys were encouraging. "Look, Shanda, she'll be gone in the morning. There was no way Matt wasn't going to fall under her power again tonight, after everything they've been through together." Wishing Josh was sitting next to him, and that things were the way they used to be, Charlie tipped back his glass for another draw on the bourbon. The soothing drink did a lot to warm his body but little to amend the pain in his soul.

Steve flipped around on his high barstool and faced Shanda. Charlie was in between them but the bar was curved gently outwards, and they were almost in the center, so when Shanda leaned morosely on one elbow she could clearly see him. "Charlie's right," Steve said, a little pissed at Shanda for being the one to cause, in his opinion, Jessie's abbreviated night with all of them. "She'll be outta here sooner than you can say 'what the hell,' heading back to the land of lobster and potatoes. You may never have to ever see her again."

"Why'd you come here, anyway? To keep her away from Matt?" Charlie sat back. "You ought to know by now, Shanda, that you need to give a guy space in a marriage. There's this little thing called trust."

"I know." Sipping on the wine the bartender set down in front of her, a robust Shiraz, Shanda added, "I'm just not sure trust and Jessie Wheeler belong in the same sentence. Not when you see how Matt looks at her."

"Hell, we all look at her that way." Steve was trying to be light, but there was an underlying tension in his voice, which Shanda caught.

She *pffftttd* at him before saying, "I'm real sorry, fellas. I guess I ruined everyone's perfect night."

"Nah," Charlie guffawed into his bourbon, swishing it around so it caught the light. "Morgan and Nadia did. A long fucking time ago."

"Speaking of Morgan…" Shanda raised her eyebrows. "Any news?"

"The plane crash?" Charlie asked, eyeballing her.

She nodded. Steve leaned in to listen.

"No real news. Ulysses was in touch with Arnie's guy inside Brody. Morgan's apparently fit himself right into the good graces of the prison population. He's—get this—teaching yoga now, and meditation and martial arts."

"Quite the little joiner." Shanda's surly comment was echoed by Steve, who took a drink while he studied her, while he thought about how pretty she was and how crazy Matt must be to even consider hanging onto troubled Jessie the way he did in the ballroom earlier that night.

"Joiner is right," Charlie agreed. "The good thing is, what he's not doing is making threats against Jessie or hinting that he agrees with the conspiracy theorists who are all spouting reasons why our plane crash was not authentic." He raised his glass. "A toast. To movie magic."

A slight grin crisscrossed Steve's pleasant face. He toasted Charlie.

Shanda was more hesitant. "What don't those theorists believe, Charlie?"

He shrugged. "They don't buy that the 'bones,'" he lifted one set of fingers as quotes, "were carried away by animals, for one, as the report suggested. We made sure we left DNA there, for all four passengers plus the pilot and co-pilot—bits of hair and blood on clothes and stuff, but you know what these Internet crazies are like. They go on and on. They think they know everything…" He drifted off.

"The important thing is that Morgan doesn't seem to be following those theories," Steve drawled, a little drunkenly. "Right, Charlie?" It amazed him that Charlie hardly appeared drunk at all. *Years of drinking bourbon,* Steve considered. *Or too much shit going down, killing his buzz.*

"Right, my man." Charlie took another pull on the soothing drink and eyed Shanda. Her suitcase was at her side. "Go on back to him, Shanda.

You'll just feel like shit in the morning if you don't. You and Matt are sweet together. You'll just draw out the pain by staying away."

"Maybe I want him to suffer," she snarled wickedly into her wine glass.

"I'm sure he's suffering," Steve determined righteously. "And so's Jessie, if that makes you feel any better. He'll welcome you back with an apology and wide open arms. You'll see."

"I hope so." With a sad sigh, Shanda melted onto folded forearms on the wooden bar, and closed her eyes. Charlie rubbed her back, and they sat in silence until the bartender waved them away, and shut the lights off behind them.

Upstairs, Shanda thanked Charlie and Steve for escorting her back to her and Matt's suite. It struck all of them odd that an ice bucket was lying outside Jessie's door, but they shrugged it off. None of them put it past Jessie to bury her sorrows in liquor the same way they just did. Maybe she started off for ice and Micah woke up so she dropped the bucket and forgot about it.

With the guys trundling off down the hallway, Shanda tiptoed in past her and Matt's door. There were two washrooms in the luxurious suite. Looking toward the bedroom, she could see that a lamp was on, but Matt didn't call out to her or appear at the door so she made the assumption that he was asleep. Not wanting to disturb him and escalate their night into more fighting, she stumbled a little drunkenly into the washroom off the living area and had a pee before going into the bedroom.

Her husband was nowhere to be seen. The bed was rumpled, as if he'd been there watching TV—the television was still on. Before she switched it off, Shanda noted a half empty bottle of Jim Beam on the nightstand. It was no secret that the Kentucky bourbon was Jessie's old standby. Even when drowning his sorrows, Matt fell hopelessly into the river of Jessie's despair.

Shanda stepped over to the window. Silhouetted there, she thrust her shoulders back. A single frustrated tear trailed down a rosebud cheek. It seemed likely there was a new treachery afoot. Dagger sharp, it twisted like a corkscrew around and around and around, eating at Shanda's insides, turning the frigid knots in her belly into a pulpy mess.

Lit only by a pallid moon, observed only by the muted sounds and dark-of-night goings-on of a forlorn city below, she bent over her hands on the window ledge, laid her forehead against the cool glass, and tried desperately to breathe.

Chapter Eleven

"It wasn't your choice to make, Matt. That's what I have a problem with. Especially not the way you made it, dropping me off like you were leaving a puppy at the pound."

Face to face, nose to nose, Jessie and Matt were having a five a.m. heart to heart, one they should have had the morning before Matt left Jessie in the Caribbean.

"You wouldn't have gone," he said, gently running the backs of his fingers down her beloved flushed cheek. "You wouldn't have given Josh a chance."

"So," Jessie stated darkly, adjusting her arms around and under her pillow for comfort, "aren't you curious how it's going now? With Josh?"

He shook his head. "I don't want to know."

"Why not?" She wrinkled her eyebrows. A furrow appeared in her forehead.

A slow smile spread across Matt's equally flushed cheeks. Their love-making had been fast, passionate and rough, up against the foot of the bed for the most part, with her legs parted and his arm around her waist to keep her from collapsing as the pleasure escalated. Then, later, it was more easy-going—Jessie rode him for a while, until Matt couldn't stand it and flipped her over so he could push himself more fully into the sweet, welcoming body he desired so completely.

The sun was peeking over the horizon now, soaking the city with the kind of promise only a new day can bring. Matt and Jessie were beyond exhausted, but neither gave a damn. It was such agonizing, perfect pleasure to be together again, with a different perspective this time now that months stood between the day Matt left Jessie angry and hurt in the Caribbean. Too, both had spent weeks dwelling on the things that mattered, digesting the changes in their lives as best they could.

"You're so damn cute when you do that," Matt said, referencing the way Jessie's brow furrowed when she wrinkled her eyes. "When your hair's all rumpled like this."

Playfully, she swatted him. "Stop. I want to know why you don't care how things are going with Josh now."

"Because…" Matt put a finger to her lips to quiet her while he pondered what he should say. "Because if it's good, well, my head would think that's good. But I suppose my heart doesn't really want to know. And if it's bad, well…" He sighed. "I'm married now, Jessie. And on a short leash when it comes to you. We've made our choices."

"No. You made our choices. The same way Josh is always making all the choices. Me, Jessie? I get none. I get no choices. And by the way," she wrapped her arms around his hard chest and wriggled closer to him, "I do hope you and Shanda make up. I really do."

He was silent for a minute. Outside, traffic noise was starting up. The room was brightening. It would soon be time to say their goodbyes again. "What about Josh?" he asked quietly. "You once said he would know if you…"

She completed his question for him. "If I slept with someone else? I don't know. He knows about us. That we were together before you took me south. He knows how I feel about you. Maybe this time I won't say anything. I'll just let it go. Maybe this time the media and the Internet will make it clear that you and I went our separate ways last night. Hey, Matt?"

"Mmmm?" He was drifting into a peaceful slumber.

"D'you ever think you made the wrong choice? Dropping me off like that?"

His heart almost stopped. Crushing her to him, he breathed in the lavender scent of her, the familiar, beloved one that encircled Jessie wherever she went. "Every day, sweetheart," he confessed hoarsely. "Every single goddamned day."

～ ～

A short nap later, Matt tickled Jessie out of bed. She pulled herself up with a giggle and a groan. Stretching widely, she entreated him to go get some fresh clothes and join her in the shower.

"Hurry." She laughed happily, tossing a pillow at him as he pulled on his pants from last night. "We can fit one more hasty little bitta love in if you hurry."

"Is this how it's going to be from now on?" he asked her, stopping. Jessie moved forward and cheekily buttoned up his shirt, crookedly, with mismatched buttons to buttonholes. "You and me meeting in hotel rooms, technically having an affair?"

"I dunno." Josh flashed into Jessie's mind. He was trying so hard to be a good husband, a good father. Shanda's pretty, hurt face danced across her eyes. There was a lot at stake here. Children, too. Her shoulders sank.

"Hey. I'm sorry." Cupping her chin in his palm, Matt touched his lips to hers. "We'll figure something out, sweet girl. I'll be back in five."

"Hey, Matt?" Jessie called as he started to move away. "All I know right now is that it feels so good, so right, being with you this way again. Okay, baby? From here I don't know. But for now…I sure as hell hope we can be together again."

His warm smile was the last thing Jessie saw just before Matt moved out of her line of sight. With a contented purr she stepped under the hot, cleansing spray of the shower, and waited for him to come back.

The first thing Matt spied when he pushed open the door to his suite was Shanda's suitcase. His heart hitched in fear.

The second thing he saw was her—prone on the couch, awakening at the sound of the door opening, rising to face him.

The first thing he heard was, "If you go back to her, we're done. If you work with her again, we're done."

Shanda held up a phone, a…burner phone. The next thing Matt heard was, "You're not the only asshole in the doghouse. I called Josh."

Marching into the bedroom, Shanda slammed the door.

Alone, Matt stood quaking until his eyes closed over. Ashamed, confused as hell, he sank back against the door. In bitter defeat, he pressed the heels of his hands into his eyes, and slid down to the floor.

Jessie was a wrinkled prune by the time she opened the door of the shower and took a curious nude wander through her suite.

*Where is Matt? Why hasn't he come back?* A sinking feeling washed over her. Shanda's accusing eyes haunted her. Josh's innocence gutted her.

Back in the washroom, Jessie buried her face in a towel, choked into it, and sank back against the counter. Soon Micah would wake and she would have to get on with the business of her new, 'normal' life.

Today she would fly back to Prince Edward Island. Today the miraculous weekend fantasy gifted by Jacob's broken clavicle would come to a screeching halt. Today she would once again leave her extended family of loved ones behind.

Today Jessie could no longer surrender—to anyone—the hurts and fears and worries she'd released last night in Matt's strong, capable arms. All of those nasty things—every abhorrent, insidious bit and piece—would rise to the forefront again today, and move back into the customary, detestable sick hollow of Jessie's stomach. Reserves of strength she sometimes wondered if she even had would once again be forcibly yanked into play.

Today Jessie would once again have to go it alone with a man she loved with a split, stinging conscience, and with a sorry lack of faith.

## Chapter Twelve

A brisk, salty north breeze was blowing in off the bay by the time Josh got the kids out the door for playtime after getting them dressed and fed. In his experience, his children worked better after some quality time in the intoxicating outdoors, and today he wanted their full attention on their schoolwork. Mondays were tough enough. This one was going to be killer.

Jessie would be home later this afternoon, maybe by four or so, depending on how early she got away from Boston. After last night's show and party, he didn't figure she'd have a super early morning. Josh had a nice dinner planned. The house would be spic and span. Hell, Oscar winner or not, he knew how to manipulate a toilet brush. Emily-Grace would help him with the laundry, and for some bizarre reason David loved to vacuum. Toys would be cleaned up, the children's faces would be scrubbed and shiny, their hair washed and combed. Even Fluffy had a new bow today, a tiny yellow one.

Yesterday Josh had gotten brave and taken his little family to some of the big box stores in Charlottetown. The pet store alone kept them all entertained for over an hour. They all made a game of using their new names, and Dylan only slipped once, when he called David David instead of Jude. After that he got super quiet and Josh had to lift him up and carry him around. The new name thing, as far as Dylan understood, had to do with his father 'going missing' and being away from all of them. Messing up was scary. Dylan hated having to use different names. It confused the hell out of him, and he was scared Daddy would go away again if he got things wrong.

They'd all gone to a late afternoon movie after cruising the stores—an animated feature. Dylan sat on Josh's lap for the entire film, which suited

Josh just fine. With Emily-Grace on one side of him and David on the other, he couldn't have been happier. The movie was about singing. What was really cool about it was that Jessie and Jacob both had roles in it—Jacob voiced a stinky old skunk, which Josh found incredibly amusing. Jessie was a gorgeous white horse with a full, sweeping mane, large pale blue eyes, an elegant, feminine carriage in the way she walked and the longest, most damp eyelashes Josh had ever seen—on an animated character. The kids got a huge kick out of the film, especially the songs sung by their mother and Jacob.

Before they went in to the theater, Josh had reminded all of them not to get too overtly excited. "We like our privacy, right kids?" he'd cautioned them. "We don't want people to know who we are or we'll have to move again. So let's not get too excited about Momma and Jacob's movie until we get back to the van."

Even with the gentle warning, the kids were bouncing in their seats, although Dylan sat sideways and clung to his father and only watched the movie from covert glances. He was old enough to understand his parents' roles in movies, but animation was still a bit of a stretch. Curious, he hardly said a peep throughout the film, and took his cues from his older brother and sister.

*My heart is full,* Josh beamed when Dylan turned around once, looked him right in the eye and whispered, "Momma?" when the dainty white horse first pranced onto the screen. "She's so pretty."

*And she sings like an angel.* Sitting there in the dark with three of his children snuggled into him watching Jessie—and Jacob too, Josh could hear his voice these days without the old jealousy sneaking in—Josh felt like he was encased in one of life's perfect moments. A chill swept over him when Dylan moved once, jarring Josh's chest in a way that brought last September's bullet to mind, but Josh pushed it away. It was too sweet of a day with his precious children to be reminded of how close he came to losing what he loved and cherished the most.

*Perfection. Finally.* All that was missing was Micah, and Jessie. Although now, Monday morning, with the raw island wind piercing his face and ominous gray clouds slumbering above, Josh had to rethink that—the perfection part. Jessie would be home later in the day to a clean house, happy kids and a tasty chicken dinner with all the trimmings. What she might not find is a receptive, glowing husband.

*I gotta be careful what I say to her,* Josh considered as he jogged down the outside steps behind Emily-Grace, David and Dylan. A few days ago, to suit the warmer summer season and to bring back memories of the family's beloved Alberta ranch, he'd installed a Victorian screen door on the kitchen entrance. It slammed behind him now with an ominous crack. Shoving his hands in the pockets of his jeans, Josh absorbed himself in a study of the red island dirt lining the edges of the driveway before he crossed narrow Sutherland Road and headed up the lane with the kids. Each child had a handful of carrot tops to feed to the horses. They were hoping to see William and Alice puttering around their place, so they wouldn't all feel so damn alone in the world. Later they would head down to the beach so the children could collect shells along with interesting saltwater-polished stones, and treasured sea glass. Each of the older kids kept a mason jar in his or her bedroom—Alice's idea—where they stored the special glass pieces that, these days, Alice told them, were becoming harder and harder to find.

This morning's early call from Shanda had thrown a helluva wrench in the day. More of a chainsaw, actually.

"Jesus Christ, Jessie," Josh muttered, kicking a stone out of the way. "Fucking Jessie." It was a quandary, this thing with Matt. Taking a big breath, Josh shoved his long hair out of his eyes. The wind was driving him nuts, whipping it this way and that so he could barely see. He exhaled in a long, slow, calculated breath. No way could he dispute what Matt meant to him, to his family. Jesus, the man pulled Emily-Grace out of their sunken SUV. Without a doubt, he had saved the child's life. If he hadn't been there, if he hadn't had the guts to dive into that mucky, freezing river and force himself to try again and again to plunge himself twenty feet deep in water so murky he could likely barely even make out the car, well…Emily-Grace would not be bouncing joyfully along in front of Josh now, the happiest he'd seen her in years. And Jessie would be dead. No doubt.

So. Given Josh's desperate action last September and this new life that Jessie was only half-heartedly adjusting to, the call from Shanda was not a complete surprise. Really, Josh figured, it was harder on her. On Shanda. This thing with Jessie and Matt was all new to her. It wasn't new to Josh.

Over the past many years, at La Casa, in backstage dressing rooms, sharing pizza at the UBC house, on the jet, whatever, Josh was witness to the deepening bond between Matt and Jessie. He was aware of the rumors that maybe the two of them had long ago hooked up, that maybe there was always something a little special between them, that maybe they were double dipping from way back, back in Charlie's time, even. The rumors were just that—rumors. Josh trusted Jessie back when he first met her, when it came to Matt and all the time the two spent alone at gigs. No, they didn't hook up sexually until Josh himself pushed Jessie away, back after Jacob's violent deed in Florida. Even that wasn't really Jessie's fault. The only thing Josh considered Jessie really ever did wrong was be a person with a big, open heart—the kind of person who couldn't stand to see a friend suffer. She went to Jacob, he was angry, shit got real, Josh got pissed and backed off and…Jessie got lonely. She turned to the one man who, all things considered, never, ever let her down, except when…

*Except when he dropped her off to me in the Caribbean.*

"Fuck!" Josh kicked another stone. It went skittering along the lane and died a good death by a wind-tossed clump of struggling lupins. "I fucking deserve this!"

There was one other person this was gonna be pretty damn tough on.

Jessie.

*Well, Matt too,* Josh considered and, being the nice guy that he was, he actually felt kinda awful for how hard all of this must be on Matt.

For a second.

But Jessie…Jesus. So. She'd spent the night with Matt, or a good part of it. Lost in his arms, in his essence, in his body. And today she would be driving home from Nova Scotia, exhausted, teary, likely frustrated and fed up, potentially hung-over, missing people she loved and coming down off the high of the big show.

Like an addict.

The crashes were always the worst. Having kids to respond to, to care for? And a husband scared of his own shadow? Who fell far, far short of the man whose arms Jessie felt safest in?

This homecoming was gonna hurt.

Home. That, too, was a stretch. Sure, P.E.I. was near and dear to Jessie's heart, but this century-and-a-half old house was new to the Sawyer-McIver family. It was big and drafty and creaky and old and quiet and lonely. Here, Jessie had no friends. ZERO FRIENDS. Here, she had to live in isolation. She was keeping her distance from the Sutherlands—maybe, Josh figured, for self-preservation, or maybe because it felt traitorous to Charles and Dee to let herself get attached to a new older couple. For Josh? Not a problem. He was quiet, sure, but he and William clicked right off the bat, and Alice was a good-natured sweetheart, always baking them goodies and giving the kids hugs, and in many ways filling Carlotta's and Dee's shoes.

Ahead, Josh saw William emerge from the barn. The older man gave him a generous wave, so Josh returned the comfortable gesture. Alice was on her knees at a garden bed. She practically leapt up when she spied the kids running toward her in their rubber boots and light jackets. At her age leaping was a subjective thing, but there was no doubt about the happy glow on her face when Dylan—aka Ben—landed in her arms.

Josh stopped about thirty feet away, turned sideways, and laid his arms over the top rail of the fence.

William made his way over. "You doing okay without the missus around?" the older fella asked amicably, settling next to the man he knew as Joe.

"Depends how you look at it," Josh answered. *And really*, he thought, *it does. I'll be okay as long as she actually comes home. As long as she doesn't start to pack her things the second she gets in the door.* He moaned, and laid his forehead on his hands. He would have flipped back around and slipped to the ground, his back against the fence, but he didn't want William to guess how bad he was feeling today.

The moan gave him away anyway.

"You okay, son?" Concern lined William's face, the little lines emanating out from his serious, friendly eyes making him appear so grandfatherly—and fatherly—that Josh almost cried.

*I need you.*

Josh turned his head to the side so he could see the man more clearly. Bitterly, he swallowed. "I don't have a dad," he said, the declaration as unexpected to him as to William, who took it as it was meant. *Need.* "Not really, anyway. I do, I actually kind of have two dads," Josh admitted. "But they both kinda let me down. In a big way."

"One would be your father-in-law? Jasmyn's father?" William asked. Raising a booted foot, he set it on the bottom rail of the fence. A little further down from the men, Alice was helping the kids feed their carrot tops to the horses, who were munching away happily, perfectly content with the brisk island breeze ruffling their manes and tails.

A gruff chortle passed through Josh's lips. "Ha. No. I'm not even on his radar." Charles crossed his mind, all business-like and professional, a man who rarely let his mask down enough around Josh to ever really let him in. Charles, who would have preferred Charlie as a son-in-law, or Jacob. Certainly not Josh. And now, Matt…Charles' best friend. His trusted advisor.

Josh was about ready to keel over.

He felt compelled to offer a brief explanation. "I was raised by a man who was not my biological father. I didn't know until about ten or eleven years ago. I knew the other guy, my real dad, and I eventually worked for him, but things went sour. We talk, but it's mostly just business between us these days."

"Is your mother still living?" William bent and tore off a blade of timothy that he stuck between his teeth and started chewing on. He was staring out over the field, cautious around this quiet man who seemed so sad and lonely today. It wouldn't do to pry too deeply, if the guy didn't want to be pried open.

Then again, Joe seemed willing to talk. He seemed to need to.

Josh shifted his feet and, like William, bent and plucked some timothy to chew on. He held it between his fingers while he talked, and chewed between words. His hair was going completely rogue in the wind, which he was thankful for since it helped hide the hard emotions from the kind man next to him. "My mother died when I was twenty," he explained. "The big C. She was a beautiful person who I miss every single day of my life."

"I'm sorry, Joe."

"Yeah. Thanks. I'm sorry too."

"And Jasmyn's mother? Is she still alive?"

"That, like my dads, is a little confusing too." Josh smiled, just slightly—

at least, one corner of his lips turned up. Jessie would have to go to the nursing home at some point. She had a wig or two stashed away somewhere. She'd have to visit as yet another incarnation of herself, with permissions to get in to see Emily and George granted via Matt's connections, as a niece, maybe, or a visiting cousin. Josh didn't give away any info about Emily's presence on the island to William. Out loud he said, "Jasmyn was taken in by a couple out west when she was twenty. They gave her some ground to stand on. She considers them her parents, and they're the grandparents you hear my kids talking about. Jasmyn and the kids are close to them. If you want the truth, as far as I'm concerned I think they just put up with me."

"It's always hard for parents to see the partners their kids marry in any kind of objective way, Joe," William offered, chewing on his blade of timothy grass. "I'm sure it's not personal. You seem like a devoted father and husband. It'll be good to get your wife back from this work trip of hers, huh? Looks like you're missing her today."

Josh grunted and rather morosely buried his face in his arms again. When he looked up, he found himself blurting out his troubles. Something about William's kind eyes just made it easy to let go. Maybe part of it was the comforting roar of the waves in the large bay behind them; maybe it was the delighted squeals of the children when the horses' velvety soft noses touched their small hands. Whatever it was, it was liberating to share like this, so openly, with someone who seemed to carry his own perpetual sorrow, who seemed to need this connection every bit as much as Josh—Joe—did.

"She loves me, but…truth is, she's also in love with someone else." With a heavy *mmpphh*, Josh looked back over at his new friend. "She was with him last night. His incensed wife called me before the birds were up this morning."

"Oh. Well, Joe." Standing back and taking that in, William rubbed his chin. "I'm real sorry, son." He liked Jasmyn, but there was definitely something about her that was mysterious and distant, that William couldn't quite put his finger on. She was making no real attempt to get to know Alice or him, that was a part of it, and she rarely made eye contact. She was great with the kids, though, and even though it seemed like there was something troubling between her and her husband, there were little touches here and there that hinted at true love, at the kind of love that was enduring and real and sweet and painful all at once for its capacity to carry a couple along the bumpy road of this thing called life. The way Joe looked at her…the way he talked about her…like a doe-eyed puppy…it was plain to see how completely taken up in her he was, at how in awe of her he was. And vice versa, although now that William thought about it, he sensed a certain distance on Jasmyn's part, a certain reticence.

In the interest of honesty, Josh said, "I know him, the guy she was with. And I know why they hooked up last night. It's not new. And it's not all her fault. I did something…" He couldn't finish. He got a little choked up, which didn't really surprise William. It made him truly sorry for this busy father who, when you added up the pieces, seemed likely to be running from something.

"That why you moved here, son? To help her gain some perspective?" he queried. "To put some distance between her and this fella?"

Josh shook his head. When he got control of his emotions he said, "We had to make a new start. It wasn't about him, but this thing with the two of them…" He stuck the timothy back between his lips and chewed for a minute before continuing. "This thing with the two of them got to the point where distance was the only way to make things go down easier, anyway. Regardless, he's still in our lives. She works with him. Technically so do I, in a lot of ways. It's tough."

"She's coming home, though?"

"Far as I know. I sure as hell hope so."

"Son…" William hopped on board his neighbor's openness on this windy morning. There were things about this family that didn't add up. With a sideways glance, he jumped in. "The campfire we had the other night, the first night your wife was away…"

Josh tensed. He and the kids had shared a really great evening with William and Alice—dinner first, a barbecue they ate outdoors at a rustic wooden picnic table overlooking the beach. After, William and Josh built up a nice sized fire on the beach. The sunset was spectacular, all pink and orange and serene, its liquid descent into the bay positively delicious to behold. The promise of the upcoming summer with all its hope and healing and sense of renewal was so chock-a-block full of peace and promise that the future was just bursting on the vine, like luscious fruit ripe for the taking.

All three children were swept up in the sweet perfection of the evening, and in the casual, easy comfort of the grandmotherly and grandfatherly couple in their midst. The buoyant sky darkened around them, morphing from an optimistic indigo blue to a mysterious twilight blue-black to a shadowy, confounded starlit dusk. The mood around the fire may as well have been tied to the transformation of the sky. Just as Emily-Grace was about to stick a marshmallow-laden stick into the low flame, she lapsed out of character and accidentally called Dylan by his real name.

"Here, Dylan, you can have this one," she'd said, swinging her legs in her little girl way from the edge of the big camp chair she was buried in. She held out her long marshmallow roasting stick to her brother, one that Josh had carefully sharpened the point of so that the gooey sugary marshmallows would slide off and on with ease, and then she stilled. What stopped Emily-Grace's movement, and made her aware of her error, was a shocked exclamation from David, the family's self-appointed police officer when it came to their names.

"Ella!" he'd cried.

All three children were constantly reminded to be cautious regarding what they shared about their family and their past. Not a soul on the planet, or at least not in North America, likely escaped the drama that unfolded not all that many years ago when David and Emily-Grace were abducted alongside their mother and remained missing for an extended time. Their names were household names. Uttering the wrong names now was not an option. Emily-Grace, in particular, was not a common name.

There were a few blessings. One, Dylan Sawyer was not a household name. Unless you were a real fan of Josh, Jessie or Jacob, he could easily slide under the radar. Two, as far as William and Alice went, they did not own a television or a computer. In the barn, a dusty radio played old country, like Mel Tillis, George Jones and Patsy Cline. Chances were slim that they would even know who the Sawyer family was.

At the fire, Josh had watched Emily-Grace without saying a word, but everyone around him suddenly went silent. Dylan, who had been animated and happily chattering away, was scared into submission, which saddened Josh because he knew the little guy was mixed up about this new rule. Flipping around to look at David, Josh had just shaken his head the tiniest bit, hoping that neither William nor Alice noticed. David fixed his eyes solidly on the fire and sank back into his chair. Emily-Grace teared up and did not say another word for the rest of the evening, nor did she make eye contact with anyone. The reason for this change was more crystal clear to her than it was to the other children. It was tied into the unspeakable terror of being trapped in a drowning car. Of the loss of an innocent, desperately loved puppy called Snow.

Now, at the fence, William was bringing it up. "At the fire," he continued, "Ella called Ben by another name."

Josh couldn't look at him. Swallowing, he took the timothy grass from between his lips and let it fall to the ground. It was all chewed up now anyway. "She did," he said, without offering anything more.

"Dylan, I think it was."

"Yep." A foul taste rose in Josh's throat. Turning his head to the side away from William, he spit into the grass.

"Look, Joe, pardon me for sticking my nose in where it doesn't belong, but you have no job, you don't seem worried about money, your kids are home-schooled, your good friend seems maybe twenty years older than you and your wife barely makes eye contact with Alice and me. Ben is obviously not your son's name. I'm not going to ask what's going on. It's your business. Unless… Joe, if I ever get the sense that your children are in any kind of danger…"

"I would never hurt those kids." Josh was struggling. What could he say? The truth? No. Not at this point. Maybe never.

"Not suggesting that, son. I would never suggest that. Your wife would not leave you here alone with them if she was worried about that."

"I've never hurt her, either. That's not what this is about."

"Good. I'm glad to hear that. I just want you to know that Alice and I are here for you, for Jasmyn and for the kids. If they have other names, if you," William studied his neighbor, "or your wife have other names, you can use them around us. We're not the kind of people to go running to our neighbors with gossip."

"It's a safety thing." *There. I spit it out. He knows what he needs to know.* Josh's stomach settled a little, but he still couldn't look at William.

"I feel like I've said I'm sorry a lot this morning, Joe. But I'll say it again. I'm sorry to hear that."

"And again I'll say me too. But there it is." Nervous, Josh finally looked back over at William. "We need to keep using these names, William. They need to become second nature to the kids. So they don't slip up in the wrong place at the wrong time."

"I understand. Joe?"

"Yeah?"

"Are you safe here? Is your family safe here?"

Josh hesitated before answering. Without realizing he was doing it, he scraped off a splinter of wood on the fence's top rail. "We think so. We hope so." He crunched down hard on his lip and wondered how much he could trust this caring man with. "We've had a lotta rough years. We need this."

"And Barney?"

"Yeah, William? His name is actually Arnie. He's a good friend Jasmyn knew years ago, who eventually started working with us."

"It's good you have him."

"Yep." *As far as security goes…* Matt leapt back into Josh's brain. He groaned again.

"Your wife?" William asked kindly.

"Yeah. You know what I need, William?"

"What might that be?"

"A bike. I need a bike. A Harley. These country roads just scream 'come ride me.' It's crazy beautiful here."

It was William's turn to stare out over the field. The kids were in the house now, being given the cookies Alice baked early this morning in anticipation of this very visit.

"Not a fan?" Josh asked after a few moments of shared silence.

"Motorbikes? No, Joe. Our son Jeffery was killed on a bike."

"Oh. Oh, shit. I wondered how…"

"Drivers here don't always pay enough attention to bikes. The roads can be hilly, blind turns…" He sighed. "Look, son. This thing about your wife.

I don't know what got the two of you to this difficult place in your relationship, but when she comes home, find a way to talk to her that helps her open up. Don't go hard on her. Most people don't just choose to step out on their marriages. Something gets them there."

Hands on his hips, staring at the ground, Josh was standing with his feet apart now, facing William. He nodded, which was the encouragement William needed to go on.

"Joe, losing our son…we lost our grandkids too and Jeffery's wife, in a way, when they moved back to Ontario. It's just…it's bloody permanent is what it is, when someone dies. What you and your family are going through, maybe there's a fix. With her, with this other man, with this safety business. With death, there is no fix. Jeffery's never coming back."

"This is the thing, William." Fixated on the ground but not really seeing it, his hair blowing all around like a wild thing, Josh inhaled for strength. "I've put a lot of thought into this whole 'end of life' thing. A lot." Somber chocolate eyes latched onto William.

*Joe's eyes are damp and needy, moist and deep, like the ocean when you look over the side of a boat,* William was thinking. *Endless. This man has suffered an endless kind of hurt. He knows loss.*

"Joe, don't tell me you would ever—look, son. Talk to her. Maybe she'll surprise you."

"No, no, it's not that, William. I mean, it kind of was. In a way. But it's not anymore. Moving here, coming here, it was the right thing to do, for me. For now. Maybe not for her, I dunno." Josh changed tack. "It's just, this dying thing…if Jeffery was anything like you and Alice…kind, I mean, and I'm sure he was cuz he chose to live near you and work with you and ride horses with you…then my guess is he was a peaceful kind of guy. He sounds to me like the kind of man who lived his life to the fullest. Who appreciated what he had. Who had a lot of love tossed his way, and who was able to give it in return. If he had that kind of peace, then maybe he was cool with going. You ever look at it that way?"

William's eyes were misty now too. The tiny lines around his eyes deepened. "You talking about faith?"

"Yeah. Something like that."

"Were you thinking about ending your life, son? That one reason why you came here, for this new start?"

Josh licked his lips nervously. He stayed locked in his new friend's eyes. "Not…not thinkin' about it. I, uh, I did somethin' about it."

"I see." William had to step aside to process that. One burly hand gripped the top rail of the fence so hard his knuckles went white. "And you survived."

Josh nodded. His eyes were wide and scared.

"Why, son? Life is s-so damn precious," William stammered. "These beautiful children…what was so bad that you would give up something…so precious…life…a life…that people like Alice and me, and Jeffery's wife and kids, would be so desperate to have back?" William choked back a sob and looked away for a second to muster up enough courage to look this father back in the eye and beg him to hang on, to his wife, his kids, to life, if it ever came to that again.

"It was for them. I did it for them." Josh was openly weeping. "William, I would not expect you to understand, because you don't have all the facts. And that's the thing with Jes—with Jasmyn." He took a cleansing breath. "I just wanted you to know that there is such a thing as making your peace with leaving here, with leaving this place, this life. It's not always dark and it's not always," he gasped, and fought for the words, "the worst thing."

William cut in quickly. "How can it not be the worst thing, son? How can death not be the worst thing?"

"Because there's something worse than death. That's why. For someone who chooses to leave a life behind."

"I can't imagine, Joe. Enlighten me. What can possibly be worse?"

Josh had to work his mouth to make the word come out. When he said it, the truth emerged husky and big, and it was the hardest thing he ever had to tell someone. "Pain." He sobbed when he said it, took two big gulping swallows to try to get control of it, and he almost lost it completely when a rough, manly hand grabbed his shoulder and gave him a gentle shake. Still with his hands on his hips, he rocked his weight onto one foot and looked back up at William to see how angry the man was at the notion of him once choosing to die, when a lot of people never have that choice at all.

William's face was slightly contorted. He was struggling. "You're not alone, son," he said, and Josh cried a little more at the sheer relief of just hearing those simple words. Of knowing they were sincere. He clapped a hand over William's on his shoulder, and mouthed a silent *thank you.*

There was nothing heavy in Josh's arsenal left to say. The emotional talk took the last vestige of strength he had in reserve after Shanda's early morning call almost completely derailed him. He took a step toward William's home where chocolate chip cookies, three blissfully happy children and a remarkable grandmotherly lady waited. The older man turned and walked alongside him.

"You know," Josh admitted as they strolled along, "I've never been able to say that to anyone. The pain part. My wife knows me better than anyone, so I guess she kinda understands, but," Josh shook his head, "she's never really asked. And nobody else has, either. They're all fixated on the other side of the story. And on their own anger and confusion, I guess."

Wisely, William didn't push Josh further. He simply expressed a more immediate concern. "Today when your wife comes home, will you be okay?"

"Yeah. I will be. All that stuff is old news now." Josh wiped a sleeve of his denim jacket across his damp eyes. "I'll talk to her. I'll bring her back to me. It's just…when it comes to her and this guy, she needed him back then, you know? She needs him. I've been a lot to handle. I get that. In some ways I'm real glad she has him, to be honest. I'm glad she has a safe place to land."

"You're one helluva guy, Joe. Or whatever your real name is." William grinned. They were walking together, slowly, casually, two good friends who anyone watching might interpret as father and son. William's hand was still clamped on Josh's shoulder, just helping him hang on a little bit longer, just letting him know that he was not, and nor would he be from this moment on, alone.

Josh sniffled and let out a nice long healing breath. The air now felt invigorating and vital. The ominous cloud cover was moving on, allowing patches of bright, crisp blue to blossom overhead in bits and pieces, opening up to let in light the way a flower does in spring.

"I know you miss him," Josh said, referencing Jeffery. "Your son. But I gotta tell you. He sounds to me like one lucky sunuvabitch. To have lived here, I mean, with you guys as his parents. With you as his dad."

"He was." William was like the blooming sky. A wondrous contentment seemed to light up his soul when this good man was at his side.

Josh laughed. "Arsehole," he said.

William opened the screen door to his and Alice's small house, and moved aside to let Josh in.

# Chapter Thirteen

Mid-morning on Monday, Jessie gave Micah a final tuck in his car seat and backed out of the shiny black Ford Escalade scheduled to drive her and her son, along with Charles and Dan, to the jet. The men would escort her back to Halifax and see her safely off toward P.E.I. while Deirdre, who had work to do at home in Vancouver, caught a lift with Charlie and the rest of the gang. Jessie stood at the open back door of the big vehicle, stared inside at Micah and pondered what to do. She couldn't quite bring herself to climb in. Charles and Dan had yet to appear. The driver was off chatting with the hotel's doorman.

Upstairs in her suite earlier, Jessie had said goodbye to Jane and Sophie. The girls, wondering why she hadn't come down to the dining room that morning, had dropped by immediately after breakfast. Evading their questions, Jessie had just said that Micah was being fussy. Now, emitting a loud growl, her belly protested her choice to avoid public scrutiny by skipping the morning meal. Hunching over, one foot crooked and resting on the doormat inside the big vehicle, Jessie forlornly leaned her forehead against the Escalade's roof.

From behind her, a cocky voice jutted into the bleak thoughts ricocheting around Jessie's brain. "Hung-over, are we?" Charlie, with lanky Steve at his side, was ambling over for a goodbye hug. "You drink yourself into oblivion after Charles escorted your rebel ass out of the ballroom last night? Didn't see your ugly mug at breakfast."

"Wasn't hungry," Jessie tossed over her shoulder to the guys, and added the lie about the baby feeling unsettled. She avoided Charlie's curious eyes as much as she could by continuing to peer into the car at Micah, who was snoozing peacefully. Charlie stopped behind his old girl and tented her where she stood by lazily suspending one arm on the open door, and by resting his other hand on the opposite side, on the mighty Ford's sparkling wax finish.

Steve took up a position next to Charlie's right hand, but swung around so his back rested against the front passenger door. "She's not hung-over," he illuminated Charlie. "She's pissed. Don't you know your 'Jessie moods,' Charlie? That dark frown oughtta give her away. It's deep enough to sink ships."

"Fuck off, Steve." Jessie ducked under Charlie's extended arm. As Charlie circled himself around so he faced the open hotel door, she whirled around to glare at both guys. "Y'all bloody suck."

"Princess Jessie still not taking responsibility for getting herself kicked out of the party?" That crude, unwelcome remark was from Steve. He yelped when Charlie sideways kicked him in the shin and pointed at Jessie. Their girl was swiping at angry tears.

"I'm not gonna miss you two freaks at all," Jessie sniffled, a second before collapsing into two sets of welcoming, friendly arms at once. "Group hug."

When she backed away, fisting at the corners of her eyes to stem the good-bye flood they all knew was coming, Jessie lifted her shoulders and let them fall in a kind of useless gesture that said *I don't know how to deal.*

Charlie took her hand and brushed a thumb over her fingers. "We're all coming down the first of July," he offered gently. "You'll get tired of the chaos real quick."

"No, I won't. I want that kind of chaos, Charlie. And my guess is that you won't all be coming."

Steve waited for Charlie to say something. When he didn't, he threw in a quiet, "Give Shanda some time, Jess. She's only been married a few months."

Jessie's eyes shot over to him. They narrowed in anger. "Almost four. Damn it."

"It's year one. They're newlyweds."

At this point neither of the guys was aware that Jessie and Matt had hooked up the night before, and Jessie wasn't about to tell them. They had to wonder, though, when Shanda appeared in the open hotel doorway and glared demons at Jessie's back.

"She does seem to be overreacting a little," Steve considered with interest.

Jessie twisted around at the waist and took a good hard look at Matt's woman. Shanda was well put together. A mid-thigh floral designer sundress hugged the *Sacred Peace* star's feminine curves. Add in the perfectly curled Marilyn Monroe locks, fancy heels, just the right touch of the season's newest shade of lipstick, and she screamed confidence and poise.

A low grrr was Jessie's reaction when she turned herself back around and considered her own wardrobe choice for the long travel day ahead with a small baby—plain black Lululemon leggings topped by the light pink hoodie she was wearing last night when Matt met her at the door to the hotel suite… the hoodie with the zipper his thumb and finger had so erotically grasped and pulled slowly down…the one that he—when she still had her back to him just as they entered the suite—yanked up over her head with an almost animal desperation, taking her tank top with it so he could cup her bare breasts in his hands…

Recalling the steamy encounter, Jessie had to force a new moan inward. Last night was unreal. Letting her eyes drift closed, she took herself back there with Matt…throwing back her head, arching her trembling body away from him, dropping her hands over his on her breasts and squeezing so she could more fully feel his hold on her…his hand moving down her stomach, in an instant clutching her body tightly back against him…then that quick movement that exposed her fully to him—both of his hands fumbling to get hold of the elastic waist of her pajama pants, a quick thrust to shove them down around her ankles…Jessie kicking them off, naked, widening her stance for him…

Matt's wet mouth on her neck, sizzling electric vibrations dancing up and down her body, him moaning again and again, his body hungry, alive, on fire, pushing against hers. A hand between her legs, cupping her, pressing against her, sliding back and forth, fingers probing, pulsing, driving her quickly to orgasm before she wanted to go there, because this was a night Jessie wanted to savor…countering his almost frantic exploring by whipping around to face him, dropping to her knees, running her greedy hands up under his shirt, over his chest, too desperate to bother unbuttoning him…pressing her lips to his hard abs, trailing downwards with her tongue, unzipping his pants at the same time…his shaking fingers on her cheeks, swiping back damp wisps of hair so he could better watch Jessie do what she told Shanda he liked the best…him lifting her, flipping her around, pushing her to the foot of the bed, forcibly spreading her legs so he could unite his body with hers while she bent over and mewled loudly into the coverlet over and over as he thrust into her…

Remembering, recalling the erotically charged lovemaking and the long, sweet moments afterward lying on the bed with her best, best friend—disappearing into the love in each other's eyes, touching, caressing, loving each other some more—Jessie groaned and grabbed the side of the open car door so she could lean into it and focus on something less painful, like the hard unfeeling bit of gravel she started toeing around underneath one flip-flopped foot.

"Hey, little girl, we'll stay in touch. You'll be okay," Steve was saying.

Charlie's eyes narrowed in intrigued perplexity at the way Shanda was walking toward Jessie…stomping almost, in those tall heels of hers…her eyes firing invisible bullets.

Shanda's vice-like hand was on Jessie's elbow before Charlie had time to call out a warning. Giving the arm an unmerciful yank, the *Sacred Peace* star ignored the pained cry Jessie discharged to the world at the unexpected action.

"What the hell?" was Jessie's next proclamation as she spun around. Rubbing her arm, she took a step backward when she saw Shanda in front of her, teetering on her heels, furious sparks shooting from both moist eyes.

"One of these days, Jessie," Shanda spit at her ex co-star's wife, "one of these days I'll get back at you. I'm going to have my night with Josh. Or my week or my month or whatever. In the meantime, I'll be practicing on my husband. MY husband. Neither of those men will ever want to share a bed with you again. Or a fucking footboard or a goddamned floor or, or… a kitchen goddamned sink, I don't know, and I don't care! You are the worst kind of person on the planet. Any woman who would willingly go to bed with another woman's man deserves to suffer the way you have. You ever wonder why things get all shitty and out of control for you?"

The boys were speechless. At that ruthless dig, they each sucked in a breath and held it.

Shanda went on. Her face was red and her heart was threatening to leap out of her chest, but she needed this. Leaning forward, she spat out the last bit. "Karma, bitch," she fumed. "Goddamned karma. And it's coming for you again. You wait and see."

With a final glare, she pressed a damp tissue to her already red eyes and wheeled around. Instantly, she stopped moving.

Shaking, Jessie looked past her to see what—who—she was looking at. Matt. *Jesus.*

…the man Jessie took to her bed last night, a man she loved with a desperation she could not even begin to label with a name. The man she last saw when he left her bedroom with the promise to be 'back in five.'

He was ten feet away and walking slowly toward them.

"Shanda," he started, but she raised a palm and stopped him cold.

"Don't you come one more goddamned step toward her," she demanded. "Don't you look at her, don't you touch her. Don't you," she was sobbing now, "don't you goddamned touch her!"

"I can't…" Matt was shaking his head. His eyes were locked on his wife, on the pain he saw in the black circles under her eyes, at the way she was wobbling a bit on the heels she usually wore with such grace and self-assurance.

"Don't." It was one word. And it spoke legions.

Everyone waited, tense as soldiers on parade, afraid to speak or move. In the Escalade, Micah was waking, starting to fuss as if he, too, understood the verity of the situation.

Jessie stood stock still. Shanda's back was to her; Charlie and Steve both saw Jessie look to the tight-fitting dress and the toned body within. They knew that look.

"Jessie," Charlie warned. It wouldn't surprise him one little bit if his old girl rushed forward in a fit of rage and gave Shanda a brutal, hardhearted shove.

Swallowing, Jessie let her eyes shift from Shanda. Grasping the open door of the SUV, she forced herself to take a closer look at her lover.

GQ perfect, with his now longer hair swept over to one side, Matt was wearing dress pants today, light ones for this hot early summer Boston day, pants that certainly suited the husband of a television and film star who now, in the stunning dress, had paparazzi cameras pointing in her direction. One thing remained Matt-like, in Jessie's opinion as she let her gaze drift over the handsome man she had loved so erotically the night before—the white linen shirt overtop, the button down kind that flowed over the waist of his pants, although this one had trendy buttons on flapless pockets on the chest, little bone or pearl ones or something…

She blinked hard and fast to keep tears from flowing. Matt wouldn't even look at her. His eyes were stuck on Shanda.

Opening her mouth, Jessie reached deep and said his name. "Matt…" It came out gravelly and thin. She tried a second time, louder. "Matt…" He blinked, but didn't waver from Shanda's piercing stare.

Next to Jessie, Charlie and Steve were frozen. They were peculiar bystanders of this strange scenario.

"For fuck's sake, Shanda." Jessie let go of the door and planted her feet on the ground. "I'm leaving. Okay? Can I just say goodbye?" This time, her voice was thick with emotion.

Behind her, Micah's wails increased in volume. His little fists clutched at empty air. Nobody moved.

Shanda fired once again at Matt. "DON'T."

Finally, his eyes blinked over to Jessie. Just the slightest shake of his head…his message was clear.

"Jesus," she gasped, and would have sunk down onto the earth if Charlie didn't react quickly and grab her arm to steady her. As it was, Jessie curled over herself and hugged her belly, which killed Matt to see. From years of experience he knew it was her way of trying to hold her pain inside. "A fuckin' hug," she begged. "A last goodbye. Jesus, Shanda, please!"

Shanda was not an unreasonable person. She was just a very hurt one at this particular juncture in time. Her husband's tragic eyes were on Jessie now, a woman whose life Shanda was well aware he had twice saved. And those deeply loved eyes were swimming. It was too much.

She turned once more to Jessie. "I called him," she seethed. "Josh. I hope he's gone when you get home. I hope he packs up your kids and leaves."

It was clear now. Steve and Charlie now understood exactly why Shanda was so incensed. Even they turned away from Jessie with slight unconscious, disgusted movements that Jessie, in her peripheral vision, caught.

She and Shanda were in lockdown position. It was a while before anyone moved or spoke again. They were, however, trembling. All of them.

Eventually breaking the impasse, Shanda tore herself away, reached for her man's hand and took him along with her. The air she left behind was hot with anger. The woman she steered her husband ungracefully away from was ice cold with grief.

Matt didn't let his eyes drift away from Jessie until the last possible second. The final image he had of her, the one he should have filed away to some dark, inaccessible place in his brain but which kept coming back to haunt him in the grief-stricken months to come, was of her sinking back against the big black Ford, turning her head to the side so she could bury her anguish in Charlie's chest, and clutching at his shirt as she gasped for air.

Chapter Fourteen

It was a long flight home. Knowing she was about to once again leave a lot of people she loved behind, Jessie spent the flight huddled up against Charles' side on the sofa at the back of the jet. She didn't speak except when spoken to, knowing that she would bear his wrath if he found out she was with Matt after leaving his and Deirdre's suite last night. She was afraid to look at him for fear of giving her secret away by virtue of her haunted, deeply sorrowful eyes.

Needless to say, Charles did not get the heart-to-heart he'd hoped for—the one-to-one chat he had announced at the after-party that he wanted.

For Jessie, silence was the best option. Crying was out of the question. Even when she left the company of Dan and Charles in Halifax, who were both trying to look composed when she pulled away but who discreetly mopped at the wetness in their eyes when they parted, Jessie held it together. She didn't lose her shit until she was halfway between the Halifax airport and the neighboring small city of Truro, when she couldn't see for tears, and had to pull off the road and vomit her guts out in the trees bordering the highway.

Leaning back against the truck afterward as Micah contentedly play-talked inside, Jessie struggled with the new-old truths she had no choice but to face. One, she was a person who hurt people. A lot of people. Through the things she said or the awful words she yelled; through sex; through an inability to accept a life she, after the weekend's magical return to the stage, now formally decreed she wanted no part of.

*Except for the part where I get to spend a lot of time with my kids.* She gasped, trying to regain control, which only served to unleash a whole new torrent of choking sobs. *I tried. I fucking tried. But I can't do it. I'm not cut out to live my life in hiding, away from people I love. Been there, done that. It fucking sucks.*

Bent over double against the truck, she slid to the grass and made herself consider the other person who, in this new agony, Jessie knew deserved her loyalty, but who, because she was torn between two men and two lives, likely now hated her guts.

Josh.

*Shanda called him. He must hate me.*

The idea of going home to him, facing him, seeing his hurt, sad eyes, was so nauseating that when Jessie passed Truro, she took an off-ramp to a market she'd stopped to pee at on her way to the airport a few short days ago. Setting Micah's carrier down on a tabletop, rocking him but unable to look even into those tiny, non-judgmental eyes, she stayed until darkness closed in, nursing a large coffee she probably shouldn't have had because she was breastfeeding.

Her new cell was on the table next to Micah. Jessie left it face up. Not a single message came in from Josh. Nobody else would dare use this phone. She had a burner phone with her, and she lied into it when Charles called and asked if she was safely home.

"Yes. Home." *Whatever the hell that is these days.* "Yeah. Drive was great. No trouble at all." *No trouble. At all. It was a perfect weekend. A perfect goddamned fucked up weekend.* Bending her face over the new cell she and Josh used to communicate with each other, Jessie watched big droopy tears puddle onto the table. A new numbness was taking over. Shanda was right. Being with Matt again was extraordinary. It was dreamy, staring into his eyes like that—she remembered when she and Josh used to do that, just lie in bed and get lost in each other's souls, just touch each other, for ages and ages. Those days seemed long gone. They got chipped away by stalkers and kidnappers and sinking SUVs. What Shanda was right about was the bit about karma. Last night's wild lovemaking was being paid off in spades with today's unrelenting heartache.

In P.E.I. it was close to midnight before Josh, from his position on the inside stairs, saw headlights come down Sutherland Road and swing into his driveway. About an hour ago, William had made his way down to the big house and sat with Josh—or Joe, as he knew him—for a half hour, just for company during the intolerable wait. He nodded off at the kitchen table. Josh sent him home to Alice and bed.

When Jessie waded in, exhausted, reeling, Josh padded over, reached out to take Micah's carrier, and turned away from her. "You hungry?" he managed. His chicken dinner was long since suffocating under cellophane; a plate for Jessie sat in submissive silence in the fridge.

She didn't answer.

Fiddling with the carrier, switching hands on its handle in the semi-darkness, Josh pressed his fingers to his lips and kissed the tips of them. He laid the fingers on Micah's tiny forehead. "Missed ya, big guy," he whispered to the baby, who was sound asleep but who likely felt the love emanating from his father anyway, it was so profound.

Josh rifled long fingers through his own hair, set the carrier down on the floor and wheeled slowly around to face his wayward wife.

He opened his arms.

Jessie was falling apart. Lifting her hands to her face, she covered her mouth and eyes, stumbled her way over to him, and crumpled into his embrace.

"I get it, you know," Josh murmured to her as he held her, as he crushed her to him. "I know why you love him. I know why you go to him."

"I just—I just…" She sobbed.

He lifted a hand to caress her hair, her cheek. "Sshhh. You don't need to explain, Jessie." The two fingers Josh used to express love to his son were pressed now against Jessie's lips, to quiet her. Josh shook his head slowly. "We're not normal, you and me. Nothing about our lives is normal and it never will be, no matter how hard we try to live in a place that should feel normal. You go to him because you need him."

Her crying slowed. Jessie sucked on a lip before she told her husband the biggest 'why' of all. "I love him," she said.

Josh waited a minute before he answered. He didn't look away. "I know, little one," he admitted, taking an emotional hiccuppy breath and running the backs of his fingers over the wetness on her cheek. "But you love me too. I know you do. It's this life you're having a hard time with. The 'letting go of the past' part."

Her nod settled his stomach a bit. "'Course I do, Josh. Love you, I mean. More than anything." Jessie let her hands fall to his hips. "On the way home, I had to be Jasmyn again," she wept. "You remember what it was like to have to play a part you couldn't quite get into, Josh? One you were glad to shed when the film was finished?"

"I know where you're going with this, Jessie."

"I can't get into her. Jasmyn. I don't like her enough to be her all the time. I hate her boring fucking hair! And the thing is…I don't like the Jessie in me either." A new round of tears cemented that truth.

Pulling her head to his shoulder, Josh sighed into his wife's big, open curls. "I don't know how to make this better, Jessie," he said. "You and Matt…"

"You weren't there," she wailed into his shoulder. "When the Lexus went into the water, you weren't there, Josh! When I saw him there, at the window, this feeling came over me. It was like I just knew we were going to be okay. The second I saw him, I knew I could shatter that window and he would find the strength in himself to haul Emily-Grace and me out, out of that watery grave we would have both died in if he wasn't there to pull us out. Not just me…our daughter, too. OUR daughter. Yours and mine!"

"I would have, too," Josh said, pushing Jessie away from him enough so he could palm her cheeks and offer what solace he could. "Little one," he implored her to listen, to understand, "I would have done the same damn thing if I'd gotten there first. I would have died for you."

It was a shock, hearing those words snake their way out of Josh's lips. They reverberated down Jessie's body and back up again, leaving a tingly fear of sordid memory in their wake.

"You almost did," she breathed, clutching his cotton Henley by the elbows. "Jesus, Josh. You almost did."

"You see?" he whispered, staring into her eyes with a determined solemnity that frightened Jessie. "Me and Matt are not all that different. Do you get it now, Jessie? Why I did what I did?"

"It's not the same, Josh. It's not the same at all. It wasn't his choice to go into the river. He felt he had to."

"And I had to do what I did, Jessie. We've been in that damn river, you and me, since the day Nadia and Morgan stole you and the kids away from me."

Josh's chest was rising with the rush of emotions overtaking him tonight, with the final relief that his wife was home safe where he could talk to her, touch her, where he could encourage her to find some way to live in P.E.I. with joy. He swallowed and tried to restore his heart rate to a normal rhythm in the hopeful certainty that Jessie would remain a part of their family and eventually find peace with him and with their children.

"You once told me you'd fight for me," he reminded her. "Do it, Jessie. Fight for me now."

"With myself." It wasn't a question. She took a stuttery breath. "I don't need to, Josh. I'm here, aren't I?"

Josh paused. "Do I take that to mean Matt hasn't asked you to leave me?"

"Oh, Josh. I would never leave you. Never. And he would never ask me to." Jessie sank her forehead into her husband's chest and breathed him in. "It's not a question of leaving you, or of not loving you. It's just a question of loving him." Tipping up her head, she peeked up at him from behind soaked eyelashes that caught the minimal light Josh left on in the mudroom, which also haloed Jessie from one side.

*A repentant sinner,* Josh thought. The big pale blue eyes worriedly searching his for answers made his knees go weak.

"There's no real solution here, babe." Jessie sighed into the creaks and cracks of the old house. It was protesting the brutal potency of the wind, echoing Jessie's hopeless appeal to Josh to understand how much this hurt. "I'm sorry. I wish there was."

"I wish there was too."

"I'm sorry I hurt you. Again and again I hurt you, Josh. You're the last person on this earth that I ever want to hurt."

Taking hold of a handful of Jessie's hair, Josh treated her to a sad smile. "Yet you do, little one," he murmured. "Again and again." With one last, tender kiss that he planted securely on the top of his wife's head, Josh backed away. His hands dropped to his sides. "Now if you don't mind," he said, "let me remind you that I, too, am far from perfect. It kinda hurts to look at you right now. So for tonight I'm gonna slide in beside David or Dylan. Whichever one's not sprawled all over the bed. G'nite, Jessie."

After picking up Micah's carrier, Josh tossed a last few words over his shoulder. "I'll get this little guy settled in his crib. You should go to sleep too. You look like shit." Swinging around, walking backward, he added, "You likely didn't sleep a goddamned wink last night, huh?" He touched the outside of his crotch. "Hope you got it out of your system. I expect you did. Matt's got a lot of, how you say it? *Je ne sais quoi*, going for him. Mystery. Suave. GQ charm. The unknown 'it' factor that rebellious misfits like you crave. Jessie? Just so you know? You won't be getting any from me for a while."

Her eyes widened in confusion. "You said you understood." It was a whisper. "You said you get it."

Josh's footsteps ground to a halt at the open door to the next room. He looked back at his wife. In the darkness, lit only by a dim half light floating down the central stairs, he was every bit as mystical, absorbing and damn well perfect as the best film crew lighting teams in the world made him out to be. "I'm not a God, Jessie," he said quietly, brushing back a long strand of tired, unruly hair. "I'm just a man. And right now I'm a confused and hurt one." Raising a hand in a salute, he added, "Good night. Enjoy that big empty bed of ours. Get used to sleeping alone." He padded off toward the stairs, Micah swinging lightly at his side in the carrier.

Slumping down into a hard wooden chair at the kitchen table, Jessie rested an arm on the top back rail and laid her forehead on it. *Matt, baby,* she prayed, *I hope you're okay. Because I'm not. I feel like shit for hurting everyone around me again. And somehow I feel that you're the only one on the planet who really understands that about me. Who knows that the only part of myself that I feel is worth loving…is the one that shows up when I'm with you.*

This time when she watched her tears fall from vacant eyes, they had a greater distance to go. Each drop puddled on the unfamiliar floor of the big old drafty house where a lonely woman named Jasmyn McIver lived. Jasmyn, who, in Jessie's mind, would always remain no more than a forlorn, unlikeable stranger.

Chapter Fifteen

An early July, as a sort of Jessie pre-birthday celebration, some of the gang flew to Halifax and made the drive to Sutherland Road. Landing in P.E.I. would have been much more convenient, but staying under the radar of curious locals and airport staff would have been impossible if the Keating jet, or any chartered jet, disembarked the likes of stars like Charlie, Steve and Jacob. Even Carter was along for the trip, since Charlie couldn't very well sneak out of *Sacred Peace* for the week and not give Carter an episode off to see his friends. All the guys had kids and spouses in tow; the only people really missing, whose absence the west coast folks felt as deeply as Jessie since their gatherings in Alberta or British Columbia usually included them, were Matt and Shanda.

The date was chosen because William and Alice had packed up and driven off to Ontario for the week to see their grandchildren, with blessings to Joe and Jasmyn to enjoy a fun time with visiting friends, and an offer to feel free to utilize their home for accommodations. Hardly another soul lived on the Sutherland Road, and the beach at the end of it wasn't one of the island's best beaches—it was small, a tad pebbly, and not entirely full of the glorious white sand that locals preferred—so the gang pretty much had the area to themselves.

Josh towed in a 35-foot Montana fifth-wheel trailer for the week. Charlie and Jane set up camp in it, Steve and Sophie took their boys up the lane to the Sutherland home, Carter and Ashley roughed it in a tent that Josh set up the morning everyone was expected, and Jacob and Kayla moved into Josh and Jessie's bed for the week. Jessie laid her head on Emily-Grace's bed each night. Most of the kids snuggled into cozy tents erected in the yard. Josh slept in a dome tent with his older boys. All told, it was a grand gathering— a fun social, private week for the good friends.

Until the last full day. It was a tough day anyway, for Jessie. In her mind her birthday was never a cause for celebration, and it had nothing to do with aging. In the past, bad things happened on her birthday. This year, with home feeling like a messed up movie, she was apprehensive well before her special day.

The last full day of everyone's visit was July sixth. Jessie's birthday was the twelfth, but the gang was having cake on the sixth since everyone was pulling out the next day. The day was so hot that by ten a.m. the moms and dads were already tired of wrangling their kids to stand still for sunscreen applications. The whole kit 'n caboodle were on the beach by then, in and out of the water trying to stay cool. At noon, Jessie headed up to the house for a pee. Sophie and Jane were already up there ransacking the dregs of what was left in the Montana's fridge, making sandwiches, gathering grapes and carrot sticks and sorting out what to feed the assembled horde on the beach.

The guys, plus Ashley and Kayla, stayed down on the beach with the kids. Creative sand structures shaped from the darker moist sand near the water dotted the shoreline in various stages of completion—a castle, a sea turtle, a peace sign, a Volkswagen van. Kayla and Jacob were hunched over one, betting on winning a friendly Sawyer-sponsored contest. Utilizing rocks, pebbles and shells for decorating, their creation was the castle, the luxury fifteenth-century kind. Josh's was the sea turtle. It immediately won the young girls over—Stella and Emily-Grace were crouched over it, sun hats covering their young heads while they carved and shaped the flippers for Josh.

Ten minutes after Jessie headed up to the house, Josh left the girls to their work, Micah to Ashley's care and Dylan to Jacob's capable hands. He wandered up the beach with David, being careful to avoid a softball Charlie and Steve were tossing between them. David needed a bathroom break. Josh figured that on the way back he and David could give Jessie and the other two gals some muscle and help haul the food down to the hungry beach goers.

While David was in the upstairs washroom, Josh peeked in at Jessie in the master bedroom. She was hanging damp towels from yesterday's beach day, newly retrieved from the washing machine, over the rails of the upper deck to dry.

"Need some help?" he asked, one eye on her and the other on the bathroom door.

"Nope. Got 'em all. Thanks anyway, Josh." Jessie was humming a new ballad she and Jacob had composed in the music room last night while the others were outside enjoying a campfire.

Josh could hear loud voices below, drifting up from the yard outside. He wrinkled an eyebrow. Sophie and Jane were having some kind of argument, which was totally out of character for both. In all seriousness, considering the sheer confusion that meal prep and child care warranted with this many people in a small environment, the week had gone splendidly. Factor in personalities, female hormones and whiny, sun-soaked, tired children, and it was a miracle they were all still talking to each other much less having a grand old time overall, with campfires every night and cards and board games on the one day and night it rained.

Josh was about to retrace his steps and leave the master bedroom when he saw Jessie stop short. With a colorful towel suspended between her fingers, she cocked her head to the side and remained still.

"Eavesdropper," Josh chuckled to himself, starting to turn away.

There was no breeze that day. Prince Edward Island was one big blistering, muggy steam bath. The girls' heated voices filtered easily up to the deck.

David was just coming out of the bathroom. He, along with his father and mother, heard every damning word.

"I'm sorry for sounding like a bitch here," Jane was saying, "but this text from Shanda breaks my heart. She and Matt would have been fine if Jessie hadn't winked her sexy little come-hither eyes at him in Boston."

Sophie jumped on her. "Jane, just because Shanda set him loose doesn't mean Matt will come looking for Jessie. He'll take some time to get his priorities straight and will go back to Shanda. Mark my words."

The voices were moving, heading toward the house. The women talked in lower tones just outside the kitchen door, but paused there as they chatted. Clear as glass, their heated words continued wafting up to the second floor.

"Are you kidding me?" The incredulous voice was Jane's. "He's a man, and you know where their brains are. Who the hell knows what he'll do? Personally, I hope he has the good sense to stay away, but get this. Jessie told me yesterday that she and Josh haven't had sex since before she went to Boston. I have to tell you, that's been worrying me on this trip."

"You? Why?"

Upstairs, Jessie hung her head. The towel dropped to the deck floor. Josh chewed on a lip and watched her suffer. David tried to figure out what he was hearing.

"Because Charlie'd hop back in bed with her in a second," drifted up to them, clear as anything. "All she'd need to do is give him the A-OK. Did you see the way he was looking at her at breakfast?"

"Depends which look you're referring to, Jane," Sophie half giggled. The conversation quite succinctly turned into an attack. "The one where he memorized the way her nipples were poking out from her white bikini top, or the misty, doe eyed way his eyes followed her around the kitchen?"

These were not the good friends Jessie and Josh knew and loved. These were women afraid of losing their men.

"Sex is different with her," Jane rationalized. Upstairs, Josh grunted and ordered David downstairs. "It's too easy. She has no clue how deep her actions sometimes cut. Not always the sex, just the way she touches our guys. The way she moves around them. The way she dresses, sometimes, like in that bikini. It doesn't leave a lot to the imagination, that's for sure."

Sophie's sigh was so pained it was probably heard down on the beach. "At least your husband's been faithful to you all along," she countered. "Has Charlie cheated on you once since you met? No. You know that Steve had his fun with Jessie when he and I were dating, right? Broke us up for a while. You weren't around then, Jane. If Jessie's looking for a new man to make up for losing Matt, we ought to toss a coin to see which way she turns."

"I hate when she and Josh are on the outs. She always needs somebody to hold, and to hold her. I'm always scared it's going to be Charlie. They're so close...their history..."

Below, the screen door creaked open. Jessie could feel Josh at the bedroom door, hovering like a shadow, quiet and thoughtful. She couldn't bring herself to look at him. At least David had understood that his father's tone meant business. The little boy was on his way back down the stairs.

The delicate Sophie had one last thing to say. It almost sounded barbaric coming from her usually sweet mouth. "Marriage is hills and valleys, that's for sure. It's just that with Jessie and Josh, their hills are higher and their valleys are deeper. I wish they'd get their shit together. Shanda and Matt are going through hell."

"I guess it's good that we're all leaving tomorrow," Jane added. "I love her but I can't deal with the jealousy that flares up when Charlie and Jessie are lost in one of their heart-to-hearts. When he walked up to her on the beach this morning and put his hand on her hip and gave her that charming smile of his, then Jessie looked up at him and laid her hand on his and started rubbing it, I have to tell you it was all I could do not to jump up and scream at her to leave my husband alone. I had to sit on my hands and bite my lip. In my head, all I could see was how hurt Shanda was in Boston. I don't think I'd be able to get past that kind of treachery. Right now, after getting this text from Shanda? I'm so upset I don't think I can even look Jessie in the eye."

"I don't know how Josh can stand it."

"At least one thing's on our side these days."

"What's that?"

"Distance."

"Thank God."

Two sets of footsteps wandered through the kitchen door. From upstairs, Josh and Jessie could clearly hear the gals start moving about below, gathering food and chattering amicably. They heard Sophie and Jane greet David before the screen door creaked open again. Jessie craned her neck over the railing to watch him jog back down to the beach.

Josh padded his way over to her. Seeing him come closer, Jessie turned away and gripped the top of the rail. Big, strong arms wrapped their way around her middle.

"They don't understand. They're not us, Jessie."

Her voice came out sounding tinny and strange. "Matt and Shanda broke up, it sounds like."

Josh tightened his hold around his wife. "They'll sort it out," he murmured from under her hair.

"Good to know what the women I thought were my best friends think of me."

"Jessie…"

Flipping around, Jessie laid her hands on her husband's arms. "No, it's okay, Josh. Occasionally it's good to get that kind of validation. It reminds me of who I really am. You know, in case I actually forget on some sunshiny day when the world feels like it's spinning on its axis again." Lifting one hand, Jessie traced the bullet scar on Josh's chest with one finger, then laid her palm over it and closed her eyes. "As if I could ever forget."

Shoving herself away from Josh, Jessie tiptoed across the bedroom floor and made her way into the en suite bathroom. She closed the door so quietly behind her that Josh had to turn to see if that was actually where she went.

Raising his head, Josh rifled a hand through his hair and looked out over the beach. He spied a cheerful group of friends enjoying their last full day together. A few minutes later he joined them, and broke the news that there was a good chance tonight's birthday party might not go as planned.

Chapter Sixteen

"She heard you."

He didn't intend to tell them. Josh didn't intend to say a damn thing, but two hours later Jessie's absence was starting to grate on everyone, and nerves were running short. By then Jane and Sophie had shared the news that Matt and Shanda split. Josh stumbled upon Sophie whispering to Jane. The whispering stopped when he drew close. Both women found shells to stare at and sand to concentrate on while they sifted it through their fingers.

It was midafternoon. Tired of chasing the kids around, happy that the younger set were being industrious sand runts, digging and playing and generally getting along, Charlie, Steve, Carter and Jacob were lounging around their women, comfortably ensconced in foldable fabric camp chairs, sucking back water and juice. Out of respect for Josh, the week was alcohol free. At Josh's extended explanation of Jessie's absence, every man and woman present—including Josh—was wishing their light drinks were coolers and beer.

At Josh's words, Jane's and Sophie's surprised eyes darted up. Josh hadn't spoken to either of them since lunch. Having just come in from the water after generally avoiding everyone, he was standing in front of them in soaked swim trunks—blue ones with a white surfboard motif on one leg. Like a dog, he shook his head to dispel the salt water from his long hair. He didn't give a shit that multiple drops sprayed like rain over the dry women in front of him.

He continued, "Jessie was on the deck outside our bedroom while the two of you were debating which of your men she would go after next."

The guys all groaned.

Charlie was the first to come to his senses. "What the hell?" He sat forward in his chair. "Jane?"

Jane buried her face in her hands. "Oh, Jesus." Giving her short pixie cut an elegant toss, she dropped her hands and sighed up at Josh. "I'm sorry. Hearing that Matt and Shanda broke up was the last straw this week."

"And the first straw?" Josh probed. "Charlie's continued adoration of my wife? That's not news."

Jane's eyes popped over to her star/producer husband. Tanned and robust, muscled and toned, Charlie was a handsome man with a lot to offer—success, money, prestige, daring good looks. "You've never stopped loving her," she accused. "That's why you keep her close by. You need to have her in your life."

Like a fish out of water, Charlie's mouth opened and closed. He had no clue what to say. In the end he went with, "This isn't like you, Jane. Where's this coming from? And don't tell me it's Shanda. You know this thing with Matt and Jessie is not cut and dry. Shanda knows that too. She'll come around."

Sophie was sitting on a beach blanket beneath an umbrella. She had a sleeping Micah in her arms. Glancing over at Steve, she recoiled when he gave her a hard look. A second later, Steve chose to avoid his wife's eyes by reaching for a towel that he tossed to Josh, who started mopping his chest with it.

"I've been watching Jessie this week." Drawing up her shoulders, Jane decided truth was the best way to go. "We don't usually all spend this much time together. It's been interesting, watching her. That's all." On the blanket next to Sophie, she leaned back on one lean arm and crossed her long legs at the ankles. "She's always been needy. I just don't recall ever thinking she was…" Biting her lip, Jane peeked up at Josh. "…slutty, before. I'm sorry, Josh. Seeing her with Matt at the party in Boston, the way she touched him and moved around him…I don't see how any man can resist a woman like that. Jessie's always touching someone. A man. With her history, it makes it easy to see why it escalates. Why she goes there so fast. She can be a predator."

Josh's eyes were darkening. The towel stopped patting his body. "You're crossing a line, Jane."

"Come on, Josh. She exudes sex. Some women do, and she's one of those women. You can't tell me she doesn't." Jane was up for a fight. Shanda had become a good, dear friend over the last few years of shooting *Sacred Peace*.

Lines were quite crisply drawn in the sand long before the gang gathered in Prince Edward Island. "All of you," she waved an arm at the quiet men around their little circle, "are under her spell. Not one of you can look away from her when she's in the room. She's not a goddess! Far from it. Exactly the opposite, in fact!"

"Jane, stop." Charlie curled his lips down and pointed his bottle of ginger ale at her. "You need a time out. You're Jessie's friend."

"Like hell she is," Josh growled.

Jane was this far in. She didn't see the sense in stopping now. "Charlie, Shanda's in agony. She kicked Matt out yesterday because he's been so despondent he won't even talk to her. Poor Josh here is hanging on by shoestrings, following Jessie around like a puppy, waiting for her to curl her little finger up and invite him back to her bed, I'm guessing, and—"

"That's not your business, Jane." To everyone's surprise, Jacob chimed in. At the far end of the men's curved line of camp chairs, he had been off the group's radar for this awkward discussion. They all turned to him. "I'm sorry about Shanda and Matt, Jane. You are right about certain parts of this weird chat. Jessie does have a spell. But you're wrong in hanging her out to dry like this. She doesn't deserve it."

"I cut *her* off," Josh stated, angrily throwing his towel on the ground. He reached down for Micah. "Sex." Folding his sleeping son into his arms, he went on. "We're sorting through this mess Morgan and Nadia made, Jane. We're working through it the best way we know how. You know who came along on this disgusting ride with us?"

Spite shone out from Jane's eyes. With a flippant, hurt stare, she shrugged.

"People who care about Jessie came along with us," Josh said. "Matt and Charlie, for instance, who knew her back in the day when she rarely spoke. Just after a time when, yes, she sometimes had to use her body to get things she needed. Like goddamned food." He took a breath. "Maybe it's hard to shut that off. I don't know. But I do know one thing. Overhearing you and Sophie basically calling her a slut to her face today—at her home, a place where we've all been trying like hell to make her feel safe—only served to send her back down into her deep, dark hole." He lowered his voice. "We were supposed to celebrate her birthday tonight, something she only does for the kids' benefit, really, so they can sing *Happy Birthday* and she can blow out candles. You know why she doesn't like to celebrate her birthday? Because people she loved died on her birthday. Her father, and her friend Rachel from Charleston. Jessie's birthday is not a happy day for her. Having all of you here should have negated at least a small part of that sadness. But I think now all that having you here has done is sent her running for cover again."

"That doesn't excuse what she did to Shanda and Matt, Josh. And to you. You're forgiving her far too easily this time."

Josh skirted over the part about him. He launched into the bit about Matt. "Matt? Jessie can no more control her feelings for him than you and I can turn off the moon. Apart from him, who I love almost as much as she does for what he's done for our family, she got through a few rough patches with Jacob along to help her feel loved, but otherwise has been a faithful wife and mother. Going back to what you two said about her needing to be touched and held? That part? You're damn right she does. You go two years with no real human connection after the boy you love is murdered in front of you, and tell me you don't need to be held. You look your daughter in the eye in a sunken SUV, not knowing whether either of you is going to survive, and tell me you don't need to be held. That touching thing Jessie does? It's her way of hanging on, her way of making sure she's still connected. I watch her sometimes when she does that, with me, with Jacob, with Matt, with Charlie…you look closely at her and you'll see that she often takes this little breath, like there's a kind of little hitch in her breathing when she makes the connection, and often she closes her eyes too. It's like when you plug in the charger to your phone. To her, touch is life. It's energy."

"It's power." In front of Josh, Jane stood and brushed the sand off her body. "I know Jessie's sob story, Josh. I know it well. Charlie spouts it like the gospel. Poor Jessie this, and poor Jessie that. She's your wife, you handle her however you see fit. Just be aware that Matt is on the loose again. Tell Jessie to keep her hands off my husband while she waits for Shanda's man to reappear and climb back into her bed."

With that, Jane marched past Josh down to the shore where Stella and Emily-Grace were building an entire castle fortress complete with a sea grass-filled moat and pretty windows made from pearlescent shells.

Charlie waited a minute before he stood. When he did, his knees were weak. Facing Josh almost side on, from a three quarter profile, he had to force himself to look over. Josh was staring at some random place in the hot pebbly sand, holding his baby to his body as if the child were a shield that could somehow protect him from this new menace the world was throwing his way. Feeling Charlie's eyes on him, he gave his hair a stormy shake and met his buddy's searching eyes.

"I would," Charlie confessed. His voice was low, subdued. "I'd go to bed with her, Josh, if she ever came looking for me. I don't think that's a surprise to you. I fucked up a long time ago when it came to Jessie. I've regretted my stupidity every goddamned day of my life. Sometimes every goddamned second." He paused as Josh swallowed back the bitter truth and held Charlie's gaze. Taking a step closer, Charlie laid a hand on Josh's shoulder. "I'd say you got lucky, hooking up with her, but I know it's a helluva lot more than that. Jessie's never wanted anyone but you. You consider this Matt thing. I know it hurts like hell, for all of you, but there are so many layers to the kind of pain that drove her into his arms that there is no untangling them. You know what works with your rebel girl, Josh. Love. That's what brings her around. Your big arms around her neck, that's the only real connection she ever really wants."

He started to walk past Josh, toward his wife and daughter and young son at the water, and stopped just beside and behind him. "Let her back in, Josh. Hold her the way she needs to be held. Sex, for Jessie, is about being as connected as she can possibly be. Jane is right. Jessie needs that connection. And, my friend, I'm sure you do too." A sad grin appeared on his face. He waded off through the hot sand, cursing a few times when the soles of his feet warmed just a little more than he was comfortable with on this scorching summer day.

"Anyone else got some crazy wisdom they wanna add?" Josh fired daggers around at the rest of his and Jessie's friends.

Steve guffawed and dug a toe into the sand. He looked over at Sophie. "Yeah. I'm disappointed in you, Soph. Jessie's been a good friend to you. Old grudges fester and leak poison. They don't do anybody any good."

"I know." Sighing, Sophie looked up at Josh. "I'm sorry. I got caught up in Shanda's drama too. I'll apologize to Jessie and I'll try to talk some sense into Jane. She'll be okay when she cools off."

Josh's heart rate slowed as his adrenaline stopped pumping in overdrive. "I appreciate that, Sophie," he said, "but I know my wife. She's likely buried under the covers having a sleep after a good cry. She's not gonna want to see anybody, and that likely includes our kids." He looked about ready to cry himself.

The quiet Jacob jumped back in. A wide smile rocketed across his face. He tapped Carter on the knee. "I know what she needs!"

The memory of his Jessie/Kayla threesome in L.A. sprang to everybody's minds. Kayla, on the beach blanket behind Sophie, at Jacob's feet, started laughing, ducked her face away from her shocked brother, and swatted Jacob.

"Not that! Not everything is about sex! Music," Jacob announced, raising his water bottle in victory. "What our girl needs is music. It's been a long damn time since Jessie and me had ourselves a good old fashioned song-after-song party jam session. The kids can help."

With a wary eye, Josh gave him a slight nod. Over Jacob's shoulder, he caught a movement on the upper deck at the house. Jessie was there, leaning against the side of the open patio door, her gaze apparently trained on the beach. "Give us a bit, Jacob," Josh said. "It's your last afternoon on the beach. Enjoy it. I'm gonna get this little guy out of the heat for a while, and check on Emily-Grace's little mutt of a dog to make sure it's got some cold water and shade. I'll see you guys in a bit."

He left them to their plotting and planning, hoping against hope that Jacob had some happy tunes in his arsenal.

At the house, Josh settled Micah and the puppy, in that order, before he found his teary-eyed girl sitting cross-legged on their bed, the bed he hadn't slept in for about a month, since before Jessie's Boston trip. She was waiting for him.

"You tune them in?" she asked, twisting a ringlet in her hair.

"'Course." Josh grinned and laid down on his side. "Ahhh," he said with a wink. "Comfy. So this is why you look so rested every morning."

"Dork." Sprawling out beside him, facing him, Jessie tucked an arm around his and kissed his fingers. "It's your choice not to sleep here."

"Probably we shouldn't talk about choices." Josh's wry response was uttered in complete sincerity. He tucked a strand of hair behind his wife's ear. "Jessie," he tried quietly, "how about we find a way to get through this last day with some sense of forgiveness and calm? We don't want to send everybody home with bad stuff hanging over all of our heads. It's hard enough not having them in our everyday lives anymore."

"Puh. I can name at least two of them who I will be quite happy to see leave here tomorrow." Petulant, Jessie laid her chin on her hand and locked herself in Josh's tender, understanding eyes.

"Make friends before they leave, little one. You don't need that kind of regret hovering over you."

"What'd Charlie say?"

Josh groaned and rolled over onto his back. Folding his arms, he propped them up behind his head on the pillow. "Stay away from Charlie. No wonder Jane's worried."

"Oh, for fuck's sake. I'm not gonna sleep with Charlie, Josh. He wasn't that good in bed anyway."

The dry comment earned a chuckle from Josh.

A sardonic upturn to one corner of Jessie's lips preceded a sultry, "I want you. We're alone here, cowboy. You're a man who knows what to do in bed. Who knows how to make a woman feel appreciated." Gleeful, she climbed over him, with her knees on either sides of his damp swim trunks. "How about we take this old wet thing off?" Gripping the top hem, Jessie started to pull them down.

Before she got too far, Josh dropped a hand over one of hers and held on tight. The trunks stayed put just below his hips. "Now's not the time." His tone wasn't mean, it was just solemn.

"You gonna cut me off forever, Josh?" Jessie let go of his trunks and sat back. "Like it's not enough punishment for me to have to see that bullet scar when we're making love?"

"Low," he growled. "Look, Jessie, our friends are only here for a few more hours, technically. And you and I, we need to reconnect on a day when we're both feeling a little better about ourselves. Okay?"

"Why aren't you feeling good, Josh?" Jessie's childlike little girl voice was back. She sat further back on her haunches. Josh grimaced, and pulled his always sore leg out from under her. "Because of me, huh? I always bring you down."

His eyes brightened with love and with moisture. Sitting up facing her, he cupped her chin in his big paw and drew her close for a long, sweet kiss. "You don't bring me down," he said in a gruff murmur. "According to the girls out there, I'm the luckiest man on this beach." Backing away, sliding off the bed, Josh got serious and said, "You told me Matt and Shanda broke up. That's why it's not the best day for me, Jessie. I don't need to be making love to my wife for the first time in weeks and wonder if she's thinking about someone else." He held out an arm. "Come on. I'll grab the baby monitor. Micah will sleep for another hour. Let's go visit with our friends."

"Stay by me?" Jessie whispered in a pleading, scared voice. "On the beach?"

"We'll share a chair. You can sit on my knee."

On the way out of the bedroom, Josh spied a sarong Jessie often used as a cover up on the beach. Grabbing it, he walked over to her and wrapped it around her body from the back, and pulled the ends up halter style so he could tie them around her neck, as he had seen her do many times.

"Charlie," he murmured into her ear while he tied it. "Can't have the bastard losing his mind staring at those beautiful breasts of yours now, can we? Those puppies belong to me." Stepping back, he frowned. "Right?"

Jessie held out a hand. Relief washed over her when Josh took her outstretched fingers. "Damn straight they do." She sighed. "Dork. Puppies. Have some respect, husband. Treat me like a lady."

"You got it, m'lady. No more puppies. Just breasts from here on in. Beautiful breasts." Josh leaned in close as they started down the stairs. "I love you, little one. We'll get back on track."

"Soon? I need a cuddle, Josh. In a big way." The wistful request almost had Josh start back up the stairs so he could pull Jessie into his arms and love her right. So they could reconnect and right the wrongs of the last many weeks.

Instead he simply said, "Real soon," kissed the tip of her ear, and smiled when she giggled and snuggled her body in close to him as they walked.

On the beach, he dropped into a chair and pulled her down onto his lap, sideways so she could sit crossways and face her friends. Holding her close like that was the only way Josh knew to make Jessie feel safe; when she was in his arms, he, too, was certain he could hold the big bad world at bay, at least for a little while.

She didn't speak, she just listened, unable to look at either Jane or Sophie. Jessie remained sitting low on Josh's lap with her cheek laid gently against his shoulder, her body slouched so that her spine was curved over into a C, her fingers restless and unsure in her lap. At one point, she moaned painfully and turned her face directly into Josh's neck. She wrapped her left arm around him, and stayed there for a while.

Everybody went silent. It wasn't a stretch to wonder what—who—she was thinking about. Josh took it like the man he was—strong, these days. Sure of his love for Jessie, and of her love for him. He dipped his nose into her hair and whispered *I love you* over and over until Emily-Grace and Stella came running through the pebbly sand, begging everyone to go down to the shore to see their quaint castle village in all its sea-weedy, shell-perfect glory.

Chapter Seventeen

Later, only so many people could be involved in the dinner prep at any one time, so Jacob took advantage of it and ducked into the music room. There were auxiliary percussion instruments in there—handheld bits and pieces, like tambourines and a cowbell. The kids came running once their parents got them showered and changed. Kayla was recruited to hand out the instruments.

Jessie was rummaging around in the fridge for spinach when the sound of twangy, bright, fast-paced strings filled the house with an immediate catchy vibe. After a few bars, dramatic Stella's giddy laughter brought smiles from every adult in the house within listening distance. Jacob's confident upbeat vocals and some not-so-confident but gaily played percussive instruments, all punctuated by the happy laughter of children, were enough to encourage Jessie to slowly close the fridge door and saunter, with an air of curious wonder, toward the music room. She stopped at the open doorway and leaned back against the door frame.

Inside, Jacob was rhythmically stomping his foot to help the kids navigate the tempo of the hardy tune he was picking. By his side Kayla spun in easy pirouettes, flanked by Emily-Grace and David, who were copying her movements.

"Dance party, Momma! I can't stay still!" Emily-Grace shouted when she saw her mother at the door. "Come in!"

"I see that." Brightening, Jessie's eyes twinkled at Dylan, who was climbing behind a child-sized drum set with Vic Firth sticks clutched firmly in his young fingers.

Shaking her head in amusement, Jessie brought her gaze back to Jacob, who was pouring his heart and soul into a rousing old-style country jazz fusion piece.

"You used to be so pouty and sulky when you sang," Jessie remarked idly to herself, crossing her arms as Jacob brought the old house to life. He was rocking it on its foundation. In his arms was, of all things, a banjo Josh had unearthed a few weeks ago at a garage sale; one he got for Jessie one weekend as a joke more than anything. She never played it. Relegated to the music room, its main purpose prior to Jacob's visit was to rest on a padded stand and watch over the more useful stringed instruments Jessie needed for her tunes.

The hardwood floor under Jacob's foot was springy; it moved every time he stomped his foot to help the kids keep time. When he spied Jessie at the doorway his eyes lit up in expectant knowing. "Come on," he pleaded between verses, nodding toward the Gibson acoustic guitar he'd bought her in New York.

"Twangy much?" One half-hearted concentrated eye roll later, Jessie was sporting a grin so wide she thought her face might crack. Charlie's wide-eyed dark-haired young son Lucas grabbed her by the hand and hauled her into the room.

"It's bluegrass! You're playing bluegrass," Jessie laughed at Jacob, who cracked a grin while picking the medium paced tune. "Take it easy! You're gonna reinjure your collarbone!" A diabolical wink from Kayla, and Jessie's guitar was unceremoniously shoved into her hand. Swinging it over her shoulder, taking the pick Kayla also gave her, Jessie adjusted a capo to suit the happy song's key and joined in, tuning as she played.

Kayla jumped in. "Two days after surgery he was playing with the sling on, Jessie. Music is this boy's soul."

"Bluegrass is the purest form of country," Jacob roared into her ear, skipping a whole line of the chorus to make his point.

"Not this stuff!" Jessie hollered back. Facing Jacob, she added, "This is a moonshine-fueled rock country pop bluegrass hybrid! I kinda love it! Hillbilly rolls!"

What Jessie loved the most was sharing the stage—the best kind, the personal, intimate, home kind—with Jacob again. What made the impromptu jam even better, more special, a memory worth keeping, was the enthusiastic chiming in of all of the children. Dinner prep went on hold. Josh even brought Micah into the mix, dancing with him in the hallway to protect his ears. Sophie scooped up Jacob and Kayla's Lily, and Carter joined in with his daughter Ayasha in his arms.

At the door, Jane paused before meeting Jessie's eyes. Catching the apprehensive look, Charlie draped an arm loosely around her shoulder. "Still think she's a problem?" he asked in the carefree tone he always used to soothe his wife's rare touchy moods. Before them was a woman the world loved, one who often brought her music to the stage to ease troubled hearts and minds, whose performances were raw, who left nothing behind, who gave the world everything she had to give and then some.

Charlie added a post-script. "Behold a side of Jessie nobody remembered to mention on the beach today. One of the reasons she's so damn captivating."

Jane had nothing to say. She stood at the door with her hands on her hips, watching the delighted children participate in a musical mayhem that could only, in the years to come, bring them rainbow waves of remembered joy.

"God," Jessie teased Jacob when they brought his unexpected bluegrass tune to an exultant, cheerful close, "that was fun. Want to switch to bluegrass all the time?"

"I've got a whole playlist of those." Holding the banjo up high, raising his eyebrows, Jacob poised his hand over the strings for another go-round. "Talia's influence. Ready?"

"Oh, yeah," Jessie agreed, grabbing a small folk guitar Emily-Grace often played on, and handing it to her daughter. "Rock on, Ryan!" To Emily-Grace she said unnecessarily, "Watch me for chords, honey."

Dinner was late that night, but nobody cared. A thunderstorm blew in just as the guys were thinking about getting a campfire going. It sent everyone running to gather up towels and swim suits hanging from jerry-rigged lines suspended between trees and on racks on the back end of the Montana; the house's usual line was already full of kids' clothes and Josh's T-shirts.

In the end, everyone hunkered down inside to watch lightning streak across the bay. Being this close to the water made for some dramatic light shows. Rain came down in torrents—quick thinking, a lot of laughs and some serious cardio got the bedding in from the tents before it all got soaked. With Josh's help, Jane and Sophie organized new sleeping arrangements for the tent dwellers on the floors in the living room and playroom.

David, Dylan and Emily-Grace presented Jessie with her birthday cake around nine-thirty. Jacob led the gang in *Happy Birthday*, even though 'happy' was subjective on that day. Hauling her children close for a family picture, Micah in Josh's arms behind her, Jessie's grateful eyes sent Jacob a sweet 'thank-you'. It was after midnight before the older kids finally let their yawns get the best of them and trundled off to bed after playing board games with their parents.

A subtle melancholy overtook the adults after the kids were settled. Quiet 'good nights' ended the unexpected day. The only couples who made love that night were Jacob and Kayla, and Carter and Ashley. Charlie and Steve both slept with their backs to their wives. Jessie curled up with Micah on Dylan's bed since Dylan was downstairs with his friends, and Josh, for the most part, passed the night sitting at the bottom of the stairs rubbing his aching leg and listening to the rain.

In the morning, the air was fresh and clear again—another perfect beach day, the kind where tinkly little wavelets made their way to shore with a casual nonchalance. Tiny white snipes rushed along the pebbly sand in mighty attempts to outrun the ripples. It was the kind of early morning air that called for fresh starts and tranquil, lazy hours on the deck with a good book or on the bay paddling a lemony kayak.

At the bottom end of Sutherland Road, however, the promise of new beginnings and a relaxing day on the beach were irrelevant. The burden of endings were upon the Sawyer family, who had no choice but to watch their friends pack up and prepare to leave them behind. Worse, with the exception of just a few shared words with Kayla and Jacob, Jessie wasn't really talking. This leaving was going to mean hard feelings and a whole new layer of loneliness.

The last two families to leave were Charlie's and Steve's. Carter and Jacob had tag-teamed their rides a few hours earlier, with plans to stop at a mall in Halifax for some quick east coast maritime shopping before the final lap to the airport.

Just before joining his family at their rented SUV, Charlie took Jessie aside in the cool shadow of the Montana camper, where he found her alone replacing Fluffy's warm water with some cooler H2O she carted outside in a water bottle. The small white puppy was exhausted from all of the hype and buzz around it all week; this quiet area behind the big fifth-wheel trailer was a perfect hiding place to sleep this time of the day.

Charlie laid both hands on Jessie's shoulders and turned her toward him. It was the only way he could get her to look at him. Before she met his concerned gaze, Jessie swiped a loose strand of hair out of an eye and pocketed her fingers in the denim shorts she'd pulled on that morning.

"Jessie," Charlie started, "don't do this. Don't shut me out. Don't make me leave worrying about you."

She rolled her eyes. "You don't need to worry about me. I'm tough as nails. I'm a rock."

"I know that," he replied dryly. "And about as impossible to break through to. A guy needs a stick or two of dynamite to get past your stony layers when you retreat like this."

"You calling me layered?" A haughty chin raise augmented Jessie's indignant, sarcastic tone. "Jane and Sophie might have another way of describing me. They'd probably just call me a stuck-up bitch. Or a slut. Either one'd suit them just fine." Blowing out an insolent *ppffftt*, she stuck her head out past the side of the trailer so she could spy on the busy throng of people over by the cars. "You better go. Jane'll think we're sneaking a sweet little fuck back here, Charlie. A parting gift."

"You don't fool me," Charlie responded in his tender, chiding, big brother way. "I see the hurt in those pretty eyes right now, and so did Jane all day yesterday and last night. She's your friend, Jessie. She feels awful about caving to her insecurities and going down that road."

Jessie tossed her head with an arrogance she didn't feel. "No worries, Charlie." Burying a new nauseous ache as deep into her gut as she could manage, she said, "I get that Jane had to pick sides. Shanda's her shopping buddy. Her wino friend. There's an allegiance between them that I used to be a part of but that I knowingly said goodbye to when I couldn't comprehend the thought of having to stand on my own two feet again without Matt by my side."

Charlie let his hands drop to his hips. Facing Jessie, he let them slide over to his pockets and hooked the thumbs over the tops. His expression grew somber. "Justify it any way you want to if it eases your conscience." He tilted his head at her. "Let's face it—Matt was engaged to Shanda when you willingly hooked up with him in Stockholm. You were married. That was bad enough, and then—"

"Boston. Right? It'll always be a dirty word now too, huh? Just like whore and slut."

Lifting a finger to run it over his bristly chin, Charlie shook his head slowly. "I honest to God don't know what to say to you right now."

"You know what, Charlie?" Finding some fight after yesterday's and today's long, numb silences, Jessie let him have it. She hunkered up her shoulders for the fight. "You and I know each other better now than we ever did when we were together. I've always counted you as a friend, a good friend, to me and to Josh. An uncle to our kids, or a second dad, even, if you asked Emily-Grace where you fit in. She worships you. It's never crossed my mind that you and I would ever go there again, to bed. To sleep together. When Jane brought it up it blew my mind although in a lotta ways I guess it wasn't really a surprise to find out what she really thinks of me. Sophie has more reason to judge me, although I thought we made our peace over what happened with Steve a long time ago. I'll never shed that old me. I know I deserve it. I earned it. It's just…"

Sucking on a lip, Jessie absently watched the puppy protest the loud voices by getting up and circling around the soft dog bed she'd brought out for it earlier. Furrowing her brows together in concentration, she looked back up at Charlie. "Matt's place in my life deserves more credit than the 'old me' warrants. He isn't some kind of game. Being with him was never about having an affair, or about fulfilling a sexual fantasy or having an adrenaline rush or the thrill of the chase or any of those things. He is my *security*." Withdrawing her hands from her pockets, she raised them in a question mark. "You see? My real life guardian angel. I love that man, Charlie. The things Jane and Sophie said…hurting Shanda…the truth is, Matt and I go so deep that Shanda barely registered on my radar in Stockholm or in Boston. Or on his, I can assure you."

Taking this in, Charlie studied Jessie with a curious twist to his lip. "You need to let him go, Jess. He's suffering. Shanda's suffering. You said it yourself—you're strong. Josh has been a rock through all of this. Let him be your guardian angel for a change. Let Matt watch you from afar."

"Matt and I have tried that! It doesn't work with us. We need each other."

"What you need is a kick in the arse, Jessie! You think I don't know how close the two of you are? I was there, remember? Way back when? I know what he means to you and what you mean to him." Charlie had to force himself to lower his voice. Sometimes Jessie frustrated the hell out of him. He glanced behind him and to the side—surreptitious looks from Jane, Sophie and Josh were all occasionally being tossed their way. "You cannot continue to drag both Josh and Matt along on some twisted game of 'wait and see' while you try to figure out if and when Josh is going to break. Neither of them deserve that. And neither does Shanda."

"I'm not." Jessie's childish foot stomp would have made Charlie smile if he wasn't quite so worried about leaving her and Josh here alone to sort out a mess that sometimes seemed to have no real solution. "Look, Charlie, I have no intention of living my life without Matt in it. It's not gonna happen. Shitty comments like the ones your wife made about me, and your obvious devotion to Shanda too, only serve to remind me that I am the only one living my life, and so I am the only one who has a say in whether it will be a happy life or a lonely life. I choose to keep in my life the one man who I have always, always, always been able to depend on. Matt has never let me down. We've had our fights but he knows me and he loves me. Even the whore me. The slut me."

The tempo of this little spat was increasing. Blood started to pound in Charlie's ears, unleashing an inability to curtail the voicing of hurtful things exacerbated by frustration and exasperation. During the drive to the Halifax airport later, Charlie's silence would piss Jane off, but withdrawing from her would give him time to reflect on why he said what he did next—it was jealousy. Plain and simple.

He started by shoving a pointy finger in Jessie's face, so close that she actually had to take a step backward. A white hot rage tore across Charlie's eyes before he let the nasty rebuttal loose. "Did it cross your stupid mind at all that maybe, just maybe, Matt has known all along who you really are, Jessie? And that's why he finally ended up in your bed in the first place?"

Apart from fisting her hands into tight white-knuckled little balls, Jessie didn't move. There was no way she could possibly respond to a dig that low with any kind of grown up poise or decorum. Her mouth opened and closed; inflexible cement locked her eyes into masks of stone, masks that stared at Charlie with sheer loathing intermingled with a 'you-went-too-far' Judas vibe.

When she could swallow again, Jessie pressed her lips together. A few seconds later, after fully absorbing the shock of what Charlie'd said, she fired back with a final, low-voiced rant. "You just couldn't let me have this, huh Charlie? You had to pull that rug out from under me too, and take Matt away? Matt, the one person who always makes me feel safe? The one person who makes me feel like I can continue to breathe just 'cause I know he's out there watching over me?"

Stunned at the capacity he had found within himself to fire such a heartless comment, Charlie shut up and let Jessie have her say.

She continued with, "Josh will break again, Charlie. It's not a matter of if. It's a matter of when. One day he will wake up and realize that his dreams are dead. It'll kill him far worse than actual death would have, because the truth will gut him. It'll bury him alive. You won't notice because you'll be out there collecting awards with the tragic Shanda at your side while my husband soaks himself in booze, and while I clean the puke and piss off him in the shower, probably with our kids helping me since none of the rest of you will be around."

Her tone changed. The words got higher pitched and thin. Jessie started to back away from her old friend. Charlie, mortified at his appalling behavior and at what he was hearing, trembled. Adrenaline surged through his body. Jessie finished with, "I will do those things for him. I will be here for Josh, and I will clean up his goddamned shit if I have to." She was crying now, her angst fueled by fear—fear of a future she felt she could predict without a shadow of doubt. "Josh knows I love him. Regardless of where Matt fits into my life, into *our* lives—us Sawyers—Josh knows I will *never* leave him to fight those demons alone."

*Never*…the word emerged heated and determined, like the navigation span on the Confederation Bridge—higher than the rest of the bridge, more noticeable from the safety of shore. A place where large ships could pass underneath, where they could navigate with safety. "Don't you see, Charlie? I need Matt. I fucking need him." The declaration was infused with a desperation it hurt Charlie to hear. "I need to know I have a place to land where I am welcome and where my kids are welcome, even if it's just a phone call, from me or from any of them. I gotta tell ya—I used to think I had you, and Steve too. But after yesterday and today? I wouldn't call either of you if I was back in that SUV submerged beneath ten thousand tons of cement."

"So that leaves Jacob for you to call. Well, well, well." Charlie wanted to hit her stubborn face. So many people were getting hurt here…

Afraid he might lose his shit entirely, he started to stride away. He stopped with about ten feet of grass—the hot, sun-withered kind, they were both out of the shade now—between himself and Jessie. "Whore like you…won't you get bored?" he threw back at her. "Oops, I forgot. You've got Kayla on your roster now too. You ought to be just fine, I'm sure sex with her mixes things up real good. As for me? I can't speak for Steve, but after years of watching you try to make some sort of life for yourself that even borders on sane, I'm glad you won't be calling me anymore. Because, your highness, I'm tired of all the drama." Charlie's voice broke on that last word—drama. He stumbled on the next bit, until he was able to get himself under control again. "I'm tired of picking up the pieces. And I bet if Matt wasn't so messed up in you now—I'm talking about the sex here, let's call a spade a spade, my memory's not that damn short—then I bet he'd walk away too. Good luck, Jessie."

He took a few more steps before whipping around again. "I was gonna say you should send Emily-Grace out west for a visit with Stella, but now's not the time. Maybe not ever."

Watching Charlie stalk away, Jessie planted her feet in the ground and swallowed bitterly. When he reached the cars, she noticed that he didn't look anyone in the eye right away. His goodbye hugs were quick and courteous, his demands terse and abrupt. "Into the car, Stella," she heard him say; his daughter and her best friend were forced to part with final, tearful hugs.

Jane and Steve both glanced over at the statue-still Jessie, each wondering what was just said that had Charlie shoving the heels of his hands into his eyes and moving quickly, accelerating his family's parting with harsh requests and brusque demands.

With Jessie observing from the perimeter, Charlie thrust out a hand to Josh. Emily-Grace was sobbing at Stella's open window, clutching at her hand, and the younger kids—Steve's boys, Charlie's Lucas, and the Sawyer boys—were running around the field. "In the end?" he said to Josh, his hand quaking, the palm sweaty. "I'm glad you got her, not me." Switching his weight to the other foot and dropping a hand to a hip, he added, "Here's the thing, Josh. If you decide to let her go, I'm on your side. And if I were you, I'd strongly consider it. Jessie's priority is Jessie. Stay here with the kids and send her out on tour or to do a film with Matt by her side. By the time he sees the light he'll be bored of the sex and she'll have found someone else's life to mess up. I'll see ya, Josh. Thanks for the hospitality."

He called Lucas to the car and loaded him in. And then he was gone.

Watching the Deacon family car disappear in a rush of gravel and red dirt, Sophie gave Steve a look of warning and went off to round up her boys. Josh stared at Jessie, trying to regulate his breathing and sort out just how bad the pieces he'd have to pick up that day were going to be. Steve didn't even try to go to Jessie. He'd tried to engage her in conversation the night before and again today, but she was like the contents of a steel safe—unreachable. Her soul, when she was in this kind of retreat mode, was tucked deeply inside layers upon layers upon layers of self-preservation.

Steve's voice got Josh's attention. "Hate to leave things this way, buddy. You gonna be okay?"

It was a struggle for Josh to speak without giving his fear away. "What I am going to do," he said in the end, "is take my wife down to the beach with our kids. We'll build ourselves a new castle and when the kids have burnt off some energy and are playing in the sand close by, I will lie on our beach blanket, curl my body into Jessie's, and tell her I love her. A thousand times, if I have to. She'll put her earbuds in and listen to music and maybe not hear me, but she'll feel me there beside her and she'll know, Steve. She'll know she's loved."

"It kills me how she does this, Josh. How she finds ways to create cyclones out of a clear blue sky. We're all leaving here feeling like shit."

"You might want to ask yourself why that is, Steve." Josh's voice was dangerously low. He looked over at Sophie, who was now on the other side of the rental car getting Caleb and Cole settled into their car seats. "And just where those cyclones actually originated in the first place."

"I know. I hear ya." Amicable to a fault, Steve laid a hand on Josh's shoulder. "Keep an eye on each other," he ordered. "You'll call me, right, if anything goes haywire? I can be here in a day."

Josh grunted. "I appreciate that, Steve. Right now I think you're the only one I can call. Maybe Kayla or Zach, I guess, and Arnie, but not Charles or any others of that crew."

"Anytime. All right. We go. I'll see ya, buddy."

A final look to Jessie, a quiet hand raised in a low half wave, and Steve slid in behind the wheel and backed away.

They weren't far behind Charlie's gang. Steve was just as quiet on the drive to the airport as his friend was.

Josh stuck to his word. Nothing was said to Jessie about the fight with Charlie. In truth, Josh didn't really want to know what passed between them. Together he and Jessie packed a picnic lunch of the week's leftovers, and took the kids—and the puppy, which they set up underneath a shaded striped blue umbrella next to Micah—down to the beach.

The next day, Josh hitched the rented Montana to his four-year-old Ford truck and drove it back to the dealer. With Emily-Grace's help, Jessie did a thorough cleaning of William and Alice's house up the road where Steve and Sophie had stayed. They left chocolate chip cookies in the fridge and a fresh bouquet of pretty wildflowers on the kitchen table before locking the door behind themselves and giving their own home an equal spit shine.

William and Alice cruised down their lane a few days later, none the wiser about the celebrities who had overtaken the end of the Sutherland Road for a week. Life went on as usual until one day a week or so later when William happened to mention a curious visitor to Josh. William's concern set yet another wild storm in motion; it careened their way with reckless abandon, whirling up all the old fears without remorse, putting Josh and Jessie back on the defensive. Only this time when the storm settled, it left a perpetual rainbow behind.

# Chapter Eighteen

"A while ago, Joe, you and I talked about why you and your family are here. About your concern for your family's safety."

Josh went cold. Something about the cautious way William was bringing this up while they fed and watered the two horses in the barn on this dewy early morning made him set his dirty bucket down and give the man his full attention.

William had stopped working. Standing at Star's stall, he was leaning against it with one long, rigid arm. Unsure, he was using his free arm to paw at stubble on his chin while quietly observing the man he knew as Joe. In his mind he was ascertaining just how scared the man might be as far as his and his family's safety was concerned. At his friend's reaction—Joe's quick look toward him, a nerve on his cheek going into overdrive, the setting down of the bucket so he could better listen—William almost had second thoughts about saying more.

"Look," he finally said, "I don't mean to scare you, Joe. It's just that after what you said about changing your names, and all that…"

"What is it, William?" Experience had long ago taught Josh not to pussyfoot around this kind of stuff. Matt flitted cross his brain. Charles. Charlie. A sick nausea settled into his stomach at the thought of having to call any of them. Overturning the empty bucket, he staunchly set a foot on the base, rested his forearms on the thigh of his bent leg, and faced William. "Tell me."

William paused. "There was a car at your place yesterday. A sedan. It showed up while you guys were tooling around up west for the day, while you were showing the kids the windmills at North Cape and climbing the

West Point lighthouse." He licked his lips nervously. "Joe, that car stayed parked outside your house for a good hour or more."

Josh tried to remain relaxed, at least in appearance. His body tensed but he remained casually poised over the upturned bucket. *No point in hitting the panic button,* he thought. "Male or female driver?" he asked. "How many people in it?"

"Male. One."

"You approach him? How old? What'd he look like?"

"He was wearing a cap. A ball cap. Skidded off back up the road as soon as I got close enough to have a better look. Alice was chattering at me not to go over, said it was just someone checking out the beach or parked so they could use a cell phone, and I thought so too at first, but after this fellow got out and walked around your place I wasn't so sure."

"Could have been a tourist," Josh stated with a hesitant frown. "There are tons of Americans on the island these days dreaming about buying property here."

"Absolutely. You're likely right." William dropped his hand from the stall door and reached for the bucket under Josh's foot. Josh took his foot off so William could grab the wire handle and take it. "Just in case, son, I wonder if you ought to inform the police."

*The police don't know we're here,* Josh considered. *Just one guy does. An old RCMP buddy of Matt's.* Unsure, he stood still, pondering the whats and whos and whys while William finished filling the horses' water buckets. After a bit, Josh said, "Did you get the make and model of the car? Just in case?"

"Joe." Setting the bucket down, William bypassed Josh, ambled over to a pile of rectangular bales of straw stacked up by the door, and leaned against them. His back to Josh, he stared out of the doorway, fixed his gaze on the big house his ancestors built and said, "How serious is this? What is it we're dealing with here?"

"William," Josh started, talking to his friend's back, "I don't want to get you and Alice involved. It's likely nothing, anyway."

"I told you before, Joe." Turning, William faced Josh. "You're not alone here. In Prince Edward Island, neighbors are family. We look out for each other."

Something flickered in Josh's eyes. Light. Hope. "Did you tell Alice?"

"She knows there's something different about you folks." William spoke a little more gently. "She's been alone with the children, Joe. Baking, walking on the beach…she's overheard a few things."

"What? Like what?" Suddenly on even higher alert, Josh paled. He scratched at his beard while he waited for William to fill him in.

"For one, your young fellow—Ben, as we know him, Dylan, as apparently the rest of you do—told her he has two fathers. One of who is apparently quite a well-known singer. I'm guessing that's not you."

"And?" The nerve on Josh's cheek was pulsating rapidly now. Josh glanced out of the open barn doorway toward his house. Suddenly the distance between the barn and there, with the road in between them, seemed immense. He was ready to vault. If Morgan…

He shuddered.

William raised an eyebrow. "Your kids are well traveled."

Josh swallowed.

"On," William added, "a private jet."

"Just spit it out, William. How much do you know?"

Studying Josh intently, William raised a foot up on a straw bale and rested a forearm on his knee, echoing Josh's posture earlier. He hoped the unthreatening pose would relax his friend. "When we were in Ontario we watched a lot of television in the evenings. Netflix. Binge watched. Our daughter-in-law's favorite show is shot in Alberta. *Sacred Peace.*"

Josh's brain went into overdrive. *We'll have to move…the man outside our house…William and Alice know I'm alive…maybe their daughter does too…*

"Josh…" The name was said lightly, with no weight to it. William watched his neighbor for signs of awareness and panic. "You need to call the police. With your history, a car parked at the end of your driveway for an extended time is cause for concern."

"How much…" Josh gulped, and looked again at his house. He could see Jessie at the clothesline, dropping a basket of wet clothes onto the lower deck. He fixed a scared stare back on William. "Your daughter-in-law… Alice…"

"Our daughter-in-law was quite captivated by the whole *Sacred Peace* story. The real one, I mean. She told us about the shooting and the subsequent disappearance of the lead actor. About how sad it was that his wife—a singer, Jessie Wheeler—was pregnant at the time her husband's plane went down."

Josh didn't look away. A dry, scratchy itch started in his throat. He couldn't speak.

"It was Dylan who gave you away, Josh." William was so understanding, so careful and sensitive in the way he was telling Josh what he and Alice had figured out, that Josh was drawn to him, to the kindness in the man's eyes, to the honesty and trust he found there. "Two fathers. One a singer. The proverbial light came on, especially when we linked Dylan's name and were shown a number of articles about you on the Internet. Articles with photos. Videos, too. Interviews. Jessie on stage. It didn't take much study of the kids or of your wife to see the resemblances. So," he added after an extended pause, "there was a plane crash. You survived, obviously."

"Was staged." Hanging his head, Josh dropped down onto a bale of straw across from William. "William, please…" Appealing to the man's good nature, Josh looked up with sad, scared eyes. "Nobody can know we're here. Nobody can know I'm alive."

"Are you happy here, Josh?"

"Sure. Trying…uh, trying to be…the horses…I'd love to have a bike. I need a bike…" Recalling William's personal loss, Josh let that go. He crunched a piece of straw under the toe of one boot.

"And your wife?"

Josh went silent. A heavy sigh preceded yet another look out the door to Jessie. Eventually he nodded toward her and said, "My wife has four Oscars. Two for songs and two for acting. She's always said she wanted a normal life but it doesn't suit her. She belongs on a stage or in a recording studio. She can still do those things if she chooses."

"But you can't."

Josh plucked a piece of straw from the bale he was sitting on and stuck it between his teeth for a chew. "No," he admitted. "If certain, uh, parties, know I'm alive, Jessie—and or me—will be at risk again."

"Parties?"

"Uh, party. One person we have a rocky history with, put it that way. Someone who has already done enough damage to warrant that we pay close attention to his demands."

"Where's this person? Vancouver?"

"Alberta. Prison."

"Prison," William repeated, sorting all of this out in his head.

"Just like me," Josh said, rising. "Living a life he never planned. Saying goodbye to his hopes and dreams, limited as to where he can move, and limited as to whom he can talk to. All those things. As to why we're still afraid of him, William, he has a network on the outside to do his bidding."

"Son, call the police."

"Did you tell anyone, William? Does your daughter-in-law know? Please," Josh begged. "This is my family here. If this person knows we're here—"

"I swear to you, Josh, we did not tell a soul. We did not alert our daughter-in-law to our suspicions. Alice and I didn't even talk about it until we got back in the car and headed for home."

"Do you trust her not to say anything? Alice?"

"I do. And she trusts me. Your secret is safe with us."

"I can't call the police, William. I have...others I can call."

"Then make your call. Go round up your family, bring them back here. We'll keep an eye on your house from here for the day. Alice, your wife and the kids can do some baking. It's a gray day, not a beach day. You can help me reupholster an antique chair in the open doorway of the shop so we can keep an eye on your house."

Josh didn't move. "I don't know, William. I'm sorry. I think maybe we should pull out of here. I think maybe we should just go."

"Go where? You want to run every time somebody figures your secret out, son? What kind of a life is that?"

Downcast, Josh hung his head and stared at the dusty floor of the old barn. He shook his head. "None of this worked out the way I planned it." Picking William out again from under the sheen of mist in his eyes, Josh said, "When I married her, I didn't think she'd come with so much pain, you know?"

William softened. "That why there's distance between you, son? Why she has her eyes on another man?"

"She's somethin' else," Josh said, in the kind of awe and wonder William recognized Josh always used when he talked about his wife. "She's really special, William. Problem is, I'm not the only one who knows that."

"Ah." William smiled openly, waving his own strand of straw at Josh. "You're not looking at it the right way, son. You're forgetting to see yourself reflected in her eyes."

"Sometimes," Josh said as he headed for the open door, "I don't like what I see. In her eyes when she's looking at me, I mean." His look back toward William thinly disguised a sad smile.

"Then, Josh, get rid of that 'poor me' filter you're using. If every man had a wife who looked at him the way your lady looks at you, the world would be a better place. There'd be a helluva lot less…" He stopped.

"Affairs?" Josh sighed. "Aye. There's the rub, my friend." Slapping the door frame when he walked past, Josh said, "Give me half an hour. Tell Alice she's about to have a houseful of excited kids at her feet."

"She'll be thrilled. It was a sad lady I pulled away from our grandkids in Ontario."

Heading down the lane at a brisk trot, Josh wondered how much to tell Jessie. By the time he got to the house she was back inside, growling at David to stop picking on Dylan. "No go-carts today," she was telling them, "if you two keep fighting."

"Go-carts?" Josh inquired, stopping by the playroom door.

"Told them I'd take them to Sandspit in Cavendish if they behaved."

Josh started chewing on his lip.

Jessie shifted her weight and crossed her arms. "Sandspit," she said with determination. "The amusement park with the small roller coaster and the ferris wheel? Duh?"

Wheeling around, Josh headed for the central staircase. Grabbing the handrail, he jogged up the stairs two and three at a time. "No Sandspit today," he declared. "Seen my phone? Is it charged?"

"What? Why?" Jessie called out over the instant rebellious cries from the kids. With a quick glance behind her to make sure the two boys in the playroom were behaving, she scooped up Micah and headed up the stairs behind her husband. A quick peek into Emily-Grace's room revealed the little girl cross-legged on her bed watching a video on her iPad. Fluffy was coiled up into a ball, asleep at her side.

Jessie found Josh rummaging through the drawer in his nightstand.

"Why no Sandspit?" Ducking into the bathroom, she adjusted Micah on her hip and came out with her husband's phone held high in one hand. She waited for him to notice it. When Josh finally turned around and spotted it he reached for it, but Jessie yanked it backward just out of range. "Speak, husband."

He averted his eyes. "We agreed we would avoid crowds as much as possible. This time of year on a non-beach day like today, that place will be a madhouse. That's why."

Jessie cocked her head and narrowed her eyebrows. Josh used his little bit of extra height to his advantage, and grabbed the phone from her hand. "Why you calling Arnie?" Jessie asked. "Since, duh, besides me he's the only one you're allowed to call on that phone. And what do you expect me to do to entertain these kids all day? Since Stella left, Emily-Grace has been on her electronics 24/7."

"We've been invited up to the Sutherlands'." Josh didn't offer any further explanation. Striding into the hallway, he peeked into his daughter's bedroom. "Emily-Grace, off the computer. We're going up to see Alice and William."

Emily-Grace didn't bother looking up. She didn't answer her father.

Josh turned back to Jessie. "Can you get her off that thing?"

"Josh, what?" Confused, Jessie wrinkled her nose. "What the hell's going on?" She'd caught a glimpse of the worried look in Josh's eyes when he asked her to light a fire under their daughter.

"They know who we are," he revealed quietly. "William says we're good— he and Alice are keeping it on the down low."

"What? Jesus, Josh!" A wild look flickered across Jessie's face. Thrusting Micah into his crib in his room next door, which immediately started him howling and Emily-Grace, who was trying to watch her video, hollering for someone to make him shut up, Jessie closed the door to the master bedroom and faced her husband. "Talk," she demanded.

Josh held up his phone. "I need to call Arnie," he said in the most calm voice he could muster after the jarring start to his day.

"To tell him we're no longer under cover? Give me the damn phone. I'm calling Matt."

"You seriously want to call Matt? Use your own damn phone. I'm sure you've got him on speed dial. Better yet, stay out of this. Arnie can talk to him."

"Low, Josh. You know Matt's not on speed dial. He's not even on goddamned regular dial. I'll use the burner." Jessie sprinted across the floor to the bottom drawer of Josh's highboy dresser and grabbed a phone. They always removed the sim card and battery after each call as a precaution, and used a new phone every week, but her hands were shaking. Sitting back on her haunches on the floor, she couldn't quite manage to get the card inserted properly. "Fuck!" she cried, tossing the phone across the room. Leaning forward, she buried her face in her hands.

Emily-Grace whipped open the door. "Can somebody puh-leeze do something about Micah?" The baby was screaming bloody murder now. From downstairs came sounds of an escalating fight between David and Dylan. Serious yelling and the occasional vociferous 'fuck' from David was doing nothing to ease the tension quickly filling the house like a thick, sinister fog.

Josh glared at Jessie. "Our son's got quite the potty mouth. Well done."

"Oh, fuck off!" she hollered, jumping up from the floor. In two steps she was at his side, grabbing for the phone in his hands. "Give me that. I'm calling Matt on yours. Like it matters now anyway if anybody tracks us down."

"Alice and William won't tell. I trust them." Josh spun around to keep Jessie from accessing his phone. "Use your own damn phone to call Matt! I need this one."

"My battery's not charged. I never use the damn thing cuz guess why? Duh! I have no one to goddamn ever call, that's why!"

"Momma." Emily-Grace's small voice didn't stop the spat right off the bat. It took her next line to make Josh and Jessie freeze up and stare at their daughter. "You're not supposed to talk to Matt."

Stunned, Jessie stammered out a, "What? Who says?" At her side, Josh bristled.

Emily-Grace started wringing her fingers together. Her wide open eyes darted quickly from her mother to her father and back again. "Stella said so.

She said you did something bad to him and Shanda and that they're not married anymore because of it."

With a low *grrrr*, Jessie shifted her weight to one foot and stared her daughter down. "And what did Stella say that I did?"

Emily-Grace rested her nervous gaze on her father. Josh was staring at the floor, but he looked up at her and started chewing on a lip. It seemed like he was always in the line of fire when it came to what his daughter thought of him. "Stella said that when you went to Boston, Matt slept in your bed with you. And that he's not supposed to. Only Daddy is supposed to sleep in your bed with you. Ever."

"Great. Even my kids hate me. Took you long enough." With a loud roar, Jessie caught Josh off guard and grabbed his phone from him. Holding it above her head, she fired it through the open sliding door of the master bedroom. All three of them watched it fly over the rail of the deck. Throwing her arms up, she started backing out of the room to retrieve Micah. "You want it? Fucking go get it."

Locking his eyes on Jessie's retreating back when she spun around, Josh growled at his daughter. "Go round up your brothers. We're going up the road to the Sutherlands' and we're going now. Leave your electronics at home."

If there was one thing Emily-Grace knew about her parents, it was when to stop pushing their buttons. Sticking the tip of a fingernail into her mouth so she could nibble on it, she went into her bedroom and picked up Fluffy before heading downstairs to keep her brothers from infuriating their mother and father any further.

Josh stomped into Micah's room. "There was a car," he informed Jessie loudly, spitting the words out from between clenched teeth. "It was parked in front of our house for over an hour yesterday. Whoever the driver was, he got out and walked all around our house. I need to let Arnie know."

Jessie was rocking Micah on her hip, trying to get him to calm down so she could change him. The baby was red faced and pissed, and wanted none of it. She had to yell over his angry protestations. "A car? Dammit, Josh! Fucking suck up your pride and call Matt! Rig up the burner phone. He'll only call here later anyway, looking for details!"

Josh brought her to her knees. "From what I hear, Matt's not in any shape to be dealing with our security right now, Jessie. His wife just kicked him out, because of you. Or did you conveniently forget that part?"

"You fucking bastard," she seethed. "That was lower than low."

Micah was finally settling. Josh glared at his obnoxious wife. "That's it. Teach 'em young. I oughtta wash your mouth out with soap."

"I dare ya. Go ahead. Do it. You're dying to get back at me any way you can, aren't you, Josh?"

"Look. One of us has to deal with this latest bullshit." Josh was reeling with the effort it was taking to deal with his obstinate wife. For the sake of the children in their care he tried to speak evenly, but his voice came out thick and angry anyway. "The other of us has to take the kids up the lane where there are two kind people who, in case you're interested, don't generally lose their shit. Who are a helluva lot more capable than us two losers when it comes to showing our kids what it's like to be responsible adults. To give them a taste of something normal, for a change! I'm making a call to Arnie, IF I can find the goddamned phone and IF it's still working! You take the kids up to the Sutherlands' place right now, before I grab you by the ear and drag you up there myself!"

"I'll take them up there, Josh," Jessie fought back, "but as soon as you get there, the kids are all yours. I need a fucking drive!"

Chapter Nineteen

Forty minutes passed before Josh landed at the small house up the lane. Alice had the oldest three kids lined up at her tiny kitchen counter rolling out their own separate mounds of dough for cinnamon rolls. She'd learned the hard way that it was easiest to give each child his or her own dough to work with. While she supervised, Jessie sulked on the floor and piled up blocks with Micah.

When Josh opened the door to look in on his family, Jessie gave him the finger behind Alice's back. His scowl would have curdled milk, but he narrowed his eyebrows and curled his finger up toward her, signaling her to come outside. "Back in a sec, Alice," he said to the home's curious owner.

William joined them outside. They talked by the barn.

"Arnie sounded weird on the phone. I think he already knows something's up," Josh said. Eyeing his wife with a perma-frown, he was relieved to see that she had calmed down somewhat. At the very least, she no longer seemed determined to take a solo drive.

"Did he sound worried?" Jessie asked. Shoving her fingers in her back pockets, she planted her feet securely in the earthy red soil.

"No," Josh answered. "Although with the exception of saying to hang tough, that he didn't think there was any cause for concern, he didn't expand on his thoughts."

"That's good," William reasoned with a reassuring nod. "Sounds like your man has things under control, kids."

"Humph," Jessie pouted. Josh threw her a scathing look.

Looking from one to the other, William added, "I can't imagine how hard all of this has been on the two of you and your family."

"You have no idea," Jessie muttered.

"Oh yes he does," Josh told her harshly. "He's got *some* idea. He's done his research."

William decided to mitigate the oncoming fight he sensed in the air. The tension floating between Josh and Jessie was, he decided, collateral damage left over from years of worry. Gently, he touched Josh's elbow. "Let's go inside. Barney…uh, Arnie I guess it is, will be calling you back, will he, Josh?"

It was odd for Josh and Jessie to hear William calling them by their real names. Jessie screwed up her lips and tilted her head at him. She posed a question. "What are we supposed to do about the kids' names? They're already confused."

"We'll use the names we know them as," William replied. "Same goes for the two of you around them, if that's easiest."

Unsure, Jessie said, "I don't know. I'm sorry, William, but we don't really know you."

"I know them," Josh cut in. Still angry, and put off by Arnie's somewhat unperturbed reaction on the phone, Josh said, "You haven't taken the time to really get to know William OR Alice, Jessie. Your loss. You'll just have to trust the rest of us."

"Trust?" Jessie guffawed. "I'm surprised you even care to use that word in a sentence aimed at me, Josh. Seeing as nobody seems to think I understand the meaning of it."

"Do you?" Rigid, Josh, who was about to go inside, turned and faced his wife. William was halfway in the door.

"Oh, for God's sake," Jessie grumbled, bypassing both Josh and William and heading inside. "For the second time today, just suck up your pride. Get laid already, will you? Shall I call Shanda? I'm sure she's horny as hell right about now!"

The last bit was muttered in Josh's ear as Jessie passed. William overheard, but politely chose to ignore the stinging comment and Josh's quickly blooming red face. In the small space, Alice got the gist of the underhanded sting too, and sent her husband a concerned look. Kindly, William headed over to the kids at the counter and chimed in on their work with the cinnamon rolls. Dylan handed him a spoon and set him to work shaking brown sugar and cinnamon over his dough.

The day passed with no further outbursts. It helped that Arnie texted a few times to tell them all was well and that he would call late in the evening, well after the kids were in bed presumably so the adults could talk in peace in a way that wouldn't upset the children. Josh and Jessie managed to be civil to each other for the remainder of the day, and even shared small hugs and quiet *sorrys* when Jessie checked on Josh in the barn later, where he was helping William restore a set of Victorian balloon back dining room chairs.

"Just nerves," she whispered to Josh when he folded her into his arms and held on tight. "I'm sorry."

"Me too, little one. I'm sure everything's fine or Arnie would have called or taken a run out here. It was probably just a tourist like we thought."

"The North Shore Music Festival started today," Jessie reminded him. "Didn't Arnie say he was going? I think he met a woman who wanted to go. Means he likely won't be calling 'til super late if he stays 'til the end of the main act and still has to drive back to Charlottetown. You're right—he can't be too worried."

"Yeah, he said he was going. Arnie and country music…I just don't see it." Josh grinned. "Must be his way of getting laid. Take her to the concert and presto-bango, he's in."

"God, you're crude." Jessie gave him a poke in the ribs. He winced playfully. "It'd be bizarre for him to have to stand out front with the crowd, don't you think?" she mused, sticking her nose in his neck and inhaling deeply. "You smell like horses. I love horsie smells on you."

Josh sighed into Jessie's hair. "Somebody's in a better mood. Can't say I mind."

From a covert bent-over position near the chair he was working on, William was touched at the intimacy passing between his neighbors. It was really special, watching Josh and Jessie make up after a hell-bent day of serious tension. Observing their tender hugs and sweet, loving kisses, William was sorry to see an undercurrent of fear pass between the two. Seemed it was always a part of their shared existence.

When he chatted with Alice about it later, William discovered that she had also witnessed sorrow in the Sawyer family—in the children, in the subtle ways Emily-Grace occasionally stood back and swiped at her hair again and again with a distant look in her eyes, or at the way David often settled fights with Dylan when Josh and Jessie weren't around to referee. Usually David grew quiet and let Dylan have whatever it was Dylan wanted. David was the peacemaker of the group. Dylan always got anxious and propelled his anxiety into whatever he happened to be doing.

Late afternoon on that stressful day, after picking up cues from his worried parents, Dylan's anxiety was getting the better of him. Recognizing his son's propensity to pick fights when forces beyond his control wound him up, Josh took him for a horseback ride just around the field in close proximity to the house. On Rusty, the smaller of the two horses, Dylan instantly grew calm and focused.

So did his father, on his mount.

"Horses for Josh, music for me," Jessie murmured to Alice next to her. From behind the fence, they watched Josh urge Star into a trot. Dylan was riding beside his father; he gave Rusty a command the women couldn't hear, and leaned forward. Rusty broke into a trot alongside the taller horse. Jessie gave Alice a sideways look. "Horses for Dylan too, apparently." Dylan was whooping with glee.

Nodding toward Josh, Jessie said, "My husband trusts you guys. He really does."

Alice raised her eyebrows. "Should I take it to mean you don't?"

Folding her arms on the top rail of the fence so her elbows jutted out to the sides, Jessie rested her chin on her hands. Without expecting it, she felt her eyes grow moist. "Hell no, I sure don't," she admitted. "I pretty much don't trust anybody anymore. It's not just you guys." With a wistful sigh, she gazed out over the field. "That's a lie," she said almost under her breath. "There's one person left on the planet that I trust. Problem is I'm not really allowed to lean on him anymore."

Alice was wise enough to let that slide by.

Much later, Arnie made his call to Josh and Jessie, at precisely 11:33 that evening. In the living room, they were both trying to read, but anticipation and nerves were getting the better of them. Today was a stressful day that would not have been manageable at all without the compassionate and gentle friendship of the older couple that lived down the lane. By the time Josh's phone rang, the back of Jessie's left hand was covered in tiny red crescents gifted from the fingernails of her right hand. Josh's hair was a tangled mess from continuous rubbing and rifling. The anxious movements were always accompanied by hefty groans, which unnerved Jessie even more.

"Arnie," Josh barked into the phone without preamble when his old Chili Peppers standby cell ring, *Under The Bridge*, lit up the otherwise silent room. Across from him, legs folded under her on the couch, Jessie was half laying down, using her forearm as a pillow. A wide yawn cracked her jaw when she abruptly sat up at the intrusive, loud ring.

Josh listened for a minute or so. Eventually he sank deep into his wing chair and closed his eyes. At the same time, he laid his head far back and cursed. "You gotta be fucking kidding me," he snarled.

Eyes wide, Jessie held her breath and started curling a ringlet in the hem of her pale pink nightdress, a cool silk slip dress perfect for warm July summer nights.

Josh grunted and rubbed his forehead impatiently before he sat up and fired a reproachful look across the room to his wife. Arnie was talking. Jessie could hear him explaining, soothing, calming, but it wasn't working. Josh's face was reddening. He was growing more angry by the second. On the plus side, he didn't appear scared. Just mad.

"What?" she mouthed over to him. "Let me talk to him."

"You gotta give me a minute to digest this," Josh said to Arnie. "Hang on a sec."

Jessie was standing now, her heart racing, pushing blood into her ears. It pulsed like a drum, fast and steady, each pulse a cannonball. Teetering from foot to foot, she was seriously thinking about grabbing the phone from Josh when he finally laid it on his knee and said with distaste, "Did you know Dallas White was playing the North Shore Music Festival today?"

"Yeah. So? What about it? He played there last year too."

"Did you…" Josh hesitated, and bit down hard on a lip before he continued, "also know that your good buddy Matt is doing some security gigs with him this summer?"

"Matt? What? No." Clueing in, Jessie started to weave on her feet. She pressed the heel of a hand to a temple. "How the hell would I know that, Josh? I haven't spoken to Matt since Boston." More puzzle pieces clicked into place. Falling backward, she collapsed back onto the couch. "Jesus," she moaned. "It was him parked in front of our house. Matt was here? Matt, uh, Matt *is* here? On P.E.I.?"

"Even better." Rising, wincing at the pain in his interminably sore leg, Josh strode over to his wife and ruthlessly tossed the phone into her lap. "He's at Arnie's place. Drinking, apparently. Having a good ole cry in his beer. I could fucking kill him. If he wanted to spy on you he should have told Arnie to communicate that to us. Of all people, Matt should fucking well know what kind of fear we're constantly living under. Fucking asshole. Feel free to share my love with him."

After turning in a circle a few times, Josh stopped and glowered at Jessie. It took her a few seconds to realize that he was waiting for her to answer the phone. More so, he was likely waiting to see if she would leave the room to speak in private. Clearly, he was not going to offer her the courtesy of making any kind of exit.

Jessie swallowed. Hard. Clutching the phone in her lap, she sat up straight and eased her back against a cushion. Eyes on Josh, she lifted the phone to her ear.

"Hey," she said, and waited to see if the person on the other end was Arnie or Matt.

Arnie was on the other end, lingering to see if Josh was going to come back on. Without saying a word, he handed the phone to his visitor.

At Arnie's place, a townhouse near the waterfront in quaint historic downtown Charlottetown, Matt was perched on the forward edge of a stark wooden chair, hunched over his knees—not unlike the way Josh was sitting now, staring demons at his wife from the wing chair across the room from her.

Jessie had to say her muffled greeting twice, which actually served to settle Josh's nerves a little, if only because he understood the many confused and anguished layers that had led to this heartbreaking call in the first place. Jessie was brave, and proud. And trying to respect Josh's position in a complicated situation that, no matter how anyone looked at it, was untenable.

Josh knew the second Matt's voice came on the line. Jessie almost collapsed, squeezed her eyes tightly shut and swallowed three times in quick succession. Her right hand gripped the hem of her pretty nightdress, clenching and unclenching it in rhythmic motions that Josh was fairly certain she was not even aware of.

And then there was her voice. Tiny. Tinny. Thin. Loaded to the hilt with pain the way the local farmers loaded their bins with grain or their warehouses with potatoes. "Hey, baby," she breathed. "S'been a while."

In Charlottetown, Matt was having a difficult time holding it together. Arnie had quietly left the room when he handed him the phone, taking a soft drink with him—no beer for him. Matt's voice was low and husky. "Hi, sweetheart," he returned. "You doin' okay?"

"I was until today, Matt," Jessie said back to him, feeling Josh's upset eyes on her. "Baby, you scared us."

Matt let out a long, slow breath before speaking. "I know, I know, I…it wasn't planned, Jessie. I told myself I could do this, that I could be on the island with Dallas and not go there, to your place. But I couldn't. I just… I needed to see where you're living. I needed to see…our house."

"Oh, fuuucck, Matt." Jessie sank deeper into the couch and curled her knees up to her chest.

Josh wasn't surprised to see her knuckle a fist into the corner of an eye.

"Baby, you can't do this. You can't…" Letting her eyes flutter open, Jessie looked over at Josh. *He's daring me to leave the room*, she thought, so she mustered up some strength. It came from the ache in her husband's eyes, in the pain Jessie knew he'd held there over the last many years. It came from the decision he made about a year ago to end his life to pay a debt that might, if left unpaid, have taken Jessie's life.

She finished her sentence a little stronger. "You can't hang on to us like this. Like in a way that digs us into a deeper hole. Matt, this was your choice. Yours. You took me to the Caribbean."

In his chair across from Jessie, Josh buried his face in his palms and rocked a little back and forth. In Charlottetown, Matt grabbed a beer and chugged a good portion of it back. "I can't live with myself like this, Jessie," he told her, wiping the back of a wrist across his wet lips. "Shanda and I…there didn't seem to be a way out. We got so off track after Boston…" The despair in his voice was overwhelming. It was like thick molasses was choking his every word. "I was wrong. I should have never dropped you off like that. It wasn't my call to make."

"But you did, baby, it's done," Jessie reasoned in her high-pitched, scared voice. She clutched a clump of hair. Anxiety threatened to do her in. The blood in her ears was still pounding. "It's long been done." She looked up at Josh, who was watching her again, fighting against leaky eyes, begging and pleading with the universe for her not to say something to Matt that might be far more terrifying than the prospect of some unknown stalker parked outside their home.

"I'm sorry about Boston, Jessie. When I got back to my room and found Shanda there, there was nothing I could do."

There was a hitch in Jessie's voice when she tried again. "I know, Matt. I know that. I'm real sorry for hurting her. But I'm not going to say that you and I were wrong for going there. Honey, I needed you. I—need—you. Matt, I will always need you."

*This is it,* Josh moaned inwardly. *We were bickering today. We've been fighting a lot, lately. We haven't had sex since she was with Matt…maybe Charlie's right. Maybe Jessie is just too much to handle. Maybe there's just been too much water under the bridge…*

Jessie was looking at Josh now, her eyes latched onto his, shaking her head. Trails of tears were snaking down her cheeks. She wept into the phone, the hand that was holding it shaking as she tried to make sense of just how bad things were, for her, but mostly for Matt. *I have a family,* she reasoned with herself. *I have children. I have Josh. I have Josh. I have Josh.*

*Matt…has nobody.*

"I need you too." There was a certain calm in Matt's simple declaration. Jessie detected a sense of peace washing over him. Just being able to say the words out loud gifted Matt a whole new harmony. Voicing what he desired most was cleansing, the same way a summer waterfall's rainbow mist ached with steamy promise. "Can I come see you? Can we meet?"

In the hallway outside where Matt was huddled into himself talking to Jessie, Arnie cringed.

In the big white house at the end of the Sutherland Road, Josh saw Jessie's eyes transform into a calm prismed film. *Please God,* he begged. *Please.* In his mind he got down on his knees. In his mind he formed words, and he prayed. *I'm sorry,* he cried. *I'm so damn sorry for wanting to end my life, for thinking about it. For acting on it. It wasn't my choice to make! It wasn't my choice.*

Forgiveness. Such a tough concept. Should be easy, but it wasn't. There in the large, drafty room, windows open because it was so warm and Josh and Jessie were grasping for any breeze they could conjure up, Josh begged for forgiveness. With every muscle and sinew in his body on high alert and every pore screaming for God to listen, he pleaded for mercy. He pleaded for Matt to let go and for Jessie to remain his, and his alone.

While Josh prayed, Jessie tipped her head and opened her ears to Matt. "Jessie, I'm still on the other side of that car," he was saying. "I still see you in there, fighting to kick that window open. And I'm still stuck on the outside looking in, pounding on the glass in slow motion like you do in dreams, sluggish and slow, and it's impossible. There is no way I can get to you when you're on the other side of that window. There's no way at all."

His inhibitions deadened by alcohol, Matt wept, bending over his knees in a futile attempt to regain control. Life had spun off its axis. Matt was a man who prided himself on staying calm, cool and composed. The day an electric sizzle rocketed up his groin in a Brussels hotel suite, things got all fucked up. Love for Jessie was never in question, and in itself was navigable water. Desire was an entirely different river. Fear and a shared history of deep, mutual trust sparked by loneliness made the kind of love Matt and Jessie shared downright explosive.

"I can't do this, Matt." Jessie was sobbing too hard to even hold the phone to her ear. She was trembling so bad the couch was shaking right along with her. Across from her, Josh had his head down and his big hands clasped over the back of his head. His back was moving in and out—his lungs. *He looks like he's praying,* Jessie thought wildly.

"I know," Matt wept. "I know." He sucked in a breath, and then another. His gasps slowed his crying to a manageable plane. "Look, I should, uh… I should go. I'll see you sometime, okay, sweetheart? Some day down the road, maybe, when all of this doesn't hurt so damn much. I love you." He said it again, because all he could hear on the phone were her hiccupy sobs, and he needed to know she heard him. "Jessie…I love you. So goddamned much, sweetheart."

She said it back to him. "Matt…I love you too. Always, baby. Always."

Sweetness. Pure sweetness. Matt closed his eyes and thanked God from the bottom of his heart when he heard those cherished words whispered to him in the muggy heat of a starlit Prince Edward Island night.

"And forever…" Jessie heard him whisper. Hearing that…it just made her cry all the harder.

When the phone went dead, it was Matt who'd shut the call down. He drank until Arnie took his beer away and sent him up to a spare room to sleep it all off, the booze and the pain.

In the Sutherland Road house, Jessie launched herself up and into Josh's lap. Wrapping her arms around his shoulders, she cried herself dry, her chest heaving with the effort it took to let it all go.

"You and him," she cried, while Josh held her in silence because he was still praying silent *thank you thank you thank yous* for the temporary reprieve, "you're almost the same person sometimes. You know what he said to me? Always and forever. That's our thing, Josh. You and me. How did it also get to be mine and his? I'm so damn confused, Josh. I'm so scared."

Josh wasn't looking at her. His face was buried in her neck, and he was clinging to her so tightly that Jessie was finding it hard to breathe. Loosening her grip on him, forcibly shoving him backward, she stared at him for a few hard extended seconds. "I love you," she gasped. "I fucking love you. And I fucking want you."

Clutching a handful of his long hair, she moved suddenly, quickly, startling him, and pressed her lips to his. "I love you," she gasped, standing and repositioning herself on his lap so that she straddled him. Both hands were in his hair now, grasping and clutching, begging Josh to return the passion, to end his reign of punishment over her, over her body, for also loving another man.

Jessie thrust her hips against him, sending clear signals that she wanted him. When Josh grabbed her thighs and pulled her toward him, falling back so he could push against her, it wasn't because he was giving in to her needs.

*It's because she finally chose me herself,* he told himself. He gasped with pleasure. Jessie was going for his belt, working her fingers to undo the buckle and take hold of him again. Her tongue pushed, probed, searched his mouth; her silk negligee hiked up around her hips, her body urging Josh to set her the 'good kind' of free.

With a guttural cry, Josh gave Jessie a push to let her know the big chair wasn't working for him. Rising, Jessie took his hand and hauled him up; in seconds he had her up against the wall and her panties down. One more quick move and he buried his face in her breasts after hoisting the pretty pink nightdress above her head. Jessie's body was free to him—not to Matt—tonight. Matt, who was agonizing over making this choice for Josh and Jessie, for bringing them back together at a time when a lot of cards were in play, complicated cards that changed destinies the way broken hearts changed lives.

Josh cupped his wife's breasts. He groped and played and sucked and gasped, his beard itchy against her body, but at this point Jessie no longer cared. When Josh sank to his knees and sucked hard between her legs, the moans that emerged from between his lips were intense and real and wanting, saturated with fiery longing, the kind a man lets loose after a time of prolonged suffering.

Jessie was as into this as her husband was. When she couldn't stand the escalating pleasure a second longer, when the blood beating in her ears was no longer fear and sorrow based and instead became erotically charged with the rare, divine love she shared with the father of her children—intermingled with the loss of a very dear man she also loved with an intensity that burned—she urged Josh back up her body. His mouth and tongue were wet with Jessie's desire for him, wet with what he took from her on this hot summer night, a night when the stakes were raised to a point where they finally broke; on a night when love turned passion turned heartache pushed and pushed and pushed until a winner burst forth the way water rushed through the car the day Matt hauled Jessie and Emily-Grace from the Lexus.

Only this time, instead of Matt it was Josh who reached for Jessie. It was Josh who held her up with a strength and a grip that knew no bounds. Sucking hard on her bottom lip, he grabbed her thigh and held it high so he could drive himself into her, into the body he'd loved since the day she first believed in him; into the soul he craved with a thirst that could only be quenched by joining his body to hers so that she could convulse around him and tell him, through the physical act of sex, that she still wanted him.

Or so he thought.

Josh was coming down off the wild ride when it hit him that the last words Jessie said to Matt on the phone were *I love you too. Always.* So when he clutched Jessie's hair and pawed roughly at her cheek with his thumb, his eyes were fierce. Accusing.

"You just make love to me?" He moved his hand down her face and grabbed her chin. He was still breathing hard with exertion, still pumping into her.

Moaning, Jessie was pressed up against the wall, her eyes still rolling, her body clenching and clenching and clenching some more, coming down off the exquisite orgasm granted—finally—by her husband.

"Or to Matt?" she heard, as Josh shoved what was left of his erection hard into her for a few last waves of pleasure.

Struggling to get some strength back in her weak knees, Jessie faltered, and tried to comprehend what Josh was asking.

He had more to say. An uncompromising, direct stare was his way of getting her attention. "Listen to me," he demanded coarsely, shaking her chin to get her to listen. "I survived, Jessie. I survived for a reason. I will not let you down. Okay? Do you trust me?"

The echo of those words…in her surreal, elevated state, Jessie heard the words come from someplace in her past…from a jet flying over the mountains after leaving Calgary in the middle of the night. From Matt…*Do you trust me?* Unable to separate Matt's words from Josh's, she nodded. "Yes," she whispered, her eyes half lidded still with just-quenched desire, her body still sucking what life she could from her husband.

"You have to do your part," he was telling her now, that disembodied voice that was her husband. "Give me a reason to still be alive, Jessie. Let him go. Once and for all, let him go."

Her eyes flitted fully open. The look Josh spied there—fear first, then sorrow…over Matt…over him…heartache…

Jessie started to sob. Pushing at Josh, she tried to get away. Struggling, she started to cry out, but Josh held her against the wall and wouldn't let her go.

"Is any part of you glad that I am still here?" he cried, holding her biceps so she couldn't escape. Josh had no clue whether making love tonight was about Jessie loving him, or if it was her way of expressing her anger with him. Or maybe it was about taking control of his punishment of her. *Or,* he shrank against his wife, *it was about Jessie sticking it to me, loving me as proxy for Matt…*

With a mighty cry, Jessie loosed herself from his arms and vaulted from the room. Confused, scared, Josh hitched his jeans back up over his hips and bent down to grab Jessie's nightdress, panties and his T-shirt, which had also hit the floor during their passionate encounter.

At the top of the stairs, he debated which way to go. Sleep in with one of the boys, or slide in behind Jessie in his own big bed and risk being shoved away?

In the end he tiptoed in behind his wife and curled his body around her. He almost cried with relief when Jessie reached up and wrapped her arm around his. A long, deep sigh said more in terms of welcome than any words possibly could.

Closing his eyes, Josh sighed too, and slept straight through the night until Micah's happy gurgling noises commingling with the morning rays of the sun nudged him awake, and ushered him into another day.

Chapter Twenty

Jessie rolled over onto her back. After almost a month of sleeping alone she needed to lay her eyes on Josh, to know that he was there in bed with her, and had been all night long, holding her, offering what loving energy he could after last night's distressing phone call with Matt.

He blinked back at her with sleepy eyes and lifted a fingertip to touch her cheek, as if he, too, needed to ascertain Jessie's presence in bed next to him. "Sleepy girl," he said tenderly, running the backs of his fingers over a cheek, a lip, her hair. "I love you."

Jessie laid a palm over his and closed her eyes. Still today, the despondency in Matt's voice haunted her.

Micah wasn't full out crying. He was doing more of his usual 'I'm awake' thing, whining, cooing and gurgling. Josh took advantage of his youngest son's easygoing mood, and leaned in to Jessie for a sweet kiss.

Moving onto her side next to him, facing him, Jessie soaked him up. Such loving affection from Josh was too few and far between these days, this last month. They lay there simply kissing and touching, rediscovering each other again, until Josh slipped his fingers inside Jessie's panties and she straddled him for some cherished early morning loving.

Later, after breakfast, Josh washed the dishes while Jessie dried. Emily-Grace had just left the kitchen with Micah, followed by her other brothers and a lot of good-natured teasing—she'd promised to get Micah changed and dressed.

"I knew we had her for a reason," Jessie giggled, leaning back against the counter and watching her go. Her smile flipped upside down. "He's pretty wiggly. She won't fall down the stairs with him, will she?"

Laughing, Josh wheeled around for a look. David and Dylan were hot on their sister's trail, ready to jump in and assist in this great operation. "She's got spotters. She'll be okay."

There was a revitalized warmth in the way he was talking to her this morning. Reflecting on it, Jessie paused in her drying and smiled at him. Really, the secret to loving Josh and receiving love in return was in their physical lovemaking. She could tell him all she wanted just how much she loved him but he, like her, needed that physical connection, the release that making love offered. Josh was a different man when they were regularly joined that way, more confident in her love for him, and in where he fit into her world. It boggled Jessie's mind since she often saw herself reflected negatively when it came to sex, despite how much she also thrived on proving her love for her men through the use of her body.

Josh clued in that she was studying him. Sighing, he bent forward for a kiss.

Jessie ducked her head, a little embarrassed at having been caught. Slowly, she started wiping the dishtowel over a pottery mug.

"We gonna talk about last night, little one?" Josh posed quietly.

"Hmmm. I'm not sure I know what to say." Jessie trained her gaze on the mug.

"He's not doing so good, is he?" With both hands suspended, unmoving beneath the bubbles in the water, Josh watched Jessie take that in.

She let out a sad little *puh*. "No, babe," she admitted. "He is not."

"You okay?"

"Not entirely." It was a high-pitched squeak. Uncertain. Nervous.

"Uh, Jess…are we okay? Cause I gotta tell you, I still don't know who you were loving last night up against the wall, me or him."

She threw him a semi-disgusted look.

Josh interpreted it as 'it's over, let it go,' and decided maybe in some ways Jessie's mind was on both him and Matt during last night's desperate, urgent lovemaking. It sucked. He flicked a bunch of soap bubbles in her direction. She flinched. "So we good or not," he asked again, in a tone that left no more room for ambivalence.

Jessie wiped the soap bubbles off her shorts. She squished a thoughtful finger into the wet spot they left behind. "I dunno, Josh." Setting the mug on the counter, she looked up at him. "Are we?"

A ten second pause preceded a long, slow exhale. Josh shifted his gaze and stared into the bubbles. Removing his hands, he gave them a shake before stealing his wife's towel and wiping his fingers on it. Sauntering across the kitchen, he grabbed his truck keys.

"Where you going, Josh?" Panic hit Jessie in the gut. *After last night's call from Matt…*

"I need to pick up a part for the lawn mower," he said without looking at her. "I won't be long. Will you be okay for a few hours?" At the door, he hop-shuffled on an old pair of dusty brown cowboy boots.

"Yeah, sure, I…we…" Jessie shrugged. "I was just gonna putter around the flower beds. Alice said she'd come down and give me a hand, show me what to weed out and stuff. You know me, left to my own devices I'd pull out the actual flowers instead of the weeds."

"If you don't, Dylan will," Josh joked, coming back for a 'see ya' kiss.

Jessie relaxed and emitted a slow yoga breath. Grabbing his belt buckle before he could move away, she laid her arms around his shoulders so she could hold him close for a longer, more tender kiss and hug. Mewling with longing, aching for him to stay nearby, she wiggled her nose into his neck, by his ear. His hair tickled her; she wrapped a few strands around a finger and kissed the inviting earlobe underneath it.

"All right, little one." Loosening her grip, Josh smiled. There was a twinkle in his eye; it was somber, but it was there. "I'll be back by lunch time."

"Promise me." It was a whisper.

One more kiss, and Josh was gone.

Jessie stood at the screen door and watched him leave. He backed out of the driveway with a casual wave and a firm, set line to his jaw. "Lawn mower part, my ass," she grumbled. "Where you really going, Josh Sawyer?"

In the truck a few minutes later, Josh punched in a text to Arnie. *You home?*

By the time Josh got up to the end of the Sutherland Road, Arnie's return text popped up. At the stop sign, Josh read it—*Yep. Still got company.*

*Good,* Josh thumb-typed back. *Keep him there. I'll be there in an hour.*

*Will do* came an instant response. *He's sleeping off a hangover.*

A few minutes later, just as Josh was turning right to head toward Kensington and then through the small town to Charlottetown, another text came in from Arnie. *Am I gonna need to call the cops?*

Josh fixed his lips in a straight line and didn't answer. To himself he said, "I sure as hell hope not." Poking a finger on the stereo, he selected 95.1 CFCY—country music—and sang along under his breath all the way to Charlottetown.

Matt had always been an early riser, but he still wasn't up and about when Josh got to Charlottetown around ten. Arnie's place was a two-story townhouse condo overlooking the harbor. He and Josh sat outside on a small first floor patio deck and talked in low tones until they heard a slow downward creak on the stairs. With an apprehensive look to Arnie, Josh got up and made his way inside. He found Matt in the kitchen glumly staring down a coffee pot, one hand on a mug that he didn't seem to really be seeing.

When the light changed at the doorway, Matt looked up and took a quick step backward when he saw Josh there instead of Arnie. Josh leaned against the door frame and shoved his hands in his jeans pockets.

"Jesus," Matt cursed. "You scared me."

Josh didn't say a word beyond a simple, "Hey, buddy."

He didn't have to. It was easy to tell what Josh was thinking simply by the way the guy's eyes softened into concern during a cautious body scan of Matt's stooped posture. Josh started at the wrinkled white button down shirt and jeans, first—*same clothes I wore yesterday,* Matt considered with a start, almost buckling with embarrassment at what Josh must be thinking. He watched Josh let both serious eyes drift upward to land on his mussed-up hair, still wet from a shower. In reflex, Matt ran long fingers through the un-styled mess. Josh paused on uncharacteristic new whiskers Matt hadn't bothered to shave. Matt's fingers landed there next; accompanied by a thumb, they absently pawed at the careless, itchy growth. Josh's scrutiny ended on Matt's bare toes.

Matt averted his eyes. Through the window he fixed his gaze on a sailboat toughing it out in the harbor. It was a windy day; waves and sudden gusts were giving the sailors a bouncy, bumpy ride. "I'd say I didn't think Arnie'd want me using his razor," he offered unnecessarily, his voice low and hoarse, "but the truth is, I can't stand the sight of myself in the mirror." He paused. "I'm supposed to be at my old cottage in Darnley. Never quite got back there last night." He gripped the empty mug with both hands, as if it were an anchor to the earth.

At Josh's silence, Matt reached for some courage, shifted his eyes sideways, and sought out his friend in the doorway. He choked out a truth he wasn't certain Josh would care to hear. "I'm so fucked up," he gasped. The admission was a strangled attempt at honesty. "So fucked up, Josh. I'm sorry. You have every right to hate me."

Josh was still leaning coolly to one side. Matt could read his confusion and anger by the speed at which the telltale nerve on his cheek was pulsing. Right now it was going at the rate of a newborn's heartbeat, rapid but regular.

"I don't hate you," Josh said. Heaving his tired body away from the door frame, he took a few steps into Arnie's small, modern kitchen and pulled the mug out from under his old friend's trembling fingers. Reaching for the coffee pot, he poured a cup and added a splash of milk he retrieved from the refrigerator. Handing the mug to Matt, Josh said, "I caused this shit, Matt. This mess we're all in. So I think it oughtta be up to me to clean it up."

Matt settled back against a cupboard. He was shaking so badly he could barely lift the mug to his lips. "This was not your doing, Josh. I went there again when I promised myself I wouldn't."

"Takes two," Josh reasoned ruefully, pouring himself a coffee even though he'd already had two. This was a multiple coffee kind of heart-to-heart. "Or three, if you want to be brutally honest. Jessie wouldn't have crossed that line with you in the first place if she was happy with me. If she wasn't feeling alone." He took a sip of the hot beverage and said, "You're a good man, Matt. She needed someone. I'm glad it was you."

A loud guffaw was Matt's response. "I betray you and you choose not to beat me to a pulp. You should be pounding me into the pavement right now, Josh. What am I missing here?"

Looking around the kitchen, Josh drew in a breath, puffed up his cheeks, and let the air out in a slow whistle. "We need to figure this out, Matt. We need to find a way for all of us to move on with the least amount of heartache possible."

A tiny light flickered on in Matt's eyes. Narrowing his gaze into a searching, curious wonder, he pointed his mug at Josh. "You're scared. Why?"

Josh switched his weight to his other foot and pocketed his free hand. "Truth? I don't think she would have come back to me this time if you hadn't made her come back."

"That doesn't help. Fuck, Josh. Jesus." Twisting away, Matt set his mug on the counter and leaned on both of his forearms. He tried to channel his breathing into some kind of normal rhythm.

"The thing is, Matt," Josh continued, taking in another deep breath for strength, "we're doing okay now, Jessie and me. We're hanging on, at least. But I gotta tell you, there's this undercurrent of fear in our household, and it's got shit all to do with Morgan. It's my bored, unchallenged wife. It's her constant worrying about me, about when I'm gonna go off the rails again and leave her alone with four scared children. And, buddy, it's you. Jessie can't stand knowing you're in pain. She can't stand not knowing when she'll see you again, and if you'll be okay. And I think a good part of the fear where you're concerned is not knowing whether the two of you could have made a life for yourselves that would have meant no more worrying. Safety, security. No more hiding. The glamorous life she's used to, surrounded by friends and family. All those things."

Josh was talking to Matt's back. When the room got quiet, Matt wheeled his weary spirit around and looked Josh in the eye. "We could have had a life together," he said. "Jessie and me and your kids. A good life. We would have made it. But always there would have been an undercurrent in our house too. And it would have been screaming your name."

Taking that in, Josh chewed on his lip before saying, "What about Shanda, Matt? How bad was it?"

"She kicked me out. That's how bad it was."

"You love her…"

Matt pshawed. "Yeah, hell, of course I do. But Jessie's under my skin. The only way I can explain it, Josh, is that I need her in my arms. I need her close by where I can see her, touch her. I need that control. It's the only way I feel like I've got any hope at all of keeping her safe." His voice cracked on the heavy emotion. "I've been with her too long. I've let her down too many times."

"She doesn't think you've ever let her down. You should know that. Except maybe when you dropped her back off to me without giving her a say in it."

"Of course I've let her down. Look what's happened to you—Deuce McCall, Morgan…"

"You're a man, Matt. You're not a god. You've always been there for us."

"Jesus, Josh!" Matt was near tears. "I took your wife to my bed. More than once. I dream every second of every day that I'm holding her…I see this image in my mind of just lying there in bed with her in my arms, rocking her after," he choked, "after making love…" Tense, he checked Josh out for signs of impending rage. Seeing only a grim set to his jaw and that ever-pulsing nerve, Matt added, "Dreaming of her that way, of us together, this peace comes over me. Then like a damn skyrocket, the second I realize she's not mine to hold anymore, it goes away." His voice got quieter. "I had her, Josh, for a time. Even before we ever hooked up, if she needed someone to hold her, I was there. I didn't need sex then, from her, in the old days. Just breathing her in was enough. Knowing she was safe when she was with me was enough."

"And now…" Josh was scared to ask.

"And now she's a drug I can't get enough of. That I crave with a desperation that's ruined me for every day living. Loving Jessie is destroying me, Josh. The same way she destroyed Jacob for a while. The same way you're a man covered in scars, inside and out. I want her. I need her. I'm consumed by her."

"I'd say she doesn't belong to you, Matt, except that you know Jessie as well as I do. The thing is…our wild girl doesn't really belong to anybody."

Something flickered in Matt's eyes. "Our girl," he whispered, swallowing, imploring Josh to elaborate.

Josh shrugged. His calm nonchalance would have been disarming to anyone else. Matt knew Josh well; he could see beneath the surface. There was hope there. Curious, Matt raised his chin and listened. "Asking Jessie to never see you would be the catalyst to an absolute and final goodbye for us," Josh said. "Shanda's not there yet. She doesn't understand how deeply the two of you are wound in and around each other."

"Yes, she does. She just can't live with it."

"Can you, Matt? If Shanda takes you back, can you live your life with her and still let Jessie in? In a healthy way that works for all of us?"

Matt's thick, scared voice lost some of its desperation. "You need to explain, Josh."

"I will," Josh said. Using his foot, he shoved out a chair from the small round table in Arnie's kitchen. It skittered backward. "Take a seat. Bring your coffee."

Matt didn't move. He blinked at Josh. "Why are you here, Josh? Is Jessie thinking of coming back to Vancouver?"

"I don't think she's focused on Vancouver right now, Matt."

Matt's shoulders sank. He picked a spot on the floor and let it go out of focus. There seemed to be no end to the ups and downs of hopes and dreams as far as Jessie was concerned. She was just one big roller coaster ride.

Josh's next words floored him. "I think she's focused on you." Matt's eyes darted back upward in a flash.

It took Matt a few seconds to come to his senses. The room spun. He gripped the counter for support until his feet felt grounded enough that he could trudge over to Josh. He dropped into the chair Josh had kicked out for him.

Josh sat heavily opposite him. Fingering his mug, twisting it around and around, he stared at the table before he spoke. "Matt, this is where I need to start. It's awkward as hell, buddy, but here it is." He looked up. That tiny, barely visible light in Matt's eyes was flickering. *Hope.* It sputtered out at Josh's first words. "You see any signs of triggers when you were with her? In bed?"

Matt stuttered out, "McCall? Her past?" His eyes grew dark and afraid. He shook his head. "No."

Josh recoiled at a wave of erotic remembrance he saw pass over Matt's face, that Matt was powerless to hide. Ducking his head, Matt focused on clinging to his mug as if it were once again an anchor, a lifeline.

"She still has them," Josh elaborated. "There are things you have to keep in mind when you're with her."

"What? I don't—I don't understand."

"You will. Listen. You can't, uh, do certain things with her. McCall for instance, the bastard, he…tied her up sometimes. And left her. You know this. You read that stalking journal she kept. Jessie told me that sometimes with Jacob some of the bad shit came rushing back. They, uh, were a little more adventurous than me and her. I know what to watch for, how to be careful with her. What not to do."

Matt let go of his mug. He wiped sweaty palms on his jeans. "Josh, don't let her go. I'll figure this out; I'll get my shit together. I don't see the two of you going your separate ways, ever. It wouldn't work."

"Not what I'm talking about, buddy."

Floored, Matt stared at him. "Then I don't know what this has to do with me."

"Settle in, Matt." Josh sat back and exhaled slowly. "It's time we talked. I mean really talked."

Matt waited a minute before he raised a hand and waved Josh on. "I'm listening," he said at last, and leaned forward to hear what his old friend had to say.

Chapter Twenty-one

At home later, Josh walked in to find Jessie in the kitchen cleaning up lunch.

"I saved you food," she said, yanking open the refrigerator door and pulling out a plate of soggy tomato and cheese sandwiches. "I made extra."

Josh was pale, uncertain. Wordless, he accepted the plate from Jessie's hand and sat in a stool behind the L-shaped part of the kitchen counter to gulp down his wife's culinary masterpieces. The sandwiches were inhaled in three bites each.

"You get what you needed?" Jessie asked him. Watching Josh lick his fingers, she knit her brow together in worry. "You don't look so good, babe."

"Caffeine poisoning," he grumbled, and looked past her to a computer cubby where Emily-Grace was poking away at YouTube. "You watching her?" he asked, nodding toward the computer.

Jessie spun around to look. "Hey, daughter," she said, sidling over to stand behind Emily-Grace. "You're not supposed to be on the Internet without myself or Daddy around to help you."

"Duh, Momma, you were right there. I can't help it if you're always off in dreamland." Bubbling, Emily-Grace pointed at the screen. "Look what I found!" Pressing the 'play' arrow icon, she let go of the computer mouse and cranked up the volume.

She had selected a video from way back, from before her mother and father were married. Jessie glanced back at Josh with a smile as a much younger version of herself stood in front of a microphone in tight jeans and a sequined halter top and told a large audience what she was about to play.

From where he was sitting a ways behind them, across the room, Josh strained to see.

Jessie's on-stage voice was confident and sure. "I've written a lot of songs for people over the years," the old her was saying. "My all-time favorite is a love song." Her eyes shone with love and twinkled with promise. "I wrote it for the man I am going to marry. For the man I am going to," blushing, she ducked her head, "have children with. For the man I am going to grow old with."

Cheers filled the computer speakers. David and Dylan heard their mother's voice on screen and came running in from the playroom. Micah was cooing contentedly from his high chair, sucking on a teething ring, stretching sideways to see as if he, too, understood the significance of this particular video.

"I love your hair, Momma," Emily-Grace cooed in starry-eyed wonder. She let her brothers each wiggle a half butt on either side of her. "It's so pretty long and curled like that."

A chair scraped backward on the wooden floor. Jessie looked up to spy Josh walking toward her and their children just as the on-screen version of her said, "This is for Josh." The stage version of her did the usual love sign for him—two fingers at her eyes, a swoop down to her heart, an outward flourish from her lips.

"We were so young and naïve," Jessie breathed in wonder. Josh wrapped his arms around her waist. From a standing position behind their three older children, the two of them watched the song play through. "This was when we were shooting the second season of *Drifters*, around Christmas, I think," Jessie mused. "Just around the time you proposed, before...before..." Her eyes started to water.

"Shhh, little one." Josh cemented his comfort with a kiss on the back of Jessie's neck. "We're here. We're okay. We've made it this far." His smile grew wider and his eyes got misty. He tilted his head toward his children. "Look how blessed we are."

"Y-yeah," Jessie agreed with a gulp, watching the younger on-screen version of herself sing accompanied by Christian's delicate touch on the ivories as well as stringed instruments that carried her through the highs and lows of the tender love song.

The frame switched to a shot of Josh, standing at the back of some fancy ballroom where the concert was taking place. Shyly dipping his head to avoid the camera picking him up in its unforgiving glare, he was licking his lips and shuffling his feet. The loose piece of hair Jessie loved forever was hiding Josh's flushed, embarrassed cheek like a waterfall.

"Ohhh," the current her in the kitchen gasped. "Look at you. So young. So handsome."

"No beard!" David called loudly, which made everyone laugh.

The ballad was rising now, hitting a crescendo that seemed to tell its own story—that some days would be diamonds and some days, in this love story, would be dust. It foretold Josh and Jessie's future the way only a true love song could—in highs and lows, and in hills and valleys.

Josh put a firm hand on his wife's waist and drew her around to face him. "Dance with me," he begged. The love in his eyes was as bright now as it was then—more so, even, because of the heavy price he paid to get to this point. And because of the worry that still haunted Josh, that wound through his heart and his spirit like a sticky spider's web.

And because of the man Josh saw just a few hours earlier, who never got the chance to face Jessie the way Josh could now, in the knowing that they were a husband and wife with four children in their care, that they could share a bed and cuddle whenever they wanted to. And because, as the song played out, a younger version of that man was present in the video too, just off camera in the wings, witness to Jessie blossoming under Josh's love, and maybe longing for her even then, but too honorable to say so.

Jessie lifted her arms and brushed her lips against Josh's before she laid her tired cheek on his shoulder and slow danced with him in the safety of their Prince Edward Island kitchen.

Overcome with what this meant, their children watched. It was sacred, seeing their parents so in love this way, unashamedly holding each other while their younger mother sang, on screen, the first love song she ever wrote for their father. The kids all knew the ballad. Since then, Jessie had performed it many, many times in huge arenas and on smaller, intimate stages.

When the song filtered to a tender close, Jessie lifted her head from her husband's shoulder and lost herself in his somber molten chocolate eyes. "So in love with you," she whispered. "So lost in you."

Josh needed the boost of confidence. After last night's crazy, bewildering sex, and Matt's reappearance in their lives, he needed assurance.

Jessie's doe eyed love for him granted it. With a long, slow exhale, Josh kissed her back, and let the song play out.

Much later that day—at seven o'clock in the evening—he handed her his truck keys.

"What?" she asked, confused. She was in the middle of running a bath for David and Dylan, to get the beach salt and sand off of their small bodies.

Josh laid a palm against her cheek. "You need a drive," he told her in a husky tone.

"No, I don't, I…" Jessie stilled. "To…to where? Why?"

A good long pause prefaced Josh's single word. "Darnley." He needed the time to repeatedly swallow and find enough saliva in his mouth to make his lips move again. "He, uh, rented his old cottage for a week, Jess. Matt. You'll find him here." Josh pushed a handwritten map into her hand and closed her fingers over it. "It's only about ten or fifteen minutes from here."

"I know where it is. I've been there, Josh. When I've been…out for a drive. That's all. I wanted to know where he stayed when he was here that time."

"You wanted to be close to him."

"Y-yep. I did."

"So go. Be close to him."

Jessie took a step back and turned off the tub's faucet. "I don't get it. That where you went this morning? To see M-Matt?" She could hardly say his name.

Josh nodded. "Yeah."

"Why, Josh? Did you fight with him?"

He shook his head. "No, Jessie. No harsh words. We just talked."

"'Bout what?" She wasn't budging, although she was fingering the keys in her hands tenderly, looking at them, wondering… Glancing back up at Josh, she bit her lip. "You want this to end. You want me to let him go once and for all."

"No. The pain," he acknowledged in a whisper. "I want the pain to end. The worry. For you and me, and for Matt."

"And for Shanda?"

"One way or the other," Josh said, giving himself away. Giving his fear away.

"How do you see it ending, Josh? I want to know how you see the pain ending."

"Go see Matt. Find it in your heart to listen, Jessie, to yourself and to what it is you need. Search your heart. Do what you need to do. You didn't have a choice before. You have one now."

Jessie held her breath. She looked at him from a rather askance viewpoint, chin raised high, mouth partially open and eyes wide. The life she could have with Matt ran through Jessie's mind with the intensity and speed of a bullet. "Josh, I…babe, are you sure about this?"

"I love you," he said. Josh didn't blink. Something honest and true had settled across his eyes. A happy-sad smile appeared on his lips before it quickly overturned. He shoved his hands in his pockets and waited to see what she would say, what she would do.

Jessie paused before she brushed by him with a prolonged squeeze of his hand. "I love you back," she managed.

Jessie didn't cry when she turned left onto the Lower Darnley Road. She dredged up whatever strength and power she could find in herself, and she forced the wetness away. It was almost seven thirty when she pulled up alongside the cottage she knew Matt had rented a few summers earlier. The view of the Darnley Basin was as spectacular as he once told her it was. Mirrored and calm, there wasn't a breath of breeze to set flight to a single ripple in the water. The earlier wind had given way to a peaceful evening stillness.

An orange sun was just starting to think about descending and going to sleep for the night when Jessie slid out of the truck, circled the hood, and picked Matt out up on the deck of his cottage. Expectant, he was perched on the rail at the far end of the cedar-shingled cottage with one knee crooked up, his back against the wall, his left foot solidly on the ground.

"Stunning," Jessie said through a semi-composed, unsteady gaze, referencing the simple summertime beauty of the magical place. She picked her way up the steps. At the top, she stopped and took Matt in with an apprehensive frown.

Shifting to face her, he leveraged his body up off the rail with a trembling arm.

Jessie lifted her hands up, covered her face, and blindly took a step toward him.

Matt crossed the verandah in a few quick steps. He pulled the lithe body he loved into his arms and gasped with the pleasure of simply holding Jessie again. He couldn't form enough sense out of all the jumbled thoughts ricocheting through his brain to speak. The interminable days and weeks since Boston were a dank and dusty no-man's-land—Matt barely remembered getting through them. Holding Jessie in his arms, breathing her in, sucking in her energy, was like stumbling across an oasis in the desert. She was the water, the life-force, he needed to survive.

"Oh, God," she breathed into his neck, equally overcome. "I can't stand this."

"Come inside," Matt said, running a hand through her hair, holding great handfuls of it so he could tip her head back and bury himself in the pale blue eyes he so desperately missed.

"C-can't," she stammered. "Can't go there right now, Matt."

He wasn't surprised. A small upward curve appeared on his lips, accented by the same tiny light in his eyes that Josh was privy to earlier. "Let's go for a walk," he suggested. "Let me show you my beach."

"Okay. A walk. All right."

At the truck, Jessie reached in and grabbed her black ball cap. With an amused grin, Matt pulled it down over her eyes. Hand in hand, they walked up the gravel lane to the Lower Darnley Road. There, they turned left and headed toward the campground.

At first, they stuck to safe conversation. "What was it like watching over a country singer?" Jessie asked. "Dallas is a good guy."

"He's entertaining," Matt said. "I liked most of his songs okay. His fans sure love him."

"I'll have to start calling you a redneck, huh?" Playfully, Jessie elbowed him.

Chuckling, Matt lifted his arm and laid it around her shoulder. "His lady is sweet. She has a son about Emily-Grace's age."

"Yeah, Ry, I think his name is. Cute little surfer blond kid."

At the main entrance to the campground, they turned right. Matt bought them both ice cream sundaes at the camp store. They ate them on a wide wooden bench just behind the store, in front of a building used as a Laundromat. Just below that was a large fenced-in playground. Jessie pulled the brim of her hat further down over her eyes when a young mom strode past, a teeming basket of clothes in her arms.

"Okay, if I knew this was here I'd have brought the kids by ages ago." Jessie spoke fast, covering up her anxiety about being recognized. "They'd love that playground."

"Bring them by tomorrow." Matt focused on the hot fudge in his sundae when he said that. *Hope.*

"Maybe," Jessie said softly. "I dunno, Matt."

They ate the rest of their sundaes in a kind of quiet restlessness. When they were done, Matt took Jessie's white sundae bowl and plastic spoon from her and dumped them in the garbage.

"Where to now?" Jessie asked when he walked back up to her and pulled the ball cap down even lower over her nose. Dropping her hands to his hips, she had to look up at him from underneath the brim. "I can barely see, Matt," she grumped amiably in her childlike little girl voice.

His smile grew wider. "God, I've missed you." Holding her elbows, he ached for a kiss so he could lick a bit of chocolate off the corner of her lip. In the end he licked the tip of his finger and used that to wipe the chocolate off instead. "Beach walk," he rasped. "We'll do a loop. This way."

"This what you and Catherine used to do?" Jessie tucked her fingers into his and they started down a central lane of the busy campground. A kid on a bike swerved around them. "Geez," she exclaimed, sidestepping out of the kid's way. "Busy spot. This place has changed a lot since I used to camp here with my mom and dad."

It was busy, all right—it was high tourist season. Everywhere there were kids, bikes, babes in strollers, older couples walking dogs, park staff in green shirts, and teens with sultry eyes wandering aimlessly on the hunt for friends. Campfires were starting up around the trailers and tents that dotted the area. The comforting woodsy smoky smell wafted through the trees like a wel-come, much missed memory.

At the end of the lane, Jessie darted into a rustic ladies' room for a pee before joining Matt for a stroll down a wooden ramp that led to the beach. When her toes tucked into the sand at the bottom, she whipped off her flip-flops and hopped up and down with delight. Seven or eight sand structures—castles and mythical creatures, mostly—dotted the beach, surrounded by happy families, yellow plastic buckets and small spades meant for digging.

"Oh, this is amazing!" Jessie yelped happily. Forcibly pulling on Matt's hand so they could start at the east end and work their way west, she had to quell a guilty wave that passed over her. *Josh would love this. The kids would love this.*

Beside one of the sand structures, someone stood and reached out to shake Matt's hand. "Hey, how are ya, friend?" he asked. Responding to the friendly gesture, Matt lit up and said to Jessie, "You remember Dallas. Dallas, you know Jessie."

If seeing Jessie and Matt together on his P.E.I. beach confused him, Dallas was too much of a gentleman to let on. He, like Jessie, was being cautious about his identity, and was hiding under a ball cap. With a wide grin, he looked to his right and then back at Jessie. A petite, elegant, tanned ponytailed blonde rose to say hello. "This is Cassie, Jessie."

"Hi, Cassie," Jessie smiled. "It's nice to meet you."

Matt nodded a nervous hello to Dallas' pretty gal. He was a mess last night, and not super social backstage at the outdoor festival gig. After the chat with Josh this morning and with Jessie by his side this evening, he was a gazillion pounds lighter, and much, much happier. Life just felt right again, when Jessie was close by. He hoped Cassie was the insightful, forgiving kind. Dallas sure seemed to be.

Dallas pointed to an industrious, busy kid in a yellow hoodie. "And that youngster working hard carving turrets on his sandcastle is Ry. We're camping over on the bay side," he explained to Jessie.

"Some of us are camping," Cassie offered. Dallas laid an arm around her shoulders. "And some of us are glamping. We're in a fifth-wheel. Showers, kitchen, all that jazz."

Jessie laughed and aimed a question at her music friend. "Sounds like the way I'd want to do it too. Will you get to stay here for a while, Dal? Or are you going right back out on tour?"

"I planned my summer so I'd have some time off," he told her. "I've spent enough time alone. I need some R & R with my girl and Ry. We're staying for a bit."

Cassie was glowing.

"I wish you all the best," Jessie said. "I really do." She started wringing her fingers together in front of her belly. There was a sadness to her words.

"How long are you here for, Jessie? Did you just get in?"

"Me? Uhh…" Unsure, Jessie untwisted her fingers and stuck her hands in the back pockets of her jeans. She looked to Matt for help. It wasn't lost on either her or on Matt how quickly they reverted to their old roles with him as protector.

"She's staying on the island for a week or so," Matt clarified quietly. "It's just a brief visit."

"What's next professionally?" Dallas asked, seemingly okay with that answer. He, of all people, understood the complexities of relationships. Seeing Matt with Jessie today was like seeing an entirely different man than the one who worked security the night before. That man was broken. This man appeared fixed, with this girl at his side.

"Not sure," Jessie shrugged. "Maybe write some songs and see where they take me. I'm still sorting some things out."

"I hear ya. You take care, Jessie."

With happy waves and promises to meet up again someday, somewhere, Jessie and Matt wandered off down the row of sand structures. After admiring the last one, they kept on going down the beach, and spent a comfortable half hour crawling over sandstone rocks and wading in rivulets of water until they got to a smaller sandy beach that Matt told Jessie the locals referred to as 'Secret Beach.'

"I'm not sure why except that it's not as popular as the main beach," he said. "It's less populated and more rocky."

"More like our beach at the end of Sutherland Road," Jessie said, plopping her butt down on a low sand-duned cliff next to Matt so they could watch the sun sink lower in the western sky. "Kind of pebbly in places. But it works, for us at least."

Matt grew pensive. After a bit, Jessie took his hand and kissed the backs of his fingers. He smiled sadly at her. "It was good of Josh to let me see you, Jessie," he said. "There are not many men on the planet who have the integrity and guts your man has."

"In all honesty I was surprised that he went to see you today, Matt. And even more surprised when he handed me his truck keys tonight. He…wants us to come to some sort of peace tonight." She sighed and pressed Matt's hand against her cheek. "He can't stand me moping around, I guess, sulking and whining about this new life I am trying to come to terms with. Being away from you. From everybody."

"He told me. He's scared."

"Couldn't have been too scared if he let me come here. This is the thing, Matt. In his heart Josh knows which way this is gonna go." Jessie was staring at Matt's hand, which she was holding in her lap now, enfolded in both of hers. There was a calm serenity to the way she was talking, as if 'choosing' wasn't as hard as maybe Josh—and perhaps Matt—thought it might be for her. "Matt, I'm here now, baby. As much as I haven't entirely made my peace with it, this is my home. The current that day, when the car was in the river…it picked me up and started carrying me, and this is where it dropped me. This is where I am, where I belong and where I need to stay. With my husband. I'm sorry if you were hoping for more. I'm sorry about how awful this has been for you, and for Shanda too."

He was still. Jessie looked sideways at him. "You're not surprised."

With a heavy sigh, Matt sat back and lifted his hand out of Jessie's fingers. He draped his arm back around her shoulders and fixed his gaze on the lowering sun. "No, sweetheart," he said. "I'm glad you've been able to come to this conclusion on your own."

"Matt, if you hadn't dropped me off I would not have made my peace with Josh and with this life as much as I have. I would have stayed with you."

"And regretted it. Missed Josh every day. Every second of every day."

"Overall it still doesn't change things, Matt. It doesn't change how I feel about you, how much it hurts to be away from you. I don't know how to live this way, torn between two men. It's not fair to either of you. I think we have to agree to let each other go. The thing is, though…" She stilled. "I'm worried about you. That call last night…"

"I've been your wing man for a lot of years, Jessie," Matt said. "I don't know how to let you go, either."

"My wing man." She smiled. "My Matt. Always looking out for me." A thought crossed her mind and she took a right turn. "Emily-Grace has been taking swimming lessons, Matt. I finally got her back in the water. You know how?"

He shook his head. "No, sweetheart. But I'm glad."

"I told her she has two choices. One, she can crumple up in a heap of fear and not allow herself joy, the kind that comes from living, from really living. Or two, she can face the fear, the current reality. She can turn it around into something useful and take control of it. So it doesn't control her." She paused. "You and me, baby…we need to take control."

"That's kind of what your husband said to me today."

"Oh?"

"The control thing. You're right, I think he was pretty sure which way you would go. Still, he wants us to find a way to make it work for all of us. I do think he's scared, Jessie, but he's willing to make a compromise that will ease some of this pain. So we don't have to let each other go completely."

"Josh said that? He's gotta be worried that we'll still end up in bed together, Matt. That's going to be what breaks us. What keeps us apart."

"Talk to him," Matt said. "We'll go from there, okay?"

Cocking her head, Jessie felt a rush of confusion sweep over her tired brain. "Ooookayyy," she said, biting her lip and wondering what Matt was alluding to, exactly. "I'll talk to him when I get back. What about Shanda, honey?"

"I don't know. She's not talking to me at the moment, and I don't blame her. I haven't had a thing to offer her lately."

"What, not even that gorgeous bod?" Giggling, Jessie nudged him.

"I should have handled things better in Boston. I should have communicated better. Then maybe we could have all talked and come to a more peaceful conclusion about things then, I don't know. The way you and I had to leave things…" Grabbing a handful of sand, he filtered it between his hands. The minuscule grains waterfalled through his fingers. "We never seem to have good endings we can live with."

"We will this time." Jessie spoke softly, with the respect the moment, and the perfect disappearing sun, deserved. "Tonight you and I will part at your cottage like the best, best friends we've been for so, so long. And if Josh is as calm as he is making himself out to be, then maybe tomorrow I can bring the kids over to see you. They miss you too, you know. And as far as Shanda goes, I will hand write her a letter—no emails, my security doesn't allow those from our secret house, nudge nudge wink wink—and hopefully she will see the light and not burn the letter and an effigy of me along with it."

No more words were shared until, in a final salute, the sun dipped into the ocean and melted into curvilinear trails of liquid, gorgeous beauty.

"Was it worth it?" Jessie asked Matt in a hushed whisper just before they gathered their flip-flops to go. She asked it without looking at him, and she didn't elaborate beyond saying, "Was it worth all of the pain?"

He waited before answering. "Yes," he murmured back to her. Cupping her chin in his hands, he pressed his lips to the welcoming, soft mouth of the woman he loved. Jessie breathed him in, and kissed him back. "It was worth it," Matt said when he finally let her go. "I love you, kid."

"I love you back, Matt. Always will." A final, tender embrace, and they turned their backs to the sinking sun, crawled up over the sand dune, and walked hand-in-hand into the alluring bluish-purple of an expanding twilight sky.

~⁓~

Josh heard the truck motor down the road before he saw it. In the moonlit night, a full moon tonight, a bright one that lit the skies almost as if it were daytime, he was able to watch Jessie throw open the driver's side door and hop down onto the grass. It was only ten o'clock. He'd half expected her to stay away for the night. Lingering against the fence where the horses got to frolic and play, down the lane on the Sutherland side, he had just said good night to William.

Josh called to Jessie just as she started up the walk toward their kitchen door. In a few short seconds, she turned around and was at his side. Jessie took up a position next to her husband, copying his stance with both elbows jutting out sideways on the rail and one foot up on the bottom rail. She winked at him. "I see I've trained you well, husband. You have the baby monitor in your hand."

"I can see their silhouettes, too," Josh said, lighting up at the way Jessie was so easily relaxing into this chat. "They always go to our room first."

"Ah. Wise husband."

She'd said it again. Josh held his breath. Then he said, "Husband? We're good?"

Inching closer to him, Jessie laid her left cheek on her joined hands on the rail, and watched Josh do the same, only with his right cheek, so they were nose to nose. "How many times do I have to tell you I love you, Josh?" she murmured. "That I will never, ever leave you?"

"Not even for strong, safe, dependable Matt, huh?"

She shook her head slowly from side to side. "Not even for Matt, babe, although we'll never let each other go. Not completely, Josh. Can't."

Struggling, Josh couldn't look at Jessie for fear of breaking down in sheer relief.

She grabbed the sleeve of his denim jacket and buried her face in it. "I'm sorry, Josh. I'm sorry I hurt you. I'm sorry this has all been so damn hard. All of it."

"It was close," he said in a knowing sort of way. In a serious, scared sort of way.

"Matt has always been a safe place to land, Josh." Jessie swiped at her eyes. "You scared the shit out of me with your terrifying attempt at honor. Please, babe, don't ever do anything like that again. And by that I mean don't ever make big decisions without me again. It's all for one and one for all in this marriage. Okay?"

Josh inhaled deeply. "I want you to know, Jessie, that if you want to leave—here, me—I won't stand in your way. I know how much you hate it here. This life."

She chuckled wryly. "That's ironic, isn't it? I thought this was what I wanted. I thought it'd be you who hated it. And anyways, I don't—hate it, I mean. Not entirely. I still need the freedom to go work sometimes, that's all. But I know how hard that will be on you, if I go. That's what I'm most afraid of, babe. You know that."

"I'm okay, Jessie. I'm dealing okay."

"At the moment, yes, you are. I'm glad, Josh."

Josh silently considered what she wasn't saying. Staying on what he hoped was safe ground, he dove in a little deeper about the whole decision-making thing. "Back to decisions," he started with a nervous twitch in his lip. "I made one last one without you. But I can't take all the blame. I talked to Matt about it too."

"Oh? Oh." Jessie wrinkled her nose. "Matt said there was something I should ask you. Something about a compromise. I gotta tell you, Josh, you're being way more understanding than I thought you'd be about me and Matt. But this compromise, if it's about you trusting us to work together again, I've gotta be honest. I'm just not sure we can, babe. Not without..." She sighed and turned her head away from him. "It's nothing against you, Josh. It's just that sometimes I really want to be held by him. I can't explain it. It's all tied in to that stupid SUV and how fucking scared I was, and seeing him on the other side of that window, unable to get to me—to us. Emily-Grace and me. It's like I knew then that there was no way we could touch each other, feel each other's skin, ever again, or our arms around each other, not with that window between us. Sometimes now, thinking of him when I'm scared..." She let out a small, sad *pffft* and stared at the grass beneath her feet.

"I hear what you're saying, Jessie," Josh said. "I'm not going to take this personally because you know me well enough to know what my weak spots are too. And you still love me and are willing to stand by me. You always try to stand by me, even when I let you down."

Straightening, Jessie tried to jump in, but Josh raised a hand and stopped her from talking. "Let me finish," he said kindly. "Jessie, if in the future you need to feel secure, and for whatever reason I'm either not around to help you, or I'm incapable of helping you, my old plan still stands. Okay? The only thing different about it is that I'll still be on this earth."

"I don't...what are you saying, Josh?"

"Look, don't jump to conclusions and please don't go bed hopping on me, like with Jacob again or Charlie or whomever, but—"

"What? I wouldn't! Well, I might with Jacob," Jessie teased, and winked happily. "And as I said, your sister is adorable."

"Not hearing this. Not going there." Chuckling, Josh put his hands over his ears.

Jessie pulled them away. "Babe, are you saying what I think you're saying?" Her eyes were as serious as Josh had ever seen them.

"I'm saying," Josh explained tenderly, "that if you need Matt at any time—to hold you, or even for sex, I won't stand in your way, and I won't judge you. It's different, what the two of you have. In many ways, Jessie, the love the two of you have for each other is nothing short of extraordinary."

"Like you and me." Weepy now, teary-eyed, Jessie stood in front of Josh in absolute awe of his capacity to stand aside and give her—and their good friend—what they needed the most.

Swallowing past the lump in her throat, her eyes glistening in the full moon, she whispered, "I won't have regular sex with him, Josh. I swear to you, I won't. Just…maybe…the odd time. Like, super rare. Thank you. Thank you for being the most incredible man on the planet."

"I don't want to lose you," he murmured back to her, his eyes as bright and moist as his wife's. "If this is what it takes to keep you, and to help Matt stay sane in the meantime and be the man we need him to be—the man who holds our lives in his hands—then so be it."

"You are loved, Josh Sawyer," Jessie breathed, leaning in for a kiss. "So, so much."

"So are you, little one." Josh lit up. "Come on. Let's take advantage of all those happily slumbering offspring of ours."

"Yeah. You bet." Arm in arm, they headed back down the lane toward the big white house. In the moonlight it was captivating, haloed in the pale light, spiritual and serene, the sacred sanctuary of a family in need of grace.

"Hey," Jessie teased, poking Josh in the ribs as she practically skipped down the lane, feeling weightless and free for the first time in forever, "I don't suppose this is your way of saying you want to get in Shanda's pants."

"Only if that's the only way Shanda will allow you and Matt to be in each other's company."

"I knew it!" Delighted, Jessie grabbed Josh's sleeve and brought him to her for more kisses. "We'll have a foursome," she purred, hopping up and down. He rolled his eyes and groaned. "We'll show Jacob and Kayla how it's done!"

"I hope to God you're kidding, Jessie," Josh said ruefully. "I'm a redneck, remember? A traditional kind of guy?"

In hysterics at his quick and vehement response, Jessie jumped on Josh the second they got in the door. Sex tonight was as inspired as last night, only this time it was more in celebration, and it left both of them gasping on the kitchen floor afterward. The baby monitor was silent while they made love, which was a good thing, because neither would have heard it.

The next day, Jessie, with Alice along for the day, took the kids to Darnley to see Matt while Josh reupholstered chairs with William. Dallas and Cassie joined the Darnley group with shy Ry in tow, which delighted Emily-Grace and the boys, who were way past tired of each other's company. They spent the day far down the beach in a quiet not so populated spot, using their own names since Alice was now fully aware of everyone's identity. A frank discussion with the children earlier that morning, at a level Jessie and Josh hoped they could grasp, helped things along.

When Josh wrapped his body around Jessie that night, and she backed into the welcoming, safe curl of his chest, they were both more content and at peace than they had been in a very long time.

In the end Jessie didn't write the letter to Shanda. Josh called Shanda instead. He reasoned with her and helped her understand the relationship between Jessie and Matt, and how Matt's peace of mind was directly tied into the woman whose life he'd saved more than once.

At the end of the week, Matt flew back to his wife in Vancouver, leaving Jessie to sit alone on the deck at his rented cottage after driving over to say goodbye. Both were quiet and reflective, but both were also at peace, finally. Did they kiss before they parted? Yes. Did they make love? No. There was something about Josh's trust in them and in what they meant to each other that almost burst that bubble; that took away the desperate need to immerse their bodies in each other. It was almost like if their souls were peacefully entwined, their bodies reaped the benefits, and relaxed into comfortable serenity too.

Jessie stayed on the deck until raindrops spattered over the Darnley Basin; until a thick fog swept over the cottages and campground and baptized them anew. When she drove down Sutherland Road in Josh's truck, the bay that bordered their home on the north side was equally immersed in mist.

By the time Jessie opened the truck door and slid to the earth, the skies were clearing. A new sun peeked daintily through pockets of moisture. It brought with it the birth of a rainbow, and soon colorful arcs of blissful promise crisscrossed the Sawyer home with a whole new hope.

Chapter Twenty-Two

*M*onths later, Jessie was kicking herself for giving up a sunny home in the Caribbean for one subject to a cold eastern Canadian winter when weekly nor'easters blew in one after the other, dumping tons of frosty white snow on her healing island. The drifts were so high in January and February that she could barely see to back out of her laneway. The kids loved it. They did schoolwork with their mother in the mornings while Josh worked with William up the lane, restoring antique chairs. In the afternoons, Josh and Jessie dressed the older kids in snow pants, hats and mittens. Josh took them outside to build snow forts and to go sliding on a low hill beyond William and Alice's home. When Micah woke up from his nap Jessie took him outdoors too, on a wooden sled Alice gave her—one with a high back to help support him—and Jessie, Josh and the kids took turns running up and down the lane towing Micah behind them until everyone was rosy cheeked and exhausted.

Evenings were for music and dance lessons. When Kayla and Jacob landed for two weeks in late January, the usual routine took a nosedive. Schoolwork got pushed aside for dance and music in the mornings. Even David and Dylan got into the hip hop style that Kayla and Jessie rocked best—some culled from Jessie's shows. Jacob was learning drums from Casey. He passed his new skills along to Dylan while Jessie worked with David on a keyboard in his bedroom upstairs. Emily-Grace took that time for extra dance lessons with Kayla.

Charles and Dee showed up on the first Sunday of the second week. Every night was a Sawyer family recital. Charles counted his millions while Jessie shook her head at him. *No. Our kids are not going into the biz.* Josh watched his children with a growing mixture of concern and confusion. Even if any of them did choose to pursue public careers on the stage, he could never sit in an audience and cheer them on unless he donned a disguise and pretended to be someone he was not. By the time the Vancouver crowd said their tearful goodbyes, Josh was no more than a silent observer during the nightly displays of youthful talent.

One freezing night a few days after their visitors left, the tenth blizzard of the season stormed in and dumped a new load of snow on top of the Sawyer family, laying it against the north side of the house in heaps and waves. Grimacing in pain even before he left the house the evening of the storm, Josh blew snow with William's old snowblower and shoveled until he was well past aching. Once the kids were settled for the night, Jessie went out to help. They were keeping William's lane cleared too, in case of emergency.

Eyes more on Josh than on her own work, Jessie winced every time he lifted snow. "You run the snowblower," she ordered. "I'll shovel."

They didn't shed their snow clothes until almost midnight. By the time Josh and Jessie yawned their way back into the kitchen, their dripping coats, snow pants, mittens, hats and scarves were hanging to dry on every hook, chair back and closet door in the mudroom.

Taking her husband's hand, Jessie led him upstairs to the big air jet soaker tub in the en suite bathroom off their bedroom. Flipping on the faucet, she added three lidfuls of bubble bath before reaching into the medicine cabinet.

"Your shoulder," she explained, handing him two ibuprofen that he stared at in his palm like they were poison. "No more of this snow clearing, Josh. Hire someone else to do it. It's too much for us."

He grunted, and turned away from her. A whole new round of muttery winces, punctuated by the occasional 'Jesus' and the odd 'fuck,' snuck out when Josh tried hauling his T-shirt up over his head with one hand.

Jessie interpreted his attempt to go it alone as wounded pride. Reaching for Josh from behind, she took hold of the T-shirt's bottom hem and lifted it off his sweaty body. Rolling her eyes, she reached around his waist to his jeans and undid the button. "You are the most stubborn man I know," she chastised. Hauling his zipper down for him, Jessie followed up by shoving his jeans down over his hips.

Josh kicked off the jeans and his boxers. Easing into the tub, he sank back against it with his eyes closed.

"You're in pain, Josh," Jessie scolded. She gave his abandoned jeans a resolute kick with her foot. "Your leg and your shoulder aren't what they used to be. Your body is protesting." It didn't seem worth the angst it'd come with to bother bringing up his chest although she sometimes wondered whether Josh suffered from the aftereffects of a bullet ripping through his lung. Not like he'd ever tell her—he never complained.

Josh couldn't deny that his leg and shoulder hurt, though. Jessie was a star witness. Some nights those two damaged body parts ached so bad that in Josh's mind it made more sense to get up and limp around the house than it did to try to find a comfortable sleeping position. On those nights, Jessie always went nosing around in the dark looking for him after the stairs and floors stopped their telltale creaking. Almost always, she found him snoring in the rocking chair in Micah's room, his feet tucked up on an ottoman, the sore leg cushioned on a pillow and the sore arm resting on the good arm, hugged to his belly.

In the tub, Josh's eyes blinked open when Jessie slid into the whirling water opposite him. "I'll get my own tractor," he declared in a sleepy slur. "The boys will love it."

"The boys?" Jessie snorted. "Heck, screw the boys. I wanna drive it."

Josh's tired eyes lit up. Underneath a pile of bountiful bubbles, he extended a hand that Jessie gratefully took. "Emily-Grace'll want in too. I'll get one with an extra seat in the cab."

"We'll have to draw straws for the kids. They'll have to take turns. Safety, babe." Twining her fingers through his, Jessie slipped deeper under the soapy mountain. "Are kids even allowed in those things?"

"I don't see why not," Josh answered. "They've got passenger seats and safety belts. Heck, they'd be as safe in a big tractor as they would be in a car. Safer, even." He shivered. Jessie didn't need to ask why. She exerted a little pressure on his hand. Josh squeezed back and they shared a moment, both grateful that the water they were immersed in tonight was only a few feet deep.

"Fine," Jessie agreed with a renewed cocky half smile. Letting go of his hand, she lifted Josh's sore leg and laid it over hers, since she didn't want to put any of her weight on it. "I'm cool with it," she added, "as long as you keep the tractor close by and don't go out on the roads." Across from her, reclining against the back of the tub reveling in the heat soaking into his sore body, Josh grinned.

"What?" A pink blush spotted the tops of Jessie's cheeks. She knew that grin. She was seeing it a lot these days, and had since the day Josh put his own fears aside and granted her and Matt the freedom they needed to be able to move on and yet stay involved in each other's lives. "I love seeing you this happy," she murmured as she settled deeper down into her end of the tub. "For the most part, I love being here with our family."

"You're not really missing everyone as much as you thought you would."

"Nope. Not missing certain people at all. I just miss the work." Jessie frowned. Reaching into the water, she scooped up a handful of bubbles and blew them into Josh's face. His grin grew wider. He wiped them off his beard.

"You're gonna have to make up with Charlie eventually, Jessie," he admonished. "According to Charles, he's pretty hurt that you won't take his calls."

"Why would I?" She looked away.

"And who's the stubborn one?"

"Puh. Whatever. He sucks."

"He's one of your oldest friends. Don't crucify him and Jane for one bad day."

Jessie balled some more bubbles between her fingers and watched them crackle into nothingness. She dipped her hands beneath the water and looked back at her husband. "Since when did you become Charlie's defender?"

"Since I tucked my daughter in the other night and had to tell her she couldn't take the jet back with Charles and Dee and Jacob and Kayla. She wants to see Stella, Jess."

"Charlie said some pretty shitty things, Josh. What makes you think he even wants to make up?"

"Seriously? You have to ask? Time heals, little one. Charlie kicks himself every day for losing you. Don't make it permanent."

"Josh Sawyer, the great mediator." Jessie's voice was scratchy and rough with fatigue. Micah's early mornings always snuck up on her way too quickly after these late nights clearing snow. "You know, babe, you blow my mind. It's supposed to be me holding you up these days. Not the other way around."

"Who says?"

"Don't you miss it?"

Then there it was, a quick blink, a tiny star-like opening into the past. Josh knew Jessie spotted it in him when she sucked in a breath and held it, and finally emitted it in a long, slow *pfffft* that came with a leveraging of her hands on the bottom of the tub so she could sit up straighter. It was a dead giveaway. Josh wrapped a set of fingers around the toes of her left foot, and lifted the foot for a kiss. Anything to avoid meeting her worried gaze, to avoid speaking out loud and admitting the truth. The past—and what they were both missing—remained as buried as their bodies underneath the bubbles.

Bedtime was already long past. Neither Josh nor Jessie spoke again. They sank back into the swirling water until Jessie nudged her husband with her toes and gently roused him out of the soothing bath.

They didn't make love. Given the level of exhaustion, both the physical and the emotional kind, when Josh slipped into bed next to his wife he simply laid a hand on her hip and let his eyes flutter closed. Facing him, Jessie dozed off before she even finished her prayers, one set of fingers tucked cozily up underneath a sleeve of Josh's T-shirt.

The following Saturday, after three hours of clearing snow from his and the Sutherlands' laneway with William's old rust bucket of a snow blower that was broken down more than it worked, Josh took his family for a drive to Stratford, a bustling community just east of Charlottetown. He stopped into a farm equipment dealer and walked out as the new owner of a spit shined brand spanking new green and yellow John Deere tractor, paid in full with a certified check signed by his alter ego, Joe McIver. The tractor he chose had a spacious enclosed premium cab, big enough so if he wanted to he could bring his kids along to clear snow with him.

The tractor was a thing of beauty. Standing outside to admire it while the kids explored the cab the day it was delivered, Jessie hooked an arm into Josh's. "This is the key to more sex," she said, puffing up her chest. "This gargantuan thing will preserve my husband's energy so he can make love to me more instead of spending all his time clearing snow with a body that hurts every time he lifts the shovel. Right?"

Josh chuckled. "The way you talk, you'd think you never get any. We're doing okay in that department, little one."

"I know," Jessie agreed, pinking up, "but we did say five." She held up a hand and pulled off her mitten. Four fingers and a thumb splayed out in front of Josh's face. "Five kids. Micah's fourteen months old. And I'm not getting any younger. We need to be having lotsa sex."

"You're bored." Josh leapt forward and grabbed Dylan, who had slipped and almost fallen in his hurry to get down from the cab of the tractor. "Whoa, kid. Easy. Slow down. I'm gonna start calling you Leapy."

"Or Climby." Jessie grabbed the knit toque on her son's head and soundly pushed it further down so it covered his ears. "Listen to Daddy, Dylan. Take it easy." Dylan was, no doubt, the most adventurous of their children. Jacob crossed Jessie's mind. Didn't seem like this was a biological connection, given Jacob's personality versus Josh's. Josh was the guy that always had to be on the move, the one with the need for speed and adrenaline.

Dylan ignored her. He twisted around in Josh's arms. "Daddy, David won't let me drive."

"I'll let you drive," Josh said with a playful wink to Jessie. He let Dylan slide safely to the snow covered ground. "Just don't tell Momma. I have to stay on her good side."

"You be careful with our children in that big thing, Josh Sawyer. Easy does it." To Dylan, Jessie added, "You kids are not to be anywhere near it when it's running, and you can only ride in the cab when Daddy—or me, ha ha, you hear that, Josh?—is driving it. Got it? Safety first." She looked up at Josh just as William approached, a little in awe of his neighbor's ability to just run out and buy such an expensive machine. "Josh, you know not to ever start this thing up with the kids outside, right? Unless I'm with them and we're all far, far away."

"'Course," he agreed. "I'll be super careful." To William, he grinned and said, "Never did get that Harley I wanted. Want a closer look at my new toy?"

Chapter Twenty-three

"Boys and their toys," Jessie grumped on the phone to Matt a month later. "I thought the tractor would free him up for more sex but we've had so much snow this winter that he's constantly out in that thing running the roads and—guess what—clearing all the neighbors' driveways! He's in some kind of unspoken competition with the guy down the road. Here, most people pay private drivers to come clear their driveways, but Josh got a line from William and Alice on all the seniors in the area and on all the single moms, and at the first snowflake he takes off and clears their laneways out of the goodness of his heart. He's having a ball. Who knew?" She let out a frustrated, pent-up breath.

Matt was at the *Sacred Peace* soundstage. The production was shooting nights for the next few days, outside just beyond the back door. Through the phone line Jessie could hear the almost dull thud of his desert boots as he walked across the wooden floor the interior sets were constructed on. Over the line she heard Matt reward the bit about a lack of sex with a triumphant grunt. "No sex. Thanks for sharing that with me, Jessie. That actually makes my day."

She jumped on him. "Did you hear the rest of what I said? Jesus. Men. Y'all hear the word sex and your bodies go into overdrive. Certain parts, I should clarify. The ears stop functioning altogether."

Matt's low laughter was music to Jessie's ears. "I hear you, sweetheart," he chuckled. "Josh sounds like he's got a few things figured out. I'm glad he's doing well. I really am."

Jessie relaxed. "Me too," she replied, "but truth is, Matt, sometimes it freaks me out." Cross-legged on her bed, she whipped closed a script she had open in front of her and crab-walked backward to lean against the headboard. Jessie had given the screenplay a good try, but the words were blurring together. She'd read every line three times before she gave up trying to focus and punched in the call to Matt instead.

"It's four in the morning here, Matt," she said, pulling on a warm quilt she was using earlier for warmth while she read, and wrapping it around her shoulders. "This latest storm is the worst one yet. The Maritimes have literally been shut down for two days. The Confederation Bridge is closed to all traffic and we lost our power hours ago. It's freezing in here. Josh has been out since midnight, from the second the wind went down enough so he could see two feet in front of him, I suppose. He goes up and down these country roads using the telephone poles for guidance cuz it's not like he can see where the hell he's going. And that's with the winds gusting at 70 kilometers an hour instead of at 90 or 100 like they were for the last two days. I worry about him. If he goes off the road I've got no way of getting to him."

"You worry about worrying," was Matt's candid answer. He was on a burner phone as usual for this call, but he was exercising caution as to what he said and who might overhear. Shanda had just left his side with a kiss and a smile, for one; yet she was the least of their worries when it came to folks in the area who might still, even after all this time, be watching him for clues or, perhaps, mistakes.

Charlie cruised by on his way to the back door. Various crew were messing about getting organized for the next shot, hefting heavy lights and gear outside. Cast and keys were just about to start blocking a new scene. Charlie would be needed on set shortly. He slowed and raised his eyebrows when he saw Matt on the burner phone.

Warily watching Charlie hit the brakes, Matt pondered him.

Alerted by the sudden pause in the conversation, Jessie wondered if someone was listening. She tested Matt with a question. "Matt?" she asked. "You're gonna be in Vancouver, right, when I fly in to record my new album?"

He didn't answer. Charlie was walking closer to him, asking quietly, "Is that Jessie?"

"Matt!"

"One sec, missy," Matt said. "Someone wants to talk to you."

"It better be Charles," Jessie grumped into the phone, "or Carter!" She groaned and leaned her forehead on a palm when she heard Charlie say to Matt, "Charles wants to see you. Something about a blog the publicist stumbled on last night."

Matt held up a finger to Charlie. "One minute." To Jessie, he said, "Don't worry about Josh. He's a big boy. A man like him needs his toys."

"He needs to feel useful," Jessie retorted glumly. Outside, the wind was fierce; the snow seemed to be changing to ice pellets. The hard little shards were whipping against the windows so loudly that Jessie was worried the glass might actually shatter. Pellets fired from shotguns would likely exact less damage.

Dylan, who had snuggled up with David earlier that night, had woken twice already and was under the covers in Josh and Jessie's bed, which comforted Jessie as much as it comforted her son. She jumped every time a new gust shook the house, and wished to hell the mighty tractor would come rumbling down Sutherland Road.

Charlie's unwelcome voice came over the line just as Josh texted on the iPhone. Jessie's eyes darted to Josh's message. *Almost done. Freezing rain starting. Home soon. You up? Staying warm?*

*Phew.* She texted back *All well pls come home.*

Dropping the iPhone on the bed, Jessie turned her attention to a friend she had quite soundly ignored since last summer's nasty fight. She was surprised to find sadness creep into her heart at the familiar warm, albeit nervous, timbre of her old friend and ex-fiancé's voice.

"Isn't it, like, four in the morning there, Jess?" *Start safe,* Charlie was thinking. *Please don't hang up on me.* "Is everything okay?"

With both hands stuffed in his pockets and a stern look in his eyes, Matt was watching Charlie. He didn't appear overly concerned, although Charlie thought that might change once he got wind of the blog Charles wanted to show him.

"Go," Charlie mouthed to him. He wanted Jessie to himself for a while. He watched Matt wander over to the craft table for a coffee, *so he can keep an eye on me,* Charlie considered, *in case Jessie goes ballistic.* Finding a battered wooden sawhorse by the wall, Charlie nudged his butt up onto it.

Jessie's voice came over the line, thick with fatigue and edged with more than a little bitterness. "Don't put on a show of pretending you care, Charlie," she bit off, referencing his comment about whether everything was okay.

Charlie's shoulders sagged. "How would you know if I care? You never take my calls."

"Not really interested in talking to you." Absently, Jessie twisted to the side and gently ran her fingers through Dylan's dark curls. She trailed the back of a finger over the healthy pink flush of her little boy's cheek. A slow smile slipped into place over her distaste at hearing Charlie on the line.

"Look, Jessie," Charlie tried, "things went haywire on us last summer. Jane is sorry, and I'm sorry. Your turn."

"To be sorry?" She straightened. "The thing is, Charlie, I wasn't meant to overhear their conversation. As far as I know, Jane and Sophie have always felt that way about me. It just took what happened with Matt and Shanda to put that shit into gear, that's all. And you went right along for the ride. I don't need friends like you guys." A little hitch jumped in her heart at saying that aloud. She closed her eyes and rubbed her forehead. "Josh and I don't need you, and we don't want you. We just want to be left alone."

"You're getting that wish," Charlie spat back at her, swallowing three times at the hurt that ricocheted through his body upon hearing those words. "Soon everyone up here will just forget about you guys. *Sacred Peace* fans will forget that Josh was ever on their favorite show. Oh, I forgot," he added in his mean-spirited 'back-at-ya.' "I forgot that you're heading west soon to record your album. And Charles just told me you are seriously considering a new film. So I guess at least one of you won't completely disappear. Why you leaving? The snow get to you? I hear it's like the true north down there. Before you know it, polar bears will be skating across the ice to your little island."

"You're a mean bastard sometimes, Charlie."

Her sad tone got to him. He deflated. "Look, Jessie, you can talk the talk all you want, but I know you've done your time out east. Charles told me all about yours and Deirdre's new plans. What I'm wondering is how much Josh knows."

"Josh?" A weird laugh made its way from P.E.I. to Calgary. "You should probably call him Joe. Sometimes he doesn't even answer to Josh anymore."

"He's settled into his character, has he?"

"You know my husband." Cocking her head to listen for the tractor, Jessie said, "Disappearing into a character is the only way Josh knows how to deal. You should have seen him when Charles and Dee were here. Watching the kids and me play music was foreign to him, even though he hears us practicing all the time. He's always been a redneck and now his life has morphed into Joe McIver's life—horses and tractors and clearing snow, and a stay-at-home wife named Jasmyn who watches his kids and does his laundry and cooks his meals."

"Jessie," Charlie started, in a more tender tone than the one he opened the chat with, "if being Joe helps him deal, then let him be Joe. Things will never change for Josh. Not if he wants to stay safe, and keep you safe too." The blog Charles had showed Charlie upstairs earlier was on his mind. He felt sick, and chose not to bring it up to her. Matt would soon know about it too.

The blog was a mean diatribe written by some psycho conspiracy theorist. The guy had painstakingly deconstructed all of the clues the trusted Keating publicist had handed to the media about the disappearance of Josh's jet. The most incriminating evidence—evidence that absolutely could not be disputed—was the 'coincidental' sighting, in a remote mining town in northern British Columbia, of Dr. Westfield.

Doc Westfield was on the 'downed' medevac plane. He was supposed to be dead.

At Charlie's reminder of their harsh reality, about the need to stay safe, Jessie's radar went on high alert. She and Josh were becoming a little careless these days, making more appearances in local communities, sometimes accidentally calling their children by their real names, sometimes forgetting to toss on hats when they left their vehicles. Had something new on the Morgan front happened? Should they go back to being more cautious?

"I love it here, Charlie." She sighed. "I do. The time with the kids, with Josh…it's been amazing. But you're right about my plans. I need to move on. I need to be making music, making films. I'm just gonna ease into it. Josh is holding his own, living in his own private little Joe McIver movie."

Relieved that she seemed willing to talk, Charlie relaxed back against the soundstage wall and glanced over to the craft table at Matt, who was spreading cream cheese on a toasted bagel yet still keeping a close eye on the phone at Charlie's ear instead of going up to see Charles like Charlie had asked him to. With a start, Charlie realized that he simply wanted the phone back so he could keep talking to Jessie. *Matt and his proper goodbyes,* mused Charlie. *Can't let her go.*

Into the phone, Charlie tossed a dose of reality. "You can't leave Josh alone, Jessie."

"Jesus, Charlie, you and me don't talk forever and still you can't help but tell me what to do."

"You're impossible, you know that?" Squeezing his eyes shut, Charlie stuck a thumb and a finger into the outside corners of his eyes. "Josh and I talk. Regularly. I agree that he sounds like he's doing amazing. Still, you can't dispute this—extended time away from each other has often, in the past, stirred up the proverbial witch's brew."

"Geez, for a second there I thought you were talking about you and me, asshole. After all, you banging all your little honeys in Europe opened up the door for me and Josh to get together way back when." Her voice hardened. "Don't bother insinuating that distance always leads to *me* screwing around. Josh and I are always fine as long as a ton of exterior shit's not messin' us up."

"For fuck's sake, princess. Take a chill pill. I'm just being honest here. You told me yourself last summer that you think Josh will always have the propensity to be unpredictable. I'm just urging you to remember that."

A hyper-extended *pffft* calmed Jessie down. She dug one set of nails into the back of a hand. "The seasons will change, Charlie. Josh will get a new Harley. Sam and Alin are thinking of coming down for a week this summer, and I'm sure Jacob and Kayla will be back around at some point. Josh won't have to be alone for long."

"And you'll run off to live an exotic, erotic life with Matt at your side. Forget about Jacob, he won't be around, he's going to be busy this summer, Jessie. He's got a film and a ton of shows lined up. I'm shooting, Steve and Carter are shooting, and I hear Arnie has a new woman. You want me to spell it out for you? Don't leave your husband alone in P.E.I. while you take off with Matt."

"Not that it's any of your goddamned business, but Josh has made his peace with Matt. He's okay with things."

Lowering his voice, Charlie took a surreptitious peek over at the curious object of their conversation before he said, "Think about it this way. Matt saved you and Emily-Grace. He saved the lives of *Josh's* wife and child. Your husband has some sort of false perception about the guy. Shit, Jessie. Josh feels like he owes Matt. He owes him you. That's the only reason he's giving the two of you some slack."

"Jealous again, are we? This is getting tired, Charlie. And you wonder why I don't want to talk to you."

"It's not jealousy, Jessie. You know what I think?" Charlie took a tired breath. "I think Josh is as scared as you are of letting Matt go. I think he's terrified of losing the one man on this planet who has proven he can handle you."

Jessie let out a roar that was so loud and unexpected it stirred Dylan at her side. "Like an untamed mustang, huh Charlie? Always needing to be reined in. That's me. I've got news for you. Josh can handle his wild horses. He doesn't need Matt to do his wrangling for him."

"Why do you always have to get so damn defensive, Jessie? You live in a secret little box and never bother looking outside!"

"Looking outside?" Jessie echoed. Her voice rose an octave. "I look outside all the time, Charlie. And guess what I see? For the last many months, mostly just a white expanse of snow! It's pretty, yes, and in the summer all I see is green, and the blue of the bay, but I see no other musicians, I see no stage, I see no lights and no audience. I see no soundstages like the one your stupid ass is on right now, I see no actors, I see no director and no cameras, and no goddamned crew! All I see, day after day, is this big old house, four small people and three big ones, and one tiny corner of a huge world I used to love exploring!"

"You wanted those things! You've always wanted that kind of life! Stop whining, you big baby, and make it work."

Jessie was sniffling. She swiped at her nose. "Not like this, Charlie. Not 24/7. Not all of the time. I need balance and it has to include a world I grew comfortable in. It has to include satisfying, rewarding work."

"And it has to include Matt."

They'd reached an impasse. By the way Jessie sucked in a sudden breath, Charlie was certain he hit the proverbial nail on the head.

"Not like before." It was a whisper, a hushed confession. "Josh and me are good, Charlie. We're so good. I don't want to mess this up."

"You will, Jessie, when you go back to work and leave Josh behind. It's that simple. You don't have the—"

"What, Charlie?" she cut in. "What don't I have? Restraint? Willpower? I must have *some*. I've never gone back to bed with the shitty likes of you! Fucking asshole."

"You…exhaust me."

"Likewise."

A few seconds passed. Craning her neck, Jessie listened to the echoey background set sounds sifting over the phone to her. Two or three hammers, all hitting whatever they were hitting at different times, were singing in their usual cacophony. Happy voices hollering directions, and other voices calling out acknowledgements from some distant part of the *Sacred Peace* set— mostly male—snuck through the line.

Charlie's shallow, anxious breathing underscored all of the much-missed sounds. It confused Jessie.

She hung her head in one hand. "As always, Charlie," Jessie sighed, "chatting with you has been a real pleasure. Thanks for this. I don't suppose Matt is still around there?" She waited for him to jump on her. Charlie remained silent. In her usual cocky self-defensive arrogance, Jessie added, "I'd like to say goodbye to the one man who we all know can handle me. I want to know if he's gonna be in Van when I'm there recording, so we can sneak off to a bathroom stall and fuck standing up."

Glancing over to the craft table, Charlie saw Matt stuff the last of his bagel between his lips. The man's steady eyes were intently focused on Charlie. "Who's handling who?" Charlie muttered under his breath. Out loud he grumbled, "Yeah. Your stud's right here, your highness. Gimme a sec."

Jessie listened to his footsteps move across the soundstage. "Charlie," she said, settling down before he had the chance to hand the phone over, "I'm sorry."

His footsteps slowed to a halt. He said nothing.

Jessie twisted a numb finger around the hem of her quilt. "None of this has been easy."

It took Charlie a second to pull himself together. He shoved the heel of a hand into his forehead. "I know, kid. I'm sorry too. What I said last summer was unforgivable. I'll never forgive myself for..." He swallowed. The saliva in his mouth had turned to sawdust. "Aw, damn."

"What you summed up last summer, Charlie, is what an awful catch I turned out to be. Look where we are. Look where my involvement in Josh's life has taken us. To the edge of nowhere. A beautiful nowhere, but still...we're so far outside the lives we should be living that our past feels like a dream."

"I—we," Charlie looked over at Matt. "We want you back as much as you want to come back, kid. I'm sorry for throwing reality curve balls into your plan."

"I'm not gonna fuck it up, Charlie. I'll be careful. One day at a time. With addictions, you know? It's always one day at a time."

"We'll help with Josh. I promise. We'll make sure he's never alone."

She paused. "I wasn't talking about Josh."

"Ah ha. I see." Matt was standing directly in front of Charlie now, in his usual Matt stance with his legs apart. The heated, intense gaze the Keating team all knew so well had Charlie captured squarely in its sight. "Your addiction is right here, waiting to talk to you again."

Charlie was about to hand the phone over when Jessie's small voice came over the line again. "Do you miss him at all around there? Around *Sacred Peace*?"

"Josh?" Charlie pondered wistfully into the phone as he studied Matt. In front of him, Matt blinked but otherwise held his cool at the mention of Josh. "Yeah, Jessie. I do. I miss him a lot, and not just around here. I miss my buddy."

"I guess that's good," she answered softly. "Thanks for that, Charlie."

"All right," he said. "Here's your guardian angel. I hope you'll talk to me again one of these days, kid."

"Talk," she bit off. "Not fight."

"Fair enough."

"I'll see ya, Charlie. Have a good night shoot." The melancholy in her voice was so thick Charlie wondered how she could breathe.

Matt talked with Jessie for another twenty minutes before she paused and straightened. The welcome rumble of the tractor's powerful engine could finally be discerned between the sharp cracks of the ice pellets hitting her window. "I should go," she said when, with undisguised relief, she heard the big machine rattle to a stop in the laneway outside. "Thanks for keeping me company, Matt. I'll see you in Vancouver soon, right? I'll be in need of a hug."

The line got quiet.

"We'll be careful, baby," she whispered, sensing Matt's reticence. "It's different now, with Josh and Shanda, with their trust. Hugs might be all we need."

"I can't," he confessed. "I can't be there."

"Can't?" she gulped. "Or you're not allowed to be?"

"Does it matter?"

"Oh fuck, Matt, really? Come on, baby. Kick up a stink."

"Jessie…"

"I know. Forget it. Shanda's not as liberal as my husband, apparently."

"Apparently."

"That sucks. Seriously? Fuck, Matt."

"Look, I love you, Jessie. That won't ever change."

"I thought we had this sorted out. Josh talked to Shanda. I haven't seen you in months and months, Matt. I just need a goddamn hug."

"We'll see each other again one of these days. I think Shanda figures the more time that passes, the easier it will be. Time…the ultimate healer, you know?"

"Tell her Josh and me are good. Tell her I just need hugs. That's all."

"I will." He forced a cheery note into his voice. "Maybe I'll surprise you, sweetheart."

"I sure hope so. Matt?"

"Hmm?"

"I love you back. So much."

"I know. I'll see you." Like a drug racing through a vein, the smile in his words zipped through the connection. Jessie's spirits lifted. They crashed the second she tapped the burner's 'end' icon. She craned her neck toward the heavy thud of Josh's footsteps on the outdoor steps.

Adrenaline was clearly winning the battle over Josh's fatigue when he landed in the master bedroom a few minutes later and started hauling off the gray hoodie he was wearing over his T-shirt. "All told, this one's the worst yet." He grinned at Jessie. "Snow, and now ice pellets starting. Messy driving out there. It's supposed to warm up and start to rain. I hope to God that means we'll be getting our power back. Are you frozen?" He tossed the hoodie on a chair in the corner. "What are you doing up, anyway? It's almost five in the morning."

Hopping over to the bed on one foot, Josh yanked down a sock so damp with sweat it was stuck to his skin. Balling it up, he arced it over the bed toward a clothes hamper in the corner. It missed, and landed dully on the floor. He ignored it. Bending over, Josh gave Jessie a quick kiss before he moved sideways and brushed his lips along Dylan's soft cheek.

"I can't sleep when you're out there. You know that. S'why you texted me, dork." Grabbing her script, Jessie tossed it onto the nightstand at her side of the bed, lay back, flipped onto her side and curled her body as tightly as she could around Dylan's lumpy body under the covers. He protested the interruption to his sleep with a little boy grunt. "Everybody's sleeping in hoodies and socks. Emily-Grace was reading to Micah so I left him in bed with her. We don't have enough extra blankets to go around."

Josh's eyes were on the script. "That what I think it is?" He leaned down and tucked the quilt around Jessie, using his fingers to poke it cozily in under her body.

Following his gaze, Jessie mussed up Josh's quilt tucking job by twisting around and locking her eyes on the screenplay she was reading before she called Calgary. "Yep," she said with just a little too much confidence. "Dee brought it."

"You serious about it?" Josh's fingers went to the button on his jeans. In a few quick motions, his zipper was down.

"C'mere, babe," Jessie said, reaching over her slumbering son to lay a hand against her husband's hip. "Lemme help you."

Josh took a step backward. "How serious are you about doing a film, Jessie? You've already got this recording gig coming up."

"Umm…"

"Look, this snow's getting to all of us. At the Food Mart in Kensington they're saying it's the most the island has had in decades. It's not the norm. We'll get ourselves to Halifax, fly south, and stow ourselves away in the Caribbean for a month if you need to get away."

"Can't do that," Jessie moaned, rolling her face into her pillow. "We can't leave William alone with all this snow."

"They've lived here for decades, Jessie. They'll be fine. Heck, we'll bring them with us if you want."

"Josh, by the time I finish the album, the snow will be gone." Another round of icy snow burst like shotgun pellets against the window. "Or not."

"Jessie…" Josh stilled. His jeans were hanging over his hips.

Jessie was fresh off her heated discussion with Charlie. The background noises of a happy, busy television crew swapping jokes and moving gear on the set of *Sacred Peace* were reverberating inside her head. She pulled the quilt tighter around her body. "This part you're playing, this Joe McIver thing."

Josh lifted a big paw and scratched an itch on his neck. "Not playing a part, Jessie. Just gettin' by."

"I swear, Josh, sometimes I think you think you're actually him." She was talking from behind Dylan's curls. Jessie's words came out muffled, afraid.

Josh shifted his balance. He lifted both hands to behind his head, elbows out to the sides, so he could interlace his fingers, lean back against his palms, tip his head back, and stare at the ceiling.

Jessie sat up. The quilt fell to the bed. "I'm not saying it's a bad thing, Josh. It's all well and good if it works for you, babe, but I am not, and nor will I ever be, Joe's wife Jasmyn. She's not a character I want to stay locked into. Her skin is not my skin." Clutching a handful of hair, Jessie said, "I can't stand this. I want my old stylist back."

Josh dropped his arms. His feet remained locked in place. "Anything else you want to complain about?"

"Depends." Jessie's bottom lip was quivering like a five year old's.

"If you're asking me, it's five o'clock in the morning and I'm beat, Jessie. You're frustrated. This isn't the best time to get into shit. Things will look better when the sun comes out again."

"Josh, please, I miss my old life. I need to be making music. I need to be playing parts that challenge me, with creatives like me who I feel are a part of my tribe. I miss the kind of discourse I had with those people. I miss the heart-beat of the cities I used to visit; hell, I miss the goddamned Noodle Box. Our kids don't have any friends here. They need friends, Josh, so they can learn to socialize with others. They need more than this island has to offer them."

"So much for me being tired, huh? Do you really want to get into this now?"

Something small and dark was on the bed behind Jessie. Josh reached for it. He held it up. "And who the hell did you call in the middle of the night?"

"*Sacred Peace* is night shooting." Jessie's voice was small and weary. She started threading her fingers together, the same way Emily-Grace always did when she was stressed. "I got scared in this stupid house with this stupid storm and with stupid you out playing in it."

Josh tossed the phone onto the bed. It bounced twice before landing right side up. "Look," he yawned, "we'll start the kids in school next fall. We'll get the boys into hockey. This is just the long winter talking. The blizzard. You'll feel better after you get some sleep."

Rounding the bed, he grabbed the screenplay and tossed it in a garbage can next to Jessie's nightstand. He waited to see how she would respond before he skirted the foot of the bed once more, scooped up his son, and carried him out into the hall and into David's bedroom, where the boys could both stay tucked under the warmth of an extra blanket. When Josh came back to the bedroom he shared with Jessie, she was standing by his side of the bed facing him, shivering profusely in the cool, unheated night, the script held high in one hand.

"This is a good part, Josh. This is one of the best I've read in a long, long time. Don't take this away from me."

Ever so slowly, Josh raised a hand and held up five fingers. "Five," he said. "Five kids. We're trying to get pregnant again, are we not? The kids we have are still young. This has been incredible, all this time with them. They're happy, happy kids, Jessie. Finally." Shifting his weight to his other foot, he added, "You can't keep your balance if you've got one foot in one world and one foot in another. Decide what it is you want. I'll support you, you know I will. Just as long as you know that if you go into that world again without me, to a place where I can't…" he gasped at the effort it took to say the next bit, "where I can't follow, that all our old crap will come right back to haunt us."

Reaching for the hem of his T-shirt, Josh hauled it up over his head. Almost instantly, he too started to shiver in the cold.

Jessie's eyes dropped to the bullet scar on his chest. Her shoulders sank. "I didn't want this, Josh. I didn't choose it. You did." With quivering fingertips, she traced the puckered skin.

"Little one…" Josh lifted her fingers and kissed them. At the same time, he took a step closer to his wife. "I don't want to be Joe McIver any more than I know you want to be Jasmyn. I'm not him. I'm still me. I'm still here."

Jessie's gaze flitted up to meet his sad basset hound eyes. "You don't want me to go because you can't. You made the ultimate choice, and so you have no choices left. You're scared you'll be left behind."

He didn't answer. He couldn't. Josh had just spent most of the night roaring through a snowstorm with the heat in the cab cranked up, working his fingers to the bone clearing snow from driveways. All through the long night he was sustained by country tunes pumping out from the radio speakers, just about as loud as he could stand them.

"Whaddaya think I was doing all night?" he asked in the somber Josh tone Jessie knew so well. The one that always broke her heart—the hurting one Josh usually tried to hide.

"Oh, babe," Jessie sighed, leaning into his body and wrapping her arms around his cool shoulders. She kissed his sore shoulder and closed her eyes at the sweet shiver he rewarded her with. "Trying to outrun the past, I suppose." She looked up at him. "Did it work, Josh?"

"Can't be done," he murmured. "It can't be done, Jessie."

There was nothing left to say. Jessie let the script in her hand fall to the ground. Desolate, she didn't resist when her husband lifted his big hand to her cheek and moved it backward to bury it in her hair. He brought her close to him and leaned his forehead against hers. "Beautiful girl," he whispered as he closed his eyes, "let's make that baby."

The wind was easing a little now; the house was shaking a little less. Dylan stayed asleep next to David while Josh brought his lips to his wife's and probed inside her mouth with his tongue, eliciting tiny mewls from her.

His hurried movements were no mystery to Jessie. They were a whole new attempt to outrun the things that hurt. This night when Josh pulsed inside her she wondered if their new baby would come nine months later, and she decided that Josh—and Charlie—were right.

*I'm foolish. It's just this gray, desolate weather. Vancouver will do me good. I'll feel better when my new album is in the can.*

The next day, the bad weather eased. The family went outside for some fresh air. The previous snowstorms had left soft fluffy snow that glistened in the sunlight. This newest snow was icy, with a crusty top. When the children forged through it they mainly found themselves walking on top; most of the snow was thick and crisp, but some broke into jagged bits underneath their snow boots. No snowmen could be built from this stuff, and no snow forts, either.

There were no more discussions about the film script. Josh had to take a step back and consider whether he was being selfish when he found the screenplay in the recycling a day later, but he shoved the notion aside. Jessie was quiet but she was functioning okay, and so the household moved forward once again.

The album was recorded in Vancouver without issue. Emily-Grace and Micah travelled with Jessie. Josh kept Dylan and David home for the two-week session. Jacob was a part of the recording, which felt like old times for Jessie, but Matt's absence was a hard thing to take. The UBC house was stale and lonely. Josh's Harley and King Ranch were there—the Mustang was stored at La Casa. The whole place felt like some sort of dusty, forgotten museum. Jessie and the kids stayed at La Casa, and only made a few visits to their old home.

Jessie forced herself to return to Prince Edward Island with as positive an attitude as she could muster. It was easier to take than she expected. The snow was finally abating, shrinking so that tufts of grass poked out here and there from underneath. Josh and the boys were happy to give up their brief bachelor lifestyle and have the women—and good-natured little Micah— back. Jessie sank into her new normal as best she could.

Eventually she took a day to drop into the nursing home. Josh had encouraged her all along to make occasional visits, which she did, saying that it was expected she would fly in to see her mother occasionally and not to worry about being followed since things seemed settled lately anyway, as far as Morgan went. Still, most times Jessie drove out to Clinton, she went in disguise.

Jessie had brought one secret home from Vancouver with her—the blog Charles, Charlie and Matt had been made aware of, the one citing issues with the staged plane crash. The crash had become, in recent weeks, a full blown conspiracy-based discussion. Josh stayed away from the papers and off the Internet. He remained blissfully unaware. Jessie wrote the whole thing off as entertainment for the masses.

It wasn't until late that summer that destiny took a hand and gave their lives a whole new twist. This time when change came, it was nobody's choosing but fate, and it all started with a little boy, a swing, and a small white dog named Fluffy.

*Chapter Twenty-four*

For Dylan's birthday, in early June Josh and William, with Jessie's help, installed a play set in the backyard. A slide, a rock wall, a sand play area, swings and a cedar framed roofed-in area killed a lot of time for the Sawyer kids, whose main entertainment was each other. Oddly enough, although the gift was meant for Dylan he was the child who used it the least. His preference was to either go riding with his father or crouch in the dirt and push small dinky cars and motorbikes around, making rrrrr-ing noises and dreaming of the day he'd have a motorbike like the one his father kept telling his mother he was going to get this summer.

Dylan had actually asked for a trampoline for his birthday. Jessie, to Josh's amused raised eyebrows, had vehemently stomped her foot and said no.

"Too many injuries," she told Josh. "I know you're all mister, like, action figure and all, and trampolines are supposed to be good for cardio, but I've heard too many sob stories about kids getting hurt and I don't want our kids part of those statistics."

"You're not thinking it through," Josh rebutted. He was just finishing up Micah's diaper change at the time. Lifting the little guy off his change table, Josh set him on the floor and lovingly ruffled Micah's straight chestnut hair. "You can suntan on it."

Micah took off. David and Dylan were on the floor of Emily-Grace's bedroom, decorating the rooms of a wooden dollhouse that Josh picked up at a garage sale over the weekend. Micah wanted in. A few seconds later, Josh and Jessie heard Dylan holler at him.

Jessie had a half full clothesbasket in her hands. When Josh started to put a few things away in Micah's room, Jessie headed toward the open doorway. "I've got a whole beach to suntan on. It's not the space that's the issue—it's the four rug rats always vying for my attention. Momma come see this, Momma let's build a castle."

Josh lit up. "And you love every second of it."

Stopping at the door, Jessie pinked up. "*Almost* every second. I'm not gonna lie. The occasional undisturbed novel, cooler and bag of barbecue chips to myself would not be unwelcome."

"So. No trampoline."

"Nope."

"Kinda sounds like a unilateral decision, Jessie." Josh's eyes were twinkling.

"Yep." She grinned adorably at him.

"We're supposed to present a united front."

"Harrumph. Since when?"

End of discussion. Jessie moved out of Josh's line of sight.

Chuckling to himself, Josh finished up what he was doing. Jessie dropped her basket outside Emily-Grace's room. Josh heard her say, "All right, do y'all remember the meaning of the word 'share?'" All these years later, it still astounded him that his wife could appear so normal, yet put the girl in diamonds and haute couture and she could dazzle millions without blinking an eye.

Quarantining himself in the living room with a computer that evening, Josh researched play sets. He found one online that he thought he could build with William's help and presto, a week later the kids had their new source of entertainment—one that garnered Jessie's approval.

In late July, the play set sat idle for days. Heavy rain dripped from every square inch of its kid-friendly beauty. Standing at the kitchen window watching rivers of water stream from the swings and puddle on the ground, Jessie was literally tearing her hair out.

"Josh," she cried when he padded into the kitchen to refill his coffee mug, "it's July! It's supposed to be summer! We've had fifteen straight days of cool gray weather and just about every one of those has had at least some rain. Would a little heat be too much to ask for? Like, would it be too much to ask for that yellow blob in the sky to make an appearance?"

Leaning back against the counter, Josh crossed his ankles and brought the warm mug to his lips for a sip. "I don't think it's the weather you mind so much," he decided. "You're a Vancouver girl. You can handle rain."

"Right on the money, Sherlock. I love our kids to pieces, but if I have to mediate one more fight between David and Dylan or try to get Emily-Grace off her electronics, I'm gonna lose my mind! The kids need to be outdoors."

"I'll take them out. It's just rain, they won't melt."

"Take Micah too, puh-leeze. He loves those red mud puddles. Let him get as dirty as he wants. I'll put him straight in the tub when he comes in."

"Working on a song, are we? You don't want to come outside with us?" There was an undercurrent to Josh's question. Last night, an earnest call had come in to Jessie from Deirdre. A new plan was afoot.

Josh didn't like it.

Now, Jessie threw up her hands. "Duh! Gotta do something constructive around here!"

Josh said something he knew would irritate the hell out of his wife. "Why don't you and Emily-Grace go do some crafts or something?"

"Seriously, Josh." Resting a hand on the counter next to him, Jessie curled a lip downward and fired him a withering look. "*You* do a craft with her." She held up two fingers. "Two weeks of this. I don't have a single craft left in me. No more paper and scissors and glittery sparkles and glue. I'm wearing that shit! I've been wearing it for days! There's glitter in my underwear. And in all honesty? I didn't have any crafts in me to start with! Crafts are Carlotta's gig, not mine."

"In your underwear?" Stepping forward, Josh reached sexily for the waist of his wife's denim shorts. "Can I see?" he purred.

"Oh. My. God. Really? Did you not hear a word I said? One track mind much, Josh?"

"Jessie. Think about this. You cannot use the words glitter and underwear in the same sentence and not think I'd wanna go exploring."

"Oh, Jesus. Make that five rug rats. Five kids, including my adorable man." Unable to help herself, Jessie grabbed Josh's mug from him and set it on the counter. "Soon to be six. We just need to keep practicing." Snuggling up to him, she lightly bit his bottom lip.

"Someone's hormonal," Josh joked. His groin tingled. "Up a hill, down a valley. In the same damn second."

"For the right reason, I hope. You and me make good babies."

A slow grin widened on Josh's face. "You might need to do some YouTube research. Find yourself a few more crafts to stick in your repertoire."

"Maybe." Jessie ran her tongue around his mouth. She could feel Josh's knees weaken and his body melt as he responded to her overtures. "Maybe we'll have a girl this time. Dylan exhausts me."

"You can't blame me for that," Josh goaded her. "Jacob's responsible for that part of Dylan. Micah's a breeze."

It took Jessie a second to spot the diabolical glint in her husband's eye. "Oh, that was low, Josh. Don't ever let Dylan hear you talk like that."

"Relax, Jessie." Josh wrapped his arms tighter around the shoulders he loved. "I didn't mean anything by it. You're hormonal as hell. I'm gonna pester the hell out of you today. I'm gonna drive you nuts every chance I get."

"Pester all you want, husband. Preferably in bed later." A few extended kisses later, and Jessie pushed her hubby away. She turned his shoulders toward the playroom. "Now go. I have work to do."

"I'll bet you do."

"Umm…" Jessie put a finger to her lips in a kind of cute but questioning way. "Who's hormonal?"

"I'm a man. I don't ride that roller coaster." With that succinct reply, Josh planted one last kiss on his wife's forehead and went off to gather the gang.

"Thank God for that." Frowning, Jessie pivoted around to start looking for coats and boots.

None of the kids were keen to go outside this morning. The drizzly, oppressive skies were getting to everyone, sapping all of them of energy. It just seemed easier to stay tucked inside when the outside air was cool and the inside of the house was dry.

In the end, Dylan was the final holdout.

"What's the matter, honey?" Jessie asked, kneeling before him, his raincoat in her hand. "Daddy's going down to see the horses. Alice probably has cookies or cinnamon rolls made."

"I want to stay with you." Sulking, Dylan touched his mother's shoulder with his finger. "You."

"Why? I'm just gonna play boring old songs."

"I wanna play music with you. Like Jacob does." Dylan rarely could bring himself to call Jacob anything other than Jacob. The whole double-daddy thing was still a mystery to his young mind.

"No, he doesn't," wise old Emily-Grace told her mother. She stuck a foot into a yellow rubber boot. "He just doesn't want to be where David is right now. David keeps picking on him."

"I do not!" protested the child under attack. "I can't help it if Dylan sucks at Mario Kart. He drives me crazy!"

Dylan stared at his boots, stuck out his chest and leaned into his mother.

Jessie tucked a finger under his chin and got him to look up at her. Sometimes his blue Jacob-eyes disarmed her completely. Now, they were damp. "You," she encouraged with a sad little smile, "will feel so much better when you see Rusty. If the rain stops, maybe you can go for a ride with Daddy." Leaning forward, she whispered conspiratorially, "You're way better at riding horses than David is, Dylan. And you'll be just as good as him at Mario Kart when you get a little older."

"I'm good at dwums too, Momma." Dylan's eyes were wide and luminescent. Even at his young age, music already offered confidence and gave him a good safe place to hide.

"Yes, sweetheart, you sure are. Now go for your walk with Daddy. I love you."

Josh rounded the corner with Micah in his arms. "Changed and spit shined," he announced. "Where's this guy's coat?"

After the last set of young footsteps faded down the outside steps, Jessie folded her arms across her chest and watched her family's backs grow smaller and smaller as they walked away from her. A serious guilt washed over her for desiring some time alone to work on a new song, especially with the knowledge that Josh was carrying a lot of the weight when it came to the kids. Last night in bed, they'd had another discussion about this new life they were living. It blew Jessie's mind when Josh tossed in the suggestion of moving back to Vancouver. She figured the out-of-the-blue suggestion was rooted in her earlier call with Dee. She figured right.

"Maybe the threat's over," he'd said. "Maybe we'd be okay."

"What? Why?" They had just made love. Jessie leveraged herself up on an elbow and stared at him with a mixture of incredulity and confusion. "Why now, Josh?"

"Because," he answered, drawing his finger down her arm and avoiding her searching gaze, "you just recorded an album. I've been thinking about that. I know what it means."

"What's it mean, Josh?" Her eyes narrowed. "You were eavesdropping on my phone call."

"Had to. Since I had a feeling you wouldn't choose to illuminate me on what all the oohs and ahhs were about." He tweaked her nose with his finger and dove in deeper. "It means, little one," he said, "that you and Dee are planning to tour the album. Am I right?"

"Busted." Jessie hung her head on crossed arms on his chest.

"And the thing is," Josh continued, "if you're going on tour, I want to be there with you. I want to stand in the wings and see my incredible wife mesmerize the world with her music."

"Bullshit," Jessie had responded with a tiny smile, crawling back on top of him for a cuddle. Lying down over his body, her knees on either side of his hips, she eased herself down carefully so as not to jar his hurt spots, and sighed into his neck. "You've got other motives."

He grew serious. Tracing her back, Josh said, "I'm cool with Matt, Jessie, to a point. Here and there, fine, steal some time together if that's what both of you need. It's just that 24/7 for six months is a whole other ball game."

"Plus the kids," Jessie added. "I can't take them with me and leave you behind. Or leave them behind and go without all of you, either."

"Or…"

"What?" Rubbing her nose and idly mumbling, "Itchy, that ugly rat's nest on your face," Jessie continued with, "I can't not tour this album, Josh, if that's what you're thinking. It's gonna happen. We'll just have to find a way to make it work. I already said I wouldn't do any films."

Josh grimaced. "For now, you mean."

She stuck her nose in his neck. Josh could feel her warm breath on his skin, reminding him that Jessie was here, was his, and that things were good.

A new ache ran up his body at the reminder of the offer he'd made her and Matt. That was before this new album was in the can. That was before Josh had any inkling at all that his wife might be, at some point, spending six months with the man.

"You're right about all this," he intoned quietly as Jessie's body stilled on his. "This is almost as much a prison as the one Morgan's in. Not P.E.I., not that part. There is a magical, laid-back quality about this place. Just the not being able to live our lives the way we want to. That part."

A small voice tickled his neck. "You still want to work, don't you, Josh?" Jessie raised her head and stole a lingering look at her man. His lips were turned down at the corners.

"We could try it. We could go and see what happens."

"Josh, babe, the second you appear in public, the world's gonna go off its axis. You'll be trending on Twitter and in every blog and Facebook post and Instagram picture. We will have zero privacy, the kids will be photographed and spied upon, and God only knows when Morgan's cronies will fire the next bullet! We'll be waiting and waiting and waiting like we were before for shit to go down. We can't live that way, babe. We can't."

"No matter how many times we have this discussion, no matter how many ways we twist and turn and try to manipulate it, it always comes out the same, Jessie. You get to work, and I stay in exile." Raising a palm, Josh held it outward toward her. "Don't tell me it was my choice. I don't need to hear that again from you."

Lifting her body higher and curling over his chest, Jessie pressed her lips to the wrinkled skin over Josh's lung. "I love you," she breathed. "So incredibly much. But babe, this is our life. I can't stay here day after day after day while you try to outrun our past with horses and snow blowers and now this new Harley you keep saying you're going to get. I can leave here. I can work."

"And play."

"Fuck, Josh." Rolling off of him, Jessie lay on her back and stared at the ceiling. "You're seriously pissing me off."

He raised himself up on an elbow and stared her down. "Look me in the eye and tell me you and Matt won't hook up the entire six months you're away if I'm not there, Jess. Can you do that?"

Her voice was small. Jessie started wringing her fingers and thumbs together. Fixating on the twined hands, she said, "N-nope. I guess I'm a sucker for love."

Josh froze. "What the hell's that supposed to mean?"

"You're a big boy. Figure it out." Throwing back the covers, Jessie slipped off the bed and headed to the washroom. She had the door slammed behind her before Josh could gather his wits—and his temper—enough to counter the not-so-ambiguous remark.

This morning, watching him outside with the kids, Jessie saw what she'd figured was coming all along. Slumped shoulders, a slow walk and, earlier at breakfast, restrained conversation and long looks out of the window.

"Signs." She sighed inwardly. "They're starting. The novelty's wearing off."

Black clouds overhead were descending on the Sawyer family once again. Josh was getting bored, and clueing in big time to the fact that his wife was nearing the end of her rope. Each time they had the conversation about work and their limited choices, she acquiesced and made concessions—record an album but skip the film, for instance. And each time, the cloud above them got darker. Today it seemed evenly spread, even dangling its foamy tentacles above the children, challenging their moods and causing some serious sibling rivalry rifts.

Only one of the Sawyers was at risk, however, of seriously crashing. Jessie could scream and maybe go to bed for a day and bury her head in frustration…the kids would fight…but Josh would go into Charlottetown and land on a stool at a bar. Not even Arnie had the power to stop Josh if and when he sank that low. No one did.

"You won't though, will you, babe?" Jessie asked his back now. Lifting her hands, she positioned her fingers into a fake camera and pretend-snapped a photo of her husband with all four of his children in tow. In their colorful raincoats and bright boots, the children were a cheery contrast for their restless, discouraged father.

                         ✎

When Josh and the kids wandered back an hour and a half later, Jessie was waiting for them. Guitar in hand, she trooped out to the kitchen and winked at Dylan.

"I've got a song for Daddy," she declared. A nervous flush spread across her cheeks. Adjusting the guitar over her shoulders, she dug a pick out of her shorts' pocket. Like a shy schoolgirl, she peered up at Josh from underneath long eyelashes and started to play.

"'Pink Houses'," Josh murmured to no one in particular at the familiar guitar hook she started with. The distinctive hook always got the eighties rock song on listeners' radars right from the get-go. "What are you trying to say, little girl?" Famously, John Mellencamp's catchy singalong tune was about the American dream or, more accurately, the corruption of it.

Crunching on his lip as he helped the kids take their coats and boots off, Josh listened to the song with a cute half grin that Jessie, watching him as she sang, wanted to swallow up. Emily-Grace grabbed Micah's arms and started dancing; even Dylan and David made friends long enough to cheer and toss in a few dance moves.

"What are you trying to tell me?" Josh asked Jessie when she brought the song to its close with a rousing final chord. "You saying that's what this is? Us, here? Some corrupted version of the American dream? Got news for you. We don't have a white picket fence."

"And thankfully," Jessie giggled, "we also don't have an interstate running through our front yard. I think Mellencamp is saying that a lot of people are living copycat lives in similar houses, but that they find comfort where they can. Like in trips south, or in whatever."

"In thrills and pills?"

"Hell, no. His lyrics, not mine, Josh. That's not what I meant."

Her sighy little girl look amused Josh more than the song.

"Play us another one, Momma." Emily-Grace tugged at Jessie's sleeve.

Jessie hitched up the guitar and ran the pick thoughtfully over her bottom lip. "Okay. One more. This one's for Daddy too. Bob Dylan this time, kids. Here's your musical education for the day."

Her loving baby blues got lost in her husband's soft expression. Josh was leaning against the wall now ducking his head and trying not to light up the whole room with how touched he was by his wife's impromptu private concert.

With an adoring smile, Jessie started into Dylan's poignant ballad *I Believe*

SUSAN RODGERS

*In You,* the tender song she and Josh slow danced to at Jacob and Kayla's wedding.

*They ask me how I feel*
*And if my love is real*
*And how I know I'll make it through*
*And they, they look at me and frown*
*They'd like to drive me from this town*
*They don't want me around*
*'Cause I believe in you*

*They show me to the door*
*They say don't come back no more*
*'Cause I don't be like they'd like me to*
*And I, I walk out on my own*
*A thousand miles from home*
*But I don't feel alone*
*'Cause I believe in you*

*I believe in you even through the tears and the laughter*
*I believe in you even though we be apart*
*I believe in you even on the morning after*
*Oh, when the dawn is nearing*
*Oh, when the night is disappearing*
*Oh, this feeling is still here in my heart*

*Don't let me drift too far*
*Keep me where you are*
*Where I will always be renewed*
*And that which you've given me today*
*Is worth more than I could pay*
*And no matter what they say*
*I believe in you*

*I believe in you when wintertime turns to summer*
*I believe in you when white turns to black*
*I believe in you even though I be outnumbered*
*Oh, though the earth may shake me*
*Oh, though my friends forsake me*
*Oh, even that couldn't make me go back*

*Don't let me change my heart*
*Keep me set apart*
*From all the plans they do pursue*
*And I, I don't mind the pain*
*Don't mind the driving rain*
*I know I will sustain*
*'Cause I believe in you*

*I could not love you more,* Jessie thought as she sang, moisture highlighting her lashes with a dewy shimmer.

Leaning against the wall, hands shoved into his pockets, long layered hair dripping still from the incessant rain, their spellbound children between himself and Jessie, Josh could have been a timid, bashful twelve year old.

*I could not love you more,* Josh thought as he listened. His breath caught in his throat. Standing there in front of him in jean shorts and a cotton patterned halter, bare toes turned bashfully inward, singing with the usual sweet, cocky, confident childlike allure she called forth for a lot of the old classics, Jessie could have been the same girl Josh fell in love with on the first season of *Drifters.*

The song's message brought both of them to their knees. *I believe in you no matter what.*

"I get it, Jessie," Josh said later, after the kids danced off to the playroom and he could take his wife in his arms in peace. "Every day I wonder how we got this far. How we've managed to make it through. So many things get in our way…so many things conspire against us."

"Love, Josh," she said, "that's how. Faith in each other that we'll always try to do the right thing. I'm sorry about everything I've ever done to hurt you. I'm sorry for not always making good choices. For not having the guts to go to you, to stand by you when things went haywire. For getting emotional when I should be calm. For complaining about stuff."

"Faith, huh? My girl and her faith. Maybe that's the ticket, Jessie. Maybe that's what'll get us out of this mess."

"Faith, Josh?" Jessie ran her fingers through his long, damp hair. "Faith is everything. Faith has gotten me through some pretty black times. Faith and prayer, babe. Heartfelt and sincere."

A wave of peace passed over her. By the look that flickered through Josh's eyes—a ripple of surprise followed by tiny pinpoints of light—Jessie intuited that Josh felt it too. "Whoa." She exhaled gladly. "That's gotta mean something."

"Faith," Josh said again. An easy nod of his head cemented it. "I believe I will work again. And that we will live in peace. How's that for faith?"

"I think that's good, Josh. I think we're good. We can relax and let the universe work in its own creative way. We've done enough worrying. It's time to kick back and just trust God or the universe or whatever energy's out there looking out for us, that has brought us this far." She lit up at the carefree glow that washed over her husband. "Now," Jessie poked him in the ribs, "I took out some chicken. How about a big old pot of Emily Wheeler's famous chicken soup for dinner?"

"Whatcha need me to cut up?"

"It's under control. One thing I have been forced to learn in my Jasmyn McIver incarnation is how to be a better cook. Go keep an eye on Micah before David and Dylan corrupt him. Or before he starts chewing on a piece of Lego."

"I'll toss him in the tub. Did you see that kid? He was up to his knees in mud."

"Throw Fluffy in with him," Jessie laughed. "Kidding. I wonder how Emily-Grace likes having a dog dyed with good ole Prince Edward Island red dirt. Do you think this rain will ever end?"

One more kiss and Josh slipped away to be the stay-at-home dad his kids cherished. In the kitchen, Jessie pulled out a cutting board, knife and veggies, and went to work with a smile.

Chapter Twenty-five

Gleeful pockets of sunshine dotted the sky over the bay the next day, parceling misty rays of welcome heated light through tears in thick, cotton clouds. Problem was, the shrinking of the gray skies happened slowly, like quilt batting being pulled apart, which meant Micah's beloved puddles were left behind to dry up in bits and pieces. They shrank up the way marshmallows do when they're dropped into a campfire, only much slower, with no sizzle and with no apparent visible destruction notable by the naked eye.

They were sinister that way, puddles left over after a rain—conspicuous only in open areas, like on the lane on the way down to William and Alice's place. Like sheets of black ice in winter, invisible patches of moisture stuck around for the first few days after the two weeks of frequent rain. The more ominous puddles melded underneath blades of lush green grass where children in summer sneakers or flip-flops ran through them without noticing, until their mothers and fathers halfheartedly scolded them at bath time for how dirty they managed to get during the day.

The Sawyer children were no exception. Josh and Jessie both cautioned their kids to watch out for puddles since the lane across the road was rife with them, although their warnings were more about trying to keep the kids clean than anything else. Josh was a little more cautious in his counsel. He took Dylan riding but made sure to lead the small horse to a dry area of the field, "just in case," he told his son. Over years of riding, Josh had fallen prey to more than one horse that slipped on wet ground.

One morning a few days after the last rain, Jessie let Fluffy out without his leash so the little ball of fur could romp around the yard with the children before Emily-Grace and David took off for the day. The older two Sawyer kids were about to jump into Josh's truck for a run into Charlottetown with their father. Rolling her eyes at Josh when he called the two to get them settled in the truck, Jessie pleaded for him not to come home towing a Harley.

"Out of respect for William and Alice," she cautioned. "Their son, Jeffery. And for me. I don't need to be worrying about you out on these little country roads, Josh. They're full of slow moving farm vehicles and anxious, impatient tourists."

"Like hell," Josh grunted, reaching out to give Emily-Grace a hand climbing up into the back seat. "You wanna cut my balls off too?" He grabbed the seat belt and pulled it securely down over his daughter's lap. "I feel the need for speed, Jessie. I need the wind in my hair. I need freedom."

She nudged an elbow toward the Ford. "Roll down your damn window if you want wind. Don't you dare go buy yourself another Harley, Josh Sawyer. Not here, not now."

"I'll get you one too," he tried. "A light little Sportster with all the trimmings. Saddle bags. Chrome. What color do you want?"

"Josh, don't you—"

Exasperated, Josh made a throaty grunting sound and avoided her eyes.

Watching, Dylan was fuming. He grabbed the bottom hem of his father's T-shirt and gave it a tug. "Why can't I go too?"

Bending to his level, Josh loosened his son's fingers from the hem.

Coming up behind Dylan, Jessie took hold of his biceps. At her touch, he writhed and kicked until she had to forcibly hold him back by wrapping her arms securely around his bony shoulders. "Divide and conquer," she told him in a voice loud enough to be heard over his wails. "Daddy needs Emily-Grace to bat her big blue momma-eyes at him to keep him from buying that big motorbike he wants, and he needs big strong David to help carry groceries into Arnie's place since Arnie will be back from a trip to Ontario tonight and we promised him fresh orange juice and eggs when he got back."

"What Daddy doesn't need," Josh said, scooping Dylan up in his arms to give Jessie a reprieve, "is to worry about my little guy here running off in the grocery store parking lot like he did last week, and almost getting hit by a car. You can come with me next time, Dylan, you and Micah. For today,

I need you to be big and tough and strong so you can keep an eye on Momma and on your baby brother. Momma's feeling a little queasy today. She needs your help."

Leaning over, a calmer Dylan in his arms, Josh brushed his lips against Jessie's. "I'll bring you some of those crackers you like, little one."

Jessie was glowing. "Could be a false alarm, Josh. Mighta just been the mussels we steamed last night."

"Nah. It's all that sex," he grinned.

Jessie yelped happily and covered Dylan's ears. "We'll see, babe. Don't get excited yet. I love you."

Dylan laid his head on his father's big shoulder. "Daddddyyyy," he moaned.

"Oh my heart," Jessie lamented, laying a hand over where she figured her heart was in her chest. "That's a tragic sound if ever I've heard one." She reached for Dylan, but Josh set him on his feet instead.

"No lifting for you today," he ordered. "Not until we know for sure. And then maybe not for eight months or so. Or seven. Whatever. Sawyer kids like to make early entrances into this crazy world."

That did it. Dylan threw himself on the ground and exploded into a full-blown tantrum. Arms and legs flailed everywhere.

Jessie raised her eyebrows in amusement and took a step backward. "Well, then." She mulled over how she thought the next few hours might go. "Josh? Wanna trade places for the day?"

"As if." He chuckled.

"You're going to see that bike. You bastard."

"Can't hurt to look." Lifting his fingers to his lips, he kissed the tips and laid them on his wife's belly. Losing himself in the haunting pale blue of her eyes, he whispered, "Sure you want more kids?"

At his feet, Dylan was outright howling. Nearby, tottering around behind a white butterfly, Micah stopped and widened his soft chocolate Sawyer eyes.

"Crap." Jessie noticed him watching, and sighed. "You're not doing a very good job of that role model thing, Dylan," she muttered. To Josh, she said, "Go. We'll be fine. I'll see you soon. Text me when you leave town so I know when to have dinner ready." She hollered to Emily-Grace and David, "Be good for Daddy. Have a fun day."

"Quite the little wifey," Josh returned with a wink. "If you go out on tour you'll lose all your new domestic engineering skills."

"Grrr. Like it'll be so hard to eat gourmet salads again instead of peanut butter and jam sandwiches. Go. Love you. Drive safe. Precious cargo."

There it was—the one moment that always reared its nasty head when Josh and Jessie were about to be separated. Like a bony skeleton hanging from a hook in a Halloween display window, thin and sinister and ghastly, a troubled pause danced between them.

Josh's lips moved as if he wanted to say something, but he bent for another kiss instead. This one was long and lingering.

"I hate this," he heard Jessie murmur. "I won't do that tour, Josh. I don't ever want to be away from you or the kids again. I like peanut butter. Really. As long as it's smooth and not that crunchy stuff you like."

The kiss moved up her cheek and landed at the corner of one eye. A heavy sigh preceded the moment the moistness of Josh's mouth disappeared from Jessie's skin. Turning, he said to Dylan, "Down, tiger. Go easy on Momma."

"Love love love you," Jessie said to his back.

Ambling toward the truck, Josh's shoulders slumped. Dark memories tried to latch their creepy hooks into his spirit. It was a sunny day, finally. Josh roused up a heavenly vision of the Harley shop, and pushed the bad stuff away.

Shortly, the truck cruised up Sutherland Road away from Jessie and the two youngest children. Dylan had Jacob's pouty, stubborn streak in him. He didn't settle for a good ten minutes. Having been schooled by her little guy pretty much from the time he was two, Jessie was astute enough to give him his space. Puttering around her flowerbeds with Micah, she yanked at stalks Alice had identified as weeds. "Moody musician," she reckoned as she worked, eyeing cranky, sulking Dylan over her shoulder. "Jacob's kid. Figures."

A while later, a vibrating white body at her side got her attention. By now Dylan was wandering around in circles staring aimlessly at the ground, inconsolable at the audacity of his precious father to leave him behind. Jessie had tried talking to Dylan but he just got mad at her, so she covertly followed his movements instead and waited for a moment she knew, from experience, would soon come—when Dylan would deflate and drop into her lap for a hug and a cuddle.

"Fluffy! How's the wild, free life?" Sitting back on her haunches, Jessie picked up the dog's small, writhing body and gave it a good scratch behind the ears. Glancing toward the general area of the new play set, her eyes followed Dylan, who was making his way to a yellow swing.

Dylan dropped his despondent frame into the curved seat and wiggled his butt backward to get more comfortable. After a dejected look back to his momma to make sure she was taking in his sorrow, he used his right foot to push himself until he got a good swinging rhythm going, back and forth and back and forth.

Dylan rarely used the play set. A little jump in Jessie's heart saddened her at the idea that he was likely just hanging out there in order to feel closer to his older brother and sister. A jarring noise from inside the house jolted her out of endless self-reprimands. Taking on Dylan's sadness was only serving to make her miss Josh and her two oldest children more as well.

The burner phone was ringing. Leaping up, Jessie grabbed Micah, skipped two of the kitchen door's steps at a time on her way up, and headed for the phone, which they left, for convenience, in an open cupboard next to the dinner plates. Lifting the phone to her ear, she kept one eye on Dylan. Through the kitchen window over the sink on the north side of the house, she could see him plain as day. Fluffy, alone now except for Dylan, started running around underneath the little boy's swinging feet.

"Hey," Jessie said into the phone, unsure whose voice to expect on the other end.

Charlie's warm timbre greeted her. "Hey yourself," he said amiably. He was chewing on something. A low crunching sound came through the line.

"Okay, that's annoying," Jessie scolded. Over the phone the muffled chomping was rather revolting. "You sound like the squirrel that got inside our walls last fall. Either swallow or spit it out."

"Annnddddd we're off to a good start." Lately Charlie and Jessie's friendship was a half and half kind of thing—half fighting, half reasonable conversing.

"Sulk wart. Early there, isn't it? What are you doing up?" Adjusting Micah on one hip, Jessie removed the phone from her ear long enough to knock on the window to get Dylan's attention. Outside, he was swinging higher and higher. Underfoot, trotting back and forth with her tiny pink tongue lolling out, Fluffy seemed to be treating the flying legs as a game. Dylan looked over at the kitchen window. *Too high*, Jessie mouthed to him. He stuck out his tongue and pumped harder.

"Ouch, that was loud," came from Alberta.

"Sorry, Charlie," Jessie said into the phone. "I just needed to get Dylan's attention. He's outside and I'm inside. So what's up?"

"Not much. It's early, yep. Couldn't sleep so I got up and toasted a bagel that apparently I am only allowed to stare wistfully at since chewing is no longer an option." In curious wonder, his voice went down a notch. "I heard that my favorite singer is going on tour. I'm not ashamed to admit that the news got me a little excited, despite concerns I've mentioned in the past and so won't repeat at the risk of coming across as insensitive or selfish."

"Insensitive? The famous Charlie Deacon?"

"Is that a dig? I know a dig when I hear one."

"Dig shmig. You're the king of digs. Look, I wouldn't book my tickets yet if I were you. I'm having second thoughts. I won't bother telling you that you've likely been right all along. Although I think I just did." Biting her lip, Jessie unlocked the window, pushed it open and gave it another good rap. "Dylan," she called through the open screen, "that's high enough, honey!"

Dylan looked over at the window a second time. Screwing his mouth into a determined frown, he pumped his legs harder.

"Oh, that kid," Jessie groaned. "How'm I gonna get through his rebellious teen years, Charlie? He's an obstinate little bugger. I swear he just narrowed his eyes at me! In kid speak I'm pretty sure he just gave me the finger."

"What's he doing out there?" Charlie dropped into a stool at his Calgary condo's kitchen island. Using his thumb and forefinger, he rotated the second half of his uneaten bagel around and around on a plate.

"He's on the swings. He's mad because Josh went to town with Emily-Grace and David and left Dylan here with me and Micah. And Fluffy. That damn dog drives me insane. I'm always tripping over it. Good thing it's cute."

Micah heard his name. He reached for the phone. "Hey Charlie, Micah wants to say hi."

"Awesome. Put him on."

Jessie was just holding the phone to Micah's ear when, out of the corner of her eye, she noticed Dylan tightening his hands on the swing's ropes. He seemed to be picking out a spot on the ground to focus on. At the same time he pumped harder and sucked in a breath.

"I know that look," Charlie heard her mutter from the distance, since the phone was at Micah's ear. "I've seen David do that a thousand times. He's gonna jump."

Jessie was only a little nervous. Like Josh, and not at all like pouty Jacob, Dylan was the master of climbing and jumping and all things adventurous. Apart from his raw emotional breakdowns and the occasional tantrums that still rocked the Sawyer household as he grew older, he had a lot of Josh in him. Not genetics, obviously, but certainly there were some aspects of Josh that Dylan seemed to somehow draw into his being by osmosis. Adventure was one. Recklessness and a need for speed—adrenaline rushes—were two more.

His mother closed her eyes, said a silent prayer, and let her eyes flutter open on time to see—almost in slow motion, it seemed—Dylan's fingers letting go of the ropes.

The second before his little boy body hit the ground, the dog darted out in front of him. Dylan cried out. Landing on Emily-Grace's beloved pet was not an option. Thrusting out his right leg, Dylan went sliding through one of the almost invisible shallow puddles left over from all the rain. The leg wrenched horribly; reddish water sprayed up on both sides of it as Dylan skittered sideways through the mud.

Jessie heard the crack through the open window.

Shrieking, she grabbed the phone from her youngest. "Charlie," she screamed into it, "I gotta go! I'm hoping I'm wrong, but I think Dylan just had a very bad landing!"

In Calgary, at the fear in Jessie's voice, Charlie lurched into efficient super-producer mode. Adrenaline ripped through his veins, calming him in what seemed like a warped but highly capable way. Over the years he'd learned to be the kind of guy who mostly rode waves instead of the one who got sucked under them. "Stay on the phone!" he hollered back to her. "Don't hang up!"

"Fuuccckkk," Jessie cursed. "I better be wrong." Running down the steps, she bolted around the side of the house.

She found Dylan lying on his back on the grass, raised up on his elbows staring oddly at his leg while the annoying Fluffy reared and yipped around him, licking his face and vying for his attention.

"Oh, Jesus," Jessie moaned. Micah was whining, trying to get the phone back. Jessie twisted to one side to haul it out of his reach. Bending down by Dylan, she set Micah on the grass and dropped the phone down next to him.

"Oh, Jesus," Charlie heard again in a distant voice, more desperate this time. "Dylan, sweetheart, don't move." Jessie's voice was a forced hushed mix of terror and worry. "Momma's got this. We're all good here."

"Jessie!" Charlie called. He was standing in the center of his Calgary living room now, and starting to pace. "Jessie! What's going on? How bad is it?"

Shock rushed over Jessie like a tidal wave. Moving her shaking hands over Dylan in a dazed attempt to figure out where she could touch him, how she could move him, in the far off reaches of her mind she could hear Charlie's tiny voice. It took her a few minutes to comprehend that it was coming from the dropped phone, which Micah had now picked up. Grabbing it from his small fingers started a whole new round of angry high-pitched wails, but Jessie ignored him.

"Charlie," she gasped, aware that the more frightened she sounded, the more terrified Dylan would be, "Dylan's broken his leg." A few sobs snuck through anyway. "Josh is gone and I've got my hands full with Micah. I have to…I have to go, I need to call an ambulance, I think. Yes, I do, I can't, I can't move him."

Small moans were starting to come from Dylan. He was still staring at his leg. It was summer; he was wearing shorts. Blood oozed from an open cut part-way down his calf.

Jessie was ready to throw up. "His leg is bleeding, Charlie. I think… oh, Jesus…there's bone there. I seriously need to hang up! Call Josh for me and tell him to get his ass home. No—to the hospital. Tell him to go to the hospital."

The second after she said it, Jessie sank back onto her haunches and closed her eyes for one brief second. Could Josh dare go to the hospital? With Jessie, Dylan and the other three children close by, Josh could be recognized. Hell, they all could, in an emergency situation that would require close scrutiny.

Hanging out at emerge would be nothing like chilling at the mall, where people buzzed around like bees doing their own thing, lost in their own private worlds.

Charlie seemed to have realized that too, because he sucked in a big gulping breath. "Jess," he said in his TV producer 'I-mean-business' voice, "you have an iPhone. Leave me on this phone and go grab the iPhone. Call 911."

"Charlie, I'm hanging up. I've got Micah in one hand and this damn annoying dog jumping all over Dylan and," Jessie was crying now, which broke Charlie's heart and just made him more worried, "Dylan's throwing up, I gotta go. Call Josh, please."

The line went dead.

"J-Jesus Christ," Charlie sputtered. He was on a burner phone he'd swiped from Matt the evening before, but even if he called emergency services in Prince Edward Island he had no clue what Jessie's actual street address was. Far as he knew it was Hicktown, P.E.I, period. He pictured himself calling and saying, 'yeah, well, it's by a beach.' The whole goddamned province was lined with beaches. "Hold it together, girl," he prayed on Jessie's behalf. "You can do this."

Two minutes later he was at Shanda's door, banging on it with a fist and shouting loud enough to send more than one curious neighbor to his or her door. He was literally quaking when Matt, blinking himself awake, threw open the door.

Matt zipped up his jeans and stared Charlie down.

Always, the tough drama in their lives—for the most part, anyway—seemed to involve Jessie. Matt's gaze darted down to the burner phone in Charlie's hand. He was scared to ask—so he didn't. Paling, blood rushing so fast to his head that he had to square his stance for stability, he tensed his body and waited for Charlie to unleash a new terror.

"D-Dylan," Charlie stammered. "He'll be okay, I think, but Matt—Jessie thinks he broke his leg." Charlie's words were spilling out like a river, tumbling over each other like water over stones. He shoved a palm up to his forehead and wiped sweat off his brow. "Jessie's alone with Dylan and Micah. Josh isn't home, he's got the older two, and—"

Throwing open the door, Matt did a quick about-face and headed into the condo's living room. Charlie followed. Shanda was up now too, her face lined with concern about the jarring wake-up call. With an air of caution she made her way slowly into the room.

Charlie was trembling so hard he could barely speak. "Sh-she's alone, Matt," he said again. "Fuck, I hate this! I fucking hate it! Shit's gonna hit the fan when she gets to the hospital. This is Dylan we're talking about. And Josh will lose it."

Matt whipped back around to Charlie. "When'd this happen?" he barked, reaching for the phone dangling from Charlie's sweaty fingers. He hit redial.

"While I was on the phone with her a few minutes ago. I think Dylan jumped from a swing."

"Who you calling?" Ignoring Charlie, Shanda stopped in front of Matt. She grabbed his elbow. "Josh? Or Jessie?"

Shaking her off, Matt gave her a hard look. She withered under it. This was not the time to be handing out judgment on close ties with Jessie. Regardless, Matt chose not to answer her and instead listened to the phone ring on forever.

"Dylan was throwing up. She's either dealing with that or she's talking to 911." Charlie put his hands on his hips and turned in a small circle. "Give her a few minutes."

Matt punched in a second call. This one was to his old RCMP buddy enlisted to help in case of emergency. As far as Matt was concerned, this qualified.

In Prince Edward Island, Jessie was growing frantic. Dylan was clutching at her hand now, crying and trying to move. It was a warm sunny day, finally; the clouds were clearing more and more, letting patchy sunlight filter through, so Jessie wasn't overly concerned about Dylan growing too cold. The thing was, though, the grass underneath him was damp and still dewy. Then there was that ugly muddy puddle to consider, so Jessie ran inside the house and grabbed a handful of coats from the mudroom. While she was running she decided she'd better call William and Alice—then it hit her that she had no clue what their number was. The couple was on speed dial on her iPhone, but that phone was charging upstairs in the bedroom and Jessie had no interest in leaving Dylan alone for too long—and Micah too, she'd left him outdoors for this quick jaunt to the mudroom. William and Alice would come running when the ambulance tore down the road, anyway.

"Dylan," she instructed when she slip-landed back at his side, "Momma's just gonna put these coats under you so you don't get a chill, baby. I'll be gentle, I swear. Close your eyes. Rest until help comes, okay? Nice people are on their way to come and help us."

The cut on Dylan's leg from where the bone was peeking through was oozing more blood. *What do I do, what do I do?* Jessie sobbed inwardly. A feeling of helplessness overwhelmed her.

A ring cut into her thoughts. The phone. It was in Micah's curious hands again. She grabbed it, quaking so hard she dropped it twice before she was able to get a good enough grip to answer it.

"Charlie?" she cried over Micah's vociferous protests. "I don't know what to do! It's bleeding a fair bit now." She'd had the forethought to turn away from Dylan when she said that.

"It's Matt, sweetheart," came a tender, loving voice from across the country.

Bending over her knees, Jessie laid her forehead on the ground and sobbed with relief. "Matt. Oh, God. Thank you, God." Matt, always Jessie's rock in a storm—until a time when he, too, was at the mercy of a roiling tempest—was on the line. The firm timbre to his tone now was exactly what Jessie needed to help her navigate this new Sawyer challenge.

"I don't know what to do," she sobbed when she got partial control of herself again, deciding right then and there that she would be nice to Charlie from now on for putting her guardian angel on the phone. "Did Charlie tell you? Dylan broke his leg."

"He told me." In Calgary, Matt sank down onto the couch and hung his head.

"It's bleeding, Matt. The ambulance is at least a half hour away. I put… I put coats under him. The grass is cold, and it's still wet—all that goddamned rain—I'm so fucking tired of rain—"

"Tell me what you're seeing, Jessie," Matt urged, cutting her off. "What's the leg look like? Is it straight?" He was about ready to puke too—his stomach was reeling—but as always, Matt had a role to play when it came to Jessie.

And he played it well. Shanda was watching, and so was Charlie, but Matt didn't give a shit. Jessie needed understanding, patience and a sweet lot of sensitivity right now. This next half hour was not going to go down well in the Keating/Sawyer history books.

"The bone," Jessie responded in a taut, scared tone. Adrenaline had kicked in, giving her the wherewithal to settle down enough to answer Matt. His sweet voice helped too; Matt was a tonic when it came to managing Jessie and her trials. "I can see it. But the leg is straight, for the most part."

Matt melted when he heard Jessie say to Dylan in the next breath, "It's Matt, honey. Matt's on the phone. See? We're okay now. Matt's taking care of us. We're just fine. Don't try to move, Dylan. Stay still."

Calm as he could muster, Matt released a pent-up breath and started issuing instructions. "This is what I want you to do, sweetheart. Go inside and grab some of those big towels for the beach that I bet you've got lying around. Roll them up and lay them next to Dylan's leg, on either side. Do you have some rope, Jessie, or, I don't know, clothesline or something like that handy? Or even a long, thin towel, something you can wrap around his leg and the towels to keep the leg immobilized? Saran wrap might even work."

"I don't know, I—I'll look. Momma will be right back, Dylan. One minute." Scooping Micah up in one arm, worried that he might land on his brother's leg, Jessie bolted for the house again. Inside she grabbed towels and a roll of twine Josh had used for some household repair and left in a tool kit inside the mudroom. At the last second she remembered to snatch a carpenter's retractable blade from the toolbox. Back outside she said into the phone, "I don't want to set the phone down, Matt. I can't lose this connection."

"If we get disconnected, I'll call you right back, sweetheart. You're doing great, Jessie. You're doing all the right things."

"Jesus, Matt, his eyes are rolling back in his head. Maybe he's hurt worse than just his leg!"

Matt's frantic, brisk look up to Charlie gutted both guys. Matt gritted his teeth so hard they crunched. "He's likely gone into shock, Jessie. My guess is he's just passing out on you, which isn't necessarily a bad thing if he's in pain. Keep him warm and monitor his breathing. Have you called Josh?"

"N-no, I can't call him. Jesus, Matt! He'll freak! I'll freak!"

In Calgary, Matt said sharply, "Charlie. Call Josh." After spouting off the phone number, which he'd memorized so nobody could 'accidentally' stumble upon it, he said to Shanda, "Grab a new burner phone for Charlie." To Jessie he said, "Where's Josh now?"

A quiet sniffle reached his ears. "On his way to Charlottetown. He's likely just about there."

"And Arnie's still away."

"He's on his way home from Ontario today. Driving. He won't get home til sometime tonight."

"What's Dylan doing now?"

"He's out cold. Jesus! Where's that goddamned ambulance? Matt, I'm laying the phone down so I can arrange these towels, but don't hang up, baby, please. Don't hang up on me."

"I'm not going anywhere, sweetheart. You're stuck with me."

Jessie almost collapsed at those simple words. "God, I wish you were here," she wept. "This really sucks."

*I woulda been. That was supposed to be our house...I wouldn't have gone to Charlottetown and left you alone...if I had you, I would never leave you...*

Dropping his head so low that he seemed about to pass out himself, Matt almost cried from the futility of it all.

Across from him, Charlie was pacing. Josh wasn't answering his phone. Charlie threw up his hands in frustration. Shanda touched his arm and tiptoed into the tiny kitchen to put a pot of coffee on.

"All right, kid," Matt rallied. Lifting his chin, he focused an eye on Shanda and resisted the urge to speak to Jessie in an even more tender tone. "Let's take this opportunity to talk about what you can expect when you get to the hospital."

"I know what to expect," Jessie sighed. "I'll be holding my breath the whole time hoping Dylan's okay and that Josh doesn't drive like a bat out of hell to get there when he finds out."

"Josh and Dylan will both be fine. My RCMP colleague is aware. He's on alert if you have any issues. He's a tall guy with salt and pepper hair, very friendly, efficient—you'll like him. You have his number. Don't hesitate to call him if you need him."

"Okay, so nobody will wonder why the hell we're being shadowed by the police if we call him in. Duh. We'll be all right. No need to go there."

"Jessie." Matt's all-business voice was a warning. *Easy does it.* He and Charles were pretty much the only people Jessie ever listened to that way. Even so, it was hard for him to step on her like that since regular sniffles were still sneaking through the line. He laid his head in his free hand and rubbed his forehead so hard that Charlie, watching, thought he might rub the skin right off. "If you end up calling him, my old pal will not be in uniform," he told his girl. "And he will be your uncle. Dylan doesn't have to know him. He can be an uncle you rarely see."

"Ok. Thank you. Fine." More hiccupy sobs.

"His name's Al. He can be there to keep an eye on things, period. Just as a precaution, sweetheart."

Jessie wasn't listening. Dylan was rolling his head from side to side and moaning, the dog was vying for her attention, and Micah was whining and trying to climb into her lap. "Micah, not now, honey!" she cried, not bothering to move the phone away from her lips. "Shouldn't I get him some Tylenol or something? He's coming to, Matt!"

"A little children's Tylenol wouldn't hurt if you have some close by."

"I have some in the kitchen."

"Jessie, grab a bag of frozen peas or corn or something too, and wet a clean facecloth or towel. You can lay those on Dylan's leg to help keep the swelling down. Not on the open wound, just above or under it."

"Okay, baby. I'm going."

Twenty minutes later the ambulance finally came screaming down Sutherland Road. By then Matt had also encouraged Jessie to take an extra precaution and grab a ball cap to pull down low over her head. Terrified to leave Dylan alone with the EMTs for fear he would say something he shouldn't, she was loathe to run upstairs and grab her phone but she needed things for Micah anyway so she had no choice. By then, Charlie still had not reached Josh.

"What the fuck is he doing?" Matt uttered under his breath to Charlie, his palm firmly over the mouthpiece of the phone he was talking to Jessie on.

Charlie got the gist of what he was saying. He felt like throwing his phone across the room in frustration.

"Okay," Jessie finally said to Matt. "They've given him some more serious pain meds and they're loading him into the ambulance. William and Alice are here now. They've offered to keep Micah but I can't make myself leave him, Matt. Dylan's comfortable with William. He's like a grandfather to our kids, especially to Dylan because of the horses. He's gonna go in the ambulance and I'll follow in the van with Micah. Alice will stay here in case Josh comes back. Did you guys reach him?"

Matt paused. "Not yet."

"Seriously? What the fuck, Matt?"

"Any idea where he was going?"

"Groceries, uh, and likely the pet store cuz the kids love it there. I dunno exactly where he was going, when. Oh, Jesus. Yes, I do. Call the fucking Harley dealership. It's on the way into town. That's exactly where my asshole husband is. Fuck, Josh."

"We'll get a hold of him. I'm going to ask him to bring the kids home and stay put, Jessie. You can handle this."

"He's Joe McIver, Matt. A.K.A. an Oscar-winning actor. He's been out and about lots without any trouble, without anyone clueing in. The beard, remember? And he never looks anyone in the eye. I need him with me!"

Matt got quiet. "No. You don't."

Jessie stopped walking. She held the phone away from her ear and stared at it. "Bastard," she said after a minute. "No words, Matt."

"Don't read more into this than is necessary, Jessie," he replied darkly. "Josh is better off at home where nobody can eyeball him too closely. He won't blend in when he's surrounded by emergency care workers, and neither will you. The two of you together in that kind of environment, especially with any or all of your children, is risky."

"Humph," she snorted into the phone. "Fine. I'll call you as soon as I know anything, Matt. And baby…thank you. As always. Always always always."

"I love you," he choked, unable to look at his wife when the words snuck out. In the kitchen, Shanda crumbled. Catching her eye, Charlie shrugged sympathetically.

"I love you back. So much. Talk soon, Matt."

Matt didn't say a word when he disconnected the call. He stared at the phone in his hands until he got his wits in gear. Two minutes later he did an iPad Google search for the number of the Harley dealer in Charlottetown. Shortly he had a panicked Josh on the burner phone.

"Jessie?" Josh asked, breathless, when he took the call. He was on a salesman's phone after having been hastily beckoned by a store employee. The urgency of a call coming in for him at the dealer's shook him to the core.

"It's Matt," he heard. In Calgary, Charlie and Shanda stilled, and listened. "Thought it was Jasmyn in those parts."

"Matt? What the—" Confused, Josh rifled long fingers through his hippy locks and rotated around to spy his kids lounging around a shiny blue and white Harley Sportster in the showroom just behind him. There wasn't anybody else within hearing distance—the sales staff was busy with other customers. "It's Jessie when some frazzled employee comes running over to tell me there's an urgent call for me," he explained, biting off the words.

"Wouldn't have been so urgent if you'd answered your damn cell phone."

"What? I left it in the truck. What the hell's going on, Matt? I can't see my wife being so desperate to reach me that she'd be asking you to call me!"

"You left it in your truck? That's convenient. Your kids'd rat you out at home about the Harley anyway, Josh."

"Is me getting a bike really your business, you sunuvabitch? Why the hell are you calling me here?"

"Listen up, *Joe*." Matt emphasized the *Joe*, and got down to business. "Dylan had an accident. Don't hit the panic button, he'll be fine, but—"

"What kind of accident?!" In Josh's experience, panic buttons were far too easy to come by. Hell, he had a whole storeroom of them filed away in his brain, in all sorts of funky colors. His voice went up about ten notches. "Why isn't Jessie calling me?"

"She's getting Micah settled into his car seat and then she'll be behind the wheel, that's why. Dylan jumped off a swing and had a bad landing. Looks like a broken leg."

The groan that came over the line from P.E.I. to Calgary was hard to take. Matt sank lower into the couch and stared at his bare toes. "Take the kids home and wait for news."

"What? Like hell. Not happening. We're heading to the hospital. Which hospital? Summerside or Charlottetown?"

"Not worth the risk. You'll be under scrutiny with that motorcycle gang look you sport so well. You don't need to bring more attention to yourself by showing up at Dylan's side when he's medicated and confused."

"Oh, Jesus," Josh moaned. "The poor kid."

"He'll recover. Go home. Wait for a call."

"And Jessie…?"

"You know her. Tough as nails."

Josh softened. "Yeah. That's my girl."

Matt got quiet.

After a few seconds, Josh clawed nervously at his beard and said, "I'll go home. I'll take these two rug rats to William and Alice—"

"William went in the ambulance with Dylan."

"Ambulance…" Digesting that, Josh closed his eyes. "Jesus. Yeah, okay. Thank God for William. The man's a saint. Alice there?"

"Yeah."

"Then I'll leave these two with Alice and go into town. I can't leave Jessie alone to deal with this. We'll be careful. We won't give ourselves away."

They talked quickly for another few minutes before hanging up. Matt promised to call Charles and Dee, and Josh promised not to speed all the way back to the Sutherland Road.

At home, Josh got his older two settled with Alice up at her place, peeked in at the dog, took a leak and grabbed a few of Dylan's favorite toys along with a couple of toddler books for Micah. He tried calling Jessie, to no avail. "Likely has her hands full with Dylan and Micah," he figured. "Or else the hospital has a no-cell policy."

He ripped back out to his truck by jumping down the last few steps at the kitchen entrance, and tore up some red dirt when he shoved his foot down on the gas and pulled a hard right to go left after backing out of his laneway. Back up the narrow Sutherland Road he went, pedal to the metal, and wondered what awaited him at the hospital.

Chapter Twenty-six

Dylan was medicated but awake in a sleepy kind of way when Jessie hurried into the hospital and asked the admissions clerk where she could find her son, Ben McIver.

The woman said tersely, "One moment, please," and disappeared for about five minutes, which just about drove Jessie around the bend. Pacing, with an agitated Micah balanced on her hip, she avoided curious glances from a scattered cluster of folks seated around the small waiting room, and yanked her cap down lower over her mousey brown hair. Weirdly, one of her songs was playing through the overhead speakers—an upbeat dance tune, a duet she did just for fun with Pitbull back in her Miami days. Hugging Micah to her body, she whispered, "Sometimes this is all just a little too surreal. Was I ever that person? Feels like another lifetime to me."

Eventually she was escorted through a waiting room door into the emergency unit and brought back to Dylan. A toned, tanned woman in a short flared skirt and sleeveless top swept toward her, meeting her at the door to a private room.

"My name is Dawn," she said, sticking out a hand by way of introduction. "I'm a social worker here at the hospital."

"Is there a problem?" Jessie asked. "I'd like to see my son."

"He's sleeping," Dawn said kindly. "Would you mind having a quick chat with me after you pop in to see him?"

An alarm bell rang in Jessie's brain. "Uhh…sure," she said. "Can I just have a minute?"

"Of course. I'll be right outside."

Ducking into Dylan's room, Jessie's heart rate went into overdrive. Intuitively she could tell something was seriously amiss, and it seemed apparent that it had nothing to do with Dylan's injury. William, who was waiting inside, affirmed it.

"There was a bit of a hullabaloo over his name," he told Jessie in a guarded kind of way. "Ben isn't liking being Ben today. He told the EMTs in the ambulance that his name is not Ben, it's Dylan. I'm sorry, Jasmyn," he glanced over at the door, "but it gets worse."

"Oh, God." Jessie sank into a cushioned wooden chair with Micah in her lap after peeking over at Dylan to ensure that he was okay, that he was dozing comfortably. "Hit me with the good news."

"One of the nurses assumed I was his grandfather, a role I was proud to assume. She then proceeded to inquire about his parents. Apparently the EMTs communicated to her that you were on your way but that his father was as yet unreachable by cell, as far as they knew. She was simply asking if he'd been informed and was on his way, so she could put out an alert to admissions to watch for him."

"And?" Jessie inhaled slowly and held her breath. In her lap, Micah wriggled. She let him down so he could wander off and explore the room.

"She wanted to know his name. I told her Joe McIver. Your son overheard. He started to cry and just kept saying 'no no no. That's not my daddy's name.'"

"Oh, God. Did he tell them…" She was terrified to ask. "Jesus, William. We're gonna have to move again."

"He didn't give away a name. I suppose Josh is Daddy, to him, but until they got him calmed down he was adamant that his father is not Joe McIver. He raised some serious flags. It didn't help when he said he had two fathers, Daddy being one, and a man called Jacob being the other. If any of these women are fans of you and your friend Jacob, you could be in trouble here. Jacob and Dylan are known names in the music and television business, right?"

"Yeah. I guess so, when they're put together. Jesus. Okay." Jessie puffed up her cheeks and exhaled thoughtfully. "I need you to wait outside for Josh, uh, for Joe." Craning her neck, she peeked around the door. "He can't come in. Nobody can see him or waylay him for questioning. Send him home, or if he won't go home tell him to grab a takeout coffee up the road at Jo Mamma's and sit in his truck in the Walmart parking lot and wait."

"Will do." Approaching the door, William looked back at Jessie. "For what it's worth, Alice and I don't like this any better than you do." Pinpricks of light had settled into the older man's eyes. Moisture. Tears.

"Aw, geez William," Jessie moaned. "Our lives are constantly in turmoil. We should have known better than to let anyone try to make friends with us. Our little family is better on our own. Everyone around us just gets hurt."

"Nobody is better on their own." William's declaration came with a mini attempt at a smile. "Every second with someone we love is worth a ton of seconds without. I wouldn't change that. Even if it meant never having you in our lives. Even if it meant never having my son when we had him."

"Thank you." The way Jessie uttered the soft statement was gratitude magnified a hundred thousand times.

Turning, William left, nodding at the social worker as he passed.

Dawn slipped into the doorway and smiled at Jessie. "He's a tough little guy," she said, gesturing toward Dylan's small body in the big bed. "He didn't complain about the pain once."

Jessie had to bite her lip. On the tip of her tongue was *like father, like son.* The injury in itself was similar to Josh's from the evening cougar attack. *That should bring Dylan comfort,* she thought. *Anything to be like his precious Daddy...*

Micah was grabbing her leg now, begging to be picked up. Sighing, Jessie bent over and lifted him into her arms. "He's getting hungry," she explained, and pulled a Tupperware container of grapes out of the bag she'd hastily packed at home. "Here, Mic, uh, Michael. Grapes. Your fave. Snack away."

"Can we talk for a moment?" Dawn asked.

"He's asleep," Jessie said, nodding toward Dylan but locking her eyes on Micah's container of grapes. "We can talk here. I don't want to leave him, if you don't mind." She was having visions of police swooping in, and Dylan disappearing forever into some obscure hospital room in a musty, unused wing. *I've worked in too many strange movies,* she chided herself.

"Okay." From a far corner of the room, the social worker grabbed a round black stool on wheels and rolled it closer to Jessie. Crossing her legs at the knees, she was about to bring the conversation to an easy start when Jessie jumped right in with a white lie she hoped would result in the dogs being called off, per se.

"He told you his name isn't Ben because it isn't. Fair enough."

"His health card reads Ben McIver."

"Yes. We're here under protection." Jessie was still staring at the grapes. "I can have this verified by the police if you need it."

"Hence the father's name also not being what your son said it is."

Pursing her lips, Jessie glanced up at her inquisitor. Dawn seemed like the compassionate sort—gentle eyes and an easy demeanor. A petite brunette with a short, cropped, trendy haircut, she was studying Jessie with a restrained, careful scrutiny.

"Look," Jessie said. "I just need to know that my son is going to be okay. If you need that verification, I can get it for you."

Dawn was hesitant before she spoke again. "That's not the issue, Jessie," she replied.

Jessie closed her eyes.

Reaching out, Dawn lightly touched Jessie's knee. "Your son let it slip that he has two fathers and that one is a singer called Jacob. There was a lot of hype when Dylan was born. A lot of music fans were polarized—Team Josh or Team Jacob fights were all the rage on social media. Your family is often on the covers of magazines by the checkout at the grocery store. Especially since the trouble in Alberta."

Jessie took a chance. Shifting Micah on her lap, she tried to keep her voice even. "You look like the trustworthy type. My children and I would like to live here in peace."

"Thank you. I keep confidences. I do. The problem is not with me. There seems to be a buzz going around the hospital. Staff is taking breaks…"

"Texting. Messaging. It's fine. We'll take a trip."

"Jessie…the man who came in with Dylan confirmed that his father is on his way."

"Not anymore," Jessie tossed in almost gaily, trying to throw Dawn off her trail. "He's been averted. I hope." The second she said it, she clamped her lips shut. "Oh, damn," she murmured in her scared little girl voice. What was left of the grapes suddenly became interesting again.

"Exactly. I happen to be a huge Jacob Ryan fan. He's playing a benefit in Washington tonight. So I doubt it's him that's driving in from Charlottetown."

"Nope. Not Jacob."

Dawn took another metaphorical step. "Might it be the man you were dating after your husband died? Because if that's who Dylan was referring to, I have to tell you that it seems a little odd, I mean that he would call that man Daddy so soon after losing his father."

Jessie bit her lip.

"This is the problem, Jessie. This is the quandary that's making its way onto social media as we speak. I'm sure you're aware of all of those conspiracy theories about the medevac plane crash."

"And the Doc Westfield sighting. You were going to pull that one up from your arsenal next, weren't you?"

"If your husband is alive, Jessie, and is on his way to this hospital, he needs to turn around and lay his head down until the heat passes. There will be media here—not a lot, at least not soon, anyway. We're a small province. But there will be curious fans, potentially a lot. By the time Dylan is treated your privacy will be seriously threatened."

"And our safety. Jesus. What about Dylan?" Jessie whispered without looking up. Crestfallen, she took Micah's small hand in hers and held it tightly. "We can't move him."

"Now that you're here, the doctor will be in to see you as soon as he's free. What I'm hearing, though, and what I've seen in these types of injuries, is that first of all Dylan will likely go for an X-ray to determine the extent of the break. As you can see, he's been temporarily patched up somewhat already, but he'll need surgery to reattach that bone. There's an orthopedic surgeon in Charlottetown who can handle some cases, but occasionally these kinds of breaks are flown to Halifax on the LifeFlight 'copter. Given what's happening on social media right now, I would recommend Halifax. However, you will need some security in place."

"I need to talk to my husband. I need to talk to Josh." Swiping an arm under her nose, Jessie had to blink back tears.

Dawn drew her attention back by touching Jessie's knee again. "So it's true," she said with compassionate concern. "Josh Sawyer is alive."

"Oh, God," Jessie breathed, managing a small nod. "I don't suppose there's anything left to argue. Yes. He's alive. We live our lives in fear. We had no choice."

"Oh, honey," Dawn sighed. "I'm so glad. For you and your children, I mean. How wonderful."

Looking up, meeting Dawn's kind gaze, Jessie responded with a forlorn frown. Her worried eyes were a troubled river, bubbling over with whirlpools of uncertainty.

Dawn took her hand and squeezed it. "What can I do to help?"

"Change the tide," Jessie begged. "Please. Get on social media and tell them it's not us. Tell them they've made a mistake."

"It might help for a bit, Jessie," Dawn offered wisely. "On a temp basis, that's all." She nodded at Dylan, who was groaning and trying to open his eyes. "Your fella here doesn't seem to support your new identities. Once he's feeling better he's likely to talk again."

"Out of the mouths of babes," Jessie groaned. "Can I make calls in here?"

"You can use the phone in my private office."

From the bed Dylan called out in a tiny voice, "Momma. Momma!"

Getting up, Jessie adjusted the grape container and Micah, and went to Dylan's bedside. "I'm here, Dylan," she said. "Momma's right here. Everything's okay now—you're in good hands, baby bear."

Dawn approached. "Will Micah come with me?" she asked. "To free your hands? I won't leave the room."

Something about the woman was indeed kind. Micah intuitively sensed that, and fell easily into Dawn's arms.

Jessie bent over Dylan. "Guess what?" she said brightly. "You get to have an X-ray! How cool is that? They're gonna take pictures of the inside of your leg. Maybe they'll let you keep one. And then you'll get a cast. Maybe one of those awesome colored ones. Emily-Grace and David can draw pictures on it for you."

"Daddy," Dylan moaned. "I want Daddy." Small sobs right from the bottom of his soul made Jessie's heart ache.

She twisted her fingers around his. "I know, baby," she soothed. "You'll see your beloved daddy soon, I promise. Hey," she added, her voice rising in pitch, "I bet Daddy would draw a horse on that new cast if you asked him to. Maybe he can draw Rusty."

A hurried swoosh at the door alerted her to the presence of the busy doctor. If the young man knew the rumors that were circulating about his patient's family, he either didn't care or he was professional and busy enough to ignore them.

"You're the mother?" he asked, consulting a clipboard he was holding in one hand and scratching an itch under his short-trimmed blond hair with his free hand as he talked.

"Yep." Jessie straightened.

"We're off to X-ray momentarily. Children tend to want a parent in with them."

"Okay. Good."

He scanned further down the clipboard. "Not pregnant, right?" At Jessie's silence, the doctor looked up.

"Uh, I might be," she admitted, deflating.

"Where's the father? Or the grandfather? He was here earlier?"

"I need a phone," Jessie whispered, blinking sorrowfully up at him. "I need to make some calls." Dylan was moaning and crying for his daddy. Wildly, Jessie appealed to Dawn for help. "I can't leave him."

The social worker stepped forward. "Give me some numbers. I'll make the calls. And if I need to, I can go in with Dylan for his X-ray."

"Says here his name is Ben," the doctor said, flipping a page. "Did I miss something?"

"You and everyone else," Jessie muttered. Turning to Dylan, she said, "Daddy's on his way, baby. Hang on. Just hang on."

*Chapter Twenty-seven*

Prince County Hospital was a hub—a central facility, the second largest hospital on the island. Smaller feeder hospitals and clinics sent patients in need of acute care to Prince County. Today was a hot, sunny beach day on the touristy island. Some prospective patients were taking detours at the beach; they'd land at emerge when the sun went down. As a result, the hospital wasn't overly busy.

Josh walked right in.

The staff pretended they suspected nothing, and took him to his son.

By then, in a sleepy haze but still inconsolable, Dylan was out of X-ray. He cried outright when his father walked into the room with a favorite worn teddy bear dangling from one set of strong fingers.

"Hey, little buddy," Josh said to Dylan. "Look who I found."

"Thank you, Daddy," Dylan sobbed, clutching the bear to his chest. He took his father's fingers in his and held on for dear life. Dylan's eyes, murky with pain and drugs, stayed open until he couldn't fight it any longer and let them close over.

Pale and tired, Jessie was standing by the foot of Dylan's bed, leaning on the rail. Trying to appear tough, Josh angled his head in her direction and worked up a sad smile. "He's never even needed stitches," he said. "He should have worked his way up gradually, don't you think?"

The worried furrow in Jessie's brow deepened. "He needs surgery, Josh. Like father, like son."

"That'll keep him off the swings."

"And off Rusty. He'll be heartbroken."

Josh pawed at his beard. He reached down and tucked the worn bear in close to his son's cheek. "Not for long. He'll be back in the saddle before we know it, if I know this kid." Looking back at Jessie, he tried to mitigate her tears—the ones that were starting to trickle down her cheeks now that Josh was in the room with her and she no longer needed to be the strong parent. "He's holding his own. He's a tough kid, Jess."

"Drugs, Josh. Remember those? He's juiced up on pain meds."

Josh chose to ignore the dig. Bending over Dylan, he pressed his lips to his forehead. "Our wild boy," he said tenderly. "Just like his father." He smiled sadly. "Daddy loves you, Dylan." Turning, he let his fingers slip out of Dylan's grasp when Jessie came around the bed and touched his hip.

"Josh…" Taking him in her arms, Jessie let more relieved tears sneak their way down her cheeks. "So glad you're here, although you shouldn't be. You weren't supposed to come in. Where's William?" Peeking behind her, she looked for the older man who had become such a good friend to the exiled Sawyer family.

"I sent William home to check on Emily-Grace and David," Josh said. "I was talking to Matt again—he called his RCMP bud back for us. Now that the word's out, we're going to need some immediate security. Al, is that his name?"

Tearfully, Jessie nodded.

"Al is on his way to our place. He'll escort William and Alice and the kids—and Fluffy—to a secluded, private house for the rest of today and tonight. Tomorrow William can go back home under escort if it's needed, to feed the horses. Al's got officers coming here to the hospital to help support the local police in case things ramp up when the sun goes down."

Jessie lit up. "Ya gotta love islanders. They'll choose the beach instead of stalking us on a day like today. Most of 'em, anyway."

Raising his eyebrows, Josh said, "You remember the winter we just had, Jess? Damn straight they'll choose the beach!"

"Yeah." She giggled. "I guess." Hooking a finger over her husband's belt buckle, Jessie asked a question that had been running around her brain since the second she realized they were no longer the incognito McIver family. "Josh…what do we do now? Where will we go?"

Hauling in a big breath, Josh placed his hands on his wife's hips. "Home," he decreed. "There's not a damn place else we can go. And to be honest, there's nowhere else I want to go."

"We can't go home, Josh. The EMTs know where we live. There's likely already a media circus happening there."

Lifting his hands to her waist, sliding them around her back, Josh latched his eyes onto Jessie's. At first there was a serious bent to his face, a flicker of doubt, but then something changed.

A light came on.

It was tiny, minute—but it was there.

He shook his head. "Not here," he said, his voice breaking. "Home."

Jessie's eyes widened. "Vancouver? You can't be serious."

"I miss my bike. I miss my life."

"Josh, we can't. It's not an option, babe."

"What we can't do, Jessie, is live our lives this way—hiding, running, worrying. If there's one thing we've both learned through all of this, it's that life is too precious to live it hiding under a rock."

"Or under mud. Bright red mud." She was catching on.

"I miss the thrill of walking onto a set at five a.m. for a hair and makeup call."

Jessie wrinkled her nose. "Ew! I don't miss that!"

Josh laughed. "I miss the sunrises I used to see on early morning set calls. I miss the bad coffee at craft service."

"I miss bossy pants Charlie running me off your set for distracting you."

"I miss Deirdre's scathing looks every time I toss David or Dylan over my shoulder."

"You do realize she only does that because she's worried about your shoulder, about you hurting yourself, right Josh?"

"As if." He laughed. "I miss the view of English Bay from Cypress Mountain. I miss downhill skiing on Sunday afternoons."

"There's a ski hill here." A playful glint danced across Jessie's eyes. It got even brighter when Josh started to protest.

From the bed, Dylan opened his eyes and piped up in a thin, medicated voice. "Daddy always says the hill here's about as big as a mosquito bite, Momma."

"And there you have it." Josh got serious again. His voice got soft. "What do you say, little one? Can we just go home?"

"Josh, what if…" Jessie pulled him away from Dylan's immediate vicinity. "As soon as Morgan hears…"

"I can't live my life this way, Jessie. We can't. It's not fair to you or to the kids. You need to do that tour to support your album. I want to be on it with you. I think we just need to live our lives one day at a time, one second at a time. Jessie…people die every day. We'll suck the marrow out of whatever we can, and just live our lives, and share them with the people we love."

Bashful, afraid, Jessie said, "There's one more risk you may not have considered, Josh."

He hesitated. "Matt?"

"Yeah, babe. It's one thing to see him on occasion. It'll be quite another to see him every day again."

"Are we good, Jess?"

"Yeah. We are. So fucking good, Josh." To prove it, Jessie gathered a handful of his shirt in her fingers and pulled him toward her. Before she kissed him, she murmured, "Well, we will be good when you shave off that nasty rat's nest. Can't stand the beard, Josh. Need to see my man's face again."

His smile flipped upside down. "Can I at least keep the long hair?"

"Umm…" Her laugh tickled his lips.

"Teasing. I'll cut it back to where it was."

"Depending on what film role you take. You're free. You're no longer tied to *Sacred Peace*."

"I didn't mind being tied to that show. It was a good one to be tied to."

"I just thought of something."

"Mmm?" Josh asked.

"Shanda. Since Matt and me…"

"Not interested. She's too thin and bony. Since you've been doing all that cooking, you've gotten a few love handles. I got used to those." For emphasis, Josh grabbed a little extra pound or two at Jessie's waist and gave her a good squeeze.

"Ow!" she yelped. "Not fair!"

Dylan was actually laughing at his silly mom and dad. When the doctor breezed back in, he was seriously amused.

"Good little patient you have there," he said to Jessie and Josh, who turned to face him. Quickly resorting to all business, he said, "I understand we may have some issues with us repairing this boy's leg in Charlottetown. We might want to consider Halifax."

Holding hands, Josh and Jessie shook their heads in unison.

"No?" The doctor leaned an arm on the foot rail of Dylan's bed, and shifted his weight to that foot. The free hand moved up to his hip. "So, shall I see if we can book his surgery with an Ortho in Charlottetown then?"

Jessie stepped forward. "No," she said. "See if you can book one in Vancouver. Please."

"Van…what?"

"Vancouver?!" Dylan yelled from the bed. "We're going to Vancouver?!" He was so happy he tossed his bear up into the air.

Josh caught it on the down swing. His eyes caught a flicker of fear in Jessie's baby blues, but she was quick to hide her concern under a smile.

"Home," she said aloud, taking the bear from Josh and giving it back to Dylan. "We're going home."

Chapter Twenty-eight

The cool light mist wafting over B yard like clingy wet dust was doing nothing for Morgan's already dismal mood. Today he'd had to go out to B yard for his single hour of daily fresh air without brushing his teeth. He'd squeezed every last little bit out of the tube, twisted it and turned it, and now it was beyond empty. There was no money for more. His money supply was toast. Caulfield had cut him off.

Morgan's teeth were coated in a revolting fuzz, like they used to be in the old days when he'd go out and suck back beers half the night. He wouldn't be surprised to look in the mirror and see woolly green blankets coating his teeth, and his tongue too. Caulfield did a lot of repulsive things to Morgan, but this was over the top. The lack of control over something so often taken for granted, stemming from a decisive cut to his money supply—as if Caulfield had twisted a garden hose to make water stop flowing—equated to the sense that Morgan's balls had been soundly sliced off.

Morgan had a serious lip on as he rolled, around and around in his brain, ideas of how to access a tube of toothpaste. He had to cut his thinking short and switch gears when he saw Vaughn striding in his direction. As usual, Morgan was at the edge of B yard, lingering against the chain link fence. Gangs left him alone if he hung out on the edge—if he kept his head down.

He'd kept the old patterns, even though in the long run they didn't really matter anymore.

Now that Morgan was teaching self-defense and yoga, and sitting in on a meditation group that he was also taking turns instructing, word was getting around that he was a more helpful sort. Mindful tools like those did a lot for a guy penned up like a rabid dog. The yoga and meditation, in particular, sent inmates back to their ranges with peaceful smiles on their faces, whereas before their stony eyes communicated only rage, or pain. Connecting to the Divine this way, or to Source, as some of the fellas called the metaphysical energy they tapped into during meditation, gave them a power far beyond the walls of the prison, and far beyond the lives they'd mapped out for themselves.

Suddenly there was light. Suddenly there was hope.

Vaughn seemed to be in decent spirits today. As the big guy sauntered closer Morgan straightened, but didn't bother taking his hands out of the pockets of his light jacket.

"Good to see ya back out in the yard," Vaughn said, halting a few feet away from Morgan. Hauling a pack of smokes out of a pocket, he nudged a cigarette into his fingers, stuck it between his lips and touched a lighter flame to the tip. "Saw what Caulfield did to ya last week. Saw ya fight back. What the hell was that about?"

Ducking his head, Morgan shrugged and toed at the dirt.

"Caulfield cut ya off, I heard. That right?"

Speaking in a slow drawl, still staring at the damp dirt, Morgan answered, "If you're talkin' about my money, yeah. You heard plenty."

Vaughn took a long pull on his smoke. He exhaled into the misty air and protected his cigarette from getting wet by curling his fingers around it. "So ya got pissed and he threw ya in the SHU again. Freeze your ass off?"

Morgan huffed. "My balls, more like it."

"Ya handle it okay?"

Morgan looked up. "The fire alarm freaked me out."

This was something. Morgan rarely spoke. On some bizarre level, he felt connected to Vaughn. Over time they'd managed to become civil to each other—Vaughn only because he kept a watchful eye on Jessie's old security, and so was able to report back to Arnie's buddy Ulysses that the kid was earning a certain respect in the prison population.

Vaughn released an exclamatory breath. "Hell yeah, those fire alarms are fuckin' terrifying. Nothin' like bein' stuck inside a cage when those things are goin' off." He turned sideways, leaned against the metal fence and casually faced Morgan. "You hear the news?"

"The plane crash."

"Sawyer's alive."

"Yeah. Waitin' on Caulfield to come on shift any minute now. I'll be back in the SHU within the hour."

Vaughn took another puff and pointed his smoke at Morgan. "Someone's grown hisself a setta balls."

"I'm tired of him. I'm tired of his games. Tired of never seeing Jessie sing anymore."

"She did that one show a while back."

"And shit-all since. Now I guess we know why."

"Ya blame her? Ya shoulda backed off. Ya can't have it both ways, kid. Ya want the music, ya gotta back off."

Morgan paused. "Did Ulysses ask you to talk to me?" For the second time, he surprised Vaughn. Morgan was looking the big black man in the eye. A rarity.

"I got called to the warden's office for a call this morning. They're coming back to Vancouver, Morgan. They're tired of hidin'. I wish to hell you'd leave them the fuck alone. I ain't never gonna get my song at this rate." He changed positions, swung around so his back was against the fence and said, "You and Caulfield hate each other's guts anyway. What's he gettin' outta all this? Likely he's already got his cut of Sawyer's money spent. What the hell's he care?"

Morgan shuffled his feet and looked away.

Vaughn tried a new tack. "Maybe what I should be asking is what the hell do you care? Huh, kid? Why do I get the feelin' ya care more than you're sayin'?"

Morgan looked back at Vaughn. "He's going to be angry at being 'had,' Vaughn. He's going to go at them with both guns blazing."

Vaughn took a long pull on his smoke and thought about that. Regarding Morgan carefully, he said, "I guess they made up their minds. They've decided to let fate take its course. To let the river run where it may."

"Fate, is it?" Taking one hand out of a pocket, Morgan reached out and grasped Vaughn's cigarette between his thumb and forefinger. "What do you say we give fate a nudge?" Placing the smoke between his lips, he took a drag and passed it back over to the big black man.

Alert and watchful, Vaughn was dumbstruck. Nobody else in Brody Pen would ever have the nerve to grab his cigarette right out of his hand like that. Who did this Morgan kid think he was?

"I'll get you your song," Morgan said to him by way of explanation, exhaling at the same time. The smoke wafted upward into the mist in tiny trails that curled in and around each other like snowflakes on a morning breeze.

"She won't be writin' any more songs if she's dead. Or if her husband's dead, in which case she won't be wantin' ta."

"That ain't the fate I'm talking about nudging. There's only one way to end this thing, Vaughn. To set that family free once and for all. You got that rigged-up excuse for a blade on you?"

"Hell, yeah. I don't take no chances out here in the jungle. I always got my blade."

"How bad do you want that song?"

Vaughn hooted loudly. "Bad. I fuckin' want it bad. You know any cons got songs wrote for them by Jessie Wheeler?"

Taking a step toward him, Morgan locked his eyes into Vaughn's, imploring him to pay attention. "You gotta back me up, Vaughn. You have to make sure I'm protected. And you gotta give me some guarantees."

"What kinda guarantees?" The homemade knife was up Vaughn's sleeve, always ready for easy access.

"These kind." Morgan leaned back against the fence. Leaving no room for conjecture, he told Arnie's old Downtown Eastside neighbor exactly what he expected from him.

After Morgan looking him in the eye, and stealing his cigarette for a puff, that was Vaughn's third surprise of the last few minutes.

Caulfield was on shift within the hour. The guard sneered at Morgan when Morgan passed by to head back inside. Right on time, a swarm of Vaughn's cronies casually flocked around the two. Something malicious and hot sliced into Caulfield's side, ripped his flesh on the way out and then viciously tore his gut wide open twice more.

Morgan's eyes were on the guard the whole time. The wide open surprise in Caulfield's eyes didn't bother him. The fresh wintergreen scent of the pink peppermint in the man's open mouth, however, drove Morgan around the bend. He vomited when he got back to his cell, and couldn't help but wonder how soon he'd get his money supply back in order. He was desperate for a tube of toothpaste.

Caulfield left the prison in an air ambulance an hour later. By the time he got to Edmonton's trauma center, his soul was waiting on final judgment at the pearly gates.

Chapter Twenty-nine

A shiny new Learjet medevac plane caused quite a stir when it soared elegantly over the runway at the Summerside air base and went wheels down. A ripple of glee filtered through the curious onlookers lined up a few hundred meters away. This new revelation—that Josh Sawyer was alive and had been living on Prince Edward Island under a pseudonym with his wife and children—had everyone in the small province aflutter. The stupefying news was spreading in the world at large like a forest fire, heating up a wild excitement in everyone who blogged and tweeted and re-tweeted and shared.

In the interest—supposedly—of preserving public safety and the safety of the injured child and his celebrity parents and siblings, the local police and RCMP had set up a security perimeter around the hospital and at the old air base with plans to stay in position until the Sawyer family was safely away. Charles Keating gratefully footed the bill.

Dylan, transported from the hospital by ambulance, waited with his father's hand in his while the jet made its graceful landing. Splinted for a few days to help monitor the swelling in his small leg before surgery, he was comfortable enough but was antsy as heck to get outta bed and get moving again. He had a long six weeks and then some ahead of him as he recovered.

The medevac jet cruised up and rolled to a stop not far from the familiar Keating jet with its welcome distinguishable gold stripe, which had landed just ahead of it. Jessie, anxiously twisting ringlets in her hair, was waiting in the Sawyer family van with Emily-Grace, David and Micah. Fluffy was snuggled into Emily-Grace's lap after having been immediately retrieved from the usual dog carrier the second the van was put into park.

Arnie wandered over to Jessie and leaned on the door after she lowered the window. "Hi, kids," he said, peering behind Jessie into the back seats.

A nervous chorus greeted him. Micah smiled adorably and clutched a bare toe. His shoes lay in haphazard disarray on the floor mat beneath his suspended legs.

"You ready for this?" Arnie asked Jessie.

"Which part?" she asked, looking past him to spy the ambulance with Dylan and Josh in it cruise closer to the medevac plane. "That's not the same medevac jet, right, Arnie?"

"Nope. That one'll sell for twenty times its price. Thanks to social media, it's now more famous than you and Josh. Even Charles wouldn't be able to swing its purchase if he were on the other end of that transaction."

She guffawed. "Charles, huh? He's still capitalizing on our family. That man won't stop til he's in his grave."

"Speaking of that man," Arnie said, standing tall again. "He'll be some glad to have all of you back in Vancouver."

"Until the thrill wears off and the fear sets in again," Jessie said in a subdued voice so her children wouldn't hear. "Arnie, how long before you plan to come back out west?"

"I need to take care of things here first," he replied with authority. "Your house, all that. I'll be out west within the week."

"Sure you don't want to stay? Got the new missus and all…"

"No more new missus. We broke up. We spent too many hours in a car together during that Ontario trip. She drove me insane with her constant need to backseat drive. At any rate," he softened, "your family is my family now. These kids are the only kids I'll ever have. I'm going where you're going, if you'll have me."

A slow smile widened on Jessie's face. "Who knew, huh?" she said gently. "All those years ago, who knew you and me would practically become family?"

Arnie couldn't answer. He was too busy turning a sweet shade of happy pink. Jessie let go of her hair and twined her fingers in his.

The door to the Keating jet swung open on a downward arc. Shrinking into the driver's seat, Jessie turned a pinker hue than Arnie when Charles and Matt descended to the tarmac just behind Deirdre, who was immediately greeted by a local publicist hired to help navigate the media storm. Blowing kisses, Deirdre waved at the van.

Jessie let a quiet laugh filter out between her lips. "The consummate professional," she said, lifting a hand to wave at Dee. "Look at her go." Already Deirdre was being greeted by local politicians eager to meet a member of this celebrity party, since Jessie and Josh had yet to appear.

With a sigh, Jessie lowered her hand. She started absently fingering the steering wheel, squeezing it, moving her hand over and around it. Charles and Matt were tailing Deirdre, although both had looked over. Charles waved. Matt just nodded and dropped his head, visibly uncomfortable at the scrutiny he was being subjected to in the press as part of the revelation of Josh's existence. Matt had been romantically attached to Jessie at a time when Josh was recovering. The media was having a field day.

A small voice interrupted Jessie's woebegone study of the much missed man she hadn't laid eyes on in about a year. "Momma, can we go see Grammie Dee now?" David was vibrating in his seat next to Micah in the middle row of the van. "I want to see Grammie."

"In a minute, honey," Jessie advised him. "For now just watch your little brother get loaded into the jet, David. You guys will have so much cool stuff to talk about when you go back to school."

"We're going back to school?"

"I hope so, honey. We have a lot of stuff to talk about, to sort out, but your dad and me hope so." Jessie's eyes were still following Matt while he and Charles assessed the immediate environment. Her heart was doing that hitch-leap thing it always did at the sight of him. Today he was showing off a hip light spring jacket. *A nylon one,* Jessie thought in admiration, *that shows off the strong shoulders I like to lean on.*

To Arnie, she said, "I'm glad I got in to see George and Emily one last time. Even though it had to be a stealthy middle-of-the-night kind of thing, for security."

"How is old George?"

"He didn't wake up. He wouldn't have known me anyway. They're both off in their own worlds now. Soon they'll both be off in a dimension we can only contemplate. Won't be long now, for George at least."

"We'll have to get you to Peterborough soon to see your grandmother too, Jessie. And Sara."

"Yep. It'll be nice not to have to do everything under the radar anymore. As much under the radar, anyway." Lifting her arm, she crooked it on the door, at the open window, and rested her head on her hand.

Outside, a roar went up in the crowd when Josh appeared at his son's side, making his exit from the ambulance. He waved but didn't look back. Focused on Dylan's safe transport, he held the little guy's hand until he could no longer safely do so when Dylan was moved inside the jet.

Calling out to Dylan, "I'll be back in a minute, buddy," Josh turned and headed across the asphalt toward the rest of his family.

"It's now or never," Jessie grumbled, adjusting the rearview mirror so she could see the excited fans lined up beyond the fence behind her. "Kids, stay in the van for just a few more minutes, please. I need to have a word with Daddy before we go to the jet."

A frustrated wail followed her when Arnie opened the driver's door and Jessie slipped out.

As Josh strode toward Jessie, a scan over the enthusiastic crowd jump-started the nerve on his cheek. It twitched in overdrive. "Jesus," he scowled when he was close enough to Jessie for him to rest his hands on her hips. "Can't say I missed this part."

"Sure you did. You're all about the ego," she teased. She bent forward for a hug and a kiss. A rousing cheer went up from the perimeter. Her smile flipped over. "Josh, there's no going back now. We either go all in or we arrange a new place to hide."

Josh sucked in a breath. "No more running. It is what it is at this point, Jessie."

"All right." Turning her head, Jessie took a quick look at the crowd. "Hey, look. William and Alice are here."

Arnie, who also spotted the older couple at the fence, jogged over to get them. He escorted the two onto the runway.

"Yeah, I called them earlier," Josh said. "I couldn't leave without saying goodbye. Without letting the kids say goodbye."

"We'll be back. I can never stay away from P.E.I. for long." Taking Josh's hand in hers, Jessie pivoted around to welcome the island couple.

In awe, William was shaking. Alice was thoroughly amused. "Do you really like this?" she asked. "This is nuts."

"It's just a game," Josh told her with a grin. "You know us. We're ordinary people."

William guffawed. "Not according to the media out there in the crowd, you're not."

"Hey, they hype us up. Trust me."

Alice held out a large Tupperware container. "I feel almost silly giving you these now."

Jessie lifted the lid and snuck a peek inside. "Cinnamon rolls? And carrot cake? Alice, you're a doll!" She enfolded her new friend in a warm embrace. "You do realize I'm gonna have to work my ass off for weeks to burn off these calories, right?"

"See?" William said to Josh. "Ordinary people wouldn't give a shit about calories."

"You're wrong there," Josh laughed. "I've seen the cars lined up at island gyms."

A kind, lingering look followed that truth. Josh tipped his head down so that his long hair cascaded over his cheeks. *It's his 'hiding from the world and from the things that hurt look,'* Jessie thought, tearing up at what she knew was coming next. She shoved her thumbs in her back pockets and tapped a foot nervously.

"Look, William," Josh started, looking up to meet his friend's eyes. "I told you that I've felt for a long time—well, most of my life, really—like I don't feel like I've ever really had a dad. Not a real one who listens to me and who likes me for who I am." His voice got all crackly. Josh glanced away before he pulled nervously at his beard and reached deep to finish what he needed to say. "I can't tell you how much it's meant to me to get to know you, to work around the horses and the houses and on all those antique chairs with you. I wish you were my dad. For real."

A tender moment passed between the two men, followed by a low grunt from Josh, who was trying to stay in control of the years of longing for a father to really be there for him.

William laid a hand on his shoulder. "I'd be proud to have you as a son, Josh," he said.

"You never had to deal with the real me," was Josh's quick response. "I suppose that might change things."

Jessie sighed and looked down. Tossing her head, she licked a lip anxiously before watching to see how the rest of this little interplay would play out.

"The real you?" William was baffled. "Are you referencing your challenges with alcohol, son? You couldn't throw me if you tried. When Jeffery died I drank myself into oblivion for months. If you want the truth, that's one of the reasons why Jeffery's wife pulled up and took our grandkids back to Ontario. I wouldn't be here today if it weren't for Alice. She's my guiding light, and has been, for decades."

Pooh-poohing him, Alice encircled her arms around his waist. "Oh, don't make me sound so old." She was beaming.

Josh's eyes danced over to Jessie. "I guess I know that feeling," he said honestly. "I know what it's like to be loved that way."

"Always," Jessie whispered, bashfully blinking up at him past long, damp lashes. "I just gotta get past myself sometimes. Past my own fears." They, too, shared a sweet lingering look that went far beyond affection; one that was rooted deep, deep down in each other's souls. Bringing them out of the sadness of the imminent parting, Jessie added, for William's and Alice's benefits, "He's an easy man to love. I'm incredibly blessed."

"Every one of those women at that fence would agree," William chuckled. "They'll all be jealous of me too, I suppose." He took a step toward Josh and threw an arm around him.

Josh didn't hesitate. He embraced his good friend fondly, using both arms so that William would feel comfortable following suit. It was a good minute before the guys backed off. Alice and Jessie hugged too, although less effusively. Deirdre was watching, and Jessie wasn't as close to Alice as Josh was to William, anyway. Still, she swiped at tears when she backed away.

Josh turned to the van. "These kids need to say their goodbyes to you guys too," he choked out. Arnie was close by. Josh appealed to him for help keeping the kids turned away from all the lenses being pointed at them. William and Alice wandered over.

Like a child herself, Jessie tugged cautiously on her husband's elbow.

"Josh," she said, taking in a quick breath. "How'd Dylan hold up in the ambulance?"

"He's a trooper," Josh told her. "He's okay, but one of us should get back to him real soon."

"S'gonna be you, right? You're gonna fly on the medevac plane with him, aren't you, Josh?"

Josh examined Jessie for signs of distress. "Hey," he said, worrying over the tension he noted lining her eyes in little cracks and fissures. "What'd we say?"

"I know. I worry about worrying. The lot of you never get tired of telling me that."

"You know the drill, Jessie. We're cherishing every moment, you and me. We're not worrying about bad stuff. It'll find us no matter how hard we try to outrun it."

"Okay." She gulped. "Okay, Josh." Dropping her hand to his, Jessie locked her fingers tightly around Josh's. A big part of her wished they could stay joined like that forever. "I probably ought to load the kids, then," she said a little wistfully, without moving. "Once I get them settled I'll run over to give Dylan a hug and a kiss."

Unable to help himself, Josh tossed in a request. "Don't get too cuddly with Matt on the way back."

Jessie's cheeks were suddenly dotted with pink. She started to vibrate. *Beloved Matt…fifty feet away…*

Josh cocked his head. "Here's a weird question for you. Did you ever have sex with Matt on the jet?" Letting go of her fingers, he pawed at his beard and turned in a restless circle before looking back at her. "Uh…I don't suppose I really want the answer to that question. Do I."

"Umm…" Jessie hooked her thumbs over his belt and found a crack in the worn leather to focus on.

"Great," Josh griped, a sour taste in his mouth. "I'm glad I'm taking the medevac with Dylan."

"Um…" Raising her shoulders in a question mark, Jessie said, "Speaking of Matt…"

"Yeah. Go." Josh knew when he was beat. His voice took on a tender tone. He laid his hands around her elbows. "The man can't take his eyes off you."

Jessie's shoulders softened. "I suppose the press will have a field day with this one."

Lightening up, Josh grinned. "I could come with you. I could hug him too; we could pretend we've been having threesomes for years."

Throwing back her head, Jessie laughed loudly. "You and Matt? Like, eww, Josh. Seriously."

"You were with my sister!" he protested. "What the hell's the difference?"

"Don't say that too loud, husband." Jessie let her fingers drop from his belt. With a saucy smirk, she started to sidle away. "I'm not sure William and Alice could get past that about us. This small island's a pretty conservative corner of the world. Not like you'd ever go there, anyway. And neither would Matt. You're both damn stubborn alpha males. Throw in another woman, maybe…" She winked. "Me and Shanda can fight over you. Ohh, that might actually be fun."

"Jesus. Tell me you're joking."

Jessie was giggling. Her eyes were as bright blue as the sky today, filled with sunshine and light. It was as if some compassionate angel had reached into her spirit and lifted the world's toughest burdens away. Watching her, Josh wished she could always be this happy. Remove worry from the equation—add friends, family and *home*, and Jessie utterly shone with joy.

*I need another moment with her. I need to hold her for one more second.*

Josh took a few steps toward his wife and caught a trailing finger. He turned her back to face him. "It's a generational thing, not a place thing," he whispered sweetly. "Threesomes. I hear they're all the rage these days. But just so you know…" He shook his head slowly. "I'm not interested. I just want you." Cupping her chin in his hand, he brushed his lips across hers. "Go, little one. Let him take you in his arms and help you feel safe. Absorb his energy. Just get off that plane and come to me, okay?"

Jessie sighed into her husband. "'Course, babe. You know I will." She smiled sadly at him. "I won't have sex with him on the jet, Josh."

Josh sobered. "Not something I really need to hear right now, Jessie— you and Matt and sex. I'd prefer not to know the whens and the wheres."

Exhaling, Jessie closed her eyes and let her man hold her. "Love you," she murmured into his shoulder.

When he got his voice back, Josh stammered out, "Arnie and I will bring the kids over to you. We'll give the media a quick family photo, okay?"

"Okay," Jessie agreed quietly. "The island's been good to us. I can get behind that."

Shoving her fingers into her back pockets, she swung slowly back around toward where Charles and Dee were engrossed in some deep chat with the local powers-that-be. She looked back at Josh once. He was watching her, that old familiar hurt look soaking his eyes. Jessie forced herself to look away.

Without so much as a glance in the direction of the crowd at the fence, she headed over to Matt. Hanging back from Charles and Dee, he sauntered toward her when he saw her making her way over.

"Oh my God," Jessie murmured into his neck when she landed in his arms. "Oh my God, Matt."

"Some circus, huh?" he whispered, enclosing Jessie tightly before pushing her back to arm's length so he could read how she was feeling, how she was coping with this strange new twist in their destinies. *Not well*, he considered as Jessie's troubled eyes grew paler by the second now that she no longer had to be the strong one.

Jessie, regarding Matt now, clinging to his elbows, started to tremble. "You know, Josh has been a rock through this latest crap," she said with sincerity. "Still, I always feel like I have to hold him up. Just in case…you know…"

"I know," Matt replied, gazing into his girl's soul the way he always did, loving her, telling her he missed the feel of her too just by virtue of holding her close.

"I haven't seen you in just about a year, Matt. You and I, we have not been in each other's physical company in a year. Our family has missed having everyone around for Christmas, for every holiday and for all of our birthdays. This birthday of mine that's coming?" She stuck a pointy finger in her chest. "I'm gonna celebrate it. I'm gonna celebrate the hell out of it!"

"That's my girl." Tender and sweet, Matt pulled her close again.

Jessie sighed lovingly into him with every taut muscle and nerve on her body. "Country music," she breathed into his ear. "What were you thinking? You'll never be able to tour with me again." For a good chunk of the last fall, Matt had taken Dallas White up on his offer to tour with him as his security.

Matt's warm chuckle was so, so welcome. "Dallas is a good guy," he said. "It was a good tour."

"You didn't fall in love with him, did you?"

That brought out an elated laugh. Matt released Jessie and they both wiped away their happy tears before Josh walked over with the kids. Micah was in Josh's arms, but Josh took a breath for strength, reached out, and kindly shook Matt's hand. Charles and Dee rushed over to smother the kids—and Jessie, and even Josh—in welcome hugs.

As promised, Josh and Jessie posed for photos with the three of their children they had close at hand, and waved a solemn goodbye to the crowd before ushering the kids into the jet.

Josh flew back to Vancouver with Dylan in the medevac plane. Jessie held Matt's much missed hand and they laughed all the way west in the Keating jet. The children sat with Grammie and Grampie. It was easy to feel celebratory and happy while riding above the clouds, with the familiar parts of their lives to look forward to. Rides on Josh's Harley were the biggest on his list. Jessie had to admit she couldn't wait to see his adorable, sexy body in his leather jacket again, and the idea of snuggling up behind him for cruises up to the lookout on Cypress Mountain made her positively wiggly in anticipation of what 'fun' they might get up to when they got there.

Still, all of the adults on the jets lapsed into occasional silences at the frightening unknowns that awaited them as Josh and Jessie merged back into their old lives. It wasn't until just before they landed that they heard about Caulfield's stabbing and his subsequent passing. While none of them knew exactly what that meant and how it would filter down to them, they all intuitively felt it meant something. The timing was too perfect.

"We need to go see Morgan," Jessie said to Matt just after Victoria announced their imminent landing. "Josh and me need to take back our power. You too," she said. "You've carried as much weight or more as the rest of us. You come too. We'll just tell him straight out that we are back and that we are no longer afraid of him."

Matt was hesitant. He brushed his thumb over the deeply loved fingers that had only let go of him briefly during the flight, and only then at moments when Jessie couldn't help letting go of him, like when Micah crawled into her lap for a cuddle and a nap. "That backfired on you last time, sweetheart," Matt warned. "I'm not so sure it's a good idea."

"I approached him from a place of fear last time. This time," Jessie raised her chin with pride, "I'll approach him from a place of power."

"That's my girl," Matt whispered. He draped an arm around Jessie's shoulders and hugged her close. "I'll talk to Charles. We'll set it up. No more fear."

Easier said than done. Terror started crawling up Jessie's legs like a horde of angry spiders the second the jet went wheels down in Vancouver.

"Home, sweet home," she murmured to Matt as the jet rolled to a stop. Turning side on to him, she buried her face in his shoulder and clung to him. "Home, sweet home."

Chapter Thirty

Overlooking the North Saskatchewan River, the Fairmont Hotel MacDonald in Edmonton, Alberta, eight hours north of Calgary, provided simple, modern accommodations on a gorgeous historic property. Sweeping landscaped grounds that resonated with the hotel's 1915 origins, including a bubbling fountain and railed terraces, added to the sophisticated feel of the place. Josh and Jessie were there with Matt and Arnie; the four shared a quiet dinner in its upscale restaurant on a Monday night two weeks after the return back west.

Dylan's surgery to reconnect his broken bone happened the day after he was admitted to Vancouver General. He was now recuperating at La Casa, where Carlotta and Deirdre were catering to his every whining whim.

"He's gonna be incorrigible when he's back on his feet," Jessie cautioned them the day she tucked him into an upstairs bed.

There was only so much restraint the older women could manage, however. The thrill of having the beloved Sawyer family back home in Vancouver was never going to wear off, as far as they were concerned.

Some of the security team had moved on. Sam and Alin, married now, had set up housekeeping in Calgary to be near Alin's parents. Alin was following through on her dream of becoming a member of the Royal Canadian Mounted Police, and Sam was training cyclists on the Canadian national team. Patin, Alin's brother—the Sawyer kids' tutor for a short time before the move to the Caribbean—was back in the Alberta city as well, teaching grade four. Ulysses was still hanging around La Casa. As Charles' and Dee's old standby, he went back into high gear doing what he did best to help

Josh and Jessie navigate the relentless, curious media during their resettlement in Vancouver. Big Dan had moved on, but he jumped back into the Keating camp eagerly when he dropped by for a visit one day and was joyfully pounced upon by Emily-Grace and David. To the kids, the big Scandinavian was family.

The old white heritage home in Prince Edward Island was turned over to William and Alice.

"Do what you want with it," Josh told them over the phone. "Rent it for income if you want. We'll come visit and if it's empty, we'll stay there. If not, we'll tuck in down the road somewhere." The horses were handed over to William as well, along with a hefty budget to keep them fed and housed. Rusty, the smaller horse, had proven to be a steady, gentle animal for Dylan to learn on. William told Josh he might take up giving lessons. All of a sudden there was a lot of interest in learning to ride Dylan Sawyer's horse, and William's life had new meaning now that he'd allowed the joy of children back into it.

Carlotta, with help from Dee and a hired team, spent a few days spit shining the UBC house, but as yet the family was not living in it. They wouldn't move back in until Josh and Jessie got back from Edmonton with some kind of assessment about what they were still dealing with where Morgan was concerned. Eventually they would have to get a bigger house. For now, though, the suspected pregnancy was a false alarm. Disappointed but accepting, Josh and Jessie just decided to have fun continuing to try for baby number five.

There was little conversation at dinner in the quiet Fairmont on Monday night. Having Matt and Josh at the same table was odd, to begin with. After almost a year without contact, in Vancouver the men were mostly staying out of each other's way. They avoided talk about Jessie and tried to be 'casually friendly' when they did meet. They had a bond. A shared history like theirs, plus the kind of men they were—easygoing and able to look past the top layers to see how each other ticked—ensured that their connection would never break. Besides, on many levels Jessie was a link between them. Caring for her meant that it was in Matt's and Josh's best interests to remain social.

Matt's and Josh's worlds were littered with shattered dreams, heartache, loss, pain, fear, worry…but mostly, what motivated them was love. Love for

Jessie, love for the children and even a kind of respectful manly love for each other. Were there hard feelings? Sure, hard feelings that were easily dismissed when one brought to mind Josh's honest trust and desire, a few years back, for Jessie and the kids to live in peace in the safety of Matt's care.

After dinner, none of the four lingered in the bar to chat over drinks or, for Arnie and Josh, ginger-ale, the way they might have done in earlier years. Tomorrow was weighing on their minds.

Upstairs, Jessie, Matt and Josh said goodnight to Arnie first, since his was the first room they passed after exiting the elevator. Josh retrieved a key card from the back pocket of his jeans as he, Matt and Jessie approached the large suite where the two Sawyers would rest their heads for the night. Jessie was on Josh's right when he stopped in front of their door to unlock it.

Head down, Matt mumbled, "Good night," and started to move past them to continue down the hall.

Jessie stopped him with a subdued, "Hey," over her right shoulder.

Josh looked over at her while Matt half turned back around.

Over weighty glasses of bourbon on the dark nights when the memory of Jessie's skin sizzling on his skin haunted him, Matt told himself he owed it to Josh to be a good man from here on in—a man of integrity. The self-deprecating lectures for what he'd done in the past, for taking Jessie to his bed at a time when he should have stood back in order to give her some perspective, came hard and fast on those drink-soaked nights. Always, his self-loathing was set to an iPhone playlist of old blues, or, when he was really suffering—when his heart was ready to disintegrate into a thousand tiny pieces and the hot, steamy, remembered desire was too ripe to bear—he selected a playlist of Jessie's slow tunes, and let those rip through whatever space he happened to be in. Those were the times when Shanda was working late shooting nights, or when Matt was alone in his English Bay condo in Vancouver. Those were the times when Matt had no choice but to tell himself the few nights and days he got to have with Jessie in his arms as his lover were worth the pain, were worth the continued agony of loss.

When Josh happened to turn to Jessie while standing by the door to their suite, these were the thoughts he saw crisscross Matt's drawn face beyond her, and settle into his lonely eyes. There was more there, too, more that Josh discerned via experience, over years of working with the man and getting to know him. It was worry. A draining, exhausting, debilitating kind of worry, alleviated somewhat over the past year and a half while the Sawyers were squirreled away, but back again in force now that Josh and Jessie were determined to take back their lives.

Jessie saw it too. Clearly. Matt wasn't astute enough to hide these things, not when Jessie caught him off guard by calling out to him to say a better good night.

Josh stood at the door, poised and frozen, alarmed at feeling like a voyeuristic witness to the cracks Matt seemed unable to force back inward when Jessie called him back to her. No light was visible in Matt's cracks at that surprised moment. There was only pain, the raw, seeping kind.

A tender, worried look passed between Matt and Jessie then, and it terrified Josh. It rocked the tenuous foundation he and Jessie always seemed to have when they were around the other men she loved and couldn't let go—Jacob, for one, and even Charlie and Steve at times although their shared love was, in the last decade or more, the friendship kind. What was even more concerning were the unspoken words ricocheting between Matt and Jessie, words telegraphed through gentle, moist eyes. Words that said *I love you* clearer than if they'd been sung in a song, written in a letter, or voiced angel-soft with a kiss.

All Matt's hurts were there at the surface. In a few quick seconds he got himself back under control with a quick intake of breath and a shift of his weight to his left foot. He dipped his head. When he raised his chin again he looked to the side just in time to see fear saturate Josh's eyes.

It was the last thing Matt wanted.

What the guys telegraphed to each other in those few heated seconds wasn't any kind of stand-off or challenge. It was a shared knowing that the woman who stood between them now loved them both, that the paths they walked in this life—past, present and future—were inextricably intertwined and, if they had any say in it, would always be so. That if they lost Jessie, they too would be lost. The look also spoke of a certain reverence for each other. There was an esteem that came with being the men most loved by Jessie Wheeler. There was a marvelous wonder in the hows and whys of how they came to be with her, even now when Matt would have to lower his head and stride down to his room alone while Josh went inside to be the one to hold Jessie through what was certain to be a long, sleepless night.

Most of all, there were sorrys afloat between them, between all three as they stood in those few seconds locked in a sort of untouchable embrace that spoke of unity and a shared knowing.

Sorry on Josh's part for being the cause of the hurts Matt was unwittingly sharing now, for Josh was the man who set Jessie and Matt's lovemaking in motion in the first place—because, Josh felt, he was not man enough to handle his wild wife and the unspeakable terrors holding his family hostage.

Sorry on Matt's part for taking Josh's wife to his bed, for thumbing her damp parts and putting his mouth over her soft lips, for tracing his wet tongue over her nipples and closing his mouth over her breasts. For moaning in ecstasy at the pleasures Jessie's body granted him, for allowing her to undo his belt, his zipper, and gift him the kind of carnal ecstasy that was only ever complete when an almost supernatural, divine love was joined in perfect harmony with bodies that relished touch. With bodies that celebrated sex and so got easily buried in frenzied oblivion, and that clung to each other because the spirits inside those bodies loved each other.

Sorry on Jessie's part because she was a person who lived life on a whole deeper plane than most people, and that level of detached existence affected those around her. Her music got her there, her tragic history kept her there and her ability to see light and hope and to separate what others thought were wrongs from what she simply believed were rights catapulted her to a place where she watched the world tick by from above. She was no more capable of not loving Matt when he was there for her than she was of not taking Josh into her arms when he was the man at her side. Or Jacob, back when she was lost and alone in Edinburgh, or when she was in pieces on the floor in New York when Morgan and Nadia started their vicious game in the first place.

Like a cyclone, the things they all had to be sorry for whipped around them. The air was fusty, incomplete; breaths were hard to come by, lungs were shallow and bare.

Recognizing the emotional interplay passing between these two men whom she loved with a desperation that gutted her, Jessie took Matt's warm fingers in hers and brushed a thumb against his.

Matt was the man who would have to go it alone tonight.

And so it was Josh who stepped up and got past his own fear and past his own habit of berating himself through hostile, revolting thoughts and actions; it was Josh who moved slightly and extended a hand to Matt.

Jessie was holding Matt's left hand, telling him through touch that he wasn't alone. A new, stronger mask washed over Matt's tired face. Reaching over their joined fingers, unable to let go of Jessie just yet, he tightly gripped Josh's extended hand.

The men shook away the past, realigned the present, and affirmed the future.

Jessie would be a part of it, of both of their lives. Both of them had given up too much, of themselves and of each other, to ever consider letting her go, or to let her come between their own profound friendship.

Matt pressed his lips into a tight line and nodded once to acknowledge his respect for Josh's acceptance of him. Letting go of Josh's hand, he placed that palm over Jessie's cheek, bent to her for a brief kiss, whispered, "I love you. Sleep well, sweetheart," and walked away.

Stepping out of the shower around nine that evening, while she toweled her hair Jessie was saddened to see Josh sitting under the window against the wall in what looked like an uncomfortable hard wooden chair. The chair, its frame delicately hand-carved, seemed likely more for decorative purposes than anything else in this luxurious suite. Bent over his knees, Josh was resting his forearms on his thighs. Hands clasped tightly together, staring at the floor, he was completely lost in thought.

Scanning him for signs of distress, Jessie let the thick white towel she was using fall to the bathroom floor, and ran a wide comb through her hair. She rummaged in her suitcase for some comfy bed wear—her lace-trimmed white tank top and panties. Pulling them on, she tiptoed across the floor to her husband.

He moved when she touched him. Sitting up straight, Josh let his hands fall to the small of his wife's back when she eased her body onto his lap, straddling him, facing him.

"It'll be okay," she whispered. "All of it. I have a feeling. I've got this, Josh."

He didn't answer. Blinking, Josh pondered this beautiful creature in his arms and wondered, for the gazillionth time, why he was the lucky man to have her while Matt was alone in his suite likely drowning his loneliness in bourbon. Shanda was at *Sacred Peace* with Charlie and the gang, working long hours. Josh, Jessie, Matt and Arnie planned to drive the eight hours south to Calgary tomorrow after their scheduled meeting, and visit the set.

The *Sacred Peace* visit would be tough to take. The meeting beforehand would be killer.

They were going to Brody River Penitentiary. They were going to look Morgan in the eye and tell him in no uncertain terms that they no longer cared what he had planned for them. Regardless of what the future held, Josh, Jessie, and Matt and Arnie too, were going to take back their power.

Jessie laid a palm against Josh's cheek. "So beautiful," she murmured. "No longer itchy…"

Once they'd gotten Dylan settled after his surgery, Josh shaved his beard off and got a haircut at La Casa, with the help of an old *Drifters* hairstylist friend who came by on her day off from some sci-fi show she was shooting up on nearby Burnaby Mountain.

"Handsome," Jessie breathed, running her hands over her husband's smooth face. "My beautiful man."

Josh's eyes were troubled. His voice was husky when he spoke. "I don't know if we did the right thing, Jessie," he said. Film offers were flying in. The children were ecstatic. Jessie's tour of her new album was in the works. If one didn't look too closely, life was just about perfect once again.

Jessie couldn't think of a single thing to say to ease her husband's pain and worry. She took action instead.

Leaning forward, she pressed her mouth to the outside corner of his left eye, following up the movement with a gentle, loving kiss in the corner of his other eye. Her lips trailed down to his mouth, and Josh felt her smile at the ease with which she could kiss him without the beard annoying her. As yet there was no urgency to her kisses; it had to do with being here, alone, in this expansive suite with no children nipping at their heels, no Matt wandering La Casa, and no Charles and Dee covertly snooping to see how Josh and Jessie were getting along.

They were getting along just fine. Being alone for so long in P.E.I. was the key to uniting Josh and Jessie in a whole new way. They were more dependent on each other now, more a part of each other in some amorphous, dreamy way, and they were also more trusting of each other—Josh of Jessie's ability to balance her relationship with Matt in a way that worked for all of them, and Jessie for Josh's renewed strength and trust in her in Matt's presence, which she was certain was not always easy for Josh.

He cemented that for her now. Sometimes it was so easy for Jessie to see the little boy in her husband, the scared, lonesome boy he used to be and sometimes still was. Josh swallowed now as Jessie sat back a little on his lap and offered up one of her woeful little semi smiles. "Will you have sex with Matt again?" he asked her. "Like we talked about a year ago?"

Taken aback, Jessie's eyes flickered with uncertainty. Her smile overturned. "Yes," she told him honestly. "I will."

"He know that?" It seemed so easy a year ago for Josh to make that offer. To tell Jessie he would not stand in her way if and when she needed Matt again. With Matt in their lives again on an almost daily basis—with him next door now—that promise was harder to stomach.

Jessie shook her head. Lowering her fingers to Josh's lap, she was the child now. Shoulders hunched over, suddenly self-conscious, she repeatedly snapped one thumbnail over another as she considered what to say. Looking up, she tossed her hair and met her husband's solemn, molten eyes. "Nothing will change between you and me. When I choose to be with him again it will be at a time when you and I have some miles between us. I won't go to him one night and you the next."

"What about Shanda?" Josh was struggling with this. Jessie was a storm who could never be tamed. With her, there was never an intention to hurt another soul. Her storm was electric, a rebel tempest in a sea of her own making. There was no refining this woman in Josh's care. There was no telling her what to do or who to go to. All Josh could do was be her compass; all he could be was her port in a storm.

"Shanda is Matt's business," Jessie answered. "I don't want to hurt her.

I won't be with him behind her back. He needs to be honest with her. She can hate me all she wants, but Josh—I need him sometimes."

"When I'm weak. When I lose my shit."

Zach's description of Josh as a child, banished to a coat closet to hang his head and weep amongst mops and brooms, played out in a black and white movie in Jessie's mind. Josh was lost in her now, in the pale eyes he loved so well. *He wants a guarantee,* Jessie thought, tilting her head adorably at him. *He wants me to tell him I will always come back. I can do one better than that.*

She smiled. Fully. Her eyes came back to life, bringing with them damp rainbows of promise. "Babe," she said, placing a palm on each side of his face and sitting up straighter so that her toes touched the floor and her back was a gentle curve, "I will be here for you. Always. I know when you need to be held. I know when you need to be loved. You will see."

"He doesn't have these demons, Jessie." Josh's voice was gravel. "Matt can drink and put the cap back on the bottle. He doesn't piss himself. He doesn't…" His voice broke. The words cracked like clay under a scorching sun in the Arizona desert. "He doesn't abandon his family so he can drink himself into oblivion."

"You know what I love most about you, Josh? Right now?" Jessie was battling her own emotions, along with the truths she uttered to Matt when she lay in his arms all those months ago. She was stronger now. Extended time alone in Josh's company gave her the strength she needed; time alone with him was time to rebuild a stronger foundation, not just for their family, but for her as his partner as well. "I love, babe, that you are not lying to me. That you can sit here and acknowledge that these demons you fight—alcohol, darkness—still have power over you. I know they always will. Addictions are like that. Matt's mine, babe. A need to be with him again is mine. These addictions of ours—they don't change a damn thing between us. They just make us honest. And I think, Josh, that this honesty is what will hold us together, you and me. Let's not be afraid anymore. Of anything, Josh. Let's just love each other the best way we know how."

The clouds in his eyes abated somewhat. Jessie was so loving right now, so in love, that she wasn't really looking *at* him. She was looking *in* him, inside the beautiful wounded eyes that captivated her so fully, that captured her heart one starlit night so, so long ago.

To show her he was done talking, done worrying, that he wanted to explore her fully now in the quiet of this large suite, Josh slipped his big hands under the bottom hem of her tank top. Moving his hands upward, he thumbed at the sides of her breasts, and relaxed when she responded by biting her bottom lip, rewarded him with a tiny nod, and granted him full dominance of her body and of her soul.

Already Jessie was moving her hips in a slow, rhythmic rocking motion, teasing Josh, raking her fingers through his hair, giving him a reason to further push his worries aside and take charge of the bliss of the present moment.

Josh let his hands move around her body, under her breasts. He lifted the white cotton lace up over her nipples and brushed his thumbs over the swell of her breasts before he bent forward and placed his mouth fully over her right nipple. Bringing her into his mouth as far as he could, he sucked and groaned, and groaned again when Jessie placed a hand behind his head, rifled her fingers through his hair, tilted her head back, closed her eyes and arched her body into him.

So many fearful things past and present were still nipping at their heels, giving them a sense of renewed urgency. Almost as if she were surprised at how sweet and intimate loving Josh could be when they had the luxury of time on their side, Jessie let her eyes flit open and looked down at her man in her arms while he suckled her. Raising a hand, she grazed the side of her breast with her fingers, brought her hand to his cheek, and whispered, "I love you."

Josh took that as his cue to take the woman he loved more completely. He gave a little grunt and took her elbows in his. Slipping off his lap, Jessie rose and turned around. Taking his hand, she led him to the bed and pulled the covers down. Lying mostly on her stomach, one leg bent on its side, Jessie almost cried in anticipation. How sweet it was—the precious moment before a man's deep love incarnated in touch, taste, sound and movement.

Josh yanked his T-shirt up over his head and unzipped his jeans. He slipped onto the bed next to Jessie, fully on his side.

"Love you back," he said in an exhalation ripe with need, tilting her head toward him for a long, lingering exploration of her lips and mouth. "I could live on this," he murmured, his lips tingling against hers. "Your body in my arms. You are my lifeblood. You are my salvation."

His honesty—his need of her—slayed Jessie. Mewling softly, she sank more fully into him and drew her bent left knee up between his legs so she could press it against him. Raising her hips off the bed, she writhed in pleasure when Josh slipped his fingers under her body and down her panties. Even better, as he kissed her Josh inched closer and slipped his right hand down the back of her underwear. Both hands played over Jessie's body, over the damp, hot part of her that ached for him. *You're made for me,* she almost wept. *Your fingers are made to fit over that part of me, and into that part of me.*

Gasping now, panting, Jessie ached for more of him, to bring him into her mouth and taste him, to give him a little suck, but the sheer sweetness of what he was doing to her was so damn spot-on that she couldn't bring herself to give it up just yet. Josh didn't seem to care; he was into this now, he was into her, into making her thrust her body against the palm of his left hand over and over and over again. The little mewling whimpers were sending him over the edge; his hips were moving too, his body pressing against her, his thighs squeezing her bent leg, his mouth releasing primal grunt after grunt as he grazed his fingers along her body, in the little curve. He plunged them inside her, urging a cry out of Jessie that he wondered whether Matt heard next door.

The thought drove him wild. *It's because I have her,* Josh told himself. *It's because I'm taking her right now. It's because—overall—she belongs to me.*

"I'm gonna come," Jessie cried, half weeping, pressing herself into his hand, adjusting her body just a little higher up so Josh could inch even closer and more urgently push his fingers into her. "I need you inside," she begged. "I need you inside." Clutching his probing fingers, halting his insistent, hungry actions, Jessie rolled over onto her back and shoved a hand down Josh's jeans. "Hurry," she pleaded. "Hurry."

Josh moved over her. Jessie widened her legs for him, and helped him along by pushing his jeans down over his hips. The first thrust was hard, the second—Josh held it, he put it on pause so he could gasp at the sensational waves of pure ecstasy coming from Jessie's body clenching hard around him; so he could tease her, and build her anticipation even more.

"Oh my abs," she moaned when her stomach clenched. The weeping feeling that overcame her earlier did an about face. Jessie almost started laughing. "The gym this morning. So sore. Oh, Jesus."

Josh's lips curled up at the corners, just for a second, but he didn't laugh along with her. *This* was the sweetest moment of all, the one that made that heart wrenching look on Matt's face outside their suite worth it; the one that made life worth it, the one that made everything worth it. This extended pause, with Jessie so desperate for release that she was pushing her body up into him, with both of their bodies taut as wires ready to shatter like glass, was akin to pouring gunpowder from a keg and standing above it with a match.

He made her beg. He made her want it. Josh made Jessie rise up into him and continue to clench around him, and he made it last. Although Jessie would never tell Josh this, to her their lovemaking—the build up, the rise toward explosion—was like one of Jacob's guitar solos. Josh played her body the way Jacob chose notes. The buildup was spectacular, albeit sometimes demanding, and right now it was damn punishing. In Josh's and Jessie's lives, all of the pain came down to this, to the trust each had in the other to bury their hurts, to set them aside when it came time to love. The pain was a screaming guitar that resolved its grueling journey with one final, perfect, explosive, orgasmic note.

Jessie couldn't stand it. She drove a finger down between their bodies and rubbed it over herself, adding another stick of dynamite to the gunpowder trail, another screaming arpeggio to the solo, and then it was time to drop the match.

Josh stopped holding back. He gave her all he had to give.

She shattered.

For sure Matt heard the irrepressible cries that followed. Josh teased Jessie later that the patrons in the bar on the first floor heard them too as she bucked and kicked and writhed in his arms.

When Jessie started to come down off her high, her heart at first racing at breakneck speed, Josh breathed warmly into her neck and planted little kisses. Jessie pressed her lips to his nipples, tonguing them while Josh moved further up her body to savor the last of this divine connection, this absolutely perfect unity of body and soul.

"I love your body," Jessie purred, moving her palms delicately over his muscular shoulders. Sliding her fingers down her husband's back, she ran them along the welcoming, concave curves at his hips. Bending both legs, she drew her knees up alongside Josh's body so that she was completely tucked into that safe place inside his arms. She hooked one baby toe into the other foot's big toe and rocked with him, loving the feel of his hair as it tickled her cheek, the warmth of his body as he cradled her.

Josh liked his lovemaking plain. They had a few toys they sometimes called forth—a vibrator, most often, but they did well enough on their own not to bother with any extras, most times.

Did Jessie want to share Josh? Ever? The way she had shared Jacob? Never. This man was one to be loved and cherished on his own.

This lovemaking had an urgency to it. It was a direct attempt to assuage a difficult tomorrow; it was a way of offering assurance.

It was a way of grasping the now instead of longing for a past that could not be fixed, or of aching for a future that could not be tamed.

It was a way of hanging on.

Rolling onto her side, Jessie curled into the treasured sanctuary of Josh's body, and slipped into a dreamless sleep.

$$Chapter\ Thirty\text{-}one$$

$\mathcal{M}$att didn't hear any lovemaking sounds. After a lonely half hour of hopeless channel surfing, he traipsed back down the hall to Arnie's room to talk over plans for the Brody visit. They went down to the bar. Both men's minds were overrun with potential scenarios of what might likely transpire. What if Josh lost his temper, for one thing? How could he, without losing his shit, possibly handle being in the presence of the man who tried to destroy his family?

Surprisingly, Jessie wasn't an issue. Matt and Arnie were truly confident she had found some kind of amity over this whole thing. She seemed to have a calm about her, a peace engendered perhaps by a lot of time to think—and maybe pray—while she lingered with her husband and children on her healing island.

During their discussion, Matt and Arnie concluded that if at any point Josh seemed to be struggling to keep his composure during the Brody visit, Jessie would be able to calm him.

*Love does that for her, for them,* Matt considered the next morning while he drew his razor over his chin. Truly, when Josh and Jessie were good, Jessie carried an aura of composed tranquility. If need be, she could easily soothe her sometimes troubled husband with a simple, loving touch.

They met the warden in his office at nine a.m. The stocky man offered coffee to his celebrity guests and sat them down to talk before they would make their way further into the penitentiary.

"You know about Oren Caulfield," he said right off the bat.

Arnie did the talking for the Vancouver group. "We do. We heard."

"Nobody's taken responsibility for it. I admit that it's out of character for Morgan. He has been involved in minor scuffles with Caulfield, but this came as a surprise."

"You think Morgan killed the guard?" Suddenly this visit was a larger threat.

Jessie's eyes darted over to Matt, who was sitting kitty-corner to her and Josh. She didn't put it past him to call this visit off entirely. He felt her eyes on him, and looked over. A slight shake of her head—he got the message. *Don't even think about it.*

The warden brought his coffee to his lips before he spoke again. "It was a swarm," he elaborated. "An effective way of protecting the perpetrator. We don't know. The weapon disappeared. Cameras didn't catch a damn thing."

"Sounds like there was a consensus." Arnie scratched the side of his neck. He seemed completely unconcerned, which Jessie, Josh and Matt all found curious.

"To kill Caulfield? Yes. It would appear that way."

"Will Morgan be in cuffs today?" That was Matt jumping in doing his thing, crossing t's and dotting i's. They'd already been told Morgan would be in cuffs, but in Matt's experience it never hurt to ask twice.

"Yes. There will be two corrections officers present as well. Morgan will be completely subdued. He won't pose any threat."

"Sure he will." Josh's husky voice caught them all off guard. Nobody said a thing in response. Jessie was already holding his hand in her lap. Exerting a little pressure, she was relieved to feel him squeeze her fingers back.

The warden studied the flicking nerve on Josh's cheek and the muscled body easily discerned underneath Josh's cream Henley. A questioning look to Arnie was rewarded with an intense, quiet, calm look back. Relaxing, the warden pointed his coffee cup at Jessie. "Vaughn's waiting on a song from you," he said. "He's got the population all riled up. His pride's at stake."

Raising her chin like a petulant six year old, Jessie bit off, "Vaughn did something he shouldn't have. He'll be waitin' a while."

A barely-there exhale left Josh's lips. He turned his face away from Jessie, to the big window in the warden's large office. Clear blue sky filled his vision. *If only,* he caught himself thinking, chewing on the corner of his lip. *Clear skies ahead…*

The rest of the coffee meet and greet was dominated by chatter between the warden and Arnie, mostly about guys with whom they were both acquainted who had passed through Brody's gates.

Matt tuned out; he spent the half hour covertly watching Josh and Jessie communicate with each other without saying a word. Last night, walking away from them at the hotel suite door? It sucked. Period. This morning was at least partially making up for it. It was like they didn't know anyone else was in the room with them. Sitting next to each other on a sofa, they were holding hands and lightly brushing their thumbs over each other's fingers. Little smiles teased their lips as if the simple, chaste thumb touches were a much deeper conversation, one that spoke of promise and hope. At one point it seemed like the touches were almost too much, as if they were somehow igniting more than just the underlying passion that always reigned between these two, as if by themselves the touches were clearing away skin, laying bare all the nasty crap of the last years.

It was easy to tell when the hard memories took over. Josh closed his eyes, let out a little groan, and moved his right hand up to place it on the opposite side of Jessie's head. He pressed her toward him and kissed her temple. It was a lingering kiss that, to Matt, appeared like Josh was trying to breathe Jessie in. In response, Jessie seemed to swallow back her own fears. She lifted an arm and clutched Josh's left elbow, and stayed in his embrace until Arnie cleared his throat to call them back to the task at hand.

When Jessie rose, she found herself in Matt's gaze. He was the last to stand. Before he did, he made no attempt to hide the adoration in his eyes. Jessie blushed and treated him to a small smile. They, too, could communicate without words. What he was saying to her was *I'm so glad. I want you to be happy.*

Twenty minutes later they were standing outside the same interview room where Jessie met with Morgan eons ago. The warden left them in the capable hands of a no-nonsense female corrections officer, a ponytailed, freckled blonde who waited, with a strong hand poised on the door handle, for Josh and Jessie to give her the word to open it and let them in.

Matt and Arnie stood back and waited too. Arnie was a rock in a place like this. This was familiar ground to him. Matt didn't like it one bit. Prisons were a world he left behind when he left the RCMP, and watching Josh and Jessie come to some kind of terms with what they might face inside was pure torture. Half facing Arnie, Matt stared at his shoes and repeatedly swiped a nervous finger under his nose.

Josh's eyes, locked on the door through which they were about to pass—into a horrid past and a nebulous future—were wide and scared.

Gripping his hands, Jessie turned him to her. "Babe, we are not giving him any more of our precious energy. We are taking back our power. Do not let him get to you. His life spun out of control the day his child got sick. It may not always make sense to us, but Morgan is a victim here too."

Slowly, Josh shook his head from side to side. "I don't always see the world the way you do, Jessie. But I sure as hell wish I did."

Her face relaxed into a Jessie special—her childlike best. The light in her pale blue eyes was moist, bright and flowing, like sparkling clear river water on a brand new summer morning. She angled her face at him. "It took me a while to bounce back this time, Josh," she admitted truthfully. "But really, when you think about it, isn't that the only way to look at the world? Any other way is just admitting defeat. Any other way is letting the bad stuff rule. Love one another. Everyone. That's the way. That's the only way."

"I love you," he said.

"I know." Cocky as hell, Jessie smiled widely, a little crookedly in her bashful kind of way. "I crazy love you back."

Josh crunched down on a lip and let himself half smile back. He looked over at the guard and nodded.

The female guard flipped the handle down, and they stepped inside.

Chapter Thirty-Two

The room was overly bright. An inset overhead light happened to be recessed in the ceiling above where Morgan sat. It ringed his short hair, giving him an odd halo effect. He looked up when they came in, which threw all four of his visitors off balance right off the bat. What they recalled about the man was a shy, solemn guy who never looked anyone in the eye.

Like, friggin' ever.

Jessie glanced at Josh before she reached for the chair by the table in front of Morgan and pulled it out. It gutted her to see the way her husband was blinking and swallowing repeatedly, although a certain pride took hold when she noted that Josh was restrained enough to stand a few feet behind her to let her have her say. He was not averting his eyes from Morgan.

Morgan sat up straighter. It killed him to have to sit in front of Jessie and the others with his hands cuffed to the table, but so be it. One of his journeys over the past few years, through yoga and meditation, was accepting responsibility for his actions. Cuffed to a table, his pride stripped so that he felt naked, exposed, humiliated, was a 'thing' the last time he and Jessie met face to face. Today it was moderately acceptable. Today Morgan was in a better place. He was on a more even keel.

Matt and Arnie took up positions beside Josh, standing a little behind him, flanking him. The female guard was inside now too, holding court at the door. A young male redheaded officer was already in the room with Morgan. Jessie and Matt recognized him from their last visit, and both nodded hello. He seemed fairly chill and was almost smiling, as if he and Morgan had been engaged in an amicable chat before the strained, nervous visitors appeared.

It was impossible to fling all of the difficult emotions off to distant corners of the room, even for Jessie. Folding her hands on the table in front of her, she faced the man who, along with his wife, had set her family on a turbulent, seemingly never ending, stormy path.

She didn't bother opening with a greeting.

"You're looking at me," she challenged instead. "Why?"

Morgan blinked. Refocusing his eyes, he tilted his head up to look past Jessie so he could critically regard Josh. There was no malice in Josh's eyes, which initially disarmed Morgan. He had no clue what this visit was about until that moment, until the second he spied sadness in Josh's demeanor, in the way the guy was standing with his feet apart, planted in the floor as if he had mentally sent roots spiraling down into the earth to hold him steady.

Spying Morgan's searching gaze on him, Josh hauled his shoulders back and replaced the hurt and fear with something stronger, with a careful determination he drew from his wife.

Wondering how much Arnie knew, if anything, via his connection to Vaughn, Morgan nodded a greeting to the ex-boxer, then let his eyes drift sideways to Matt. There was something different in Matt today too, in the way he looked done-in and tired, in the way his lips moved just slightly and his body tensed when Morgan shifted in his seat.

"I wouldn't hurt her," Morgan said to Matt in an attempt to appease him, to calm him.

Matt wanted to speak, but Jessie had asked all of them to stay silent and keep their emotions in check. She was in control of this difficult gathering. Her chaperones respected her enough to let her see the meeting through.

Twisting around to Matt, Jessie waited until his eyes met hers. She messaged him a silent *It's okay. I've got this.* He forced the dire waterfall of remembrance in his gut to stay put.

"Thank you," Jessie whispered to Morgan when she turned back around to face him. "For saying that."

His eyes flicked back to her. A wish was in them. Jessie could see it plain as day, hovering just beneath the surface. It was accompanied by genuine sorrow and a sprinkle of peace.

All of a sudden the room seemed to brighten there at the table, as if someone was capturing the two people sitting across from each other with a spotlight. The source was a beam of sunlight floating in the small, high window. It isolated Jessie and Morgan in a way that helped facilitate what needed to be said.

"You're probably wondering why we are here," Jessie started, her voice steady and true.

Morgan hesitated. "I can guess."

"I don't think you can. The last time I was here I begged you to spare my husband's life. The lives of my children. Today I am not here to beg."

"I'm listening." Again, that almost serene tranquility in Morgan's voice, his eyes…

*Huh,* Jessie said to herself. Her wondering eyes settled into a peace of their own.

Her declaration emerged slowly, each single word a testament to the weight it carried. "We came back to Vancouver because we no longer want to spend our lives in hiding. We want you to know that we are not afraid of you anymore."

She waited.

Morgan was silent, watchful.

"Morgan…we're taking back our power."

At first Morgan's lips moved and he looked away, but no sounds emerged from him. After a bit he found enough self-assurance to make his brain and body respond. "S'good, Jessie," he murmured back to her. The honesty in that, in the intent way Morgan searched for and held Jessie's gaze, floored her. "I'm glad."

Nobody expected that, except perhaps the redheaded guard who, when all was said and done, was in all honesty Morgan's good friend.

Jessie sought a little more courage. Clasping her hands so tightly together that her fingers whitened, she tossed her curls and repeated her assertion. "We are no longer allowing you to have power over us, Morgan. We've decided…what will be…will be."

With a quick look to the table, to his cuffed hands, Morgan let out a stiff breath, lifted his head again, and gave her a silent nod. He didn't offer anything further.

"I—I hear you've been doing well. Yoga. And that kind of thing. Teaching others." Jessie was reaching for more. The decision was made before they even flew to Edmonton for her to simply say her piece and leave, but that was proving difficult to do. *Maybe I can engage him,* she was thinking. *Maybe I can take my battered army home to live in peace.*

Still, Morgan was silent. To him, Jessie barely seemed real. It was odd to have her sitting there across from him smelling of her familiar lavender—and dotted with sunshine—telling him she was summoning up her courage and deciding to live a life of her own choosing as opposed to a life dictated by fear.

Jessie tried a few more times to engage him. Morgan seemed interested; his eyes worked as if they had things to unleash, to say, but he was either still cowed by her or he didn't know how to say what he wanted to.

"I guess that's all," Jessie said softly in the end. "I wish…I wish…" Her eyes were pleading. Resigned. Closing them, she inhaled deeply and sucked up her resolve. *It's okay,* she told herself. *We've decided. We can move on.*

Behind her, all three men supporting Jessie ached for what it was she couldn't say.

Just as she rose and turned to go, a quiet voice emerged out of the space behind her proud shoulders.

"You…were always nice to me."

Jessie wheeled slowly back around. "Of course," she mumbled. "You were nice to me back then too. We used to…" She shrugged. "We used to go to the gym together."

Morgan had enough leeway with his cuffs that he could stand. He looked behind Jessie at Matt, kept his eyes on him, and eased his sturdy body upright in a non-threatening way. Matt recognized the gesture. His body was rigid and taut, but he didn't vault forward.

"Jessie," Morgan said, refocusing on her. "You can live free now. You and Josh, and your children. There's nothing more to fear."

For a second she believed him. The others did not. Morgan saw the surprise, the light, the hope in her eyes. It all vanished at once, sucked down a vacuum into the hands of time.

"Why would you say that to me?" she asked him. "Is it because your minion—Caulfield—is gone? We know you have a network, Morgan. We know you can find a replacement."

He blinked. His lips parted. The peace in his eyes…

The truth hit Jessie like a lightning bolt. She almost collapsed, and had to grab for the chair she'd just vacated before she could speak again.

"There's a peace in your eyes, Morgan, that I've never seen before. Even when we worked together, I never saw peace in you." She hesitated. "You've connected to a higher power. You've connected to God."

"I was always connected," he answered carefully. "Back then I just… I just forgot to ask for help."

"Morgan…I prayed for you. Every night."

He smiled. It was gentle, barely a curve on his lips, but it was there. It reached his eyes and, way back in the deepest, darkest depths of them, set a tiny light aglow. "I prayed for you too, Jessie. For all of you."

"Jesus, Morgan." Clinging to the chair, clutching the top rail for support, both shoulders hunched over, Jessie breathed, "It was never you. Was it? That last while, all the shit that happened while Josh was working on *Sacred Peace*…it was never you."

He didn't need to answer. The flicker in Morgan's eyes was enough.

Behind Jessie there was movement from Josh, and movement from Matt, although it was barely-there shuffles, as if both were as thrown by this new revelation as Jessie was.

She forced herself to stand taller. In front of her, Morgan stilled. A wet sheen formed across his eyes. He held Jessie's gaze as if he were afraid she would bolt if he looked away, if he lost contact.

"If not you, then…"

Still, Morgan stayed silent. His mouth was working, but no words emerged. Jessie's chest was heaving with the effort to digest this unbelievable eye-opener.

A voice from the far wall broke the silence. The redheaded guard— Morgan's friend. "It was Caulfield," he told them quietly. "Caulfield thought he could buy friends in the prison population by evening the score for people. It was Caulfield who decided to go after you guys. Once he realized Morgan wasn't alongside, he got frustrated and started to punish him." He waved at his buddy. "Morgan here spent a lot of time in the SHU this year, trying to fight back. Trying to convince Caulfield to leave all of you alone."

An unexpected grateful look from Morgan to his friend was enough to convince Morgan's visitors that there was some sincerity to what they were learning here today. Without exception, all four were stunned.

Morgan faced Jessie again. Willing the others to listen as well, he glanced past her at Josh, Arnie, and then at Matt before he spoke. "Nadia and I caused you and your family enough pain, Jessie. No more. To honor you, and in my son's memory, I've issued a directive. Nobody in Brody Pen will ever have anything further to do with hurting you. Caulfield's power died with him. The network outside these walls is also on your side."

Nobody spoke. In the hallway, somebody wearing heavy boots strode quickly by. In the room the only sound was the creaking of the chair Jessie was leaning on while she struggled to find her breath.

"I don't know what—I don't know what to say," she said in the end. "All this time…Morgan, we thought it was you."

Morgan rescued her. "Caulfield forgot something when he decided to go after your family. He forgot how barren the world is without you on stage sharing your music with those of us who need it. Without your films to give us hope. Guys in prisons like Brody—we need you. We need the kind of hope you bring to the world, Jessie."

Floored by the change evident in Morgan that he himself credited to a connection with a higher energy—one fueled by light and love—Jessie whispered tearfully, "I'm nothing without my husband, Morgan. I've got nothing to give the world when he's not with me."

"I think I learned that when I was with you that first while, Jessie. Back when Josh got sick and ended up in the hospital in Toronto." Morgan regrouped, and raised his hands toward his old boss in an appeal from his heart. "I wish I was stronger back then. After I lost my son I had no strength left to fight Nadia. After…Langley…I had no strength to fight Caulfield. Jessie…" Morgan's eyes flitted back to Josh again. "Josh…I know it's not enough…it will never be enough. But I am sorry for the pain I caused you." His gaze slipped over to Arnie and then to Matt. "For the pain I caused all of you."

Josh, Matt and Arnie could not look at each other. If they did, the feeble bond of strength all were calling up from the depths of their toes would have crumbled and betrayed their attempts to be strong for Jessie. Once again, to nobody's surprise their brave, often childish, magical girl schooled all of them.

"What about forgiveness, Morgan?" she asked. "Do you need forgiveness?"

Morgan's knees went weak. The moisture in his eyes, heightened by the light above, was shining brightly now, too brightly. "I can't…I wouldn't ask. I've done too much…I've hurt you all so badly…"

The table between them was suddenly too much. It was a brick wall, a symbol of what held all of them captive for far too long. Jessie didn't hesitate. Striding around it, she faced Morgan and took his cuffed hands in hers.

Watching, Josh couldn't breathe. A tight rope seemed wound around his neck. He kept swallowing in an attempt to struggle past it, to let some air in. He was ready to pounce if Morgan took one step out of line, yet Josh was also completely transfixed. On his left, Arnie was humbled. Years on the Downtown Eastside had taught him a long, long time ago that surprises like this, these kinds of transformations in a man's character, and forgiveness on the part of those with merciful, transcendent hearts like Jessie's, can lead to incredible, beautiful things. Matt, on Josh's right, was immobile. Later he would tell Charlie that his heart stopped the second Jessie touched Morgan.

Morgan started to sob. His crying was a low sad sound filled with years of loss, and now—renewal. He couldn't stop staring at Jessie's hands on his. The feel of her skin—it was not in the least a sexual sensation or a sexual yearning. It was the much missed simplicity of being touched by another human being, one with the capacity to care far, far beyond the worldly bonds of earth.

"I want you to know, Morgan," Jessie started, her eyes soft and doey in his, "that I hope I never get blindsided by the kind of pain you live with every day at the loss of your son. And at the loss of the woman you loved. I cannot begin to imagine how devastating that must be."

Morgan's low-key snuffling disarmed everyone in the room to the point where, even if they could breathe, all of the men—and the female guard, too—didn't want to, for fear of missing any of the thick, emotional, visceral moments that, beyond any doubt, told them a power larger than themselves was at play.

"The world can be a dark and frightening place," Jessie was saying, her eyes latched securely on Morgan's dipped head as tears trailed down his cheeks. "Bad things happen to good people. People hang on to old feuds and darkness and all it does is build hopelessness and despair and anger and rage." Shifting her weight, she rocked back on a heel. Jessie's eyes were a rich blue now, a richer blue than even Josh had ever seen them. She was glowing from the inside out. "What's the good of that?" she said to her old workout buddy. "I can't speak for the others in this room, or in my life, Morgan... but you know something, honey? There was some good that came out of all this bad. The time us Sawyers just spent together as a family was a precious, precious gift."

Astonished at Jessie's capacity to look at such darkness this way, Morgan looked up from their joined hands.

"All the time I had my husband to myself was an incredible gift." Jessie smiled and peeked over at Josh, who was as still as a statue, in complete awe of the woman he had the honor of calling his wife.

Shyly, Josh ducked his head and stared at his toes when Jessie looked sideways to Matt and added, "My relationship with this man here," she nodded at Matt, "is so, so beautiful now. So deep and perfect and beautiful."

Matt had to talk himself out of melting into the floor.

She looked over at Arnie. "This man has become a part of our family."

Arnie drew his shoulders up taller and allowed a small smile to pass between him and Jessie.

"We made our own light," Jessie continued, turning back to Morgan. "All of us. We had to."

Morgan choked back a few last sobs. "You're my inspiration, Jessie. All this teaching I'm doing is meant to honor you. It's to honor you and to honor my son."

"I want you to live in light, Morgan. I want us to live in light, not in darkness anymore. I forgive you, honey. I forgive you."

He couldn't put his arms around her, but Jessie wrapped hers around him. That simple cleansing hug sustained Morgan for years.

"Will you be okay?" Jessie asked him when she finally let him go.

"I will," he answered. "Yes. I will."

One last little smile, and Jessie let her fingers drift away from Morgan. Spying Josh watching her, she tilted her chin up just slightly, and her eyes sparkled.

From behind her, just as she reached the door, she heard Morgan's voice one last time that day.

"Namaste," he said.

Over her shoulder, Jessie smiled widely. Morgan was glowing. He was, indeed, learning to live in joy.

"Namaste," she sent back to him on wings of peace. "Namaste, my friend."

Arnie left Josh, Jessie and Matt to go outside and wait for him. He was led to another room where he met with Vaughn, alone. There, he got the whole story the way Morgan had eventually told it to Vaughn. There, Arnie was asked one last time for the song Vaughn felt was owed to him.

Outside the prison in the parking lot nobody was yet ready to speak. All the way back through the long, narrow halls, nary a word had passed between Josh, Jessie and Matt. Words were completely inadequate. Words were of no use in a world they thought was dark that had quite suddenly and surprisingly become a divine and magical place.

Matt was the first to break down. Josh was the first to notice.

"Go," he whispered to his wife. "He needs you for a change."

"You," Jessie murmured to Josh as she let go of the hand she'd been holding since they left Morgan's side, "are the most remarkable man on the planet. You hold my soul in the palm of your hand, Josh Sawyer." Tipping her face to his, Jessie sighed. Josh smiled under the kiss she pressed against his lips. After touching his lips with a finger, Jessie turned and made her way over to Matt.

Josh leaned against the side of the Lincoln Navigator Charles had rented for the group. Shoving his hands in his pockets, he fixed his gaze on the thirty-foot high razor wire topped walls of Brody River Penitentiary, and on the gun turrets spaced periodically along the perimeter. Morgan would spend his life here. What a miracle that he had made the choice to make it worthwhile.

Today was a day of miracles.

Matt was shaking profusely when Jessie approached him. Bent over, he clutched his knees and trembled, trying not to vomit.

Jessie crouched before him and grasped his face in her palms. "Matt, honey. I think it's over now. I think it's really over. You did good, baby. You did real good."

"Not good…enough…" he gasped. "Jesus, I can't…I can't breathe."

"Look at me, Matt. Just look at me." Exerting some pressure, Jessie got him to meet her eyes. There was so much worry there, still, so much troubled water running through those beautiful, gentle eyes. "Count with me, baby," Jessie said, employing a trick Matt often used with her in the past. "Just breathe. One…two…three…four…better? Come on, baby, breathe with me. Five…six…"

By the time they got to ten he was able to take full breaths. Standing, Jessie took his left hand in hers and eased him upright. "It all just caught up to you, huh?" she asked tenderly.

Josh was close by. Over Jessie's shoulder, Matt saw him make the occasional furtive glimpse in their direction. Placing his hands on Jessie's hips, which seemed like safe enough places to keep Josh from becoming upset, Matt buried himself in the eyes he loved. "I shouldn't have left in the first place," he said. "All those years ago just before Josh got sick, if I hadn't left, Morgan would never have been hired."

"Are you kidding me?" Jessie quickly harrumphed him. "Matt, what's the point of looking back and riding yourself about that now? We can't undo time, baby. Punishing yourself—me punishing myself for all the stupid shit I do—what good does it do? The river's already run its course. Morgan's making good. Look at all the people he's helping. There is good shit coming out of this mess. Real good shit."

"Josh will be okay. You and the children…you'll be okay."

"Y-yeah. I sure as hell hope so. It feels right, Matt. It feels like the world is back on its axis again."

Her back was to Josh. Matt glanced over her shoulder at him again. Josh was staring at the ground, lost in thought, likely contemplating what he almost threw away, Matt figured. A heavy sigh preceded his next words to Jessie. "I thought I was going to lose it last night, Jessie. At your door."

She swallowed. The old electric buzz was still there. "That agreement Josh and me came to last summer," she said, stunning him for the umpteenth time that day, "still stands, Matt. Time hasn't eroded how I feel about you. Not one bit. Discretion and reason," she added, "can make it work. You and me will never have to say goodbye. As long as you can work things out with Shanda." Jessie shook her head slowly. "I won't sleep with you behind her back, Matt."

Matt was so thrown he couldn't speak at first. Eventually he said, "I don't get why Josh would still agree to that, Jessie. After you've had so much time together, why would he grant you that kind of freedom?"

"Because, Matt," she explained softly, "he loves me. That's why. He knows what you mean to me. He damn near almost handed me to you before."

"He feels indebted to me because of the river. He thinks he owes me."

"Doesn't he?" She bit down hard enough on a lip to make it bleed.

"Jesus Christ, Jessie. Do you realize what you're asking your husband— and my wife— to do?"

"Tons of people in this world have open marriages, Matt."

"And tons of people lose their minds with jealousy."

Jessie lowered her voice. "I want to be with you again. I loved being with you that way, baby. That look you gave me in the hallway last night…"

"Sex, Jessie, the way you look at it—"

"Is probably the most healthy way anyone can look at it," she interjected. "This is not about how I feel about myself, Matt. This is not about me behaving like a whore. This is about me taking my life in my own hands. I love Josh and I will always love Josh. I will never leave him and I pray he never leaves me. But somewhere along the line when our lives spun out of control it became very clear to me that the arms in this world I feel the safest in are yours. Yours, Matt."

She waited for him to take that in.

"I know I'm a selfish bitch. But I am not willing to let that magic between you and me go. Not when…" Again, Jessie bit her lip. "Look, I pray Josh never spins out again. If he does I'll be there to pick up the pieces. I won't leave him alone. But if by chance you and me find ourselves alone in a hotel room in goddamned Transylvania, I'm gonna love you up one side and down the other. This is what all of this shit with Morgan has amounted to for me. This is where it lands. On love. You okay with this?"

Matt was crumbling again. The tide turned. He was indebted to Josh now, although this was something he was quite certain he and Jessie's husband would never speak aloud of.

Clutching Jessie to him, he whispered in her ear, "Yes," and in his heart, a tiny butterfly took flight.

Chapter Thirty-three

*H*ours later, dinner at a Calgary steakhouse seemed like just the right place to end the long, emotional day. A whole new peace encircled the small group of folks who took seats at a round table in a dimly lit restaurant when *Sacred Peace* wrapped for the day.

"Was it weird?" Charlie asked Josh as the server cleared away their dinner dishes. Jessie shot him a look. "What?" Charlie retorted.

"'Course it was weird," Jessie guffawed. "Jesus, Charlie. Have a heart."

"Yeah," Josh chuckled lightly, tossing back a sip of water with lemon. "It sucked." Jessie took his free hand and entwined her fingers in his on his thigh, where she tenderly relished the feel of his skin on hers.

Matt was there, keeping an eye out for celebrity-hungry photographers and newshounds. Shanda, quiet to a fault, was clinging to Matt's side. Jane was in Canmore with the Deacon children. Charles was home in Vancouver to help keep an eye on the kids. Jon was away, and Arnie would join them shortly.

Charlie responded to the critical looks Jessie was shooting at him and took the group in another direction. "How're the kids doing without you guys for a change?"

"Great," Jessie answered, tipping back her glass to coerce an ice cube between her lips. "They don't even miss us," she crunch-talked. "Even Micah's having a blast at La Casa, or so we're told."

"How long are you staying?"

"Flying back in the morning."

"Bummer. Jane would like to see you."

"Too bad, so sad," Jessie quipped. "I don't want to see her."

"From what I heard, today was all about forgiveness, Jess."

She shrugged. "Apparently I get along better with men than I do with women." Still crunching away on the ice cube, she touched a curious finger to her lip and narrowed her eyebrows. "I wonder why that is."

Beside her, Josh groaned and looked away.

Shanda snorted in a very unfeminine way.

Jessie's eyes darted to her.

"Oh, shit, here we go," Charlie grinned, a twinkle in his eye. "Catfight."

"So," Matt chided him, "as long as it's my wife in the catfight and not yours, you're okay with it."

"My wife is ready to talk it out. Yours looks ready to spit."

"Shut up, Charlie." Shanda couldn't help but smile. Even she was not immune to the high energy and simple joy that permeated the set the second the cast and crew heard that Josh was alive and no longer in hiding. His visit to the set today was absolutely surreal—a carnival atmosphere. She couldn't take her eyes off of him, which Jessie found amusing.

"You wanna reach out and touch him, Shanda?" Leaning forward, both elbows on the table, her chin balanced on clasped fingers, Jessie raised her eyebrows in a question mark. "Do you want to run your hands all over him like he's some kind of prized stallion?"

Shanda's nostrils flared in anger. "Some of us can stop at *looking*, Jessie. We're not all slut-wired the way you are."

Charlie elbowed Matt. "See? Told ya."

Matt shot him a dirty look.

"Like you wouldn't go there if you had the chance, Shanda."

Josh grunted and shifted forward in his seat. "Enough, Jessie. This is not the time."

Curious, Charlie rested an ankle on a knee and fixed a look on each of his table mates in turn. Matt and Jessie were locked in each other's gazes now. Matt's usually gentle eyes were firm and urging caution.

Jessie touched her hair with an absent kind of grace and backed down. Crunching the last few bits of the ice cube, she swallowed.

"All right, what am I missing here?" Charlie asked.

At this point neither Jessie nor Josh had any inkling of how much Shanda knew about Matt's and Jessie's hopes for continued, albeit very occasional, personal liaisons. Neither said a word as Charlie's eyes narrowed.

Shanda started to fidget. Matt let out a breath and draped an arm around her shoulders.

"All right, since nobody's talking, how about this?" Charlie switched their gears, since the current conversation seemed to be leaving a hostile imprint on what was, overall, a happy occasion. "How about you ask me what I worked on over the winter?" The question was directed at Josh.

Jessie jumped in before Josh had a chance to say anything. "Have you been writing, Charlie?"

Ignoring her, Charlie pointed his bourbon glass at his old co-star and lead actor on *Sacred Peace*. "You ready to get going again, buddy?" He was grinning like a Cheshire cat. "I can't tell you how much I'd like to work with you again."

Everyone at the table melted when the tops of Josh's cheeks bloomed pink and he stole a glance up at Charlie from behind the still-layered-but-not-quite-so-long hair he always used as a barrier for protection from the world. "Got horses in it?" he asked in a low, hopeful tone as the corner of one lip turned up.

"Oh, Jesus," Jessie swooned under her breath. Nobody was a sucker for seeing Josh aglow more than she was.

For Charlie's benefit, Josh added a sweet addendum. "I'm here. I'm still on the planet. Damn straight I wanna work."

"It's got horses." The emotion in Charlie's voice took him by surprise. It blew his mind just how much over the years Josh had come to mean to him. Charlie had no siblings. Josh had, somewhere along the way, become a brother. He perked up. "It's even got a saloon and wooden sidewalks."

"And mud!" Jessie cheered the second she realized what Charlie had in mind. "A period film? I hope you got a good budget, Charlie, for all those wagons and costumes. Can I be in it?" Her face darkened. "Oh, shit. That would mean corsets. I never wanna wear a corset again."

"You won't need to," Shanda countered. "Charlie wrote the female lead for me." With a conspiratorial glint, she leaned to the side and winked at

Josh. "It's a love story." Raising her hands to cradle her small breasts, she gave them a few uplifts. "Corsets are sexy as hell."

"All those half-exposed breasts," Charlie added, to Jessie's dismay. He lifted his hands to form rounded claws. "So touchable. Lucky Josh."

Blushing, Shanda kicked him under the table.

"What?" Charlie laughed.

Matt, Josh and Jessie had gone silent again. There were covert looks flying around that Charlie wanted to understand. He ran his fingers over the stubble on his chin and gave each of his friends a good, long study. "Okay," he said in the end. "I want in on this. What's up?"

Shanda, too, was confused. Suddenly a light came on. She shoved back her chair. "You two slept together again."

Lightning quick, Matt's arm darted out. He grabbed her wrist before she could bolt. She was already halfway out of her chair. "No," he said. "Sit down, Shanda."

Shanda's heart was racing. She appealed to the one person she figured she could trust. "Josh?"

A solemn shake of Josh's head was her answer, but Charlie was astute enough to recognize a flicker of truth in his eyes. He just didn't know it referenced the future.

Josh had a power over Shanda. Inwardly growling at his wife, he used it to restore a sense of civility. "Shanda, I'd love to work with you again." Unable to help himself, Josh raised his hands in grave surrender and tossed in, "You can run your hands all over this bod. Just note that it's got its share of scars."

"Ouch," Jessie breathed. "Fuck." Her eyes widened just the littlest bit and she met Matt's amused eyes. *I guess we deserve this,* she thought wildly. For one quick second she wanted to throw herself on her husband's lap the same way she had the previous night, and run her hands lovingly, sensually, over every square inch of his body, if only to take ownership of him away from whatever desires Shanda had. She shivered at the thought of Shanda actually touching Josh again. *Matt and I are under control—but those two could still fall in love...*

Catching the brief panic darting over Jessie's face, Matt allowed himself a small smile. *It's good,* he told himself, *to see her react this way. It's good to see her be a little bit afraid.*

"Josh," Shanda was saying when Jessie and Matt tuned back in, "you don't ever need to hide your scars from me. I know where they come from." Bitterness lined the hard stare she aimed at Jessie, who shrank back in her seat at the not-even-remotely-veiled accusation.

"Fuck you, Shanda."

This time Charlie held his tongue. With Jessie, it was easy to tell when a line was being crossed. Joking around would only serve to piss her off further. The only thing to do now would be to wait and see where this new round would land.

Matt's gaze hardened. Positioned staunchly between the two women, metaphorically speaking, he waited for Josh to issue another warning to his rebel wife. It didn't come. Josh was hanging his head. He knew damn well where his scars came from too.

Jessie hauled her hand away from his and looked away from him, toward the wall. Shanda was the only one there who didn't crumble at the self-loathing that passed over Jessie's features in suddenly moist eyes and in fingernails Jessie dug hard into the backs of her hands.

Matt shoved back his chair and moved behind Shanda. He touched Josh's shoulder in a bid for solidarity and to offer support before he reached out a hand to Jessie. "Come, girl," he demanded. "Let's go cool off."

Her chair scratched hard on the wooden floor of the upscale steakhouse. Avoiding the eyes of Josh, Shanda and Charlie, Jessie took Matt's hand. Matt didn't give his wife a second look.

Josh puffed up his cheeks and exhaled. He looked over at Shanda. "At this rate it'll be a long film if I don't send my jealous wife out on tour or out to shoot a film of her own."

"I'm sorry, Josh," Shanda mumbled. "I don't know how you do it. Her and Matt."

He was quiet for a second. "It's not gonna get easier, Shanda," he confessed. Charlie's eyebrows arched upwards.

Resting an elbow on the back of his chair and his head on his crooked arm, Josh faced Shanda from a three-quarter profile and continued. "Their blood runs in each other's veins. Trying to separate them is like trying to separate oil and water."

Shanda clued in. She folded her arms across her chest. "Are they still sleeping together?"

Josh shook his head. "No. Not at the moment."

She tested the words on her lips. "Not at the moment. And how am I supposed to interpret that?"

"If you want to hang onto your marriage, Shanda, don't get between them," Josh advised. "That's how you interpret that. Find a way to make peace with how Matt feels about Jessie. Find a way to make peace with her. Jessie is a very, very big part of Matt. Of who he is, of who he has become. You love who he is. We all do. He's an incredible man. He wouldn't be the Matt you fell in love with if he hadn't spent a good chunk of his adult life with Jessie."

"Seriously?" Charlie broke in. "You're telling me you're okay with Jessie and Matt banging each other?"

"Don't go there, Charlie," Josh cautioned. "This is not about having an open marriage. It's about two people whose lives are so inextricably intertwined that they breathe each other's air. It's about allowing them to hold each other when they need to, in a mutually agreed upon arrangement that's already proving to reduce conflict in a marriage that means everything to me."

Charlie's retort was spoken in a low, serious tone. "And it's about giving you a guarantee that the woman you love will always have a safe place to land if she needs one."

Josh sat back. "Hell, yeah."

Charlie's voice rose in pitch. "You're scared you're gonna fuck up again. You're scared this shit with Morgan isn't over. You need an absolute."

"I feel like it's over, Charlie," Josh admitted honestly. He raked his fingers through his hair. "I really do. Morgan's found some kind of peace with everything. I just know me. That's all."

"So you want me to share my husband with her." Shanda's eyes were on fire.

Josh's gaze lingered on Charlie for a long while before he fixed a hard stare back on Shanda. "No, Shanda," he said quietly. "Jessie is sharing Matt with you."

At that, Charlie couldn't bring himself to look at Shanda, to see the truth register in her already wounded expression. He had to look away. Outside the restaurant's large main window he spied Arnie approaching Jessie and Matt, who appeared to be lounging against the brick having a heart-to-heart.

Josh drew Charlie back to the intense looks passing between himself and Shanda. "Matt is the kind of man who will never let you down, Shanda. He knows that you are his priority. But if you try to take a stand between him and Jessie, you will lose him."

"And what about you?" She bristled.

Charlie guffawed lightly. It was fascinating for him to witness this conversation. Josh and Shanda both glanced over. "What?" he said, chuckling. "Shanda, you're not fooling anyone. You sit there all righteous and indignant about Matt's feelings for a woman he's cared for over a lifetime almost, yet you'd throw your husband under a train for a chance to be with Josh. Face it. You'd be over the moon if Josh and Jessie split, and if Matt left you for Jessie."

The table went silent. Josh, too, couldn't deny that he cared for Shanda. They'd worked two seasons together on *Sacred Peace*, and if Carter hadn't come along and got added to the cast when he did there was a chance Josh and Shanda might have spent more time together and maybe eventually crossed a line.

Josh touched her hand to get her to look at him, since she was staring at her fingers in her lap all of a sudden. "Shanda, I won't even things out here by going to bed with you. What you and I have is a friendship I cherish. What Jessie and Matt have is another thing entirely."

"I know," she agreed softly. "They're almost the same person. I knew that when I hooked up with him in the first place. I knew what I was getting into." Peeking up at Josh she said, "I couldn't tell where one ended and the other began. Still can't."

"Me either half the time." Taking her fingers, Josh brushed his thumb over them. "You want to know how I live with it…it's easy. I trust my wife's love for me. That's how."

"It's that easy, is it?"

"Yep. It is. I'd advise you to do the same."

"Trust your wife's love for me?" There was a twinkle in Shanda's eyes now.

"Kidding. You'd better get laid pretty good tonight for smoothing things over for your wife, Josh. I have my moments when I don't think she deserves a whole lot of grace."

Josh's eyes softened into a watery chocolate river. "You should have seen her with Morgan today, Shanda," he said. "You should have seen how beautiful and forgiving she was with him. You're looking at my girl through the entirely wrong filter."

Shanda lost herself in the love in Josh's eyes—as he was thinking about Jessie—before she looked back over at Charlie. He, too, was alight now.

Charlie thumped the table lightly with a fist and sat back. "I've seen it," he told Shanda. "Jessie and her magic. She's not all piss and vinegar, Shanda. You know that. You know her."

"I know.  It's just that back then I wasn't married to one of the men who has her heart."

Dejected, Charlie sank back into his chair.

Josh tossed him a bone. "Lighten up, Deacon. You're in there somewhere too. She's got a big heart."

Matt was escorting Jessie back to the table, his arm around her waist. By the careful, apprehensive look on her face, it seemed he had straightened out a few things. Arnie was alongside them, and slipped into a chair they had been saving for him. What he had to say brought the conversation to a more even ground, while at the same time it reminded everyone present that there were bigger things in their lives to be concerned about than who loved who the most.

"Are you ready to hear what Vaughn had to say?" he asked the group. At their consent, he crossed an ankle over a knee and said, "He affirmed everything Morgan said. The dogs have been called off. You guys are home free."

"Are we ever home free?" Jessie mumbled.

"As home free as we get," Josh assured her. To Arnie he said, "Because of this Caulfield guy, right? Did your guy Vaughn agree that all that shit was never Morgan's directive?"

"Yeah. Caulfield was pulling the strings, Josh. Morgan suffered for it."

"Grrr." Jessie shrank down deep in her chair. "All that negative energy we sent Morgan." Everyone looked at her. "What?" she said, throwing her hands up.

Josh sighed and took her hand in his. "Not all of us have the capacity you do to so easily forgive someone who has done that much damage, Jessie."

"Too bad," she replied. "The world would be a much better place if y'all could."

"You talk the talk. Now walk the walk. Start with my wife." A happy light was dancing across Charlie's eyes. Sucking on a toothpick, he rocked back in his chair.

"And mine," came from across the table. Matt's remark was accompanied by a swat.

Their playful teasing wasn't lost on Jessie. "I'm gonna start," she lit up, and settled her happy gaze on Arnie, "with a song. I'm gonna play it at a place where forgiveness needs to happen on a much bigger level than on our own little playing field."

Matt went rigid.

Josh straightened.

Charlie, as always, was amused.

Shanda was curious.

Arnie knew. "Vaughn'll be happy to hear that," he said.

Jessie's eyes lit up with anticipation. "I'm gonna call Jacob. I need him to talk to Dee and clear his schedule. We've got a concert to plan." Digging in her purse, she hauled out her phone.

"And where, pray tell, will this concert be?" Shanda had a vested interest in wherever Jessie went. Jessie's shadow was always alongside. Distance, after the post dinner conversation, was not Shanda's friend.

"Don't worry, Shanda," Jessie beamed, scraping back her chair. "It's not far. Near Edmonton, in fact. We won't be gone long."

"Jesus Christ. Why don't you start with a pre-school, Jessie?" Matt was already running potentially threatening scenarios around and around in his head. "You want to do a concert at Brody Pen?"

She was standing again, hovering over the table, practically vibrating with glee. "I'll be right back. I gotta call Jacob." It was late and most of the restaurant patrons had finished their meals and were gone. Jessie tucked herself into a shadowy corner. A few minutes later, Josh and the others heard her singing lyrics into her phone.

Josh laughed outright, caught Matt's eye, and nodded toward his wife. "She's all yours, Kelly," he said, "you lucky bastard. Have fun. A penitentiary, no less."

A wide grin spread across Matt's face. Grabbing the linen napkin he'd discarded on the table when he finished his meal earlier, he twisted it into a ball and fired it across the table at Josh. "I'm only human," he countered. "She's your damn wife. Feel free to come along and stand in the wings."

"Oh, I'll be there, Matt. With bells on."

They shared a common bond then, the two men who colored Jessie's life with love and promise in a way she, not all that long ago, would not have dreamed was possible. Jessie, who hadn't done a live show since the one in Boston that got her into all the trouble with Shanda, was making plans to sing in public. Prison, shmison. Josh didn't care if the show was on the moon. He hadn't seen Jessie play live since the summer before he was shot.

Magic would happen there, in a place where so much healing was needed. Magic would happen and Josh wanted to be a part of it.

He caught Shanda's eye. "Come with us to that show," he encouraged. "Change up that filter you see my wife through. She might be a rogue wild child a lot of the time, but here's the thing about Jessie. She's bigger than us. She's bigger than all of us. The kind of hope she brings to the world is nothing short of miraculous."

"How'm I ever supposed to compete with that?" Shanda swallowed back tears. She couldn't bring herself to look at her husband.

Eyes still twinkling, but a little less dramatic and a lot more sober, Josh glanced at Matt before he looked back at Shanda. "You don't," he told her in a low murmur. "You just don't." Lifting Shanda's hand, Josh brushed his lips over her fingers.

A second later, he shoved back his chair, saluted his friends, and wheeled around to go join Jessie in the corner. Jacob was at La Casa tonight, helping Charles and Dee manage the kids. Josh was hoping for a word with each child and an update on how Dylan was feeling.

Shanda was in that place between confusion and anxiety.

At her side, Matt echoed Arnie by crossing an ankle over a knee. "What do you say, big guy?" he asked him. "Can we do this?"

Arnie reached for a breadstick left in a basket in the center of the table. Sticking it in his mouth whole, while chewing he said, "You want a guarantee that the population of that prison will leave her family alone? And that the word spreads to the rest of the world's inmates?"

Matt's voice was barely discernible. "Damn straight I do."

"Then fasten your seatbelt, Matt. We're gonna pull ourselves a Johnny Cash."

Matt looked past Arnie to Josh and Jessie. They were both on the phone now. It was between them, suspended in Jessie's fingers, and both Sawyers were absolutely alight. One of the kids was likely on the other end. Their foreheads were touching, and both of Josh's hands were resting on Jessie's hips. His hair cascaded over his cheek. While Matt watched, Jessie reached up and gently pushed it behind Josh's ear. Neither seemed to even realize that she did it, the tender movement was so automatic after all these years.

Matt's breath caught. His heart hitched. There was a streetlight outside the window. It ringed the window side of both Jessie and Josh with light. He nodded, only once and just slightly, but it was enough for the universe to receive his 'thank you' loud and clear. Beside him, Shanda, too, caught the perfection in the moment, in having the two Sawyers back in their midst again, joyous and free. She laid her head on Matt's strong shoulder, took his hand in hers, and smiled.

*Chapter Thirty-four*

The Brody River Pen concert was the hottest bill on the Alberta live music scene. It only took a few weeks to pull together. Charles' and Matt's relationships with the warden, and Arnie's with the acknowledged leader of the prison population, Vaughn, sped things up. The Keating team footed the bill, which included building an outdoor stage that was erected on the north side of B yard, one of the largest yards on site.

At noon, Jessie and Jacob rolled in for sound check.

"You nervous at all?" he asked her on the way in as they watched the guys in their band raise their arms to officers who were checking for concealed weapons.

Jessie was leaning on her forearms on a counter top, laughing at Christian who was confidently telling a burly black corrections officer that he'd left his weed at home. "No," she answered Jacob. "I'm not nervous. They're just people."

"People who've done bad enough stuff to land them in prison," Jacob maintained.

"People who've either been misunderstood and treated wrong from the time they were born or people who've run into hard luck. People, Jacob." Jessie hoisted herself away from the counter and spread her arms and legs for a lady officer who scanned her with a wand before patting her down.

Charles appeared at her side. "The instruments and amps we're donating have arrived. They're being unloaded now. The warden asked if you and Jacob would sign some of them before sound check."

"Gotcha." Jessie looked up at the serious officer doing her weapons check and decided against cracking a joke. She grinned at Charles. "Grab me a sharpie. C'mon, Jacob."

There were a lot of instruments to sign—guitars, drums and keyboards. By the time Jessie and Jacob rolled into sound check, it was thirty minutes late starting. Just as they were wrapping up, Arnie brought a young man on stage and introduced him to Jessie.

"This is Skins," he said. "He's your guest star."

Skins had waltzed onto the stage with an air of excited confidence. A twenty-something with light brown skin and mocha eyes, he hitched up his baggy jeans with one set of fingers and shook Jessie's hand with the other. Coarse black dreadlocks framed his face. Jessie forced a cringe inward when she noted that a thick, grisly scar ran from his left eye to the top of his lip, marring Skins' otherwise smooth complexion.

Arnie retreated into the wings to stand by Matt who, as always, had his eyes locked on his girl.

Jessie greeted the inmate with a friendly air, treating him as if he was a new session musician at the Robson Street studio. "We've been told you play a mean guitar," she gushed. "So I don't get why you're called Skins."

"Cuz I also rip me a good set of drums," her guest replied with an enthusiastic bounce-shift from one foot to the other. "Just ain't had none to play for a while."

"Jacob," Jessie called over her shoulder, in the general direction of where Jacob was easing a brand spanking new rust and white Telecaster guitar out of a plush case, "what was the best set of drums in that shipment today?"

"The walnut Pearl set at the back of the truck. The Masters Maple Reserve. No question."

Skins started dancing from side to side. "Hope you remembered to toss in some sticks." He was beaming.

Jessie laughed. "We'll send some extras. Damn things splinter all over the place. I've had to tread carefully over many a broken stick, on stage in sky-high heels, at that. It ain't fun when a few thousand people are watching you, believe me. Especially when you're trying to sing at the same time." As an afterthought she added, "Thank God I get to wear my boots for this show."

"That only happens when we pull out our Metallica vibe for warm-up.

Don't be telling stories, Jess." Wandering over, Jacob thrust out his hand. "Jacob," he said by way of introduction. "So what are we playing today, man?"

"You tell me, I play."

"Know any Chili Peppers?"

"All of 'em."

"*Don't Forget Me* and *How Long*?"

"You got it. Hey man, can we also do *Under the Bridge*?"

Alight, Jessie poked Jacob in the ribs and spoke for him. "Yeah, but we gotta send that one out to Josh. It's his theme song. His choice," she maintained. "It's a hard reminder of how far he's come. Gives him strength. Hey, Jacob, are we gonna play any of our own stuff, doofus?"

Her musical soul mate's eyes were shining like a little boy's at Christmas. Both he and Jessie had already heard Skins play, via a YouTube video featuring the band the guy was playing in before he got busted for an armed robbery gone wrong and was sentenced to Brody. Jacob couldn't care less if they played their own stuff. This unexpected addition to their show was a guitar hero.

"I'm a little rusty," Skins admitted with a loose shrug as if it pained him to say so.

"Rusty to you is brilliant to us," Jacob assured him. "Trust me. You nervous?"

Skins hitched up his jeans by grabbing them at the waist in the back. "Meh," he said, and hopped up and down three times. His jeans sagged again. Grinning, he ignored them. "Stoked."

"Fuck, yeah. Let's hear ya play." After handing their guest the Telecaster, Jacob fist-pumped Skins and went off to the side of the stage to grab his own guitar.

Jessie spent the next half hour effervescent and vibrating in the wings in the direct company of Matt and Arnie. "I don't care if I never play again," she confessed. "Look at Jacob. He and this guy are soul mates. Skins sure can rip on that guitar."

Arnie illuminated her. "He hasn't played since he was incarcerated, Jessie. Two-and-a-half years."

"That kind of brilliance belongs on a stage. What the hell's he doing wasting away in here?" Sadness imbued her voice at the unwelcome reminder of where they were, that men like Skins had no more choices left to them apart from when to piss and brush their teeth.

"Hey," Matt, at her right, cut in. "He's got music. He'll get to play again now that he's got that sweet Telecaster you're about to give him. That's more than a lot of these guys have going for them in places like this."

Three hours later, Jessie had to agree. Just as Jacob brought their famous *Sacred Peace* ballad to its perfect orgasmic, singing halt, with Skins alongside helping out with the guitar solos in the tune, Skins raised his arms in jubilant euphoria. His fans—the prison population out front—roared their approval.

*This concert's doing more for these men than years of therapy can do, Jessie* mused. *Music heals. Music is forgiveness and,* she turned her head to the right and smiled effusively at Matt in the wings, with Josh by his side now for the show, *music is hope.*

Joy was on the scarred, life-hardened faces of the men snugged shoulder to shoulder out in the yard before her. It radiated outward from souls that many people around them likely thought were buried and black, proving to those from the outside world who had the pleasure of watching this unscheduled show—including Charles, Dee, Shanda, Charlie and Jane, who were nestled into comfy seats in the admin area that overlooked B yard—that music was a universal healing power.

*Just wait'll more of these guys learn to play,* Jessie thought, thinking about the donated instruments. *Those who will pick up a guitar for the first time will bury their pain in their music. Even the sad songs will absorb their hurts, and they'll all come out feeling inspired and hopeful. Life will begin anew because they will have an outlet for the things that hurt. They'll have somewhere to turn when life becomes too much.*

Skins left the stage in a reluctant haze of glory. "We'll come back and jam with you," Jessie hollered in his ear so she could be heard above the crowd. "You keep working on those riffs. You need the practice!" She was laughing wholeheartedly.

Skins passed by Josh on his way off stage. He stopped by Josh and said something to him. Jessie almost missed the intro to the next tune when she saw Matt, who overheard, clap her husband on the shoulder and hang on tight. Josh looked down and punched a thumb and finger into the outer corners of his eyes.

"What?" Jessie mouthed to Matt.

Matt smiled—a warm, happy smile that read *it's all good. Play on.*

So she did.

Christian was picking out an arpeggio on the piano, leading her into a brand new song. It was the one Jessie finally finished for Vaughn. The only verbal introduction she offered was a single word—the man's name. The sea of guys in blue before her went nuts. It took a while for them to settle down enough to listen, but when they did they were as apt an audience as Jessie, with Jacob beside her, ever had.

Jessie sang of forgiveness, and wondered in the tide of blue where Morgan was and if he could make out the lyrics.

She sang of hope and wondered, in the hardcore men in the yard before her how many of them were here because they, like her, had sometimes been abused and ignored.

She sang of healing and wondered, in the multitude of skin colors and eye colors and body types and sexual preferences and backgrounds before her whether unfettered love—freely given—might have changed the direction of any of these men's lives.

She closed her eyes and sang about a river. About darkness and fear and courage and love and security and rescue. She sang of a river's natural tendency to bubble along over polished stones, making its way to an unknown destination; and she sang about how a river, like true love, is never the same river twice. She sang about how love is endless, and about how love, like a river, flows in its own special way. She sang about how important it is to stop moving and thinking and pondering. About how important it is to close one's eyes and simply listen.

*Close your eyes, and listen to the river.*
*Open your heart, and let it in.*

Let love in.

*Listen To The River* was a message of personal triumph. Josh almost died in a river. Jessie and Emily-Grace almost died in a river. Matt risked his life to pull Jessie and her daughter from the river that very nearly claimed them.

*We did it,* Jessie thought, grasping the microphone with one hand and raising her second arm in glorious triumph while she sang. *We survived the deepest, darkest parts of our rivers. We beat back the currents that tried to consume us. And we did it with love.*

The song faded as all great songs do into a single final, sweet, satisfying note. Jessie was still in her river. It took Jacob walking over to her and whispering in her ear to get her to come back to them.

"Perfection," Jessie murmured to herself when she felt Jacob's warm breath on her ear; when she opened her eyes and saw the men on their feet before her, all cheering *Vaughn, Vaughn, Vaughn,* recognizing that it was his doing that got this inspirational message to their ears—a message they could forevermore call their own since it was written for one of their own.

"Perfection," Jessie breathed when she looked to the right to see Josh and Matt side by side, friends despite the heartbreak they had both endured on her behalf. "Perfection," she breathed, when she thought about her children at a nearby hotel in the care of Carlotta, with trusted Dan outside their door, and Sam and Alin hanging around with them today just for fun. "Perfection," she breathed when she looked up to see faces in a window, watching from above the yard—Charlie and Jane, Shanda, Carter and Ashley today, too, with their daughter, and Kayla with Lily. Charles and Deirdre were watching from above, also.

Jessie reached down and took Jacob's hand. Together they raised their arms in salute to the forgotten men of Brody Pen—society's outlaws, men who exist mostly on the fringe, who create their own protocols in order to survive harsh existences their younger selves likely never considered. Jessie sent a silent prayer to the heavens to give these men the strength to continue their lives in whatever meaningful ways they could.

That night, curled up in the gentle curve of her husband's body, her children safely asleep nearby, Jessie whispered a question to an almost slumbering Josh.

"What'd he say to you when he left the stage? Skins? That incredible guitar player?"

Josh's answer was slow to come, and it was thick with the need to sleep. "He told me we're under their protection now. He told me wherever we go there will be men on the streets watching out for us. For all of us. To help keep us safe."

Jessie stopped breathing. "Why?"

Josh cuddled his wife's body in closer. He wrapped his arm tightly around her and buried his nose in her hair. Jessie had to listen closely in order to hear what he said next.

"Because of you," he murmured. "Because of your music. Because, even after everything that happened to us, after all that shitty diabolical crap that Caulfield orchestrated for us, you had the guts to go there today and play. And beyond that, you invited one of their own up on stage to play with you. And because you wrote a song for a man they respect."

"Weird how things come around," Jessie sighed. "Vaughn cut me all those years ago. I thought he was going to kill me that night."

"You didn't report him. Why? He killed other women."

She paused. "It was an everyday thing back then, Josh. You did what you had to so you could eat."

Behind her, Josh's eyes blinked open. A sheen of moisture made them glisten in the moonlight.

Jessie had one more thing to say. "I was always scared back then. I'm so tired of always being scared."

"Yet you weren't scared today. In front of the kind of men you used to fear."

"Sure I was. I was terrified."

He stilled. "So why'd you do it?"

In answer, Jessie took Josh's arm and pulled it close. Bending forward, she kissed the fingers she loved so well. "It's like that feeling of being in the car in the river, Josh. Or of crouching over you when you were shot. You don't know how things are gonna turn out, but when you're in the heat of the moment with adrenaline racing through your body, you have no choice but to go with the flow and hope for the best. I listened to my heart and I went with the flow."

"Good girl," Josh said softly. "Soooo proud of you."

"You're slurring your words. Too bad. Since it turned out that I wasn't pregnant." Jessie could feel Josh's smile tickling her neck.

"Got something besides sleep in mind, little one?" he asked.

"Nah. You're too tired."

"Never too tired…to play."

Jessie was just about to roll over to give him a kiss when a low rumble alerted her to the fact that Josh was snoring. Giggling, she brought his fingers to her lips again, tenderly kissed every single one, and drifted off into peaceful slumber in the arms of her deeply loved man.

Chapter Thirty-five

At La Casa, Charles was pestering Jessie.

She threw up her arms in defeat. "Okay? You really wanna know? I'll tell you, then! I never want to celebrate another special day without friends and family around. That's why. No more birthdays, Christmases, Easters, Thanksgivings, you name it, without Grammie and Grampie and as many friends as we can muster at our sides in whatever city we happen to be in. That's why."

Folding her arms across her chest, Jessie rocked insolently back on one heel.

Charles had a sleeping Micah in his arms. The producer was glowing. "You don't have to convince me," he said, his smile growing wider by the second. He had finally gained enough courage to ask her, on behalf of Deirdre and Carlotta, why Jessie agreed to celebrate her birthday at La Casa in big style for once. Everyone in their close circle was invited, and some, like Maggie and Sue-Lyn and their partners, had even flown in from out of the city to attend. The guests were arriving in bits and pieces. Jessie and Charles were upstairs in the pretty Spanish villa; Charles had just rocked Micah to sleep for an afternoon nap so he wouldn't, in Emily-Grace's words, "be too grumpy-pants for the party."

Jessie reached for her son. "Let me take him, Charles. You've done your part. Go greet your guests while I put him down."

"I'll wait with you," he said agreeably.

Jessie laid Micah in his crib and drew a light blanket over him. She touched his cheek with the backs of her fingers. "He looks like his daddy," she sighed. "So adorable."

"Ah," Charles replied. "So you and Josh are good, then."

"So good. We're always good, Charles. We just have to fight to be together sometimes, that's all. We've never stopped loving each other, and we never will."

"That makes me happy." He dropped an arm over her shoulders. Leaving little Micah to doze comfortably, they started out of the room and headed down the mahogany stairs. A baby monitor dangled from Jessie's fingers.

"Someone finally likes Josh. Should I kiss your feet?"

"Never disliked him, Jessie."

"Nah." She shook her head. "Don't lie. I think it's more that you accept him."

"I do believe a man belongs with his family."

"Talk about skirting the issue."

"I just worry about him. That doesn't mean I don't like him."

"Don't we all. The worry part. Thankfully, I love him." Almost skipping, Jessie slipped an arm around Charles' waist, but she squealed with glee when they got to the bottom of the stairs. There in the landing were Steve, Carter, Maggie, Sue-Lyn and Josh, all with children tugging at them, all beaming with joy at this happy reunion. Jessie practically leapt into the center of the ecstatic group. "This is hands down the best birthday gift ever!" she cried.

It was July twelfth, a hot summer day in the hippie city of Vancouver. La Casa's large back garden and pool were decorated for the gathering. A few hours later, the adults were happily exhausted and the children were running around wired on sugar.

Wiping sweat from her brow, Jessie sat her butt down on the front edge of a makeshift stage where she and Jacob and the kids had jammed earlier.

It was a blissful viewpoint.

Jacob and Kayla were entertaining at least half the kids on Deirdre's large garden swing. Dylan, in his cast, was in his glory in the center of the pack.

To the left, at a round patio table, the *Drifters* gang was lost in happy chatter. Josh was there too, balancing Micah on one knee and Lily on the other.

Charles and Deirdre were off to the side arguing film and television politics with Jonathon and Giselle, and Jack and Lydia. With her left hand,

Deirdre was holding her right elbow so as to keep that arm steady. Some ambiguous lime-colored slushy tropical drink was suspended in her raised fingers.

Not all that far beyond them, Matt and Shanda were playing a teasing game. Laughing brightly, Shanda was leaning back against the fence surrounding the pool. Matt had her tented in one tanned arm, his hand suspended against the fence. With the other, he was brushing a thumb over her cheek. He looked about as happy as Jessie had ever seen him. She sighed in idyllic acceptance.

A quiet body landed next to Jessie. *Jane.*

"Mmm," Jessie said, proudly raising her chin. "I knew I was missing somebody. I'm scanning Dee's oasis and counting my peeps. Where's your doofus husband?"

"Inside on the phone."

"He better be talking to the pizza delivery guy."

"You know Charlie. He's always working." Jane eyed Jessie quizzically. "Didn't you get enough to eat?"

"Us whores got used to pizza." Jessie slouched on her arms.

"Jessie, look…"

"Save your breath, Jane. Nothing you can say will ever claw back what I heard that day. Suffice it to say that I know how you really feel."

"Honey, don't throw away a perfectly good friendship based on one cranky PMS day. It wasn't that long after Boston and the stuff that went down with Matt. I was having a hard time dealing."

"Jesus, Jane, you're married to a goddamned movie star. If you haven't figured out how to deal by now, you're in trouble."

"I trust Charlie. Or…I thought I did, until…" Jane bit her lip.

"Until I hooked up with Matt in Boston." Jessie ducked her head. "I guess I don't blame you. It's just that it's not like you think it is. It's not like I'll ever end up in Charlie's bed again."

"He would, you know. He told me," Jane admitted. "We had too much to drink one night at the Canmore house and we got talking. I asked him if he would ever cheat on me and he said he would, but only with you. I think I've always known that. We met on the Downtown Eastside, for God's sake, where he used to go so he could feel close to you. Charlie will always be in love with you, Jessie. He's never gotten over losing you."

"Look, Jane." Sighing, Jessie sat up straighter. "Charlie and I were young and stupid when we were together. We've both moved on. We're the best of friends but I won't be going there again. And frankly, even thinking about it kind of exhausts me. Thinking about how you feel about me exhausts me."

"I heard that you and Josh made some sort of arrangement about Matt, so you and him can still be together sometimes. Is it true?"

"Not really your business, Jane, but yes, we did. Have I been with Matt since Boston? No. Do I see that happening anytime soon? No. It's not like that. It's more like knowing I can be with him if things go haywire again. Or if either of us is lonely and needs someone to hold. That's all. Although I suppose in your mind you can't see it that way."

"I don't suppose it matters what I think."

"Nope. Not even remotely." They stared out over the large yard for a while longer. Charlie eventually appeared at the sliding door that led back into La Casa. Seeing his two girls in close proximity on the stage, he leaned against the door frame and watched them.

"Look," Jessie said, gesturing toward him. "He's lost his boyish looks. He's now a handsome movie star of a certain vintage."

The corners of Jane's lips curved up. "He's got those little wrinkles at the corners of his eyes now."

"I've long decided those are the road maps to a man's life," Jessie determined staunchly. "Little rivers that extend outward." Her voice quieted. "Trails left by the tears they've shed over their lifetimes."

"You're looking at it the wrong way," Jane corrected. "Think of those tiny little lines as representing tears of joy."

"Ah. Wise Jane. Yes. They could be both."

"Think positive, Jessie." Taking a chance, Jane slipped an arm around her friend. "They *are* both."

"Defeat, hope, fear, worry, desperation, pain, joy and at times light…real, true light…that's what I see in those little eye trails on all of the men I love."

Arnie had wandered over beside Charlie. The two men were chatting amicably.

Jessie pointed to them. "Arnie the savior," she said softly. She smiled at Charlie. "Charlie the older brother." She looked over at Charles and his friends. "Jack the discoverer. Charles the father." The *Drifters* table was next. "Carter the friend. Steve the best friend." The swing… "Jacob the musical soul mate." She sighed happily when she gestured to Matt. "Matt the guardian angel."

Jane waited. After a while she said, "And Josh?"

"Josh." Jessie thought about her husband for a minute. Her eyes were bright beacons of hope while she contemplated who he was, to her. "Josh the…lover. Friend. Soul mate. The sweetness of his mouth…the grace and beauty in his touch…the love in his eyes when he looks at me…the beautiful body like water I want to soak in…Josh is everything, Jane." Laying a cheek on her folded arms, which were supported by her bent knees, Jessie smiled sadly at Jane and murmured in an imploring kind of way, "He is everything. You see? He is all of those things."

It took Jane a second. Her brow furrowed in thought. "I think what you're telling me is that nobody else will ever come close."

"On the contrary." Jessie took a breath and said, without wavering from Jane's kind gaze, "What I am saying is that they all come close. It's just that Josh is more. He's all of them. That's all."

Josh seemed to hear his name uttered on the wind. Looking up, he pondered the two women sitting there not all that far away, maybe contemplating him, talking about him. Catching Jessie's eye, he didn't smile, nor did she. Instead, they dove into each other's eyes and swam to the bottomless depths they found in each. Once there they united in the way only those truly in love can, with souls built the same, on equal foundations.

Josh and Jessie's foundation was one of hurt, and sheer, brutal loneliness. Over the years, like a river that foundation changed; it flowed with time over different stones, some polished and true, and some vicious and jagged. Today their river was calm, a peaceful place of unequalled bliss. It came from spending the day surrounded by people they loved, who knew them, who trusted them and who loved them back.

Josh lifted Micah off his lap. The little guy wandered over to his mother and climbed into her arms for a snuggle.

"Did I hear you two are trying for another baby?" Jane asked.

"We are indeed. We said five." Jessie cuddled Micah in close. "Just before we left P.E.I. I thought maybe I was pregnant. I wasn't. I guess the up side is that we get to keep trying."

"Don't you get tired?"

"Of all this love?" Embracing Micah tightly, Jessie smiled in contented ease. "Never." Her moist eyes drifted over the capacious backyard of elegant, cozy La Casa. A contented, friendly hum emanated from friends and family. It was, quite literally, music to her ears. "How could I ever get tired of this?" She sighed dreamily.

Rising, Jessie reached for her friend's hand. "Come on, Jane," she encouraged warmly. "Let's go find us some more cake."

"What about that pizza?" Jane teased.

"That's for tomorrow," Jessie laughed. "When we're all too tired and lazy to cook."

Leading Jane to the table where extra pieces of cake awaited, Jessie caught Matt's eye. His arms were around Shanda, and he was glowing. Shanda's head was resting on his shoulder. They were, beyond a shadow of doubt, a happy couple in love.

Jessie touched a finger to her lips and sent him a little more love. *Just a wee little bit more,* she told herself. Matt accepted it with a smile.

Twisting around, Jessie saw Josh get up and sidle casually toward her. Micah squirmed to get down from his mother's arms, so Jane took his hand, took Lily from Josh too, and wandered off with the little ones to meet Kayla and Jacob across the yard.

"Josh, we're back," Jessie breathed as her husband wrapped his arms around her waist from behind. He planted a kiss on the top of one ear. "Can you believe this? Is this Heaven or what?"

"Heaven is anywhere my girl is." Closing his eyes, Josh soaked her up. "Heaven is anywhere with you."

Pivoting around, Jessie laid her arms on his shoulders. "We're good now," she determined. "You and me and our kids. We're safe and we're good and all will be well forevermore. You're here in Vancouver with us. You're taking care of us."

Josh's eyes fluttered open. He couldn't speak. A big old lump in his throat was getting in the way.

Easing into him, Jessie leaned her forehead against his. "I need to hear you say it," she whispered, drawing a finger over his lips. "I need to hear it from you."

Over her shoulder, Josh spied Matt and Shanda cuddled up together, sharing tender kisses and adoring looks. Clearly, Matt had a woman of his own to take care of.

*I can do this,* Josh told himself. *I can do this.*

"Yes," he murmured, lifting a hand to hold her wrist steady so he could kiss her fingers. "I am here. And I am taking care of you." Josh brushed his lips over his wife's forehead next, and closed his eyes again.

Jessie melted into the shelter of his body. "You're not alone, Josh. I'm with you all the way, babe." A silent prayer of thanks left her lips and made its way to wherever it is such prayers go.

The happy buzz at La Casa seemed to fade away then. It was there, but the more Jessie and Josh disappeared inside each other, the more they trusted that it remained, and the less they listened to it. They focused on each other's heartbeats and on the faith and belief they had in a future suddenly filled with promise and lined with love.

Somewhere south a seaplane buzzed gracefully over Burrard Inlet, its pontoons dripping water like rising silvery stars. It eased up into the air and banked left to head over the lush mountains toward northern B.C. To the east, a steady hum of traffic was barely discernible in the late afternoon Sunday rush.

Happy couples and joyous children dotted La Casa's cozy backyard as the sun, above, ever so slowly drifted west. Smack dab in the center of the people she loved, Jessie angled her face toward her husband for a kiss. Josh pressed his hands to the small of her back, and placed his mouth on hers. Together they stood that way, tasting each other, aware only of each other, oblivious even to their children bouncing around them, until Jessie finally sighed and pulled far enough away to lose herself in Josh's peaceful gaze.

"Are you glad?" she asked. "Are you glad you're still here?"

"Yeah," he said. "I'm glad."

Jessie tilted her head in the adorable little girl way Josh loved. "You got your Harley back," she reminded him. "And your horses. You can ride like the wind again, Josh Sawyer."

Somewhere in Josh's heart a dreamy, eager joy took root. "And ride like the wind I will." He grinned.

A white butterfly floated lazily past, its fairy-like wings almost pearlescent in the late afternoon light. It drifted away on the light Vancouver breeze. Josh encircled Jessie fully in his arms, whispered a thank you to God for granting him the sustained gift of life, and took in a long, slow, steady breath.

When next he spoke, his repeated words were thicker. They were drenched in the emotion of all that came before, all that was in the now, and all that was yet to come.

"And ride like the wind I will."

*Let me taste the sweetness of your mouth,*
*let me soak in the river of your body,*
*let me dwell in the essence of your soul.*

*You are mine, and I am yours.*

*Always & Forever.*

The End.

*Thank you!*

If you liked this book, please take a few moments to leave a review on Amazon or Goodreads, and consider sharing your thoughts on social media. Self-published authors like myself count on your support to help us continue our writing journeys!

Have a wonderful day ☺

*Susan*

Join the *Drifters* family by signing up at **www.susanrodgersauthor.com**. As a welcome gift, I'll send you a free bonus/deleted chapter from book one, *A Song For Josh*. Happy reading!

**www.susanrodgersauthor.com**

Facebook: search **Susan Rodgers, Writer** and **StillTheWatermovie**

Twitter: **@srbluemountain**

Instagram: **SusanDrifters**

Pinterest: **Susan Rodgers**

email: **fatcat@pei.sympatico.ca**

Susan Rodgers' first novel *A Certain Kind of Freedom* was a Finalist in the Writers' Federation of Nova Scotia Atlantic Writing Awards for unpublished manuscripts. Her short story from the novel of the same name, published in two anthologies, has received rave reviews, as have the Drifters novels, Susan's all-time favourite books to write.

Owner/Operator of Bluemountain Entertainment, Susan is a 'Diploma With Honours' graduate of Vancouver Film School. She produces mostly documentary style client films and short dramas with plans to one day shoot a Feature Drama based on the novel Atlantic Blue.

Formerly a Museum Curator, in winter Susan lives with her partner Steve and her striped cat Oliver (Lucy Maud Montgomery once said the only good cat is a striped cat) in Summerside, Prince Edward Island, Canada. In summer, she hides in a small trailer in Darnley, P.E.I., where she writes novels, paddles kayaks, and crafts sandcastles on the beach. She makes frequent trips to Vancouver to visit her son Christopher, where she enjoys life in the hippie city while listening to great music and sipping on good espresso.

*Books by Susan Rodgers*

**Drifters series:**
*A Song For Josh*
*Promises*
*No Greater Love*
*Riptide*
*Whispers of Home*
*And Then There Was Silence*
*Let the Music Cry*
*If I Could Sing You Home*
*After the Rain*
*Into the Blue*
*A Sacred Peace*
*Watch Over Me*
*The Light In Me*
*When The West Wind Moves*
*Listen To The River*

**Feature Screenplays:**
*The Story of Jack & Emma*
*Still the Water*
*Beautiful Jane*
*They Were Dreamers (adapted)*

**Short Stories:**
S12
A Certain Kind of Freedom
A Gentle Peace